DYNAMITE ROAD

DYNAMITE ROAD
ANDREW KLAVAN

A TOM DOHERTY
ASSOCIATES BOOK
New York

This is a work of fiction. All the characters and events portrayed in this novel are either fictitious or are used fictitiously.

DYNAMITE ROAD

This book is printed on acid-free paper.

A Forge Book
Published by Tom Doherty Associates, LLC
175 Fifth Avenue
New York, NY 10010

www.tor.com

Forge® is a registered trademark of Tom Doherty Associates, LLC.

Library of Congress Cataloging-in-Publication Data

Klavan, Andrew.
   Dynamite road / Andrew Klavan.
      p. cm.
"A Tom Doherty Associates book."
   ISBN 0-765-30785-5
   1. Private investigators—California—San Francisco—Fiction.   2. California,
Northern—Fiction.   3. Assassins—Fiction.   4. Airports—Fiction.   I. Title.
   PS3561.L334D96   2003
   813'.54—dc21

                                                                2003009213

First Edition: November 2003

Printed in the United States of America

0 9 8 7 6 5 4 3 2 1

This book is for Spencer.

AUTHOR'S NOTE These days I always call it the Agency. WEISS INVESTIGATIONS, that was the name on the door. But my wife, my children, my friends have all heard these stories so often that the Agency is enough. They know what I'm talking about.

They've been badgering me to write about the place for a long time. "When are you going to do something serious?" they say—something factual, they mean, instead of the fictional thrillers I've made my living with. But the more I struggled to find a way to tell about the Agency, Weiss and Bishop and the rest, the more I came to feel that the facts were actually a poor substitute for the truth of the matter. And now that the moment finally feels right for me to set all these events down on paper—these actual events that I saw or was told about and even participated in to some extent—I find myself essentially making them up, writing them as yet another novel, that is, complete with dialogue I couldn't have heard and thoughts I couldn't have known and even one or two incidents that only might have happened or might not have.

The risk of doing it this way, of course, is that you won't believe me, that you'll think the whole business is so crowded with novelistic *Danger!* and *Mystery!* and *Romance!* that I must've made it all up. And that would be a shame because, for the most part, this is the way it happened. Not just the incidents and places. The internal stuff too, the personal stuff. People actually shared a lot of it with me. I think I must've been a good person to confide in at the time. I was young, after all, just out of school, an eager listener. I was an outsider in the place, an Easterner adrift on the West Coast, a struggling writer who'd taken the agency job only for the money and the experience; I had no permanent stake in anybody's life. Plus I was, as I think I still am, slow to pass judgment on my fellow mortals. Unlike so many people who condemn and thunder among us nowadays, I never thought a man despicable because he harbored some bigotry or unkindness in him nor would I treat a woman with less respect because she acted unwisely or made herself miserable. If there's anyone, man or woman, who has never done these things, I'll let him or her look down on Weiss and Bishop and Kathleen and the others in this story. I hope the rest of you, small as your numbers may be, will sympathize with them for all their flaws and even come to like them more than a little as I did when I knew them back in the day.

PROLOGUE

Killing the girl was worth forty-nine points. In a lot of ways, it was the easiest job the man called Ben Fry had ever had.

The victim was no problem. It could've been anyone: a man, a child. A young woman alone just seemed right to him somehow. And it was simple to pick her out. He went down to the Pennywise Supermarket by the freeway. Haunted the aisles for a few minutes. Spotted her in the produce section finally. Young, attractive, small, shapely. Wearing a business suit, shopping for one. Exactly the kind of thing he had in mind. He followed her home from there.

He watched her off and on for the next three days. Tailed her to the art gallery south of Market where she worked. Observed her through the large front window. She seemed to sit at a desk most of the day, at the back of the room but in plain view from the street. Sometimes another, older woman joined her in the place. Sometimes visitors would come in and she would show them around. Sometimes she went into a back room out of sight. But mostly she sat at the desk alone.

When the gallery closed at six o'clock, she would set the security system, pull down the steel shutter and walk up to Market to catch a homebound trolley. She watched television at night, talked on the phone a lot curled up on the seat by her bay window. She didn't seem to go out much.

One afternoon while she was at work, the man called Ben Fry let himself into her apartment. He went through her clothes, her papers, her computer files and the rest. Her name, he found out, was Penny Morgan. She was twenty-three. Engaged to a young man named David Embry who was working on his MBA down at UCLA. Her mother and father lived with her younger sister in San Mateo. She wrote a lot of e-mails to them and to David and to a large circle of female friends. The man called Ben Fry found these e-mails to be very warm and affectionate. He formed an impression of Penny as an enthusiastic and cheerful person. In photographs around the apartment, he noticed she was always smiling or laughing, her eyes bright and glistening with pleasure.

He figured he'd need another two or three more weeks before he was ready to kill her.

So while Penny Morgan went to work at the art gallery, wrote e-mails to her friends, spoke to her fiancé for long, romantic hours over the phone, the man called Ben Fry prepared for her murder. He did this, as he always did, with elaborate caution. Flew to five different places under five different names. Gathered some of his materials in one location, some in another. He never used anything but pay phones. He rarely used computers. He rarely returned to the same source twice. He never left a trail.

He practiced anonymity like a religion. No one alive knew the name he was born with. A plain man to look at, he seemed so average he was almost invisible. Thirty-five or so. Five-ten or five-eleven. Dull brown hair, dull brown eyes. Soft, uninteresting features. His body was stooped and pudgy. He didn't look strong, but he had a broad, powerful chest and muscular arms and he was rattlesnake-quick when he wanted to be. He didn't look intelligent either, but he was; he was very intelligent in a relentlessly analytical sort of way. He was always taking a situation apart, examining it piece by piece, calculating the odds of this or that, assessing the possibilities of this or that. He thought it kept him sane.

When he'd gathered the materials he needed, he returned to the city. He had no home but he'd taken a shabby studio in the Mission district for the job. There, one Saturday night, he sat nude on the edge of his metal cot. There were several kidney-shaped stainless-steel tubs on a table beside him. There were needles and blades in the tubs, soaking in disinfectant. There was plastic sheeting on the floor and the furniture to prevent bloodstains.

He pulled on a pair of surgical gloves. Removed a syringe from one of the tubs. It was already loaded with lidocaine. He slipped the hair-thin needle into a shaved patch on his inner thigh, the soft flesh just beneath his balls. He slowly drew the needle out as he pressed the syringe's plunger so the anaesthetic would spread through all the layers of his skin. He repeated the process three more times. Then, when the area was numb, he reached into another of the kidney-shaped tubs. This time, he drew out a scalpel.

The man called Ben Fry paused with the blade in his hand. He closed his eyes. He imagined a tower. He had learned to do this over the years. Whenever he was idle and his thoughts strayed beyond his work and his analytical planning and he suddenly found himself clutched by some emotion that unsettled him, he would imagine the tower and trudge up into it. He would stand at the top and look out over the parapet, out over the plains below. Down there was the red turmoil of life. Purple nakedness and silver tears, agonized cries and pitiless laughter. But in the tower he felt cool and blue and far away. In the tower, he became himself again.

It was a good technique. It worked every time. Every time, that is, but once.

He climbed into the tower now. He drew a breath. Opened his eyes. Then he pressed the scalpel into the numbed flesh of his thigh and sliced himself open. He let out a strangled grunt. The incision was barely an inch long but even with the lidocaine it was agony, his nerves burned white-hot. He pulled out the blade. The wound stayed clean for a moment, then it began drooling blood. The blood ran down the inside of his leg. Staring at it, breathing hard, the man called Ben Fry let the scalpel fall from his trembling fingers. It thudded and crackled softly on the plastic sheeting.

A car horn sounded on the street outside. Night rain pattered at the windows. His chest heaving, the man called Ben Fry went on.

From another of the steel tubs, he removed a capsule. It was about the size of the top joint of his thumb, made of some sort of soft, gel-like plastic, like the stuff they use for contact lenses. But this was hard and sharp around the edges, as if someone had forgotten to file away some excess material. One-half of the capsule contained something red, the other half something blue. He had had it made in one city, and purchased its contents in two others.

Inserting the capsule into himself was even more painful than making the incision. At one point, as he worked it deep into the fatty tissue, the agony seemed to sweep down over his eyes like a curtain and he was almost blind with it, almost gone. He gave another strangled grunt. Imagined the tower, looked down at his scarlet suffering from the cool, blue tower far away.

Finally, it was done. There was a wet, sucking noise as he drew his finger from the bloody hole in his leg. The capsule was in.

He had to wait a few minutes for his hands to stop shaking before he could manage to sew himself shut. Then, when that was finished, he reached quickly—almost frantically—for another syringe, this one full of morphine.

A short while later, he lay curled up on his side like a child, his two hands resting beneath his cheek. He slept a long time. All his dreams were nightmares.

A week later, he took the stitches out. The scar was clean, the hair beginning to grow back over it. But even after another week, it was still too red and raw, too noticeable. So he waited. One week more, taking antibiotics against infection. March was over, April had begun, before he returned to Penny Morgan's apartment.

He went on a Monday evening. It was a little after 6:00 P.M. The girl, he knew, would be home around 6:30. Seated at the bay window, he would be able to see her coming, to make sure she was alone. Then he would stand by the kitchen so he would be hidden from her until she'd closed the front door. He was wearing a navy blue track suit, easy to move in. His gun sat comfortably under the waistband. He could draw it in one stride and in another he would be close enough to shoot Penny in the head. When she was down, he'd shoot her twice more just to be certain.

He'd taken no caution in getting the gun. It was a street .38 someone had sold him out of the trunk of a car. There was no suppressor. It would be good and loud when he fired. A neighbor was sure to hear it. And in a respectable part of town like this, a neighbor was sure to call the police. That was the way the man called Ben Fry wanted it. No chase, no long, drawn-out investigation. They'd arrest him a block or two from the scene.

While he waited for Penny to arrive, he rifled her apartment. Dumped the drawers, stripped the bed, pulled the books from the shelves. He found some gold jewelry, a pearl necklace; some cash, about forty bucks. He stuffed whatever he found in a plastic bag he'd brought along with him. Stuffed the bag in one of his pants pockets.

Then it was time to go to the window. He sat there on the same window seat where Penny sometimes sat when she talked to her fiancé on the phone. He was hidden from the street by the sheer privacy curtains but he could see out through them. He studied the pedestrians passing on the sidewalk three stories below. She wasn't there. It was still a little too early for her.

He settled in with a waiting sigh. He watched the street. Once his glance drifted to the framed snapshots on the lampstand. Penny with David, his arm around her, she laughing. Penny's kid sister with her golden retriever. The whole family, Mom and Dad, Penny, the sister, the golden, smiling in front of a lighted Christmas tree.

The man called Ben Fry looked away, back down at the street again. Automatically, he began to think about the next phase of the operation, going over his plans, rechecking them. It soothed him.

Then there she was. It was 6:27 and there was Penny Morgan walking up over the hill from the trolley stop. She was carrying the oversized purse she used as a briefcase. The white gauze of the curtain made her figure hazy to him but he could still follow her approach. He sat there and watched until she turned into the building. Then he got up off the window seat.

He stood waiting in the kitchen doorway exactly as he'd planned.

Penny Morgan paused in the vestibule to pick up her mail. She leafed through the envelopes as she climbed the stairs. She climbed slowly. She was tired and a little depressed. She was beginning to feel that working at an art gallery was not as glamorous as she'd hoped it would be.

She sighed. The mail: all bills and flyers. She tucked them into her purse's outer pocket. Worked her keys out of the same pocket as she reached the third-floor landing.

She went down the hall to her door. She unlocked her three locks, the dead bolt, the inter-grip and the police bar. She decided she would call David before dinner. She promised herself she wouldn't complain or anything. She just needed to hear his voice to cheer her up. She didn't like these dull evenings at home. She wished he would hurry and finish his degree already so they could get married and start their life together.

She pushed the door open. It was nearly Easter, she reminded herself. In another few weeks, David would be coming home for the holiday. They'd have almost a whole month together.

She was beginning to smile a little as she stepped into the apartment.

PART ONE The Case of the Spanish Virgin

ONE

It was one hundred and five degrees the day Jim Bishop roared into the north country. The sun burned merciless on the dead meridian. The mountains rose brown and barren on either side of the freeway. The heat pooled like water on the pavement up ahead.

Bishop rolled the throttle of the Harley Road King. The big bike crested seventy-five, pulsing between his legs. It was a long-haul dresser, built for comfort, but Bishop was aching beneath his jeans. His gray T-shirt was black with sweat beneath his leather jacket. His hair was soaked beneath his helmet. His sunglasses were smeared—his windshield too—with what bikers call "protein spray"—splattered bugs.

He veered off the freeway at the end of the long valley. Exit: Driscoll, California, population sixty-seven thousand, the last great outpost before the mountains and the woods.

The Harley grumbled as Bishop forced it down beneath its touring speed. He rolled at forty-five along a bland four-lane, hemmed in every which way by a steady stream of cars. Gas stations lined the road and sand-colored malls and more gas stations and motel after motel and then fast-food outposts, Taco Bell, Burger King, McDonald's, and more gas stations and more malls with their stores in sand-colored boxes and the big screaming letters to tell which store was which. The Harley went down one road, turned onto another and then turned onto another and the scenery stayed the same. Gas stations, hotels, restaurants and malls. From behind his aviator shades, Bishop's pale eyes searched for the city center. Then he realized: This was it, this was all there was. Driscoll was just a starburst scar of concrete and stucco at the base of the big mountains. A tourist stop on the way into the wilderness.

He chugged over a white bridge, still hemmed in by traffic.

Beneath him, the Sacramento River glinted painfully in the sun. On the far side of the water, around a bend, the cars began to fall away a little. Bishop opened the throttle some, split the lane and wove between a couple of cage-drivers. He wound round the corner onto Main Street—or what was called Main Street. Main Street was pretty much dead. The malls and their chain stores had sucked the life out of it. Now there was a gutted theater here and a desperate bar called the Clover Leaf and a hotel that might have been open or closed, he couldn't tell which. A one-armed man in an army cap was staggering drunk on the sidewalk. A fat man with a bushy beard was planted at the corner, brandishing a cardboard sign that said: *Homeless Veteran. Give what you can.* Bishop and his big motorcycle cruised on by.

He headed into the neighborhoods. On branching roads, slanting houses of wood or aluminum huddled on scraps of lawn. Fat women in sleeveless blouses hosed down patches of desert garden. Their grubby children danced laughing through the water.

The laughter fell away. The city fell away. A few last gasping shacks and then an empty field, burnt dry by the heat, ran shimmering into the foothills. Far away, as in a dreamland far away, the whitewashed walls of holiday mansions gleamed down at Driscoll from those hills on high. Bishop had reached the edge of town, the border of the northern forests.

He rounded his bike onto a gritty little lane and rode the last half mile to the airfield.

There were two men in the hangar, both in overalls. One was an older statesman, bald, craggy. The other was a young fellow with a face lit by brainless contentment. They were chatting over the low wing of a Piper Tomahawk. Chatting, chuckling. It was the older man, wiping his hands on a rag, who first looked through the hangar door and saw Bishop heading in.

Bishop had left his helmet hanging from the Harley's handlebars. Stripped off his leather jacket and slung it over his shoulder. He was strolling across the parking lot slowly, slowly surveying the airfield with the pale eyes behind the aviator shades. Bishop was around thirty then, I guess. Not a big man, five-eight or -nine maybe but broad across the shoulders and muscular, pecs and biceps stretching the sweat-dark tee. He had a way of moving, easy and tense, so you sensed his speed and his compact power. He had a round face with chiseled features under sandy hair. And though he looked as if he had his tongue in his cheek, as if he was laughing silently at a joke you were too thick to understand, the older man had been around some and had seen guys like this before. His stomach sank and he swallowed dry as he watched Bishop come on.

Bishop stepped out of the hot sunlight into the hangar's cooler shadows. Stopped at the Tomahawk's rudder.

"Either of you Ray?" he asked.

"Yeah," said the older man. "I'm Ray. Ray Grambling."

"I'm Frank Kennedy," said Jim Bishop quietly. "I'm your new pilot."

TWO If Ray Grambling was tense when he saw Bishop coming, he was really nervous now. He laughed too much—ha-ha: like that—and he spoke too loudly like a bad actor just learning his lines.

"We're a small operation—ha-ha. I can't offer you full-time work. But summer's the busy season, that's for sure, spring and summer. Ha-ha."

He walked Bishop through the doorway in the hangar wall, into an air-conditioned hallway. Bishop followed him along the hall, giving a hard stare to the back of his head, willing him to just calm the fuck down.

Ray babbled on over his shoulder. "We got the usual lawyers flying back and forth to Arcata—that's the county seat—for their trials and whatnot, ha-ha. Then in the hot weather we got the forestry department doing smoke watches, running equipment up into the woods. We get some cargo runs, store inventory, canceled checks down from Weaverville and the like. You wear your beeper and make sure you get your flight and duty breaks, ha-ha, we'll have you up in the air every day through September most likely. Here's Kathleen."

They had come the back way into the front office, a broad space divided in half by a counter. On the far side of the counter, a storefront window looked out at the small planes lined up on the airport's apron. There were chairs by the window and a table covered with magazines, a waiting place for the paying customers, when there were any, which there weren't. On this side of the counter, the working side, there were desks, computers, filing cabinets and a mess of paper. Kathleen was at one of the filing cabinets, slotting a manila folder into a drawer.

As the two men came in, Ray's voice got even louder, his laugh more frantic. "Kathleen Wannamaker, this is Ji . . . No, Frank it was, wasn't it? Wasn't it Frank? Ha-ha. You get old, you can't remember a thing anymore. Ha-ha. Frank Kennedy, that's it, our new pilot. Kathleen here's our director of operations and sometimes our dispatcher when we need her to fill in. You gotta be nice to her if you want to get those hours, ha-ha. Right, Kathleen?"

She looked up without smiling. A glamourless woman and hardboiled but not unattractive. In her thirties, small, trim at the waist, heavy at the breasts and hips. She wore a tan skirt and light white blouse. Had long, limp, mouse brown hair parted in the middle. When she saw Bishop, she unconsciously lifted her hand to brush some strands behind her ear.

"Meetcha," she said. Her eyes went up and down him. Her face was smooth and regular and would've been kind of sweet except somehow it wasn't.

Bishop took his sunglasses off, met her gaze for gaze.

Ray kept babbling. "Frank's the one I told you about, needs a place to stay? Kathleen here has a house she rents, so there it is, ha-ha. Right, Kathleen, that's good for you, right? You said the house is open and all. Kennedy's gonna be here through the summer, at least. So it works out perfect, ha-ha."

For a moment, Kathleen didn't answer. She was still looking at Bishop, looking at Bishop looking back at her. You might as well know this right away, there's no point being coy about it: Women fell in love with Bishop. It happened again and again. They fell in love, dropped, plummeted into love with him like stones out of the clouds, like stones falling out of the clouds into the depths of some murky pond. Part of it, sure, was the looks, the muscles, all the cool stuff, the bikes and the planes and whatnot. But there had to be more to it than that. Maybe it was simply the fact that he was a genuine *bona fide* coldhearted bastard. He was a bastard and he just didn't care.

Men were glad he didn't care. They just wanted him to pass on through without wrecking anything. But women? They seemed to want to make him care. Each one of them seemed to want to be the first to make him care.

So anyway, Kathleen did that thing where she hesitated before she answered Ray, she hesitated and went on looking at Bishop. And Bishop went on looking at her, indifferent and easy within himself, smiling slightly and sizing her up for the doing.

Then finally Kathleen took a breath, blinked as if she were waking up. "It's four fifty," she said. "The rent. Four hundred and fifty a month. Ready to move in, if you want it."

"Sounds good," said Bishop.

"Well, there you go," Ray practically shouted. "That was easy! Ha-ha. That's all settled. So—uh—uh . . ."

"Kennedy," said Bishop.

"Kennedy! Frank, right! I swear, ha-ha, my memory for names . . . Frank. So we'll get you started on your training, check you out in all the planes, you'll be good to go."

Bishop said nothing. He looked at Kathleen. She looked at him back and her chest rose and fell.

"Oh, hey, Kathleen," Ray broke in. "Here comes your husband."

Bishop glanced up, out through the storefront window. A twin engine Cessna 340 was gliding in through the wavering heat, settling onto the runway with a slow flare. The pulse of the props made the big pane rattle.

Kathleen didn't turn to watch at first. She let her eyes play over Bishop another second or two. Then she forced herself to look over her shoulder.

The plane taxied onto the apron. The engines shut down, the props stopped turning. The three in the office watched as the pilot unfolded himself from the cockpit, as he walked from wing to wing to tie the aircraft down.

"That's Kathleen's husband Chris," Ray told Bishop. "He's my chief pilot. He's a check airman too, so he's the one'll be checking you out in all the planes."

Chris Wannamaker came swaggering toward them now, his flight bag dangling from one fist. A big son of a bitch, Bishop observed calmly. And mighty mean-looking too.

Yeah, he thought, *and I'll just bet he's not gonna like it much when I start in fucking his wife.*

THREE

Kathleen's house—the house she rented out—was not far from the airfield. A shabby two-story clapboard slumping on a patch of heat-brown grass. There was a living room and a kitchen downstairs, a bedroom upstairs under the low eaves. What furniture there was was musty and faded.

It was evening when she brought him here. From the houses clustered all around came the sound of laughing children and whizzing sprinklers and barking dogs and mothers shouting "Dinnertime!" through one screen door and then another. The light in the sky lingered—it was still only June—but the first cooler breeze of the day came in through the living room windows, stirring the thin curtains.

Upstairs, though, it was stifling. When they stood together in the cramped bedroom, crowded under the slant of the roof, Bishop could smell Kathleen's sweat laced with her perfume. He liked the smell. He liked the sensation it gave him.

"You're gonna need the air conditioner up here most times," Kathleen told him. "It rattles a little but it works okay."

Bishop looked out the window. He nodded slightly to himself. From here—and from the southern window downstairs too—he could see right into the living room of the house next door. That was the house Kathleen lived in with her husband. This was going to work out well.

He turned to her. He moved close.

"Any furniture of your own you want to bring in, go ahead," she went on, lifting her face to his. "I can always store this stuff at my uncle's place. I just keep it here in case the tenants want to use it. You can set the place up any way . . ." Her voice trailed off as Bishop studied her, studied the fall of her hair down her cheek, the contours of her full mouth. "Any way you want," she finished finally.

Bishop let his gaze trail lazily up from her lips to her eyes, to her hairline, down to her eyes again.

"It's just fine the way it is," he told her.

FOUR

That very first night, the man with the gray moustache came. Bishop sat in a wooden chair in the living room, sat in the dark. He smoked a cigarette, cupping it in his hand so that the glow wasn't visible from the house next door. He watched Kathleen's living room through the stirring curtains.

The man with the gray moustache sat with Kathleen's husband Chris. Chris sat hunch-shouldered on the sofa, his features twisted in a surly and submissive smile. He drank beer. Beer after beer. Bishop could hear him when he shouted to Kathleen to bring him another bottle.

The man with the gray moustache sat in a stuffed armchair. There was a glass of whiskey on the coffee table in front of him but he only sipped it once the whole time Bishop watched.

About an hour and a half went by. The man with the gray moustache rose and left. Bishop could see him come out the front door and move to the silver Mercedes parked behind the Dodge pickup in the carport. Bishop could also see Chris sitting where he was, meanwhile, sucking the last out of his beer bottle. Then, when Chris was done, Bishop saw him lumber to his feet and stagger drunkenly out of the living room. After that, Bishop couldn't see him anymore.

But he went on sitting at the window, watching. And in a little while he heard the sound of Chris's voice from the back of the house. It spiraled from a snarl to an angry bark. Kathleen answered him loudly. She must've been near the screen door to the kitchen because her words were clear:

"It's my house. I don't have to ask your goddamned permission, y'know!"

Chris cursed and Kathleen cried out and Bishop knew that he had struck her. He heard her sobbing raggedly as they struggled. He heard her sobbing cry as Chris struck her again. Chris cursed again and Bishop heard his stumbling footsteps. For a few minutes, Kathleen went on weeping miserably by the kitchen door.

"You bastard," he heard her say.

After that, the house was quiet. Bishop lifted his cupped cigarette to his lips. He took a long drag. A bead of sweat rolled down his temple. The quiet went on. Finally, Bishop crushed the cigarette out in an ashtray. He got to his feet. He climbed the stairs to the bedroom.

He was glad to get into the air-conditioning. He knelt beside the black travel bag he'd set on the floor by the bed. He dug through his clothes. He dug out his handheld computer. Brought it to the table against the wall, set it into a portable keyboard, switched it on.

The computer was one of those palmtop things that can send e-mail. Bishop preferred e-mail. It was harder to snoop on. No one could simply overhear it or pick up another line and listen in. The portable keyboard was small but Bishop was used to it. He typed quickly, using his index fingers.

Weiss, he began. *I'm here. . . .*

FIVE

"Someone is going to kill me," the Mousey Guy said.

The formidable body of Scott Weiss swelled and subsided like the sea. "I'm a private investigator, Mr. Spender," he said. "If someone is trying to kill you, that's a matter for the police."

"I can't go to the police. I can't."

"Why's that?"

The Mousey Guy leaned forward urgently. "Because this person—this man who's going to kill me: The reason he's going to kill me is because I raped his sister."

Weiss's deadpan was as good as laughter. He didn't believe this shit for a minute.

They were in his office on Market Street, on the eighth floor of a concrete tower with a red mansard roof. A bank took up the tower's ground floor and the next six floors of offices above it. Then there was us, the Agency, on eight, and then a law firm on the two stories up under the mansard. The law firm, Jaffe and Jaffe, gave the Agency a lot of its business, and they rented us the space below them for their own convenience.

But it was a break for us, too. The downtown location was valuable and the eighth floor was the nicest in the whole building. Most of its charm came from its big arched windows. On a clear summer day like this we got the morning sun slanting in. We got a hearty chunk of the famous skyline: a foreground of ornate stone office buildings with a heartbeat chart of modern towers rising behind. We got to watch the city's walls flare red and yellow with the morning light and start to sparkle when their own lights came on in the gloaming.

In Weiss's office—his spacious office with its massive desk and its massive client armchairs and his massive self tilted slightly backward in a massive swivel chair of his own—the backdrop of the radiant city in its vaulting window frame served to emphasize the sweep and size of the scene.

It was a scene that dwarfed our client this morning. Wally Spender. A little man and thin with jug ears and frightened eyes and a long, slender nose: A mouse enchanted into human form.

"It happened in Spain," he went on in his high voice. "The—the incident with the sister, I mean. I—I don't know what came over me. Uncontrollable passion, I guess." He wrung his small hands, fretting on the edge of his seat like a schoolboy in a jam.

Weiss maintained his deadpan.

"I just saw her . . . down by the water. In Malaga. This is about a year ago. I was sitting in a cafe there, enjoying a coffee, and she just went walking past. Just a poor, local girl but . . . very beautiful. Very—I don't know—beautiful, like I said. I just saw her, Mr. Weiss and—and I just got up. I just got right up from my table right then and there. And I—I followed her. Right then and there. I followed her right down the street, right along the water. I remember she stopped along the way. To do some errands, you know. To buy some—some fruit or . . . Yes, fruit, that's what it was. And I just stood there, Mr. Weiss. I just stood there and—and watched her. There was something about her. I don't know. And I kept following her. I followed her all the way back to her humble dwelling on the edge of town."

"Her humble dwelling." Weiss drew the words out slowly.

But Mousey Guy completely missed the irony. He kept right on. "Yes. Yes. It was down these streets. I followed her down these streets in the old quarter. Lonely, empty, cobblestone streets between crumbling old Spanish buildings. And it was like . . . The thought came into my head that in a place like this, it was, like, *anything* could happen. I mean, we were all alone on these empty streets. And there's lots of crime there. No one would think anything of it. And I was following her, you know, down these streets, and these thoughts just started coming into my head. I couldn't help it." He licked his thin lips, stared into the middle distance. He was getting excited. His story excited him.

"So—so we reached her house after a while. And, well, there was no one, no one around anywhere. And she opened the door and I . . . I just pushed—I just pushed right in behind her. That's right. Right in. And I—I grabbed her. And, well, let me tell you, she—she pleaded with me. Oh yes, Mr. Weiss. It was terrible to hear. She was—she was on her knees, on her knees begging me, pleading with me. Crying. That's when, you know, she told me . . ." He licked his lips again. Swallowed hard. His fearful eyes were bright. "She told me she'd never been with a man. She had never . . . you know—before. Ever. But I wouldn't listen. I wouldn't be stopped. I was—I was like a wild animal or something. Oh, she fought me. Oh yes. She fought me very fiercely at first but then . . . Then, you know, she began to respond. After a while, she couldn't help herself, you know, she began to respond, if you see what I mean. And then—then we did things. . . ."

Weiss cleared his throat. Nothing human was alien to him but this was getting distasteful.

"Wonderful, wonderful things . . ." murmured the Mousey Guy.

"Why don't you tell me about this man?" Weiss said. "The one who's trying to kill you."

"Oh." Spender blinked a few times, coming back to himself. His gaze focused again on the detective. "It wasn't until—you know, afterwards, that she told me she had a brother. She told me she had a brother who lived with her."

"In her humble dwelling."

"Yes. That's why she said I had to hurry away."

Weiss nodded gravely.

"And—and, well, that was it," Spender said. "I mean, I never saw her again. I left Malaga the very next day. Oh, I was quite ashamed of myself, let me tell you. Letting my passions get the better of me like that. I just—I just tried to put the whole thing out of my mind. And I did, at first. A year went by and there was nothing. And then . . .

Then, a few weeks ago, I started to get these phone calls. At night, at my house. First there was just no one. I would pick up the phone and there would be no one there. But the other day—the other night I should say—I got a call and a man was on the line. And he said, right out, 'I am coming to kill you, *señor.*' Like that. With an accent, a Spanish accent. 'I am coming to kill you, *señor,*' he said, 'for you have destroyed my sister's honor and the honor of my family.' That's the Spanish, you know, that's what they're like. They're very passionate about keeping their family honor."

Weiss rested his cheek against his palm. "It's their hot Latin blood," he said.

"Exactly! Exactly. And the other night? The other night, I woke up around 2:00 A.M. Just woke up for no reason. I couldn't tell why. And I got out of bed and went to the window. And there he was. This man, this Spaniard, this Spanish-looking man. Just standing there. Standing there on the sidewalk. Staring right up at me, right at my window. And when he saw me, you know what he did? He took out this knife. This just—enormous, great big knife. And he drew it—like this—drew it right across his throat, as if he were cutting himself. And he was looking right at me when he did it, Mr. Weiss. Right at me. I'm sure of it."

Weiss had a wonderful face, made for the business. His expression of world-weariness and human sympathy was absolutely impenetrable. He was fifty about. Had thick, weighty, sagging features. Deep brown eyes with thick black brows above and deep gray bags beneath them. Salt-and-pepper hair, unkempt but somehow authoritative. He was big—really big—six-foot-three or -four, with huge shoulders and a dominating paunch. And because of his cop background—or maybe in spite of it—he often gave the impression that he was hovering over you protectively. Which sometimes I think he actually was.

Now, after long consideration, he asked, "What exactly can I do for you, Mr. Spender?"

"Well, find him!" Mousey Guy blurted at once. "You've got to find him, stop him. You've got to, Mr. Weiss. He's coming after me, I just know it. And if you don't do something—do something fast—well, by this time next week—I'm sure of it—I'll be dead."

"So you figure it's total bullshit," I said.

Weiss blustered like a horse. "A hundred percent reality-free, I guarantee it. I should've called you in to play Spanish tunes on a guitar while he was talking." He made a face. "Her *humble dwelling*! He had to *hurry away* from her *humble dwelling*! I mean, for fuck's sake."

I was in an alcove down the hall from Weiss's office. It was just a little nook that served the Agency as a mailroom. There was a copying machine in there and a fax machine and a stamp machine. And my desk and me.

Weiss often wandered by like this. He often paused distracted here, hands in his pockets, half-lost in thought. He liked to talk to me, to tell me things, about his cases, about his life. I'm not sure why. He knew I was an aspiring author so maybe he hoped I'd remember what he said, write it down one day, preserve it, make it matter somehow. Or maybe he was anticipating that and he wanted to make sure I heard his interpretation of events, his spin. Then again maybe I just seemed so harmless and arty to him, so far out of his orbit, that he didn't even take me seriously. Maybe he felt that talking to me was like confiding in the empty air.

"Well, he could've done it, couldn't he?" I asked. I was standing at the copier, watching a report go whirring and flapping through. "I mean, it's possible, isn't it?"

"This guy? If this guy raped someone, I'm telling you, I'm the king of Romania. If he's ever even been to Spain . . ." He shook his head. "*I will kill you, señor.* I mean, for fuck's sake."

"So why'd you take the case?"

He shrugged. "Well, I gotta make sure. I mean, the guy lives out in Sunset with his mother. What'll it cost me to go talk to her? Make sure he's not gonna hurt anyone or get hurt himself. Who knows? I could be wrong. Maybe every word out of his mouth is the living truth. Maybe one day you can write a book about his adventures. *The Case of the Spanish Virgin*."

The copier stopped whirring. I started to extract the report pages from the collater. Through the open door to Weiss's office, we heard his computer play its little three-note song. An e-mail had come in.

"Must be your update from Bishop," I said.

He nodded. As he wandered back to his desk, I heard him muttering, "*She began to respond*. I mean, for fuck's sake. I'm the king of Romania."

SIX

Weiss. All well here but slow. Chris Wannamaker checking me on planes so we spend time together in the air. But he's very sullen, silent. No way to question him. Watchful of his wife Kathleen too, suspicious, doesn't want me close. Always home when she's home so far. I managed some chats with her at work. Tough crust but lonely, abused. I just need a chance to get to her, pump her for info.

"Uy," Weiss groaned softly. *Pump her for info.* Bishop's e-mails were always full of stuff like that. Weiss was probably the one person on earth Bishop cared about at all, the one person whose good opinion he actually wanted. But he knew the older man didn't approve of some of his methods and I think he liked to rag him about it a little. The wild son giving the dig to his stodgy father sort of thing. *Pump her for info. . . .*

Weiss put a hand on his stomach and groaned again. With the other hand, he scrolled the e-mail down. Read on.

Another sighting of gray moustache, out at airfield this time. Now confirmed: moustache is Bernie Hirschorn. VBM. Heads Driscoll Foundation, which pretty much runs the city, maybe more. Lots of money, drug connections. A lot of dead bodies on his way to the top. Local businesses pay him off or he burns them out, maybe whacks them, takes them over. Owns most of the airpark now, half of Ray's business.

And Ray's right—something's going on. Some of Hirschorn's front orgs. have been chartering Chris to fly. Sometimes with passengers, sometimes with Hirschorn, sometimes just with freight. Destination mostly Arcata, the county seat, according to the manifests.

But Chris's plane keeps returning from the north—Arcata's to the west. Plus the flights take too long—the Hobbes time is way off.

Weiss swiveled back and forth in his chair a little, thinking. He didn't know what Hobbes time was exactly, but he didn't like the sound of this. It seemed pretty clear what Bishop was telling him. This Hirschorn character was hiring Chris Wannamaker to fly somewhere in secret, falsely listing Arcata as the destination. But what for? North of Driscoll there was nothing but forest for miles and miles. Was it some kind of smuggling deal? Drugs, cigarettes, CDs in and out of Canada, something like that?

Whatever it was, it made Weiss worry. Hirschorn sounded like a VBM all right—a Very Bad Man. A lot of dead bodies in his wake. And he knew how hard it was to rein Bishop in once he was onto something. Weiss would have to keep an eye on his operative, make sure he didn't get himself into this too deep.

The last paragraphs of the e-mail didn't reassure him any.

Working a possible angle. Chris Wannamaker's a boozer. Big mouth, hothead, out of control. Hirschorn may want a better pilot, more reliable. I'll see if I can find a way to move in there too.

BTW, our client, Ray Grambling's a fucking idiot. Scared, talks too much. Nearly blew my cover—called me by my real name—three times. Could get me killed. Seeya. JB

SEVEN

Chris Wannamaker was waiting by the twin engine. He had his back propped against the fuselage, his thumbs hooked in the pockets of his jeans. Bishop—his flight bag slung over one shoulder—walked toward him across the baking tarmac. Behind his shades, Chris watched Bishop come.

Chris had half a foot over the smaller man, easy. The sleeves had been cut off his NORTH COUNTRY AVIATION T-shirt showing the brutal muscles corded on his arms. He had a tattoo on his right bicep: two snakes twined around a death's-head; *Born To Raise Hell*. On his left arm he had a long, white, jagged scar. He had handsome curly brown hair and smooth features and a cruel half smile.

"She's preflighted," he said when Bishop reached him. "Let's fly."

Bishop nodded. They climbed into the cockpit.

Chris sat silent in the copilot's seat. He brooded on the view out the side window as Bishop fired the engines and taxied for the runway. Both men wore headsets but it was a Delta field. There was no tower, no ATIS, and in the quiet of morning, no traffic, nothing on the air. The men sat shoulder to shoulder and made no conversation to break the muffled rumble of the plane.

It had been like this between them all week. They were natural enemies. They knew it the second they met. Chris was assigned to check Bishop out in the company aircraft. That was required for insurance purposes. But Bishop could've flown an anchor and Chris knew it. So all week, they had gone through the motions, saying only what they had to say.

At the head of the runway, Bishop tapped the brakes. The Cessna paused. Bishop pressed the mike button.

"Driscoll traffic, five-zero-four's rolling off the active," he said.

With a smooth motion, he throttled up the engines. The plane started forward, gathered speed. Just as it red-lined, Bishop drew back the yoke. The wheels broke away from the pavement. They were airborne.

"Zero-three-zero," Chris muttered, still studying the window.

At five hundred feet, Bishop banked the plane toward the north. And he thought: *Well, there's this anyway.* The feel of the earth released beneath him, the way the landscape floated down like a handkerchief dropped from a lady's hand. The way the stubble fields around the tin hangar became pristine and geometric as they receded in the vertical distance. The whole depressing city off his right sinking to a dim glitter. In the sweep of his windshield, from his ten o'clock to his two, Bishop surveyed the sky and the wild hills billowing away into it, green forest into blue mist into the white horizon. Moment after good moment, he edged the plane skyward.

"Level her off," Chris said.

Bishop glanced at him. They were only five thousand feet above sea level now. The hills beneath them rose to three thousand and more. Bishop could still make out the riffled contours of the treetops. He could see the cars on the winding mountain highway, see their windows flashing in the sun. They were not supposed to do maneuvers less than three thousand feet above the ground.

"Do a steep turn to the right," Chris said. Then he went on brooding, turned away, his face propped on his fist.

Bishop took a quick look at the directional gyro. Their heading was exactly 030. He rolled the plane into a forty-five-degree turn to the right. He set the nose on the horizon line and the Cessna swept around quickly. The mountains circled past the windshield. The city sparkled pleasantly far away and then was gone. The plane kept turning. The sun glared in through the glass. There were the mountains again. Bishop edged the yoke over, eased down on the rudder pedal. He checked the DG once more: 030 exactly as the Cessna's wings came level. His glance flicked to the altimeter. He hadn't lost a foot in altitude. *A good maneuver,* he thought.

And just as he was thinking that, Chris's hand suddenly snaked for one of the throttles. He shut down the right engine.

It was part of the checkride—procedures during engine failure. Because when you lose the thrust in one engine, there's nothing to balance the thrust produced by the other. Driven by the working engine, the plane yaws hard toward the dead spot and eventually starts to spiral toward the earth. Or it will unless you correct the yaw, jamming your foot down hard on the appropriate rudder pedal.

Which is what Bishop did. But the rudder pedal didn't budge.

Which caused Bishop to remark: "Shit."

He stomped the pedal again. Nothing. The Cessna's nose slid to the right, tilted down. Bishop's foot battled against the pedal. It gave a little but then battled back. Bishop didn't understand—and then he did understand but he could hardly believe it: Chris was stomping on the copilot's controls, holding the rudder in place.

"What the hell're you . . . ?"

Chris laughed. "Ride 'em, boy!"

With a great, heaving, sickening roll the plane turned over. The green hills spun up toward them. Bishop reached for the right throttle but Chris was holding it tight. The plane spiraled slowly round and round but it plummeted faster and faster. The air began to whine as they fell. The g force pulled hotly at the flesh of Bishop's cheeks.

"Yee-haw!" Chris shouted into the headset, shrill, deafening, like a cowboy on a bucking bronc.

Bishop cursed again and hit him, drove a knuckle down into the side of his thigh.

"Ow, fuck!" shouted Chris.

His leg went limp. The rudder pedal gave way under Bishop's foot. He jammed it. Grabbed the left throttle and yanked it to idle. Now, with zero thrust on both sides, he could haul the yoke over to roll the ailerons level. The nauseating spiral stopped but the plane kept diving down toward the mountains. The sea of trees bubbled up on either side of them. They were sinking toward it fast. A low ridge of brown rock loomed huge in the windshield.

His jaw clenched, Bishop pulled the yoke back, pulled the nose up by main strength. He throttled up both engines at once, full power. He felt his balls go cold as the brown-rock ridge shoved itself at his face for another second and another.

Finally, the Cessna began to rise. It lifted, roaring, over the ridge, back up toward the sky. Bishop glanced quickly at his airspeed indicator—V-x—then to his nine o'clock. The treetops seemed to brush the bottom of the wing. He could see the individual leaves on them. But a second more and they were clear. The earth was falling away again.

Bishop looked over at Chris. "What the fuck's wrong with you, you son of a bitch?" he said.

Chris rubbed his thigh where Bishop had hit him. He glared at the other man darkly. Then the darkness passed. He chuckled. The sound was deep and breathy in Bishop's headset.

"Take her back up to five thousand," he said. "Let's try some more."

And he turned away to stare sullenly out the window.

EIGHT

JB. Just to remind you on procedures. Keep me well informed about nature of criminal activity, if any. I'm aware of the danger to our client but want my operatives safe as well. Also, as regards Mrs. Wannamaker, I'm sure she's a good source of information but I expect you to gather that information in a reasonable and professional manner.—W

Bishop saw his chance to begin gathering information in a professional manner that very night.

He was sitting at the table in his bedroom upstairs. He had just finished reading Weiss's e-mail on the handheld. He looked up through his window. Saw Kathleen step out through her door onto her front porch. In the glow of the half-moon—and in the glow from her porch light—he could also see that Chris's truck was gone from the driveway.

Bishop sat still. He watched her. She was wearing a blue T-shirt and khaki shorts. He liked how big her breasts were and the roundness of her hips. Plus he was still pissed off at Chris about the stunt he'd pulled in the plane that morning. He wanted to fuck the woman twice, once to *pump her for info* and once to get back at her goddamned husband. Looking down at her, he thought he'd enjoy it both times.

Kathleen set herself on the railing. She lit a cigarette, took a drag.

Bishop deleted Weiss's e-mail. He pushed away from the table.

A minute or two later, he strolled outside. Full dark had fallen. The heat, which had come down like a sledgehammer all day, now just lay on the night like a blanket. Cicadas were rattling in the sycamores. Insects zigged like electrons round Kathleen's porch light. Bishop saw the faint shadows of them on her face and her bare arms as she turned to smile at him. He crossed the thin border of lawn between their houses.

"How's it going?" he said.

She gestured vaguely with her cigarette. "Just getting some air. I don't like to smoke with the AC on."

"Yeah, me either. Chris off somewhere?"

"Down at the Clover Leaf. Bar in town."

"I've seen it."

"Fucking dive, right?"

"Did look pretty gnarly." He gestured at the porch steps. "You mind?"

She shrugged but he saw in her eyes she was interested. He came up the steps. Perched on the railing across from her. From there, he looked her over—a good long look so there'd be no mistake about it. She curled her lip as in: Who gives a shit? But she breathed more carefully and he knew she was aware of him.

They smoked together a while, quiet. They could hear a phone ringing through an open window nearby.

"Chris says you're all checked out," she said. "Ready to fly."

"That's a helluva checkride he gives," said Bishop.

"Yeah, he told me. Don't mind him. He's just an asshole."

Bishop raised an eyebrow. "He's your husband, right?"

"Sweet fucking mystery of love, what can I tell you?" She flicked the ash off her cigarette, indifferent. "Thinks it's a big yuk to see the rookies wet themselves. Then he pulls it out at the last minute. I told him: He's the one'll spin in someday."

"Be honest with you, I don't give a rat's ass if he does," said Bishop, "so long as I don't happen to be in the plane at the time."

"Right." She gave a rueful little laugh. Shook her head at the night. "Look, don't get me wrong. He's a good pilot, a hell of a pilot. Been at it since he was a kid. Flew helos in the service and everything. That Cessna—he could pull her out at twenty feet, no question. He had your back the whole time. He just likes to dick around, that's all."

"Sure."

Kathleen stood off the rail. Dropped her smoke onto the porch, crushed it under the tip of her shoe. Glanced at him. "Hey, do me a favor, willya? Don't mention this to Ray, all right? This is Chris's third job in two years. If this doesn't work out . . . Christ, I don't know what."

"Is that right?" Bishop said. "I heard Chris was golden. I heard Ray'd never fire him."

"Oh yeah? Where'd you hear that?"

"Around. I heard he was in with Ray's partner. What's his name? Hirschorn."

Kathleen gave a weary look at the empty street: There was plenty she could say on that subject. But she didn't say it. "Chris always thinks he's fucking golden. Then next thing he knows, he's out of work." She puffed her cheeks and sighed. "Look, I'm just saying. He's young, dumb and full of come, that's all. He doesn't mean anything by it. He's had a hard time these last few years. Ever since the Army bounced him, he just . . . that really tore him up, y'know? Then he had the freight job and he lost that. It's not like this is San Fran or LA or something with a million places to work. I'm just worried if he washes out here . . ."

"Yeah, I get you." Bishop dropped his cigarette now too. Stepped on it too and stood up as he did. "And hell, I'm not gonna say anything." He pretended to examine the moon as he ambled toward her. Then he was right beside her. She looked up at him and he was very close, standing relaxed with a hand in one pocket of his jeans.

She looked in his eyes and his eyes held her. "Well, thanks," she said.

"But I'll tell you something," Bishop pressed on, "if I had a woman like you waiting for me at home, I'd fly a helluva lot safer than that." He lifted a finger as he said it and laid it against her cheek. Mesmerized, she never took her eyes off his.

"Don't do that," she murmured.

He stroked the finger slowly over her cheek to her chin. She finally forced herself to say it again, "Don't, Frank, I'm serious."

Bishop let his hand fall away. Kathleen broke the hold of his gaze. She studied the porch floorboards.

"Like I need that shit," she muttered.

He was about to answer, was about to say that she did need it. Was about to say that he was looking right at her and he could see plain as day that she needed it bad—needed something anyway. But now he saw her look up, look past him. He heard the engine coming. He turned and there was Chris's pickup moving slowly down the street. The way it was moving, Bishop knew right away that Chris was drunk.

He didn't hurry though. He drifted away from Kathleen but he took his own sweet time about it. Then the two stood and watched as the truck pulled into the carport.

"What's this? What's this? What do I find?" Chris spoke loudly, rolling out of the cab. Swaggering toward them. He was drunk, all right, very drunk, well and truly drunk. "I go away for a couple of hours and what do I come home to find . . . ?" He smacked his fist into his palm five times fast to indicate fucking. "Huh? I ask you. Is this what a man should come home to?"

"God damn it, Chris," said Kathleen. She turned away, disgusted, ashamed of him.

Chris came reeling up the porch steps. Loomed up in between them. He stood swaying over Bishop. "You move in fast, my friend."

Bishop answered him with that tongue-in-cheek look he had and those pale, uncaring eyes. "Just being neighborly."

"Neighborly!" Chris cackled. He swung round unsteadily to his wife. "He's neighborly. That's all he is. Shit, anyone can see that, right? How 'bout you, Kathleen? You neighborly too?"

"Fuck you, Chris. Just shut up, okay?"

She was still turned away. He reached out savagely and gripped her jaw in his big hand, held it hard. He forced her to face him. His fingers crushed the place on her cheek that Bishop had stroked.

"I asked you a question," he said. "Are you neighborly or not?"

"Get off me!" She tried to get him off her, pushing his wrist. He resisted, held on hard. "God damn it," she said. She dug her fingernails into him.

"Ah . . ." said Chris. He let her go and casually cuffed her above the ear. The blow made Kathleen's head snap to the side. She stayed like that, faced away, to hide her tears. "God *damn* it, Chris," she said again.

Chris smiled. Now that she was crying, he was satisfied. "Neighborly," he said. He snorted, swaying over her. Then he staggered around to confront Bishop.

Bishop had not moved. He stood a little apart on the porch, watching, his thumbs hooked behind his belt buckle.

Chris sneered at him. "You say something?"

There was a long silence. Bishop standing there with that smile and those colorless eyes. He didn't answer. The bigger man took a step toward him. Bishop could smell the beer on him.

"I asked you a question, man. You say something?"

Slowly, Bishop shook his head: no.

Chris shuffled closer. "You even think something?"

The night heat hung heavy over them. A plastic trash can lid thudded somewhere down the block a ways. A screen door slammed.

"Well, for one thing," Bishop answered mildly, "I think you probably oughta stick to beating up women."

Kathleen wedged herself between them quickly. The porch light glistened on the tears on her cheeks.

"Just don't now, Chris. Okay? Just fucking don't. He wasn't doing anything. We were just talking. I swear." She put her two hands on his chest. "Please. Okay? I swear to God. Please."

Chris and Bishop stared at each other over the woman's head. The drunkenness was washing down over Chris in waves now, forcing his eyes closed. He was blinking hard, swaying hard, just barely keeping his feet. He grinned stupidly.

"You're lucky she's . . . lucky . . . she's standing there," he said.

He staggered up close against his wife. She put an arm around him.

"Come on," said Kathleen. "Come on, let's get you inside."

She began to guide him toward the door. She glanced back over her shoulder at Bishop, gestured with her head, telling him to go. Bishop nodded. With a lingering smile, he strolled away casually down the porch steps.

"Neighborly . . . fuck," he heard Chris say behind him. But he didn't turn around. Soon he heard the door shut.

A dog barked in the distance. The cicadas rattled in the trees.

NINE

Weiss waited in front of the small white house. Hands in the pockets of his wrinkled pants, his wrinkled jacket unbuttoned. It was a gray day, and the wind from the Pacific stirred the narrow tie on his white shirt. Weiss could see his reflection in the glass on the storm door. With a twinge of pride, he saw that he still looked like a cop for all the world.

But in fact, when the Mousey Guy's mother finally opened up, she took one sorry glance at the large, ugly specimen on her front step and said, "Oh God. Let me guess. Another private detective."

"Mrs. Spender?" said Weiss.

"Come on in, come on, let's get this over with."

She was a tired, sour old woman. Small and narrow and sharp like her mousey son. Her hair was gray and framed her gray, wrinkled face. Her rheumy eyes watched Weiss miserably as she stood back to let him in.

Weiss knew the smell of the house as soon as he stepped across the threshold. Airless, old, oppressively respectable. There would be floral prints inside and worn rugs and suffocating curtains. Some sentimental painting of Christ somewhere. The furniture would be hers from the larger house she'd lived in with her husband till he died. He knew all this just standing in the little foyer without even looking at the rest of the place.

"I take it your son has hired detectives before," he said.

"You're joking, right? Around here it's an annual tradition. Hey, why not? I mean, we have money to burn, don't we? This way, Mr. . . . ?"

"Weiss."

"Come upstairs, Mr. Weiss, and I'll save us both a lot of time and expense."

The narrow stairway was dark and so was the second-floor landing. Weiss followed the woman's dim figure to a closed door at the end of the hall. Mrs. Spender threw the door open with a flourish.

"This is my son's room," she announced. "This is where he concocts his nonsense."

She didn't bother to turn the lights on in here either. But the gray daylight came in through the windows. Weiss could see clearly when he stepped in.

The Mousey Guy's room was like a child's room, like a twelve-year-old's. There was even a model spacecraft on the dresser top and a pair of Giants baseball pennants on the wall. There was a single bed made with hospital corners, the blanket pulled drumhead tight. There was a desk-and-shelf unit against one wall. Weiss scanned the books on the shelves, books about coin collecting, picture books about Spain, a long row of well-worn science fiction novels.

Suddenly, there was a loud, startling *whap*. Mrs. Spender had pulled a stack of notebooks from her son's closet and thrown them down on the desk.

"I'm not supposed to know where he keeps them," she said dryly.

Weiss came forward. He tipped the stack of notebooks over, splaying them across the desktop. They were ordinary spiral notebooks, not many of them, four or five. And there were magazines in the pile also. What else: naked girls. Weiss heard Mrs. Spender give a derisive snort as he leafed briefly through one magazine's pages. The girls, he saw, were all Hispanic.

At the bottom of the stack, there were some coin-collecting folders. Weiss opened these too. He smiled wistfully at the familiar blue interiors with the circular pockets for the coins. Even the coin collection was like a twelve-year-old's, he noticed: All the best stuff, the really valuable stuff, was missing—because who could afford those coins when you were a kid?

Finally, Weiss put these aside and opened the first of the notebooks.

The pages were filled with writing, Spender's painfully cramped hand. Weiss read a line or two and saw what it was. The little man's fantasy of the Spanish virgin was worked out here in detail. How he spotted her in the cafe, how beautiful she was, the whole story. Weiss paged ahead slowly. The rape, he saw, was lovingly described, especially the part where the woman's resistance melted and she succumbed noisily to Mousey Guy's overpowering virility.

She trembles in my embrace. You are too much man for me, señor, she whispers in her thick accent. She grips me helplessly as I carry her to the bed.

Weiss smiled to himself as he tried to imagine Mousey Guy carrying a grown woman anywhere.

I think I have a hernia, I whisper in my thick accent. You are too much woman for me by about thirty pounds.

He kept turning the notebook pages. There were other fantasies written out. Most of the women in the fantasies were Hispanic. The Mousey Guy would describe how he forced them into some sexual act or other. They'd resist at first, then end up being wildly orgasmic. There were also some crude pencil drawings of naked Latina girls sprawled on the floor with their legs splayed.

"Disgusting," said Mrs. Spender with a sniff.

Weiss shrugged. Flipped the notebook closed. "People have all kinds of fantasies, Mrs. Spender," he said. "I just want to make sure your son hasn't done any actual harm to anyone? A real person, I mean."

The Mousey Guy's mother let out a laugh. "Wally? Of course not. He's a bookkeeper."

"Well . . . that's not always a guarantee."

"Oh, I know but . . . I mean, he goes to work every day at eight, comes home every day on the button, five-forty-five. Some days he works at the pharmacy, some days at the electrical supply store, some days at the—whatever-it-is—the artsy crafts store. I always know where he is, he always calls to say. We talk three and four times every day over the phone."

"His cell?"

"Sometimes, but I call at the places he works sometimes too. Not that I'm checking on him—he's a grown man—but . . . He's always there, right where he says he is."

"Weekends?"

"He takes me shopping. We go to the movies. We live a quiet life."

"What about Spain? Your son ever take a vacation there or anything?"

"On his income? If my husband hadn't left me a little something to live on, we wouldn't even be able to afford this house. We take a week at the beach in the winter, that's all. Wally doesn't even have a passport." Her pinched expression softened a little. She searched Weiss's eyes for some understanding. It was easy to find: Weiss understood everything.

So she went on more softly, "It's not much of a life for a grown man, Mr. Weiss. It's not like I don't know that. Wally always did *want* to go to Spain. Even as a little boy but . . . Something always came up, this, that . . . It's nobody's fault. Wally just is who he is." She tilted her head at the notebooks on the desk. "As God is my witness, he could never actually rape anyone. He has fantasies. Like you said. It's not a crime."

"No, ma'am. If it were a crime, everybody would be in prison."

"Exactly."

"What about this man, this man your son says is trying to kill him. Could he be real?"

Mrs. Spender rolled her eyes. "The famous man. With the big knife outside the window."

"That's the one."

"I'll tell you what it is," she said. "Three years ago, my son turned forty. Every year since then, it's the same thing. One year it's the girl's brother, then it's her father, her husband. Whatever. Always with the knife outside the window."

"Always out for revenge?"

"That's my Wally—the world's most hunted man."

"So you're sure the man's imaginary."

"The man's imaginary, the woman's imaginary. The whole thing's imaginary. You're the fourth detective he's hired. I'll give you their cards, you can call them. They charge eighty-five dollars an hour, I can tell you right now. Eighty-five dollars—plus expenses! One of them phoned Wally's employers, asked if he'd had any unexplained absences when he might've been off raping people. Nearly got him fired. And in the end? Lo and behold, what do they find out? Big surprise. It's all in my son's head. In his doodlings. Not real. Thank you very much, the bill's in the mail."

Weiss nodded absently. Ran his fingertips over the cover of one of the notebooks. He didn't tell Mrs. Spender that he had had a friend get him her son's phone records. He knew there were no midnight phone calls, hardly any incoming phone calls at all, certainly nothing out of the ordinary or threatening.

What a crazy thing, he thought. *What a crazy kind of thing.*

He straightened. Turned so that his large body, his great, saggy face, hung over the sour old woman in that sheltering way he had.

"I'll deduct my expenses from your son's retainer," he said, "and make sure the rest is returned to you."

That reached her. The money, I guess, reached her. Her thin lips tightened and her rheumy eyes got rheumier still. "Thank you, Mr. Weiss," she said. "That's very kind of you. You're a very nice man."

"Thank you for your time, ma'am. I'll show myself out."

Bearlike, he lumbered sadly away, leaving her alone there in that small strange room with the pennants on the wall and the spaceship on the dresser and the notebooks and magazines splayed across the desk.

"Well," I asked later, "did you break the news to Spender that he wasn't really a rapist?"

Weiss stood over my desk now, his hands in his pockets, his chin on his chest. He watched me absently as I ran the Agency mail through a stamp machine. The machine went *buzz-thwack*, as it laid the stamps on the envelopes. Weiss nodded slightly, thinking. "I went and saw him at the pharmacy. He had a little cubbyhole in the back. We had a private chat."

"How'd he take it?"

"He cried."

"You're joking."

"No. He was very ashamed."

"Because he's not really a rapist?"

Weiss lifted his shoulders. "He told me that, once, several years ago, he hired a hooker to play out the fantasy with him? She'd be the Spanish Virgin, you know, and he'd force himself on her and then . . ."

The *buzz-thwack* of the stamp machine cut him off as I slid another envelope in. "So what happened? That didn't work for him?"

"No. When it came down to it, his Johnson deserted him."

"His . . . ?"

"He wasn't up to the task."

"Ah." I shook my head. "So now he does this every year? Hires a detective, spins this whole yarn about I raped someone and her brother's after me?"

"Every year since he turned forty."

I shook my head. Tossed the last freshly stamped envelope in the Outgoing Mail basket. "I guess it's tough to let go of a dream," I said.

"Well, forty's not so old," said Weiss. "He could still be a rapist if he set his mind to it."

"You think so? I don't know. I mean, a man is what he is, in the end."

"Right. Right. That's the moral of the story, I guess." Weiss heaved a big sigh. I fiddled with a pencil, watched as he wandered away, back toward his office.

Just as he reached the threshold, I heard him give a husky laugh. "So ends the Case of the Spanish Virgin," he called back to me.

And he went in, shutting the door behind him.

TEN

Weiss had two vices. One of them was whiskey, good single-malt scotch. After nightfall, he would pour himself a Macallan's—the twelve-year-old; he found the older vintages too smoky. He'd sip it and replenish it steadily till bedtime, sometimes consuming as much as half a bottle, sometimes a whole lot more. He was a big man. He could manage it. I don't think I ever saw him drunk. But I don't know whether he could've given it up either or if he ever would have. He once told me it was one of the things that made life worth living.

His other vice was prostitutes. I won't tell you how I know this but I do. His sex life consisted of the occasional incall services of an escort agency run by a woman named Casey. Now I call this a vice out of deference to the delicate sensibilities of my readers. (You do have delicate sensibilities, don't you?) Because in my own coarser view, it was pretty hard to find anything blameworthy in it. Weiss was an ugly man. He was ungainly. And he had absolutely no romantic way with women at all. I heard he'd been married once a long time ago but apparently it was a pretty toxic affair. Since then: nothing. Nothing, that is, with any possibility of becoming real.

He was too much in awe of women, that was the problem. It was really kind of odd when you think about it. I mean, here was a man who'd seen more than his share of depravity in both genders, but somehow he was still saddled with this idealized view of the opposite sex. For him, ladies were by nature tenderhearted and sweet-tempered and nurturing—all traits which he cherished and which he craved. As a result, he treated most females with elaborate gentleness and respect, an almost courtly kindness. He was protective toward them. He fell in love with them only from a distance, only when they were impossibly engaged or out of reach. Women could immediately sense how desperately romantic he was about them, how he glamor-ized them, yearned and longed for them, dreamed of holding them and shielding them from evil and so on. So, of course, they came to regard him either as a sexless father figure or as a rather nice but silly old pain in the ass.

And here he was: a man who probably would've been deliriously happy married to a plain Jane homemaker with a couple of kids in a house on the peninsula, but he was baffled by his own imagination, left alone. At the same time, he was a man. He craved women. Not just the sex but the sound of their voices, the way the light hit their hair—like most of us—the whole package. So he called on Casey's girls.

He was a favorite with them, I understand. Why not? He paid without complaining. He tipped well. He was generous with liquor, even food. For the ones who gave a damn, he was tender and solici-tous, genuinely interested in what they had to say. Plus he never asked for anything complicated or difficult. He basically just wanted to hear them talk, hear them laugh, see them move, catch the scent of them—and have the comfort and pleasure of holding them, being inside them. You know.

Anyway, that night, the night after he read the Mousey Guy's notebooks, he went home and poured his whiskey and then called Casey.

"Hey, where've you been?" she said when she heard his voice. "I was afraid you'd found true love or something."

"Must be a problem in your business."

"Nah. But it is good to hear from you." Casey liked Weiss, or seemed to. She knew a good customer when she saw one anyway. Every now and again she'd come by herself and provide him with services at no charge. But Weiss was never sure whether this was an act of affection or one of those buy-ten-get-one-free deals. "What can we do for you to-night, my dear?" she asked.

"That Mexican girl, Ynez—she still there?"

"No, sorry, she's long gone. She got married, in fact. She had to move to Dallas to be with her husband."

"Well . . . Good for her."

"Uh-huh. I'll give you her number if you ever go down there. Meanwhile, I have got Carmella. Am I getting the theme of the evening right?"

"Carmella sounds good."

"A little darker than Ynez, more up top."

"Terrific."

"You want anchovies with that?"

Weiss snorted, hung up the phone.

Casey always instructed her girls carefully in what Weiss liked. No pretense, no routines, no porno poses. Everything friendly, easygoing. Some of them couldn't pull it off, but Carmella turned out to be good at it. She sat on the sofa and told funny stories about her sister's children, cracked herself up. Laughed so hard she doubled over, slopped wine over the rim of her glass. Weiss's eyes sparkled with pleasure to see her like that, to hear her laughing.

When she was gone, though, he was depressed. He returned to his whiskey. Put on his bathrobe. Sat in the chair by the bay window. Looked out at the street, glass in hand. The fog had come down from the water, down into the north city. Weiss watched it folding over the streetlamps one after another, glowing with the light of them then swallowing the glow. He nursed a half-pleasant melancholy, the sadness of desire, his own and other men's, everyone's. He thought of the Mousey Guy. He thought, with some self-disdain, that they were not all that different, Spender with his spiral notebooks, Weiss with his whores. But then maybe that had been the object of the exercise tonight—the whole business about Ynez, Carmella—maybe he'd been trying to punish himself with the similarities.

Anyway, he thought about the Mousey Guy for a while and then his thoughts drifted to Jim Bishop. Which just made things worse. Because the thought of Bishop just now only brought on envy, a gnarling pain. Bishop wanted nothing from women—or just the one thing—and he seemed to be able to call them to him with the snap of his fingers. Weiss wished that he wanted nothing too, that he could snap his fingers too. That, finally, was his fantasy tonight.

He set his scotch glass down on the end table. He pushed out of his chair. He went to his desk, to his computer. Turned it on. This was also perverse of him, more self-punishment. He knew there might be an e-mail from Bishop. He knew it would probably rub salt in his wound. But he couldn't seem to stop himself. Soon he was on-line.

Weiss. More action here. Chris getting daily flights—cargo and passengers, new faces. Can't tell how many are assignments from gray moustache—Hirschorn—but some. Hobbes time all off whenever I can check. Client Ray very scared, nervous. Might not stay on board so we need results. I see two avenues. One: Chris is drinking hard at local bar, the Clover Leaf. I hear he's mouthing off about "big plans, big success in future." If Hirschorn gets wind of this, could be rift between them, I could move in. Two: I'm getting closer to the girl. She knows something, maybe a lot. Lonely, wants to unburden. Almost there with her. All professional, of course. Hope you're well. JB

By the time Weiss rose, his hound dog face was at its hanging-down hound-doggiest. Stooped, he lumbered back to his chair by the bay window. Settled into it. Picked up his scotch again, sipped it.

All professional, of course.

He watched the rolling fog.

ELEVEN

The sun was sinking. The air was still. Bishop was in the Skyhawk, a single-engine. Sailing home over the treetops at forty-five degrees to the active's downwind. The clouds above the western foothills were bright orange against the deep, deep blue. The stubble fields around the runway looked shady and peaceful from above. Something in Bishop felt quiet and good.

He turned base leg, his hands light on the controls, the plane descending almost by itself. A light tug on the yoke and the Skyhawk was on final approach, angling for centerline. Bishop had no thought of anything else, just this. A last glance at the sunset sky, the hills and trees rising up over it as he floated down. Then the runway was before him. The airplane's gear touched the surface without a noise, without a jolt at all. As the plane rolled over the pavement, Bishop drew a deep breath in through his nose as if awaking.

That's when he noticed Chris with Hirschorn, the man with the gray moustache.

They were standing in the car lot, standing off from one corner of the hangar. Bishop, suddenly alert, was looking right at them as he brought his plane around onto the taxiway. Hirschorn was a sturdy, elegant man in his late fifties. The face of an old charmer, tanned and strong and square. A lot of silver waves up top, the thick moustache darker, iron gray. He wore a white sports jacket, an open-collared polo shirt, gray slacks. All very crisp and dry, even in this heat. Chris hulked over him, muscles bulging out of his sweaty tee. But the way he had his hands slung in his belt, his stance slouched and sullen, he looked more than anything like a scolded child.

The older man wagged his finger at him. He locked Chris's eyes with his own. He seemed to be talking quietly but he never stopped talking. And Chris didn't interrupt him either. As the Skyhawk taxied nearer, Bishop saw how Chris shifted uncomfortably where he stood, trying hard to look cool under the steady barrage.

Bishop parked the plane behind the hangar, just out of sight of the two men. On the apron, tying down the wings, he tried to hear what Hirschorn was saying. The voice didn't carry. Bishop finished up quickly, hoisted his flight bag and headed into the hangar.

It was late. Most of the staff had gone home. Ray, the older guy who half owned the place and ran it, was in there by himself. He was standing in the shadows next to a v-tailed Bonanza. He was supposed to be working on it but he was just standing there. Standing there, looking out through the hangar door at where Hirschorn was wagging his finger at Chris. Ray's eyes were wide. His eyebrows were way high up on his bald head. The horizontal lines on his brow ran clear up the sweaty dome.

Bishop strode past him without a word. Ray practically jumped when he saw him.

"Bishop," he hissed.

Bishop stiffened at the sound of his real name. "Shut the fuck up," he hissed back.

"I mean, I mean, *Kennedy* . . ." babbled Ray.

"I said shut up. And stop gawking." Bishop never broke stride.

Ray called after him in a stage whisper. "They been out there ten minutes. I can't hear 'em but it looks like Hirschorn's reading Chris the riot act."

Bishop would've liked to read Ray the riot act. Or better yet just thump the old idiot, just club him to the ground. But Ray was the client, so Bishop just kept moving. He went straight through the hangar, out into the car lot on the other side.

The lot was a small square of macadam. Most of it had been busted up over time into gravel. Hirschorn's Mercedes was parked on the one smooth spot near the road, not far from Bishop's Harley. There was a man leaning against the Mercedes. A bodyguard, Bishop thought, a dyed-in-the-wool goon. Blocky and solid, arms as long as a gorilla's. Hatchet-faced with slick black hair. He was dressed just like Hirschorn, only in the big boy sizes. He was smoking a cigarette, smiling down at his shoes.

Bishop walked casually to his bike. Opened a saddlebag, laid his flight bag inside. The goon watched him but only because he was there to watch. Bishop took his time, squinted off toward the setting sun. Squinted up at the sky as if weighing the heat that still sat on the day like a slab of stone. He took out a cigarette. Dug in his pockets as if he couldn't find a match.

That's how he approached the goon. "Got a light?"

The goon took out an expensive-looking lighter, flicked it for a flame. Bishop leaned into it.

"Nice scoot," said the goon.

"Butt ugly but it's fast," said Bishop, drawing back, blowing smoke. He glanced off toward Hirschorn. Hirschorn had his finger flush against Chris's chest. "Looks like we got a dissatisfied customer," he said.

The goon just shrugged, just smiled.

"That your boss?" Bishop asked him.

"I'm his chauffeur, yeah."

Bishop narrowed his eyes in Hirschorn's direction. "Hey, that's that guy, what's his name, Hirschorn, isn't it? Guy who owns the place with Ray."

The goon just went on smiling.

"Shit," said Bishop. "I guess Chris is in it ass deep. What'd he do?"

"I just drive the car," the goon said.

"Right," said Bishop. "Right. Poor old Chris. Now you mention it, I heard he had some business with Hirschorn. . . ."

"I didn't mention it."

"No? Guess I heard it somewhere else then."

"Guess so."

Bishop drew smoke. He waited.

"Where, you figure?" the goon asked.

"What's that?"

"Where did you hear it, do you figure?"

"Oh." Bishop made a face. "Fuck if I know. One of the pilots who hang at the Clover Leaf probably. That's Chris for you, right? Mouths off when he's drinking. It gets around."

"Yeah," said the goon slowly. "That's Chris for you. So what's he been saying?"

"Nothing much. Not that I've heard. Mouthing off. You know. Some deal him and Hirschorn were cooking up. The big payday of it all. That kind of thing."

"Sure," said the goon.

"You figure that's what this is about? Chris talking?" The goon didn't answer. Bishop felt that he'd pushed it as far as he could. "Well anyway . . . Thanks for the light," he said.

The goon nodded. Bishop ambled back to his bike. When he glanced over his shoulder, Hirschorn had finally broken off. The dapper little man was striding back across the lot toward his Mercedes. The hulking Chris was slinking out of sight around the hangar like a whipped dog.

Bishop gripped the bike's handlebars, slung a leg over the saddle. He watched as the goon hurried to pull the Mercedes's rear door open for his boss.

When Hirschorn reached the car, Bishop called out. "Hey, Mr. Hirschorn."

Mr. Hirschorn paused, looked at him, one foot in the Mercedes, one on the macadam.

"You ever need a pilot who can hold his liquor and keep his mouth shut, the name's Frank Kennedy," Bishop said.

Hirschorn had a bright smile, extra bright against his sun-dark skin. His narrow gaze seemed to take in everything about a man. "Thanks anyway," he said. "Chris and me have a history."

Bishop nodded. Hirschorn lowered himself into the car. The goon shut the door, got in himself behind the wheel.

Bishop looked away. He slipped the key into the motorcycle's ignition. He was about to throttle the bike to life when he heard the Mercedes window buzz down behind him.

"Hey, Kennedy."

Bishop turned. The man with the gray moustache was framed in the window opening. "What're you rated in?" he asked.

"Any damn thing that flies," said Bishop. "Jets, props. I flew helos in the service."

Hirschorn gave his bright smile again. "Well, you have a nice day now," he said.

Bishop sat astride the Harley, watching as the silver Mercedes crunched over the gravel, pulled out and was gone.

TWELVE

It was deep twilight when he reached home. There were three boys on the sidewalk, arguing over a skateboard. They stopped to watch as the motorcycle veered off the road into the driveway of Bishop's house. By the time Bishop locked her up, the boys were gone, one boarding off through the dusk neighborhood, the other two chasing behind him.

Bishop watched after them absently as he walked to his front door. He was still thinking about Hirschorn.

He stepped inside the house. The living room was hung with dark. The air was stale, the heat was stifling. He started to reach for the light switch and stopped. Even with the windows open, he could smell the cigarette smoke.

Bishop scanned the shadows and saw her. She was propped against the windowsill. He could make out her shape on the fading daylight at the pane.

"Leave the lights off," she told him.

He let his hand fall to his side. "Okay."

"So tell me something," Kathleen went on. "Just who the fuck are you?"

Bishop felt his heart speed up. He was glad she couldn't see his face. "What do you mean?"

He watched the glowing tip of her cigarette travel with her gesture. "I mean, you come here, and you're all . . . moving in on me right away. Out of nowhere like that. I mean, what've you been here—a week? I mean, shit, what's that about? Who are you? That's what I'm saying."

Bishop was thinking fast, measuring his words. Was she onto him? Or was it just talk? He couldn't tell. "I felt a connection," he told her. "That's all. I thought you felt it too. If I was out of line . . ."

"Well, shit yes, you're out of line!" she said. "I mean, I'm fucking married, aren't I?"

Bishop relaxed. He smiled a little, hidden in the dark. Yeah, it was just talk, after all. The usual thing. She had to talk—women had to talk before you had them. But he would have her, he was sure of that now. And then she would talk to him some more.

"Yeah. Yeah, you're married." He crossed the room toward her, stood over her, close. "But he's not around tonight. He's got a flight tonight, hasn't he?"

She half laughed, hissing smoke out at him. "Oh, you're bad. Jesus."

He brushed her hair back with his fingers. She didn't stop him. He'd have her. He could make out her waiting lips by the window light. He could see her eyes gleaming.

"He shouldn't hit you," he said. Stroking her hair back, playing her.

"Oh, what're you, my white knight?" She sniffed, frowned. She had one arm across her middle, the other resting on it. She had her cigarette held down now off to the side, out of his way. She let his hand stay on her hair, on her cheek, stroking her. "You're no white knight. I know that much. I can see that much with my own eyes."

Bishop leaned down to kiss her. She turned her head so he only caught the corner of her mouth. "No," she said. She looked past him into the shadows of the room. "I mean it," she said. "I mean, who the fuck are you? I don't even know who the fuck you are."

"You know enough," he whispered. He kissed her neck.

"Stop it. I mean it," she said, breathing faster.

"All you gotta do is tell me you don't want to."

Another moment passed. He drew away a little. Her eyes shifted back to his. He moved in again. He got the whole kiss this time. First touching his lips to hers and feeling them soften. Then moving his tongue deep into her open mouth to taste the smoke.

When he pulled back, she pressed her head against his chest. He felt her shudder under his hand. "What the fuck am I doing?" she said.

"No, it's good," Bishop answered softly. "It's right."

"He'll kill us if he finds out." She didn't sound as if she cared. She was breathless. "I'm not joking, Frank. He'll kill us both."

Gently, he drew her up off the windowsill. There was no more resistance. When he kissed her again, she melted into it, pressed her body against his, lifted her arms around him. Her cigarette, held up behind his head, sent a spiral of smoke to the ceiling.

Later, upstairs, when he was inside her, she cried.

THIRTEEN

Weiss. The girl gave over. Good stuff. She's been eavesdropping on Chris and Hirschorn for weeks, worried what her husband's getting into, etc. Overheard: Operation goes down soon. Sounds major, lots of security, material involved. Overheard Hirschorn say: Secrecy very important. Overheard him say: Timing essential because operation's base is beyond communication, no phones, etc. Chris's role unclear, possibly just flying supplies and personnel into op base somewhere in the woods but maybe more.

Can't get a handle on op's nature: Kathleen says maybe smuggling or drug-running but it sounds more like a onetime deal, a heist or something. Not sure. Kathleen has also heard certain names mentioned: Whip—a man's name, she thinks. Also: Harry Ridder, somewhere near Sonoma. Hirschorn laughed when he mentioned Ridder. Nothing more on either of these. ID on your end, if possible, thanx.

Kathleen confirms: Hirschorn pissed re: Chris's drinking, talking. But so far sticking with him—family connection, Hirschorn knew Chris's father—and he may not want to replace him so late in the day. Maybe I can give it a push though. Still working on it.

Meanwhile, I told Kathleen she had to keep eavesdropping, to protect herself and Chris, blah blah. She bought it, says she will—but may be unreliable due to guilt, divided loyalty, etc.

Get back to me with Whip, Ridder IDs ASAP, thanx. JB

Of course it sat on Weiss's stomach like a fast-food lunch. *The girl gave over. Good stuff.* He tooled his sensible gray Taurus across the Golden Gate. He stared at the pavement ahead. The sky was blue again. The air was washed clean and the water was sparkling beyond the bridge's orange-red cables. The cities of the East Bay looked like fairy-tale villages on the far horizon. But he only stared at the pavement ahead and all he could think about was the indigestible e-mail roiling in his gut. *The girl gave over. Good stuff.*

The thing was, Bishop was right. It *was* good stuff. He was onto something, something big maybe. Whatever operation Hirschorn was planning, breaking it up could be the key to saving their client's life—not to mention boosting the Agency's reputation, bringing in more clients from around the state and so on. And if this operation was going down soon, they needed all the information they could get as fast as possible. So the setup was perfect: The girl would continue to spy on her husband and report back to Bishop, now her lover . . . even if she was *unreliable due to guilt, divided loyalty, etc.*

"For fuck's sake, Bishop," said Weiss aloud as he drove.

Because, of course, though he wanted to protect his client, and he very much wanted his Agency to expand and bring in more income, he couldn't help seeing things from Kathleen's side too. That's how he was. It was a large part of how he operated. He could imagine how she would appease her *guilt, divided loyalty, etc.* by convincing herself that this was not just some tawdry affair she was having but a grand passion, even a great love. Then, to keep that fantasy alive, she would start to remake Bishop in the image of her own daydreams. She would know it was a lie but she would do it anyway so she could live with the way he was using her. She'd tell herself: *Oh, he does really care.* Looking smack at the snake-cold indifference he showed so openly in his eyes. She would think: *No, he does care, really, I know it, this is just his way.* And instead of facing what she'd become—a cheat, a pawn, a traitor in her own house—she would believe that she was working to escape her circumstances, to get away with Bishop, to be with Bishop in some future time, some future relationship where there would be no more loneliness and no more abuse.

That was how Weiss imagined her anyway. He'd seen women act like that with Bishop before, and what a hell of a fall there was when the blinders came off. Bishop didn't seem to give one hair on a rat's ass what happened to her or any of them, but Weiss—Weiss now had to shoulder his own burden of *guilt, divided loyalty, etc.* because he was responsible in part, he was the boss, he was the one who had assigned Bishop to the case.

And he sure as hell wasn't going to call him off either. He could have. Maybe for Kathleen's sake, he should have. But Kathleen was not his client. Ray Grambling was his client. It was Ray, the half owner of North Country Aviation, who had hired the Weiss Agency to find out what the other half owner, Hirschorn, was doing with North Country's pilots and planes. Ray was the one who'd have to face the FAA inspector. Who'd have to answer the questions about the false manifests and Hobbes time and so on. Ray was the one who might end up out of a job. Or in prison. Or just plain dead, if Hirschorn wanted to keep him quiet. And, from a more selfish perspective, Ray was the one who would spread the good word about the Weiss Agency if they could keep him out of all that trouble.

"Uysh," Weiss groaned, massaging his belly with one hand as he drove.

The Taurus came off the bridge and rolled north in the shadow of the headlands.

FOURTEEN "Mr. William Ridder?"

"Yeah?"

"You had a son," Weiss asked, "named Harry Ridder?"

"Well . . ." said the old man. "What's this about?"

They were standing outside a crumbling barn by a crumbling farmhouse near the freeway. There was a field beyond the barn but not much of a field. Weiss knew fat zip about agriculture but as far as he could tell, the main crop here was dust. Tough to see what a place like this could have to do with Bishop's investigation. But Bishop wanted IDs on the names he'd gotten from Kathleen—Harry Rider and "Whip"—and this was the Ridder farm, sure enough.

The old man, William Ridder, was leaning on a garden hoe, giving Weiss a sharp once-over. The noise from the freeway traffic was loud, cars rushing by, trucks grinding gears.

"I'm a private investigator," Weiss said. "Your son's name came up in connection with a case we're working on. When I tried to track him down, I found his obituary. The newspaper said he committed suicide five months ago."

"Suicide." The old man spat the word. "They just got him to pull the trigger for 'em, that's all."

"What do you mean? You're saying he was murdered?"

"Good as. What is this case you're working on anyway?"

The old man was wizened and brown, skin like a walnut. So thin his shirt and pants billowed around him. He put on a good suspicious glare but he had a victim's eyes, waiting for the worst. A man used to getting bulldozed, Weiss figured. So he bulldozed him.

"My clients are running a security check on a landscaping outfit they want to hire," he said. "Your son did some work for the outfit and they used his name as a reference. I'm sorry to bring up painful memories, but if his death was suspicious, that could be important."

It didn't make a hell of a lot of sense, but it was probably more explanation than the old man usually got for what happened to him. Good enough anyway.

"I told him," said Ridder sourly. "I told him there was plenty of work for him right here." He gestured at the dead, dusty fields. "But that was Harry. Had to go off. Down to the city." He grimaced into the distance. The traffic noise went on, filled the air, rushing, grinding. "Got himself into something down there, that's for sure."

"How do you mean?"

"Well . . ." The old man tamped the dirt with the flat of the hoe. "Harry, you know, he always had a real hand for the garden. *Landscaping,* I guess is what they call it. There's plenty of rich people who'll pay to have *landscaping* done around their houses. Harry, he worked for one man, a rich fellow named Moncrieff. Cameron Moncrieff, always remember that: Cameron Moncrieff."

"Cameron Moncrieff," repeated Weiss slowly—and the way he said it made Ridder ask:

"You know him?"

Weiss knew him. "I've heard the name. He died a while back, didn't he?"

"Well, that's the story," Ridder said. "See . . . Harry went off. Wife and me, we didn't hear from him much. But he'd call from time to time. Said he was working for several people—landscaping—but mostly for this Moncrieff, keeping his garden, y'know. Then, one day, Harry calls us and it seems this Moncrieff fellow's gone and died. I don't know what of, but something. Got sick and died. Well, Harry just sort of called, just sort of mentioned it like that, and about how he's gonna have to find other work and so on. Then, next thing we know, all of a sudden, up he shows. One night, dead of night, front step, thin as beans, trembling like a leaf."

"Scared, you mean?"

"Yeah, oh yeah. Something scared him. Someone. That's for

sure. Hardly came out of his room after that. Strapping young man when he left. Thin as beans when he came back, trembling like a leaf, I mean it. Wouldn't leave his room for anything, love or money. Took my old rifle in there and would just sit there, watching from the window. You'd look up and you'd see him, day and night. Just watching, just sitting there looking out."

"Like he was watching out for someone," said Weiss. "Like he was afraid someone was coming after him."

The old man went on tamping the dirt with his hoe. He considered the dirt a while, considered the hoe. Then he looked up and considered Weiss—Weiss and his grave, heavy features, his deep, baggy, sympathetic eyes.

"Come here," he said then. "I'll show you something."

Weiss went beside him round the edge of the field. The dirt was hard and dry under his shoes. The old man walked slowly, bent over, staring down, using the stick of the hoe for support. Weiss had to mince his long strides to stay with him.

They came to a toolshed. Old planks hammered together, six feet by five. A corrugated tin roof rusted brown. The door creaked as the old man pulled it open.

"He came out here after a while," he said.

"Your son?"

Ridder nodded. "Brought the gun out. Just sat in here for hours. A whole day and night sometimes."

Weiss's expression didn't change. But he could imagine the young Ridder: huddled in this box, trembling in there, clutching his gun.

"Wife says I oughta tear it down now. Guess I oughta. Can't do it though somehow."

The old man held his hand at the open doorway. Weiss had to duck his head to get through. Inside, he had to stand hunched and even then he could feel the grit of the rusted roof against his hair. The noise from the freeway was muffled. It was dark. It took a moment for

Weiss's eyes to adjust. Then he looked around slowly. He saw what was on the walls.

"Did the whole thing with nails," the old man said. He was still standing just outside. Leaning on his hoe, looking away, off into the brown hills. "Just old nails he found fallen here and there right on the ground. Then I guess he colored some of it in with chalk and red stone he found."

Weiss could've sworn that was fatherly pride he heard in the old man's voice. He went on staring at the walls.

Harry Ridder had carved patterns into the wood. Patterns, drawings, words. Dug painstakingly into the rotting planks. Spirals beside figures, figures over names. Each nestled neatly into the next so that every inch of space was used, every clear spot between the shears and the weed scythe and the rake hanging from their rusted nails. Weiss turned slowly, his head bowed in the cramped shed. He squinted through the shadows. He saw more and more of it. It was everywhere.

"Kind of artistic, wouldn't you say?" came the old man's proud voice from outside.

Weiss didn't answer him. He felt a chill in his stomach, a hint of nausea. Thinking about the kid in here hour after hour. Carving at the old boards, digging at every empty space. Like a man desperate to write his life story on the last piece of paper left in the world. It was eerie to see. It was madness.

Weiss heard the traffic passing somewhere in the distance. Cramped in the musty darkness here, he was sharply aware of the light of day beyond the walls, the good light of day. He bent lower, leaned closer. Tried to pick out one design from another, to separate the images from the letters from the shapes.

He discovered the face of a woman with long hair. The hair became a series of waves. The waves became a name of some kind—*Julie Angel*. The name, in turn, grew into a forest, a house, a wild wolf howling at the moon. Weiss's eyes moved over the patterns. The sweat gathered on his temples. He could hear his own breathing. *Julie*—he found the name again—and then the other word—*Angel*—molded into an angel's form. The angel's wings became a complex circular maze with more writing hidden in it. The word *Life*. The word *Hope*. The word *Death*. It made no sense that Weiss could see.

His eyes kept moving. He noticed a spot, one spot in one corner, where the sun came through a hole in the wall. It was a ragged hole. All around it, the wood was darker, the carvings were stained an unpleasant shade of brown.

The exit wound, Weiss thought.

Harry Ridder had blown his brains out in this hut. That hole—that was where the bullet came out the other side of his head and punched through the shed's wooden wall. The brown stain—well, that was the last of Harry.

And it was a funny thing: As Weiss stood there looking, it began to seem to him that that hole, that stain, were the center of the bizarre mural on the wall, as if everything chiseled into the planks around them was designed to draw his focus there. He shuffled toward it over the dirt floor. Bent closer to it. Let his fingers trail over the splintery edges. There was a word here, he saw. He felt it under his fingertips, a single word alone. It was worked closely round the hole, fit perfectly into the jags of the broken wood. As if young Harry Ridder had known, when he put the rifle in his mouth, exactly where the bullet would emerge from his skull when he pulled the trigger. *Weird,* Weiss thought. He narrowed his eyes, peered through the hazy sunlight.

The word—the sense of the word—came clear to him all of a sudden. Weiss felt the jolt of it. He felt the breath catch in his throat, felt the blood drain from his cheeks. He squinted through the haze at that single word for a long, long time. He read it over and over:

SHADOWMAN.

FIFTEEN

Sissy Truitt was another of Weiss's people. A golden blonde with a fragile face, a gentle voice and milky, deep blue eyes. One of the Agency's best investigators, especially when it came to doing interviews. She was just so damn warm and maternal, anyone would've told her anything. Weiss, of course, was crazy about her. Would've wrapped his big old self around her and shielded her from every wind and weather if he could've. An extreme example of his painfully chivalrous approach to women in general. But Sissy always took it kindly. She treated him to her tinkling laugh, her nurturing smile, the affectionate tilt of her head—as if her boss were some faithful St. Bernard who flopped around protectively at her heels. She was just good like that, good with everyone.

Weiss's vast office with its towering windows on the city and its enormous desk and its likewise enormous Weiss always seemed to intimidate her when she first came in—her with her meek manner and her schoolgirl clothes, her pleated skirt and cardigan and so on. She was clutching her case folder to her chest with her two arms as if it were her algebra textbook and she was on her way to high school.

"Oh," she said, taking one look at him and hurrying to perch anxiously on the edge of one of his client chairs. "What on earth's the matter, Scott?"

Weiss, in fact, looked drawn and pale. No sleep. *Shadowman.* The name haunted him. It had for a long time. But as much as he loved it when Sissy fussed over him, he brushed the question away with his hand. He tilted back in his own chair, the huge high-backed swiveler. "What've you got?" he asked her. "So far all I know is that Harry Ridder was a gardener for Cameron Moncrieff."

Sissy lowered the folder to her lap. "Well, you know who Moncrieff was, right?"

"Yeah, sure. Little *faigelah* smuggler, pimp, whatever. Liked to wear turtlenecks and talk about art like he knew something."

"Oh, he knew something. He did a good trade in black market art; he was a real collector. Plus he ran women, guns, coke. He was just a middleman for anything coming this way. He must've been very good at it too: He lived in a mansion, practically, over in Presidio Terrace."

"Foof. Nice part of town. I guess we're in the wrong business."

"No fooling," said Sissy with her sweet laugh.

"I remember the feds got him on something once. Counterfeiting, was it?"

"Yeah, they traced some funny money to him. He did a year."

"Okay," said Weiss. "So our young friend Harry Ridder was Moncrieff's gardener. And . . . ?"

Sissy's narrow shoulders rose and fell under her cardigan. "And nothing. Nothing I can find out about Ridder anyway. No one seemed to notice him at all except to say the garden always looked nice. The only mention of him I can find is in the coroner's report: He was present at the house when Moncrieff died."

"He died at home?"

"Yeah, liver disease."

"AIDS?"

"I don't think so. If it was, they kept it out of the report."

Weiss mused on that a second, rocking in his chair. "Who else was there at the time he died?"

"His attorney, Peter Crouch."

"Sure, I know Crouchy. A good old-fashioned lowlife mouthpiece. I heard he closed shop a while back, scuttled off to some retirement cabin someplace."

"Yeah, I tried to find him. No one's heard from him in months. No one seems to care much either."

"That's Crouchy," said Weiss. "No one would. Okay. So

Moncrieff died in bed attended by his lawyer and his gardener. Anyone else? No one named Whip by any chance."

"No, no Whip. Just a woman the coroner described as 'Moncrieff's live-in caregiver.'"

"You mean like a nurse?"

"Not professional, not an RN, not as far as anyone knows anyway."

"She have a name?"

"Julie Wyant. Which is pretty much all anyone seems to know about her."

Weiss remembered the words written in the toolshed where Harry Ridder had killed himself: *Julie Angel.* He repeated the name aloud, "Julie Wyant. So where is she now?"

"Well, that's the thing," said Sissy Truitt. "She's gone too."

Weiss lifted one big hand. "Gone? As in . . . ?"

"As in gone. As in dead," said Sissy softly. "A suicide, it looks like. About three months ago, they found her car abandoned in the Vista Point parking lot. Cops figure she walked out onto the bridge and threw herself off. No one's seen her since."

SIXTEEN

Alone, Weiss sat swiveling slightly in his chair. Staring absently at the skyline through the high-arched windows. *Shadowman.*

He thought it over. Tried to get it straight in his mind. The way it shook out so far was this:

Bernie Hirschorn—the murderous crime lord who owned most of the city of Driscoll—was paying one his pilots, Chris Wannamaker, to take mysterious flights into the middle of nowhere and back. Wannamaker's wife, Kathleen, was worried about what her husband had gotten himself into so she'd been eavesdropping on the two of them. She told Bishop that they were planning some sort of large operation scheduled to go off soon. She had heard them mention the names Harry Ridder and Whip.

Okay. Ridder was a gardener for a criminal named Moncrieff. He'd been there when Moncrieff died. Now he was dead too. He'd blown his brains out in a toolshed, gibbering with fear. Another person who'd been present at Moncrieff's death—a woman named Julie Wyant—also seemed to have killed herself. And another—Moncrieff's lawyer, Peter Crouch—was missing, or at least making himself scarce.

So the obvious questions: Was there any connection between the disappearances and Moncrieff's death or was it just a coincidence? And was there any connection between Moncrieff and Hirschorn and Chris Wannamaker and their mysterious flights into the woods?

Weiss breathed deeply, gazed blankly, swiveled slightly. *Shadowman.* His instinct, that cop instinct, told him it was all one picture. He just couldn't fit it together yet. He didn't have enough of the pieces.

Which led him to think about the other name: Whip. Now there was a lead for you. What the hell was he supposed to do with that?

Weiss was generally known as one of the best locate men the city had ever had, one of the best, it was said, in the country. He seemed somehow to get into the minds of the missing, to follow their trails by instinct. Track-downs that would take the cops a month of phone calls Weiss sometimes pulled off in an hour. I'd seen it happen. But even he, who could find anyone, would have a hard time finding a guy with only the name of Whip. On the other hand, if there was a connection to Moncrieff, the cops might know something. . . .

He swiveled away from the windows, faced the desk. Cast a sad eye on the telephone there. Still he hesitated. Swiveling, gazing, thinking.

He was worried about Ray—his client, Ray Grambling. Ray was terrified Hirschorn would find out he was having him investigated. He claimed Hirschorn would have him killed if he got wind of it. Have him killed, then kill his wife, his children, his parents, cousins, distant acquaintances . . . Ray was plenty frightened of Hirschorn.

But Weiss still had some friends on the force, and one good friend, his former partner, Ketchum. Ketchum could be trusted to listen to his story and go deaf and dumb in all the right places. Weiss thought he could tell Ketchum at least some of this without risking his client's life.

Finally now, he reached for the phone. And as he did, the phone rang. He picked it up. Spoke to our receptionist, Amy, "Yeah?"

"Inspector Ketchum calling for you," Amy told him.

Weiss was only mildly surprised. This happened to him and Ketchum a lot. "Yeah," he said. "Put him on." Then he said, "Ketch?"

"Hey."

"I was just about to call you."

"Well, see, that's how good a cop I am. I knew that."

"What's happening?"

"You know a guy named Wally Spender?" Ketchum asked.

For a moment, Weiss didn't. He'd been so immersed in the other case, he couldn't place Spender's name at all. Then he could: the Mousey Guy. *The Case of the Spanish Virgin.*

"Yeah. Wally Spender. Sure. I know him," he said.

"Well, you better come over and see him."

"Why? Is he in some kind of trouble?"

"No, he's in some kind of alley off Mission Street," Ketchum said. "Somebody stabbed him to death."

PART TWO Julie Angel

SEVENTEEN

North Wilderness State Prison is a security housing unit, a "Super-Max" lockup in the language of the trade. Its buildings stand in desolate isolation on 250 acres of nowhere. There are miles of mountainous forest on three sides. On the fourth side, there's a screen of trees and then rocky cliffs battered by the roaring sea.

Alone in its clearing, the prison is surrounded by three perimeter fences. Two are electrified, all are motion sensitive. All are under continuous video surveillance. The tops are lined with razor wire, the bottoms are sunk five feet deep into the earth to prevent tunneling. The entire expanse is covered with crisscrossing wires to keep out helicopters.

Three hundred and seventy guards patrol the place, inside and out. They are an elite corps, chosen from among corrections officers with at least five years' experience, at least two in maximum security. Once chosen, they undergo four extra months of training in weaponry, security, tactics, even psychology. The best marksmen are stationed in the guard towers, which are set every seven hundred yards around the perimeter. These towers contain small armories of shotguns, sniper rifles, pepper gas launchers and M-16-type assault weapons. There are four larger armories sunk underground. These store everything from truncheons to Stinger-style missile launchers to a couple of genuine M-1 Abrams tanks.

The prison was built only a few years ago at a cost to the state of around 200 million dollars. Its purpose is to house the worst of the worst of the state's inmate population, men too violent to be with other violent men. Basically, if you're so bloodthirsty you're unfit to share space with the gang members, drug enforcers, career killers and

Mexican mafiosi passing their lives at Pelican Bay, you are shipped off to North Wilderness SHU.

In order to determine which convicts should go to this prison and which to others, the state has developed a point system. If you're a criminal with one to eighteen points, for instance, you're sent to a minimum security or Level 1 facility, a farm or a "prison without walls" like the California Institution for Men. With eighteen to twenty-seven points, you've made it to the fence-enclosed dormitories at Level 2. With twenty-eight to fifty-one points, you're at Level 3 in a cell secured by armed guards. After that, you're in maximum security, Level 4—a "soft four" to begin with. But if you cause trouble there . . . well then, my friend, kiss your sweet ass good-bye because you are headed for North Wilderness SHU.

Now, how many points you get depends on a number of different things. Gang affiliations count against you. So do prior convictions, sex crimes and a dishonorable discharge from the military. You also get points for being young—under twenty-six—unmarried, uneducated or unemployed. But, of course, your initial points—and often the most points—depend on your sentence. For every year you're sentenced to prison, you get three points to a maximum of forty-nine. Those sentenced to life get the whole forty-nine points automatically.

The man called Ben Fry got his forty-nine points for the murder of Penny Morgan, just as he had planned. In a plea bargain that spared him the death penalty, he confessed to the crime and was sentenced to life without parole. He was then shipped to the reception center at San Quentin. There, a team of "correctional counselors" reviewed his life history and assigned him his points. His record—containing periods of gang activity and previous incarcerations for battery, violent rape, and attempted murder—had been carefully manufactured to ensure Level 4 incarceration. His points were toted up and, just four weeks after Penny's murder was committed, he was assigned—as he knew he would be—to Pelican Bay.

He had a bad moment when he first reached this prison on the wild coast just south of Oregon: the first strip search. He'd known it was going to happen, of course. His planning for this, like all his planning, was analytical and meticulous. He knew that the North Wilderness authorities used to x-ray new arrivals, but that they'd been forced to abandon the practice because of health concerns. All the same, they could still take an X ray with a doctor's order, and he'd secreted the capsule in his inner thigh to avoid the usual thorax, abdomen and pelvis scan used to find drugs and weapons inside the body.

But a body search—especially that first thorough body search given to the new men—that was dangerous. The scar on his leg was small, mostly healed, completely grown over. You had to press very hard on the spot to feel the pocket of pus that had formed around the capsule inside. Still, there was a moment, that one bad moment, right before the guards led him into the processing room, when his imagination ran ahead of him and fear flashed through his mind. What if they saw the scar, felt the abscess? What if they got suspicious? What if they found the capsule?

Because the thing was: The man called Ben Fry had committed over a hundred murders in his life, but this was the first time he had ever been in prison. And so far, he didn't like it. In fact, it surprised him how much he didn't like it, how much it got to him. The confinement, the constant noise, the constant humiliation of taking orders from other men, of presenting your balls and exposing your asshole to them for the "nuts and butts" searches—all that irritated him, but it was not the real problem. The real problem was the time. The empty time. Even in these few weeks it had begun to unnerve him. The vast minutes, the hours—unbelievable, endless. Each hour like a flat plain going on and on and on with no vanishing point; a flat, unlimited plain somehow contained within four walls. You sat and you stared at the plain of the hour, and when you closed your eyes you found you were still staring at it, and when you tried to read, there it was, just beyond the page, the words fading until you were staring at it again. So in the end, that's all you did, second after second after second. You stared at the endless plain of hours. There just wasn't anything else you could do.

The man called Ben Fry's mind was like a shark: It had to move to breathe. He had to be planning every moment, analyzing the logistics of an operation every moment or else . . . Or else other thoughts came to him. Not just thoughts; images, emotions, memories—they rose up in him, rose out of his belly into his throat, threatened to choke him, suffocate him. His head became filled with a kind of silent noise, a high, steady sirenlike sound that he couldn't hear but which he knew by the way it made his skin feel too tight and his blood feel as if it were boiling. Whenever he stopped analyzing, the images came. And the noise. And the face. That one face. That one laughing face.

He worked hard to make it all stop. He would imagine his tower. He would climb up into his tower, and look down on the cruel, laughing world from his cool distance. Like a coroner, say, looking coolly down at a maggoty corpse.

But how long could the tower hold? That was what worried him. Time was so vast here, the plain of every hour was so immense, that he sometimes feared the tower would simply crumble. Already there were hints of it. In the past, for instance, he'd always slept like the dead, but here, he was beginning to have bad dreams. He dreamed about that face, those cruel eyes, those red lips laughing at him in the dark. He dreamed about fire and woke up terrified that he was about to burn.

So although his dull features and his slumped figure betrayed no emotion when the body search was over, inwardly he sagged with relief. The capsule had not been discovered. Everything was going to work out exactly as planned—just like always—just as it always did.

The man called Ben Fry went to his cell at Pelican Bay calmly. He knew now it was going to be all right. He knew he would soon be free.

The guards who escorted the man called Ben Fry smiled at one another as the cell's door slid shut. The man called Ben Fry heard them snickering as they walked away. Mildly puzzled by this, he turned to face his cellmate. Then he understood. His cellmate was grinning at him. Lying on the upper bunk. Holding a comic book but looking at the new arrival. And grinning a predator's grin.

The cellmate's name was Rip. He stood six-foot-five and weighed 260 pounds, most of it muscle. On the outside, he had kept himself busy murdering rival motorcyclists, beating them to death, usually with a tire iron or his fists. But in here, whether because there were fewer motorcyclists to murder or just fewer tire irons, he found he had more leisure in which to pursue other hobbies. One of these hobbies was creating weapons. Over the past two weeks, for instance, Rip had been making a shank—a lethal knifelike object. He had done this by rolling up a newspaper and smearing it with his own excrement. When the excrement dried, he would sharpen the point of the object by rubbing it against the concrete walls. Then he would repeat the process. After fourteen days, the thing was razor-sharp and hard as iron. Rip kept it hidden in a space behind the toilet until he could use it to assist him in another of his hobbies: rape. Rip was what was called a booty bandit. He enjoyed raping and brutalizing his fellow inmates until he had transformed them into punks, sex slaves. Then, when they were punks, he could either collect them—or trade them with his friends for such luxuries as cigarettes and extra food.

Rip took one look at the flabby-looking white man who'd just been assigned to share his cell and grinned because he felt he had just been handed a fresh punk for his collection.

Which was ironic actually—because the man called Ben Fry took one look at Rip and felt he had just been handed his ticket out of here.

The two men's cross-purposes resolved themselves in the watches of their first night together. Lying on the bottom bunk pretending to be asleep, the man called Ben Fry opened his eyes to find Rip standing over him. Still grinning. And brandishing his homemade shank.

"There's gonna be shit on my dick tonight, dude, or blood on my shank," Rip grumbled. "You choose."

The man called Ben Fry chose. By the time the guards reached his cell, the gigantic Rip, covered in both shit and blood, was lying comatose on the floor.

After three weeks in "the bucket,"—solitary confinement—the man called Ben Fry was shipped out of Pelican Bay—exactly as he had planned—and reassigned to North Wilderness SHU.

By now, it was June. Just about the time Jim Bishop first came roaring into Driscoll. The man called Ben Fry was brought to his new home at North Wilderness and given a cell alone. The cell was eight feet by ten feet. It had a window to the outside but it didn't open and was too high on the wall to give him any kind of a view. It also had a concrete bunk, and a sink and toilet of stainless steel. The sink and toilet were computer controlled. The toilet, for instance, was generally set to flush three times a day. That prevented inmates from flushing it at will in order to speak to each other through the pipes. The door was run by computer too. It could only be opened by the officer in the unit control booth. The door was made of wire mesh so it was hard to throw things through it. It was hard to see through it into the gallery. It was also hard to call through it to the nearby cells because echoes distorted the sound too much. The man called Ben Fry spent almost twenty-three hours in this cell every day. He rarely saw or spoke to another human being.

The cell was part of a pod. Each pod had two tiers of four cells each. Six of these pods were arranged in a semicircle around a control booth enclosed behind Lexan windows. The control booth officer had a clear view into the pod galleries. He had four video monitors with alternating views of the cells. He had another monitor with alternating views of the pods' exercise yards. All this the man called Ben Fry knew, having learned the architectural plans and engineering designs of the place by heart.

The man called Ben Fry was allowed an hour in the excerise yard each day. His cell door would open electronically and he would walk to the yard alone, watched on monitor by the CBO. He was alone—watched on monitor—once he arrived. The yard was only a little larger than his cell, twelve feet by twenty-six. It was a concrete box with a wire mesh ceiling. Just enough sunlight came in to make it hot as an oven. The man called Ben Fry would pace there for an hour or do push-ups and jumping jacks and then return. He was also allowed out of his cell three times a week for showers.

But for the most part—twenty-three hours a day—it was the cell. The cell and the time. The plain of empty time stretching on and on in front of him. Twenty-three hours a day, the man called Ben Fry lay on his concrete bunk. Lay there and climbed into his tower and looked down across the plain of time without caring. Some hours, some endless white hours, the tower felt so real to him he was afraid he was going mad. But it was better than what he felt when he was below, in the world, not thinking, just staring at the vast emptiness in front of him. It was better than the red, crawling, laughing world of his dreams.

He lived through a week like this. Then one day, two guards came to his cell. They handcuffed him, forced him to his knees and shackled his ankles. With a guard gripping each of his arms, he was led shuffling down the corridor toward the control booth.

This was an important moment for him. For about twenty-five seconds, as he was led along, he could see two of the video monitors through the control booth's windows. He watched a picture of a cell come on and counted in his head. He counted ten seconds before the picture changed. Then the guards moved him past the booth and down another corridor.

He was brought into a room. There was a metal chair here, bolted to the floor. The metal chair faced a wall of clear, bulletproof Lexan. The guards sat the man called Ben Fry down in the chair. They fastened his shackles to iron rings in the floor. They cuffed his hands to the chair arms. Then they stood behind him.

On the other side of the Lexan wall, a door opened. A man came in. He was a slender man in an expensive charcoal gray suit. He wrinkled his nose at his surroundings. He kept his hands clasped in front of him, his elbows pressed tight to his sides. He seemed a fastidious and disdainful character.

The slender man sat in a chair facing the man called Ben Fry. He spoke—and his high, nasal voice was carried through a microphone, one of those voice-activated microphones that shuts down between words and makes speech sound brittle and robotic.

"How are you today, Mr. Fry?" said the man.

The man called Ben Fry nodded, his eyes stupid, his face dull.

"I heard that you were here," said the man. "I wanted to make sure before we proceeded with our arrangements. But now I will."

The man called Ben Fry nodded again.

"I'm glad to see you looking so well," said the man. Then he said, "Anyway . . ." and he stood up to go.

The guards unchained the man called Ben Fry from his chair. They led him back down the corridor. He watched the video monitors through the control booth windows as he passed. He saw a picture of his own cell come up on one of them. He had arranged the blanket on the bunk so he would recognize it. When the picture appeared, he glanced up at a clock on the wall.

Back at his cell, the guards unshackled him and ordered him to strip off his clothes. When he was naked, they searched him, nuts and butt.

Then it was the cell again. The cell and the time. The seconds, the minutes, the hours. Silent, isolated, observed.

It would go on like this for a while yet, he knew. Few diversions, little pleasure. No freedom, no gentleness. Caged days, caged nights. The cell and the time and the tower.

Exactly as he had planned.

EIGHTEEN

Mousey Guy lay dead on the alley pavement. His little corpse was sprawled prone, the right arm reaching out past his head, the left bent awkwardly back against his side. His face was turned, the profile visible, one jug ear, the outline of the long nose, one eye. The eye, open, still looked frightened as it had in life, staring, glassy. He'd been gut-stabbed and the blood pooled out around his middle.

Weiss and Inspector Ketchum of the SFPD stood at his feet, looking down at him. They stood shoulder to shoulder, their hands in their pockets.

"Okay," Ketchum said, "so you're telling me an imaginary killer stabbed this dead fuckhead in revenge for a fantasy rape of a woman who doesn't exist."

Weiss nodded. "Yeah."

"But the dead fuckhead's real, right?"

Weiss cocked his head uncertainly.

Ketchum snorted. "Jesus."

He was a small, thin, wiry black man. He had a deep, muttery voice taut with anger. His face was generally set in a scowl, except sometimes when it was set in a snarl. As far as I could ever tell, he hated everything and everybody. Except Weiss. He liked Weiss. I think.

He nodded now at the coroner's man standing off to one side. The coroner's man knelt down and began to put Wally Spender's body in a plastic bag. Weiss and Ketchum turned to walk away. Ketchum shook his head, disgusted.

"Mousey little bastard wasn't even robbed," he said.

"Well," said Weiss, "he was murdered though. I mean, that's something. I mean, at least it's not all fantasy: Someone must've done it."

"Hey, thanks," said Ketchum, as they came to the end of the alley. "I'm glad he had your card in his pocket. Otherwise, I couldn't've called you, you couldn't've come here and illuminated me on that point. 'Someone must've done it.' Why didn't I think of that?"

They stepped from the shade into the sunlight on Mission. Walked together, two rumpled suits, hands in the pockets, big man and small. They passed a line of boarded shop windows. The boards were covered with bills. The bills were ripped, unreadable, black with graffiti.

"So who's your witness?" Weiss asked.

"You kidding? One of the most honest, observant, reliable crack-heads ever to pick an old soda can out of the gutter. Swears he saw the perp running out of the alley. Swears he saw the knife in his hand."

"He give you a description?"

"Yeah. Says the guy was Latino. Light-skinned. Twenties. Black shirt."

"Well, that's him, all right. That's the imaginary girl's imaginary brother. That's a dead solid ID."

"Except imaginary."

"You can't have everything."

They sat in a donut shop on seventh. They drank coffees at a table by the storefront window. Weiss looked out through the glass. A small woman went by, bent and old, lugging a bag, what looked like a ton of groceries.

"I got something else going," Weiss said.

"If it's real, I can't help you," muttered Ketchum. "I'm working strictly fantasy homicides here on in."

"Bishop's on a case up north."

"Good. Anytime that motherfucker's out of town it's a positive thing for the city of San Francisco."

Weiss ignored this. "My client has part ownership in what's

called an FBO up there—a fixed base operation—a small aviation company, does charter flights, cargo and so on. My client thinks his planes are being used by his partner for something illegal, but he's afraid if he goes to the cops, his partner'll whack him. He tried a local agency, but they felt he needed a flier and referred him to me."

"Great," said Ketchum. "What's Bishop's plan? Fuck every woman in sight till someone tells him something?"

Weiss manged to ignore this too, close to the truth as it was. "I've got three names of people who might or might not be involved," he said. "The trouble is so far they tend to be dead. One, a gardener named Harry Ridder, shot himself. The other, a mystery woman named Julie Wyant, threw herself off the Golden Gate Bridge."

"Must've neglected to read the NO JUMPING signs."

"The third name I got is Whip."

"Whip?" said Ketchum. "Whip what?" Weiss turned over an empty hand. Ketchum rolled his eyes. "Wonderful. Every tattooed fuck who's been anywhere west of Philadelphia's been AKA'd Whip at some point. That the best Bishop can do? Christ. The only thing that bastard knows how to investigate is poon."

"You remember . . . ?" Weiss started.

"You oughta dump that fuck, you ask me," Ketchum said. "Belongs in prison. Shit, he'd *be* in prison if you hadn't saved his psycho ass."

"You remember . . . ?"

"You know he's not the son you never had, Weiss. He can't go out there and live your life for you, live your wild side or whatever the hell you think he's doing."

Weiss sipped his coffee Set his cup down. Said, "You remember Cameron Moncrieff?"

"Sure. The fag smuggler. Wore turtlenecks."

"You know he's dead."

"Hell, yes. It's the best thing about him."

"Okay, well, the other two names were connected to him, so I'm thinking this Whip might be connected to him too."

"You know what it is with Bishop?" Ketchum answered—answered as if Weiss hadn't spoken at all. "It's like he's some kind of zombie rottweiler. You know? It's like you're his master because you kept him out of Pelican Bay. But you're it, you're all the conscience he's got. You tell him to fetch the paper, he'll fetch the paper no matter what. Some poor bastard gets in his way, he rips his throat out. Some poor bitch gets in his way, he humps her. *Get the paper,* that's all he thinks about; *Weiss told me to get the paper.* He's a criminal piece of shit, man, I mean it, he just happens to be on your leash, that's all. You can't teach a man like that to know right from wrong. You can't teach him to have a soul."

Weiss waited, drumming his fingers on the Formica tabletop. Ketchum seethed.

"And what is this shit he's working on anyway?" the cop burst out finally. Again, Weiss showed him his empty hand. "'Cause you get yourself mixed up in something federal I can't protect your sorry Jew ass, you know that."

"C'mon, Ketch, what've you got?" Weiss said.

It was a moment or two before Ketchum could answer him. First he had to mutter curses under his breath while shaking his head disgustedly. Then he had to look around the shop as if searching for a witness to the sort of bullshit he had to tolerate. Then he had to sigh with a resignation only a fucking saint could bring to this miserable world of ours. And only then, finally, did he say, "All right. Jesus."

Weiss rested his cheek against his fist. Waited.

"There's a guy named Lenny Pomeroy," Ketchum went on. "Pled out on three counts of accessory to murder a couple months ago. Sometimes he's AKA'd Whip. Whip Pomeroy."

"Any connection to Moncrieff?"

"Well, yeah, why the hell do you think I mention him? See, Pomeroy was an Identity Man. A good one too. Kind of an artist at it.

The word was when Whip AKA'd you, you stayed AKA'd. Fresh name, fresh face, fingerprints, social security number, job—the whole package. And no one who's trying to find you—like, say, your friendly local constabulary—is ever gonna be able to locate your sweet ass ever again. That's where he got the name Whip. Short for Witness Protection. He's the Witness Protection Program for the bad guys. Once he gets ahold of you, that's it, man, you disappear."

Weiss nodded. "What's the link to Moncrieff?"

"Well, that's the thing. Pomeroy was Moncrieff's boy, his in-house asshole. Lover, assistant, all-around Igor."

"He lived with him?"

"Sometimes. Stayed with him a lot anyway. Moncrieff was the only friend he had, the only anything he had, family, friend, anything."

"Was he with Moncrieff when he died?"

"I don't know. How the fuck should I know?" Ketchum said. "The point is: Along with sinning against God and man through his biblically forbidden sexual practices, Pomeroy's just kind of an all-around weirdo. Liked to hunker down. Never dealt with his customers directly. Anyone who wanted to get a fresh identity from him, had to go through his auntie Moncrieff. That's how we got him on accessory charges. Moncrieff died and the second Whip went out on his own—end of story. He's a nutcase."

Weiss went: "Hmpf. Sounds like it could be my guy. Where is he now?"

Ketchum hesitated, shaking his head. Cursing again. Sighing again. "This is on the way down-low, okay? You never heard this from me. You don't even know who you never heard it from."

"Sure."

"Apparently, they've got this scumbag PC'd up somewhere but big-time."

"Protective custody," said Weiss, shifting in his seat. "Why? And who's got him?"

"I don't know. The feds, the state. It's one of those everybody-with-his-head-up-everybody-else's-ass type deals. But on the way down-low. Way."

Weiss sat quietly, the gears in his brain turning. "So that means he's got something, right? Whip, I mean. He's offering something to the feds and . . . Oh, I get it: He's rolling on his AKAs."

"Buh-bingo. That's what I hear anyway. Law enforcement's stepping on their tongues 'cause the guy seems to have a line on every missing criminal fuck in the country. Remember the Salmon River killings fifteen years or so ago?"

"Sure. They busted the guy for that just last . . . Oh."

"Right: oh. Pomeroy gave up his AKA. And next month I hear they're going after Johnny Guardo."

"Johnny Guardo." Weiss let out a low whistle.

"I shit you not," said Ketchum.

"What is he, doling them out one by one?"

"One by slow fucking one," Ketchum said. "Feds think he could keep going for years."

"In return for what? What's he after?" said Weiss. "A knock-down on the accessory raps?"

"Oh no. Oh no. He wants the accessory raps. He loves the accessory raps. It's his favorite fucking thing. As far as Whip's concerned, they can keep him inside till Jesus comes again. Protective custody, that's all he wants. Deep PC. If they could dig him a well, he'd sell his soul to live at the bottom of it."

Weiss let out a short laugh. "That doesn't make any sense. He could go undercover. He could go WITSEC, get protection."

"Not good enough. He wants slam. The deepest prison bucket he can get."

"Come on. That's crazy," said Weiss.

"Well, I told you: He is crazy. All that cocksucking drives you mad, man."

"No, no, no," said Weiss. "To stay in prison? When he could

bargain his way out? He must be fucking terrified of something. Of somebody. Somebody must be after him. Who the hell is it? Godzilla?"

Weiss had spoken quietly enough, but Ketchum said, "Shit. I knew this was gonna get you all frantic."

"I'm not frantic."

"Oh, yeah, you're frantic, Weiss."

"I'm not fucking frantic."

"You are. You're frantic, you just don't know it yet."

Weiss snorted. "Why? Go ahead. What's this Whip guy afraid of? Who the hell is he so afraid of?"

Ketchum's snarling eyes met his. "He's afraid of the Shadow-man," he said.

NINETEEN

It was sweet to have her in the summer dark. He liked the play of her heavy breasts in his hands. He liked the way her lips hunted hungrily over him. He liked her strong fingers grasping at his shoulders and his back. He lifted up on his arms. He looked down over her belly to see her sturdy thighs parted for him. She was very wet inside and it was good to feel it. He liked the sound of her short, soft cries.

At the end, they locked together, a single held breath. Then he rested on top of her. He listened to her breathing. He felt her body lifting and falling under him. Minute after minute, it was good.

Finally, Bishop rolled off her. Kathleen tucked herself under his arm. She toyed with the hair on his chest and said nothing. He rested with her in the shadows. The noise of the air conditioner cut off the sound from outside. The room felt to him like an island of silence in the whispering sea. Minute after minute, he felt the way he did in a plane or on a motorcycle going fast: clear and straight instead of coiled up and tense with his mind worrying at him. He lightly kissed Kathleen's soft hair. He liked a woman who could be quiet for a while.

The minutes passed. She stirred against him. "Hey," she said, "can I tell you something?"

Bishop drew a deep breath in through his nose, let it out through his mouth slowly. Back to work. "Sure."

"Well, it's just . . . I dunno. Maybe I'm getting paranoid or something." She tilted her face up to his. He kissed her forehead. "It's just things are getting kind of scary, that's all."

"Scary how? About Chris?"

He still had his lips to her brow. He felt her nod. He felt her warm breath on him when she sighed, when she spoke again. "I think someone's following him."

Pressed against her like that, Bishop had to keep his own breathing slow so she wouldn't feel his excitement. This was something. This could be important. "Yeah?" he murmured.

"The last few days? I keep seeing this car outside the house at night. This dark car, real nice, like a BMW I think. I just sort of noticed it, you know, 'cause it's not the kind of car people drive around here. Whenever Chris is home at night and I look out the window? The bastard's out there. Then if Chris is out on a late flight or something, he's gone. I don't know. Maybe I'm crazy. You think I'm being crazy?"

Bishop's lips moved on her warm skin. "I don't know," he told her. He was lying. He knew. "Have you mentioned it to Chris?"

"No. Christ. I don't wanna get him started, you know, make him any more tense than he already is. He's already acting nuts lately. Never goes out anymore. Just paces around the house like some kind of animal in a cage. That's why I've been having such a hard time getting over here to see you. Unless he has a night flight like tonight, he's just *around.*"

Bishop held her, massaged the small of her back. Stared over her head into the dark. Thinking. "He doesn't go out to drink at the Clover Leaf anymore?"

"Not lately. Freaking wish he would. Just sits there, hogging the TV with his baseball. Sending me out for more beers." She drew away from him. Settled wearily onto her back. Looked up through the shadows at the ceiling. "He rumbles around like some kind of thundercloud. I mean, it drives him ape-shit, just hanging around like that. It always has." She smiled. "I guess that's one thing, at least. I'm pretty sure he won't last much longer before he's gotta hit the Clover Leaf again."

Bishop was pretty sure too. He rested on his elbow, looking down at her, stroking her hair back behind her ear. This could be his chance, he thought.

"I wish I could just stop thinking about this shit," Kathleen said softly. "The thing is, you know, with Chris? It's not even fun anymore. I mean, Chris could be really fun when we first started dating. Before he got thrown out of the Army. We were always laughing. That's practically all we did."

It was Hirschorn, Bishop thought. It had to be. Hirschorn was having Chris followed to make sure he didn't start boozing it up again, start flapping his mouth off in the Clover Leaf again, bragging about their big operation. Hirschorn had handed Chris the word that day he yelled at him out at the airpark: Stay home, stay clean, stay sober and quiet until the operation is over. Chris knew he had to try to rein himself in. But Kathleen was right: He couldn't hold out much longer.

"I wish it could be like this all the time," Kathleen was saying. "You know what I mean? Just like this, we're lying here talking, me and you. Without all the bullshit, all the complications. You know what I mean?"

Bishop wrapped a curl of her mouse brown hair around his finger. Soon, Chris would crack, he thought. A day, two days. He'd be out at the Clover Leaf again. Boozing again, talking, bragging. And this time, Hirschorn's goons would be watching him. If Bishop could be there too, maybe he could stir things up a little. Egg Chris on, get him to cross the line somehow. Send a message to Hirschorn that he'd hired the wrong pilot. That Bishop himself might be the right man for the job.

The idea made something glitter in Bishop's heart, some hard, cold, brilliant thing.

"You know what I mean, Frank?" Kathleen said again. She reached up and stroked his cheek. "You ever feel like that? Like it could just be you and me all the time?"

The touch of her hand brought Bishop back to her. What the hell had she been saying? he wondered. He hadn't been paying attention at all. Stalling, he took her hand and brought her fingers to his lips and kissed them. He went back over her words in his mind. Then he understood.

"Sure," he answered her. "Sure, I do. But it's like you said, Chris is your husband."

Her hand slipped to the back of his neck. She drew him down to her, close. "Maybe I don't care," she whispered. "Maybe I don't care anymore."

He kissed her cheek. "You said he'd kill us."

"I don't care. I'm not scared of him. I don't care what he does." Her fingertips trailed down his spine. "You're not scared of him, are you, Frank?"

His hand played over her breast. He kissed her neck. "Hell, yes, I'm scared of him. He's twice my size." His body slid over the sheets to press against her.

She held him tighter. "Frank," she whispered. "Frank, I know it sucks, but I'm falling in love with you. I don't care if it sucks. I just am."

Bishop's lips moved up over her lips. That stopped her talking anyway. Plus he was hard again so, what the hell, he climbed onto her, went into her. But this time his mind kept going. He was still thinking about Chris, about Hirschorn having him watched, about how he could push Chris over the line and send Hirschorn a message that might get him in on the action.

Kathleen whispered his name, his phony name. "Frank." Bishop moved inside her.

They held each other close in the summer dark, he thinking his thoughts, she dreaming her dreams.

TWENTY

After she left, Bishop sat on the edge of the writing desk, sat in the dark. The window was open a crack. Naked, he felt the heat from outside mingle on his skin with the cool from the air-conditioned room. He lit a cigarette. He watched the smoke trail out into the night. He watched it float over toward the house across the way.

He drew on the cigarette, distant in his mind. It was funny, he thought. Funny about her being in love with him. Funny how people don't really see each other. Men and women. They invent each other in their minds and then they see what they invent. They don't really see each other. Now she was in love with him and she didn't even know his real name, didn't know anything real about him.

Well, it was almost over. Soon he would know what Hirschorn was up to. He would have what he wanted, what Weiss had sent him for. Then he could go home and that would be the end of it.

Still. It was funny. He flicked an ash at the open window. Considered the yellow lights of Kathleen's house through the trees. He hoped she'd keep her mouth shut about it. He hoped she wouldn't go around telling people that she was in love. She might. Women did. Maybe she would even tell Chris in the hope that Chris and Bishop would fight it out over her. Maybe she wanted Bishop to be her white knight after all.

He thought about that. He thought about the way Chris had grabbed Kathleen that night on the porch. He thought about the way he had cuffed her, like it was nothing, like she was nothing. He thought about it and there was a flow of sour heat inside him.

His cigarette was done. He crushed it out in the ashtray, stood off the desk. He went to the closet. He had his traveling bag in there, wedged behind some boxes. The bag was empty except for his handheld computer. He kept it hidden in there. He brought the handheld out. Set it on the desk. Sat down in front of it.

He signed on to check his e-mail. There was the latest from Weiss.

JB. Investigation here shows your situation could be very dangerous. The names you sent me seem to revolve around Cameron Moncrieff, a pimp and smuggler of drugs, women, guns, etc., now deceased. Harry Ridder was Moncrieff's gardener. He's dead too, a suicide. Moncrieff's "live-in caretaker," Julie Wyant, is also missing, presumed a suicide. Whip was Moncrieff's lover and kind of aide-de-camp, also a top Identity Man, in slam for accessory to murder and now PC'd up by law enforcement. My concern is there seems to be a connection between these people and a major whack specialist sometimes called Shadowman. If Hirschorn is also connected to him, you have to proceed with caution. I'm very serious about this. Until I know more, do not go undercover into Hirschorn's op. Do not. If you try to get close and he gets suspicious, your life could be in danger as well as the lives of Mr. and Mrs. Wannamaker, especially Mrs. Wannamaker, as she has talked to you. I'm serious. If this involves the Shadowman, it's dangerous stuff. Proceed with extreme caution until further notice. W.

Bishop read the e-mail. Snorted. Smiled with one corner of his mouth. He stretched his arms in the air and yawned.

Finally, he deleted the mail, turned off the handheld, replaced it in the bag. He replaced the bag in the closet.

He went back to bed. He lay with his hands behind his head, looking up at the ceiling. He thought about Chris and Kathleen, about that night out on the porch when Chris had hit her. He thought about how he was going to call Chris out, how he would push Chris over the line, and how Hirschorn's man would be watching. . . .

He smiled up into the dark as he thought about it. He was hungry for action and the hard, brilliant thing inside him glittered and shone.

TWENTY-ONE

The next day, Weiss found the love of his life.

"Oh, come on, don't just fall for her, Weiss," Casey told him. "Have some originality." But it was too late. The minute he saw the photograph, he was gone.

Casey, you'll remember, was Weiss's procuress, the woman who supplied him with whores. She was forty or so. Silvery blonde. A cheerful face, deeply lined from sun and cigarettes. Short, trim, liked to wear form-fitting slacks and sweaters that showed off her great ass, her great tits. Always had a warm smile for Weiss, what seemed for all the world like real affection.

They were sitting in her living room, in her penthouse in the Heights. The late morning sun streamed in through one wall of windows, through the other they could see all the way out to Alcatraz on the glittering bay. Casey was posed on the mod white sectional, leaning back, chin up, legs crossed—you know—arm stretched out along the sofa back. The good body displayed.

Weiss, across the glass coffee table from her, was in the armchair. Looking at the photograph. Gazing at the photograph.

"Oh, Jesus, Weiss, you are such a pushover, I swear. Such an old romantic." She had a rich, sensual voice. That was also from the cigarettes. She was never without a cigarette. She brought one to her lips now. Shook her head as she watched Weiss moon over the snapshot.

Finally, reluctantly, he put the photograph down on the coffee table. He couldn't stop looking at it though.

"I figured you'd know her," he murmured. "Mystery girl with no background, hanging out with Moncrieff. I figured she'd been a pro at some point."

"She was never one of my girls," Casey told him. The smoke

uncurled slowly from her mouth as she spoke. "But a friend of mine ran her for a while out of one of Moncrieff's operations. She loaned me the picture and . . ." The pause was for dramatic flair. She had her tongue in her cheek as she lifted a computer disk from the sofa table behind her. ". . . a video!" She placed it down by the photograph. "Don't wear yourself out."

Weiss glanced at the disk. Touched his tongue to his parted lips. Swallowed. Casey, watching him, let out a pretty, musical laugh.

Embarrassed, Weiss forced himself to look away finally, to look up at her. She pulled on her cigarette playfully.

"Oh, you don't have to get all blushy," she said. "Believe me, you're not alone. She was like that apparently. Guys fell in love with her. Older guys especially. She had that look, you know: like she just wafted down from Heaven. According to my friend, she had middle-aged gentlemen practically parked outside her window baying like hound dogs. Bringing her flowers, the moon, whatever. Which is kind of a pain in the ass, believe me, if you're trying to run a business." She leaned forward, tilted her head, as if to get a rightways look at the snapshot herself. "It's the face of an angel, all right. Nice hair too."

Yeah, it was. Very nice hair. Strawberry blond. Natural—you couldn't fake that color. Flowing, silky, gleaming. And the face it framed—just as Casey said—an angel's face. Wistful, distant, sweet. The sight of her struck Weiss to his hankering heart. She could've stepped out of one of his secret daydreams.

"Did she call herself Julie Wyant then?" he managed to ask.

"Oh yeah," said Casey. "Just the one name, as far as I know. But my friend says there was never any paper on her. She just showed up for work one day, no background, no past to speak of. My friend says that's how she acted too."

"Like . . . What do you mean?"

"As if she'd just been born—that was the way my friend put it. Just kind of dreamy and far away, you know. As if she'd just suddenly opened her eyes and found herself here on earth with the rest of us."

"And she never told anyone anything about herself? The other girls . . . ?"

"Nope. Moncrieff tried to check her out once but no luck. Apparently he was in love with her too."

"Moncrieff . . . ?"

Casey laughed. "I know." She arched her eyebrow wickedly. "But in his own way, I mean. He worshiped her. Went into raptures over her. As if she was one of his works of art."

"She was his live-in caretaker, right?" said Weiss.

"Yeah, the minute he saw her, he took her out of the game. Said she was too good for it. Brought her to his house to live with him."

"How long? Do you know?"

She shrugged, paused for thought, her cigarette halfway to her mouth again. "Couple of months, I guess. She was with him right up till the end."

"How about her? Do you think she loved him?"

"I wouldn't know. How the hell would I?"

"I mean, do you think she went off the bridge because he died?"

"Beats me," said Casey. "You think she went off the bridge at all?"

The question had crossed Weiss's mind too. No reason to be suspicious really. Except that there'd been no body. And maybe it was hard for him to believe that any face that beautiful was gone for good.

Without meaning to, without wanting to, he let his eyes wander back to the photograph again. Again, he licked his lips.

"Oh God!" said Casey. "Now what've I done? Forget I said it, Weiss. I was just kidding around. I'm sure she went off the bridge. She obviously went off the bridge. Don't make some kind of quest out of it. It'll just fuck you up, believe me."

Weiss picked up the snapshot. Slipped it—tenderly—into his jacket. "I can take the video?" he asked.

"Like I said: Don't hurt yourself."

Weiss swept the disk into one big hand. Put that in his pocket too. Stood up. Casey watched him from the sofa. Amusement in her eyes, maybe a little jealousy too.

"Thanks, Case."

"I live to serve you, sweetheart. You know that."

He smiled. Went to the door.

"Weiss." He paused with his hand on the knob. Looked back at her. "Baby," she said to him—gently, really gently. "Plenty of girls go off plenty of bridges. That's the way of things. Dollars to donuts, she's gone."

TWENTY-TWO

I worked late that night. I thought I was the last one left in the office. But as I slung my backpack over my arm and started for the exit, I saw Weiss's door ajar, a dim, shifting light spilling out of it. I went over to see if he'd gone home, if he'd left something on by mistake. But no, he was there. Sitting in near darkness. Tilted back in his big chair, swiveling slightly to and fro. He had a glass of his beloved scotch in one hand. His computer was on, he was staring at it. The monitor was out of my eyeshot. I couldn't see what he was watching. I could only see the dim light from it shifting on his face, in the air, on the carpet. That—the light from the monitor—was what I'd noticed spilling through the door.

I peeked in at him but, for some reason, I didn't want to say anything. Something in his expression made me feel I should just sneak away, go home, leave him undisturbed with whatever it was he was looking at. Some sad or dreamy something in his eyes. But as I pulled back from the door, I guess he caught the movement. He glanced up, saw me. Waved me in.

"Turn the light on as you come," he said. I did. Weiss rubbed his eyes against the glare. "Have a seat."

I dumped my pack on the floor. Sank myself into one of the client chairs, the one at the near corner of the desk. I still couldn't see the monitor.

"Want a drink?"

He tilted forward to slide open a low drawer. Drew out a bottle of the good stuff he liked, the Macallan. Drew out a second glass. Poured fresh shots for both of us.

"Whiskey in the desk drawer," I said. "Like a private eye in a novel."

We tipped our glasses to each other. "You can put it in your book when you write about me," he said. We drank. Then Weiss reached out casually and swiveled the monitor around towards me. "Here, what do you think of this?"

I sipped my drink and watched. It was the video Casey had given him. An Internet ad for an escort service. Just a ten-second loop playing over and over again.

"What am I looking for?" I asked.

"The woman," said Weiss as if it were obvious. "What do you think of her?"

She was beckoning from the screen. Bending forward slightly, crooking her finger, the clichéd motion. She was shown from the waist, dressed in some high-necked lacy white thing, somehow prim and sexy at once. Because Weiss had asked me, I felt I was supposed to notice something about her, so I tried. She was beautiful certainly, there was no question about that. The red-gold hair, the ivory-and-rose complexion, the uncannily deep eyes, meltingly blue. Plus her expression was interesting. Not the usual thing, I thought. None of the routine mischief, the forced sensuality you get in most of these sex ads. Very ethereal instead, almost otherworldly. Not as if she was beckoning you to some hot triple-x party. More as if she was inviting you to float off into the clouds with her and fade away to fairyland.

She didn't do much for me, I have to say. She was a little wan and romantic for my taste. I was about to make some childishly sardonic remark about her. But when I turned to Weiss, when I saw him, watching her image, saw the world-weary yearning, the sadness and the desire there, whatever comment I was thinking of died on my lips.

"So what about her?" was all I said.

Weiss blinked at my voice. Sat up straighter. Clicked the mouse to shut the video down. "Her name is Julie Wyant," he told me. "She's missing."

I knew about this. I had overheard two of Weiss's operatives talking about it in the hallway. They'd said she was a suicide. Dead. I found it strange that she was only missing now.

"The cops think she threw herself off the Golden Gate," Weiss went on.

"You don't? Think so, I mean."

He lifted one shoulder. "I don't know. They're probably right. That's probably what happened. It's just hard to tell with these things, that's all. No one ever found her body. No one even knows who she really was or where she came from."

"Did you run a check on her?"

"Yeah. There's nothing. No paper, no past. Phony name, phony background. Nothing to follow. I talked to some girls who worked with her, and a couple of guys. They all described her as sort of an odd personality. Distracted, preoccupied—as if her mind was always far away. Anyway, she never told anyone anything about herself."

"Hmph," I said. "A mystery girl."

I got only a long silence in answer. Weiss—himself distracted, preoccupied, far away—raised his glass with one hand, lightly drummed the desktop with the fingers of the other.

"She have any reason to kill herself?" I asked.

After another moment, he glanced over at me. "Fear," he said. "That's what I think. I think she might've been afraid of someone."

"Afraid of . . . ?"

He shook his head as if he didn't know. But then he said: "Well, there's this guy they call the Shadowman . . ." and he hid himself in his scotch.

Now, back then, as an aspiring author, I always liked to think of myself as a fly-on-the-wall type of guy: a quiet listener, an astute observer. I tried to be that way at any rate. And, in fact, hanging out on the wall at the Agency, I had actually heard, or overheard, this name—the Shadowman—spoken from time to time. Or *uttered*, I would say. Uttered in a tone of great mystery and melodrama. From all I could gather, he was someone from an old case Weiss had worked when he was on the force. In fact, it was supposed to have something to do with the reason he'd left the force. I'd never have been bold enough to ask him about it outright. I was young and, to be honest, Weiss, with his street wisdom and gravity and expertise . . . he kind of overawed me. But here he'd mentioned it himself. Plus I sensed he'd called me in here to talk things out for his own sake, his own clarity.

So—trying for a worldly, ironic tone—I said, "And who, pray tell, is the Shadowman?"

The big man leaned out of his whiskey, leaned back in his chair. "Well," he said, "depends who you ask." He gave an expansive wave with his drink hand. "According to the cops—most of the cops—he's bullshit. Not a real person. Or a composite of several different people. Or just something a journalist made up. A—whatdayacallit—fantasy."

I nodded. I sipped my scotch thoughtfully. I nodded some more. "Kind of like the guy who killed Wally Spender, you mean."

At that, Weiss's chin rose and fell. Which, coming from him, was tantamount to a burst of raucous laughter. I think I'd actually managed to amuse him. "Exactly. Exactly like the guy who killed Wally Spender. Only this guy . . . You remember the 'South Bay Massacre'?"

I didn't remember. I was on the East Coast when it happened. I was just a kid. But this had also been mentioned in Agency gossip now and then, it was part of the stuff I'd overheard and half heard. "Yeah," I said. "Something. Illegal immigrants who were drowned or something."

"Eight of them. Eight children." Weiss's chin remained sunk on his chest now. He frowned down at his desktop. "They weren't drowned. They were shot. Twice in the head, each one. Their bodies were dumped in the ocean, washed in on the tide. Woman went out to walk her dog on China Beach one morning, there were the corpses bobbing in the surf a few yards offshore."

I let out a soft whistle. "Jesus. Who were they?"

"Just kids. From Thailand. The theory was they were being brought in to sell as . . . you know: slaves, sex slaves. Whatever. No one ever really knew. The theory was that the deal had gone wrong somehow and the seller needed to get rid of the evidence. That was the theory. The oldest one was maybe eleven. They probably killed her first while the smaller ones watched and waited for their turn."

I didn't say anything. But I felt it; I felt it go up my spine. Images, you know: the children waiting helplessly; the red line of sunrise lying on the water and the little bodies lifting and falling on the waves. It was chilling to think of it, especially sitting there like that, with Weiss, alone. The Agency around us was dark and empty and silent. In the night, through the wall of high-arched windows, the city's skyscrapers were a haphazard checkerboard of light and dark. The clouds—these huge, moonstruck clouds—were tumbling past on the wind. Traffic noise rose to us, muted car horns, rumbling engines, the shock and sizzle of the electric streetcars. It all played on my imagination, gave me a sense of tumult and frantic hurry all around us and us isolated in this one place, this one good, bright, warm place alone in the wild world. Sitting there, talking about those corpses in the surf—it was an eerie feeling, like listening to a fireside ghost story on a stormy night.

"We had nothing," said Weiss. "The media went nuts but . . . what could we do? We had nothing. No leads, no way to trace the kids. One witness. A Chinese fisherman. He said he saw a boat, a thirty-foot cruiser, anchored off the South Bay the night before. He saw a man on deck, moving around. But in the moonlight he was just a shadow. That's what the press picked up: the shadow of a man. The Shadowman." Weiss made a face, brushing off his own thoughts. "You know the media, the way they are. With something like that, a slaughter like that, kids involved . . . All the feature stories that keep the thing going. They started speculating about the Shadowman, was he a hired gun? A whack specialist? You know the sort of thing. Then this one guy, Jeff Bloom, did this big Sunday feature in the *Chronicle*. He had, like, one unnamed source and he did this huge piece. According to him, the Shadowman was responsible for half the unsolved murders on this side of the country. 'An unstoppable Death Machine,' that's what he called him. No matter who you were, no matter how much security you had, if you were in Witness Protection, if you were in Fort Knox—didn't matter—he could get to you. Even the bad guys who hired him were afraid of him. That was the story anyway."

I glanced over my shoulder as a sudden gust rattled the windowpanes. "Sure," I said softly. "Sure."

"And meanwhile the cops are saying, 'Bullshit, bullshit, bullshit, this is all made up. . . . ' But at the same time . . ." He finished with a shrug.

"At the same time, someone actually did kill those children," I said.

"Well, that's it," said Weiss. "That's what made it so hard to deal with. In the end, it was like: There actually was a Shadowman even if there wasn't."

I hesitated a moment before I responded to that. I was always a little careful around the Agency. Careful, I mean, about what I said. I never wanted to wax too philosophical, sound too erudite, like a snob or an egghead or something. I mean, this wasn't college anymore and I wanted to fit in. But again, the atmosphere—the two of us alone in the bright center of the night—it seemed to lend itself to philosophizing.

"Well, you know, the experience of being human isn't necessarily a rational one," I ventured. "Some things are real whether they're real or not."

Weiss gave a hard laugh. "What the hell's that supposed to mean?" Immediately, I saw I had made a mistake. "What is that? Is that, like, if I turn my back on the table is it still there? Is that what they teach you at Berkeley?"

I felt my cheeks get hot. "Well, I'm just saying . . ."

"What, are we supposed to smoke some dope now or something?"

"I just mean that . . . Part of the reality of a thing is our perception of it. It's . . . it's an interface."

"An interface. You're an interface. Real whether it's real or not! For fuck's sake." Weiss blustered out another laugh. "I'm the king of Romania."

I spent, oh, a good half hour that night banging my forehead against the wall of my apartment. To punish myself for being such a callow buffoon in front of him. I thought for sure the story of my brilliant philosophical insight would spread throughout the Agency by morning and I'd be a laughingstock. Which just killed me, because I wanted so much to be a part of the place.

See, they were big figures to me in those days, Weiss and Bishop both. They loomed large in my youthful imagination: men who had touched evil and seen death and were wise to the wheelwork of the world. Some days I even talked like one or the other of them, or walked or dressed like him, tried him on for size. In any case, I thought about them a lot, about who they were, about what they were like.

I could be sanctimonious about Bishop at times. He was a hard man to warm to, very intimidating. It was pleasant to feel morally superior to his violent nature and that cool and peculiar conscience of his. But I was honest with myself. I knew I admired him. And I envied him too. Hell, just his way with women—I'd have sold my soul for a piece of that. Not to mention his physical courage, the bikes, the planes, the fear he inspired in other men. He had an air of danger around him, a lethal virility—traits much to be coveted by a bookish young man who was trying to make some kind of person of himself.

As for Weiss, he was older, more a mentor or father figure or what have you. I was better educated than he was, probably even smarter in some academic, theoretical way. But I could only stand in awe of his mean-street wisdom. That heavy deadpan of his, that deep, weary, sympathetic gaze: You could just tell he understood humanity to the bone. He knew people cheated, even the best of them, and that even the best of them lied. He knew they eyed each other jealously and dreamed foul dreams. He knew they were keenly aware of the corruption of their neighbors and wonderfully blind to their own. But more important than any of that, he knew how to accept this in them, in each person and in all of them together and in himself. Nothing human was alien to him, none of it shocked him. He was no cynic—the good things mattered to him—love and justice—they mattered to him a lot. He just knew how things were, is all. Stone stood still and water ran and the earth was a kingdom of deception and that was that. In those days I would've given anything to have seen what Weiss had seen, to know what Weiss knew.

So the idea that I'd made a fool of myself in front of him, that he'd laugh at me, talk about me, spread the word that I was a shit-talking college boy who thought trees fell in forests without making a sound, well, it was pretty crushing stuff.

But, as it turned out, I underestimated Weiss's generosity. Oh, he told the story all right, a little while later. And I did get nudged and chuckled at around the office for a while. But in Weiss's version, the foolishness of my university education redeemed itself by its surprising usefulness. Because, while I hadn't added anything to his thoughts about the Shadowman, he always maintained that, sitting there babbling my philosophy at him that night, I had accidentally solved The Case of the Spanish Virgin.

TWENTY-THREE

Bishop, meanwhile, walked into the Clover Leaf Bar.

He scanned the place as he stepped over the threshold. It was a rathole, he thought. The rathole heart of this rathole city. A narrow corridor dead-ending at the shithouse doors. A room just wide enough for the row of stools at the rail and a couple of four-man tables behind them. Grime-black linoleum on the floors, scarred wood paneling on the walls. Country music on the jukebox. Even with the front door propped open to let the night air in, the place was stifling. It stank of cigarettes and beer.

There were a couple of mountainous hoohas at the bar, one in his Airborne jacket, the other in hunting camouflage. They lifted their bushy beards out of their Millers. Glanced at Bishop, figured, yeah, they could take him, and sank back into their drinks. There was another veteran there, a wiry hophead. And then the goon, down at the end, in the shadows: Hirschorn's goon—the hatchet-faced gorilla Bishop had talked to at the airport. He made no sign to Bishop when he entered. He just raised his bourbon to hide his smile. His eyes gleamed.

As for Chris Wannamaker, he was at a table at the rear. One arm flung over his chair back, legs stretched out. Jeans and a cut-off tee, a white cowboy hat. Muscles and his snake tattoo. He was with a couple of other guys. They were all three laughing loudly. One of the other guys was also a North Country pilot, a guy named Matt. Matt lit up when he saw Bishop.

"Hey, Kennedy," he shouted. He waved Bishop over.

Chris froze where he was when he heard the name. The grin dropped right off his face. He never took his eyes off Bishop after that. Bishop stopped at the bar, ordered a beer, waited for it, lit a cigarette, walked over to the table—all the while, Chris never took his eyes off him.

Bishop pulled a wooden chair up to the table, sat down with the others. He'd just come from Kathleen, just then. He gave Chris an easy smile. The easy smile said: *Juice from your wife is still drying on my dick.* Bishop wanted Chris to sense that so that Chris would get even angrier. Chris got angrier all right. He wasn't even sure why. He just did. He looked at Bishop's easy smile. He took a long pull of beer, seething. Bishop thought: *Good.*

"Hey, Kennedy," said Matt. He spoke loudly, right in Bishop's ear. He made expansive, swaying gestures where he sat. He was drunk. "You can settle this right now for us. FAR 121. Does the reg say 'Eight hours bottle to throttle'? Or is it, 'I got my bottle, gimme that throttle'?"

Matt and the other guy laughed hard. Bishop smiled with one corner of his mouth.

" 'No pilot shall adjust his bottle and throttle at the same time,' " said the other guy. "Isn't that it?"

"Or with the same hand," said Matt.

More hearty laughter, Matt and the other guy both, rollicking back in their chairs, slapping the table. But not Chris. Chris kept glaring at Bishop, studying that easy smile, that tongue-in-cheek look of his, not knowing exactly what he was seeing, not knowing that he was seeing the thing about his wife's juice, or maybe knowing and not really wanting to know.

"Seems to me Chris is the one you want to talk to here," Bishop said quietly. "I've seen his eight hours go by like it was no more'n lunchtime."

Ha-ha-ha, went Matt and the other guy. "Yeah," said Matt. "I heard old man Hirschorn himself showed up to kick your ass on that one, Chris." Ha-ha-ha, they went.

"Now, Chris, I'd sure hate to think he was wasting his breath on you," the other guy chimed in.

"Hey, you know the three most useless things in life?" said Matt. "The altitude above you, the runway behind you . . ."

". . . and tits on a nun!" both men finished off at once.

"Well, telling Chris to lay off the bottle—that's the fourth one," said Matt. "The fourth useless thing."

Bishop looked at Chris. Even with the laughter, even with the country music on the juke, he almost thought he could hear Chris breathing. He shifted his gaze past him to the goon at the bar. The goon hid his smile in his drink again. His eyes went right on gleaming. Bishop looked back at Chris. He wondered just how drunk he was, just how stupid.

"Of course, they say altitude's the one thing that'll sober a man," Bishop said. "At ten thousand feet, even a drunk won't beat up his plane too bad."

"That's for sure," said Matt.

"Not like he beats up his wife."

Matt and the other guy hardly knew what the fuck he was saying at this point. They were just laughing at everything. They were still laughing when Chris sprang to his feet.

"What the fuck is that supposed to mean?" Chris said.

"Whoa, sit down, you're making me dizzy," said Matt.

"Relax," said Bishop mildly. "These are the jokes."

"That's right, these are the jokes," said the other guy. "Sit down."

"Well, just shut the fuck up about my wife," said Chris. That was as far as he was going to take it. He wasn't that drunk. He was about to sit down again. "And you can stop sniffing around her too," he muttered. "Just stop sniffing around her."

Bishop dropped his cigarette to the linoleum, crushed it under his heel. "Well, sniffing around her's a tough job—but someone's got to do it."

That was it. That was all it took. Chris stood over him again. "Get up," he said.

"Aw, cut it out, Chris," said Matt, trying to keep it light. "He's just giving you shit."

"Stay the fuck out of it," said Chris. "Get the fuck up," he said to Bishop.

"Now why would I do that?" Bishop said, tongue-in-cheek. "I'm right in the middle of drinking . . ."

Chris grabbed Bishop's T-shirt in his two hands. He yanked the smaller man to his feet. As he came up, Bishop punched Chris quickly in the throat. Chris's eyes bulged. His cowboy hat flew off. He fell to the floor, gagging.

Bishop sat down again. ". . . a goddamn beer," he said.

He sipped the beer. On the floor, Chris raised himself up on one knee and one hand. He clutched his throat with the other hand. He gagged, his tongue hanging out of his mouth.

Matt tried on another weak laugh. But as he looked at Chris, he finally stopped laughing. He turned to Bishop.

"Jesus, Kennedy," he said. "You hit him in the throat."

"Did I?" said Bishop. He sipped his beer again.

Over at the bar, the two fat hoohas had turned on their stools to watch. So far, they seemed to be enjoying the show. They glanced at each other from time to time and chuckled in appreciation. The hop-head, meanwhile, bounced around on his toes and puffed a cigarette quickly. Hirschorn's goon hid his smile in his bourbon.

The bartender was a giant with a shaved head. The rest of him was all muscle and all of his muscles were covered with tattoos. Drying out a glass with a towel, he was watching like the others.

"Don't make me come over there, ladies," he called over the music. He had a voice so deep it sounded as if he'd swallowed a bullfrog.

Chris had now reached up, got hold of a chair back. He was pulling himself to his feet. Bishop came out of his beer with a satisfied "Ah!" and set it down.

"You know I got a theory, Chris," he said loudly. "Know what my theory is? My theory is: Any man that's gotta take a hard hand to a woman must be 'cause he's got a soft dick." He looked at Chris amiably as the big man got his feet under him, stood. "That's my theory. What do you think? You got an opinion on that?"

Chris rubbed his throat, trying to get his breath steady. "You psycho motherfucker. You coulda killed me."

"Yeah, in fact, I could've killed you twice," Bishop answered. "Once when you grabbed me and then again for good measure when you were down on the floor making that funny choking noise."

That made the bartender laugh, a big deep bullfrog laugh. "Oh brother," he said. The hoohas chuckled too.

Chris's face was already red from gagging. Now it was turning purple with rage. He was still too shaky, though, to make his move. He pointed at Bishop.

"You got a big fucking mouth, little man," he said. "You better remember I've got friends in this town. I've got people I can call."

Bishop bared his teeth. He didn't look at the goon. He knew the goon was watching—watching with his gleaming eyes. He knew the goon had heard that. Chris and his big talk, his drunken threats.

"Is that right?" Bishop said.

"You bet your fucking ass that's right," said Chris.

Bishop went into the watch-pocket of his jeans. He brought out a quarter. He flipped the quarter at Chris. It hit Chris's chest and fell, pattering on the linoleum floor.

"Why don't you run along and call them then," Bishop said.

Matt said, "All right, Kennedy. Knock it off, will you. That's enough. Let's all have a drink here and be friends."

But Bishop went on grinning up at Chris. He wasn't going to stop. Not yet. He said, "Hey. I'm friends. I'm friends with anyone. Even a limp-dick, wife-beating patch of cow piss like him."

"Oh boy," laughed the bartender again. "That wasn't nice."

Chris was still shaky, but now he was too angry to care. "Come

on," he said hoarsely. "Come on! You don't have the element of surprise now, sneaky little shit."

"That's right," said Bishop quietly. "You're all ready for me,
aren't you?"

"Well, come on, stand up then. Stand up this time like a man."

Bishop lifted his beer and took another sip. Chris trembled,
watching him. His whole body trembled with rage.

Bishop set the glass down slowly. "I'll stand up like a man for a
man," he said.

Chris snapped up a chair and drew back to swing it at Bishop's
head. Then he was on the floor again, groaning and his face bleeding.
Bishop had pivoted out of his seat and turned inside the blow, block-
ing it off with his arm. Then he'd sprung his elbow back into Chris's
mouth and stomped on Chris' shin to make sure he went down. Once
Chris had fallen, Bishop kicked him in the stomach too.

"That's gotta hurt," chuckled one of the fat hoohas, shaking his
head.

"Jesus, Kennedy," said Matt.

"Jesus, man," said the other guy. "Come on now."

Bishop picked up his beer. He drank it standing.

The bartender leaned on the bar. "Hey, mister?" he said in his
bullfrog voice. "I figure you made your point."

Bishop nodded. "I'm done." He stood over Chris, holding his
beer. "You got more to say to me, you know where I am," he said
down at the fallen man.

Chris didn't answer. He was curled up, groaning, holding his stomach, spitting blood. Bishop considered him dispassionately. The piece of
shit would beat his wife for this, he thought. He'd been humiliated. He
would take it out on her. But there was no help for that. Not in Bishop's
mind. He'd wanted to show the guy up in front of Hirschorn's goon, to
send a message to Hirschorn that he, Bishop, was the better man. Now
that was done. If Chris went home and took it out on Kathleen, that was

his business, that was too bad. That was the way Bishop thought about it.

And yet . . . yet, all the same, he stood there another second. He thought about Kathleen and the beating she would likely get. Again, he felt that sour heat inside him. The idea of her getting hit like that pissed him off more than he would've admitted.

He turned his glass over and dumped the last of his beer on Chris's face.

"You have a pleasant evening now," he said.

As he walked out of the Clover Leaf, he stole a quick look back at the goon at the end of the bar.

The goon was hiding his smile in his bourbon. His eyes were gleaming.

TWENTY-FOUR

"I don't believe this shit," Inspector Ketchum muttered.

Weiss took a deep breath. "Just wait," he said.

They waited, the sinewy little black man bristling beside the bear-sized Weiss. They were in a coin shop in North Beach. Seymour Hinckel's Rare Coins. It was a small store, pleasantly dark, crowded with display cases. From time to time, a collector would wander in and stoop to look into the cases at the rare coins lying on black padding. Right now though, there were no collectors, there were only Ketchum and Weiss. And Seymour Hinckel, the owner of the place, round of head and body. Bald, bespectacled, breathy, mild. Thrumming with excitement at being in on police business. They were all of them watching the street through the storefront window.

"Well?" Ketchum said. "Here I am. I'm waiting."

Weiss nodded.

"And you're telling me the guy who killed Wally Spender is just gonna come walking in through that door."

"Right."

"Even though he's just a figment of Spender's imagination."

Weiss lifted his shoulders. "It's an interface."

"An interface," said Ketchum. He shook his head. "I don't believe this shit."

"Here he comes! Here he comes!" said Seymour Hinckel in his breathy voice. He bustled uselessly behind his counter, arranging his calendar here, his receipt pad there, then rearranging them. Weiss raised his chin expectantly. Ketchum sneered, but then he always sneered. All three of them looked out through the storefront window at the man who'd murdered Wally Spender.

The killer was tall, slim-waisted, broad-shouldered, with coffee-and-cream-colored skin. He was classically handsome and arrogant about it. You could tell by the way he strutted along the sidewalk doing a heavy eyeball number on anything female coming the opposite way. He bebopped up the hill across the street, past a row of Victorian apartment houses. He reached the corner. Stepped off the sidewalk without bothering to look for traffic. As if he figured the cars would just naturally stop for someone as pretty as he was.

"Let me get around him, then give him the motion," said Weiss.

"You fucking well better explain this to me when we're done," Ketchum muttered.

"Just badge him when I'm at the door."

Ketchum was about to say something else, but stopped. He settled in with an angry sigh.

The killer had reached the shop. Weiss moved away from the inspector. He stood over a display case, hands behind his back. He pretended to peer down at some silver dollars.

The killer pushed in. A ribbon of bells attached to the door tinkled merrily. Still strutting, even in that confined space, the killer high-stepped past the display cases toward Seymour Hinckel. Seymour Hinckel held his breath. He was puffed up like a balloon. Approaching him, the killer smiled a big, white, handsome smile.

But Weiss was already at the door behind him. And now Ketchum stepped in front of him. He flashed his badge.

"Carlos Rodriguez . . ." he said.

That was all he had time for. The killer spun away, thinking to make a run for it. Weiss was there, towering over him. In the blink of an eye, the killer had a stiletto in his hand. Another blink, and Weiss had the stilletto and the killer was gripping his own wrist and grimacing in pain. Weiss had a flash of temper. He backhanded the guy across the face. The slap was loud in the little shop. The killer reeled back against a display case. Then Ketchum was on him. The wiry cop forced him down over the case. He yanked his arms behind his back. He worked his handcuffs onto him.

"Congratulations," said the cop. "You're fucked for life."

The cuffs clicked shut. The killer was still down over the display case. Weiss watched him, unsteady in his rage. Then he took a deep breath. He closed the knife and held it in one hand. With his other hand, he tugged his earlobe distractedly. Seymour Hinckel watched too, peeking out from behind Ketchum. He was so excited he looked as if the tubby Seymour balloon might just come undone and go spitting this way and that around the shop.

"What's this for, man?" the killer cried out—the first words he'd been able to speak.

"Shut the fuck up," Ketchum explained. "The only thing I wanna hear you say is 'ow' when I bust you upside the head."

"But what the fuck's this supposed to be . . . ?"

Ketchum busted him upside the head.

"Ow, man!"

"And watch your fucking language when you're talking to a fucking law officer. Ya fuck."

"But I didn't do nothing."

"Now that's just bullshit. Use your head, *caballero*. Would I be standing here arresting your ass if you hadn't done anything? You killed that little mousey guy in the alley, that's what you did. You're a stone murdering fuck."

"No, man, no!" said the killer.

"Not 'No, man, no,'" said Ketchum. "Yes, man, yes. You're a stone . . . Say it with me now. A stone. Murdering. Fuck."

By this time, a little telegram of fear, dispatched from Carlos Rodriguez's brain, had arrived at his eyes and they became so wide they seemed to take up a good 50 percent of his formerly handsome face. He looked desperately from man to man for help or comfort. Weiss gazed down at him deadpan. Seymour Hinckel watched him, scarlet with the thrill. Ketchum's perpetual sneer had become his occasional scowl. There was nothing for the killer anywhere.

Finally, in despair, Carlos cried out the truth.

"He paid me to do it! Dude was psycho, man. The guy—the little mousey guy his own self. He wanted to die. He paid me to kill him!"

TWENTY-FIVE

The murderer was still shouting when they put him in the back of Ketchum's road-weary Impala.

"Dude, I swear it to God! You gotta believe me, man! He paid me! He told me how to do the whole thing. Said I was supposed to pretend he raped my sister. He was psycho, I'm telling you!"

Ketchum slid behind the wheel. Turned over the ignition while Weiss settled in on the passenger side. The car's rusted front doors creaked as the two men pulled them shut.

"All right, Weiss," Ketchum said. "Let's hear it. This better be good."

He steered away from the curb. Pointed the front fender straight down the steep hill. At that angle, Weiss had to lift his head to see the Bay glittering in the near distance.

"Nobody else had a motive," he said quietly.

"Man, what was I supposed to say?" Carlos Rodriguez shouted from the backseat. "Tell me! Psycho offered me money, man, I'm gonna turn him down? I mean, I wasn't even doing nothing. Just sitting at the tittie bar minding my own . . ."

"Hey!" Ketchum shouted. The killer jumped in his seat and shut up. "We're trying to have a conversation here."

"I'm just saying . . ."

"Don't make me stop this car, you hear me?" Ketchum turned half-around and wagged a finger at the killer. "If I have to come back there, I'll fucking kneecap you."

Rodriguez sagged into silence. Weiss, meanwhile, narrowed his eyes at the windshield with concern. But Ketchum faced front just in time. The Impala swerved around the old Asian lady who'd lugged her vegetable cart into the middle of the street.

"Crazy Chinese bitch," muttered Ketchum, wrestling the car back under control. "So anyway . . . ?"

"Right. No one else had a motive," said Weiss. "Spender was all his mother had, she wouldn't kill him. And no one else cared a damn about him. He wasn't robbed, so it wasn't about that. The only one who would get anything at all from his death was him."

"Him," Ketchum echoed. "Spender himself. Because he's gonna get . . . what?"

"Well . . . He wanted his fantasy to become real, I guess."

"Dude was psycho," Rodriguez muttered.

"Hey!" said Ketchum, shaking a finger at the rearview mirror. And then to Weiss: "He wants his fantasy to become real even if it means he gets iced."

"Yeah. That was the easiest part of it to make real. All he had to do was pay someone to play the avenging brother."

"Should've paid someone to play the girl, would've been a helluva lot more fun."

"He did. He tried. It didn't work out."

"Oh yeah?" said Ketchum. "His Johnson . . . ?"

"Deserted him, yeah. This was the next best option. So it got me thinking how he'd do it," Weiss went on. "Because the Spenders had no money to speak of, not enough to pay a killer. But I did notice when I was in Wally's room that he had some coin-collecting books that were missing all the most valuable coins. Which I figured was just normal at first. You know, like he couldn't afford them? But after I started thinking along this line, I thought, well, maybe he sold off the coins to get the money to hire himself a hit man."

"A hit man. Against himself," said Ketchum. "I swear. The shit people pull."

"I found out what coins they were and called around to various coin shops. Then I find Hinckel. And big surprise. Spender didn't sell the coins himself, he let the killer do it. Hey, Carlos," he called over his shoulder into the backseat. "How did you guys work it? Spender tell you the coins would become more valuable if you held on to them?"

"Yeah," said Rodriguez sullenly. "Psycho mother."

"I get it, I get it," said Ketchum. He raised his eyes to the rearview again. "He tells you to hang on to them and you're such a dumb shit, you hang on to them for what? Forty-eight hours?"

"I wanted to make sure they were really good, man. How'm I supposed to know?" The handsome killer's voice sank away in a string of muttered obscenities.

"So," said Weiss, "Hinckel got ID for the sale and so on. Our boy back there gave a false address but a real cell phone number."

"'Cause he's stupid."

"Right. So I had Hinckel call him up and say he'd made a mistake and underpaid for one of the coins, that he owed him another couple of thousand dollars."

"And that's it, in he walks," said Ketchum with a grim smile. "How do you like that, Carlos? Only reason you got caught is 'cause you're such a dumb shit. That oughta make you feel better when you're pulling your twenty-five-to."

They drove on for another while, each with thoughts of his own. The Impala reached the base of the hill, bounced through the flat intersection, took on the next hill, a nearly vertical climb. Blue sky filled the windshield and one lofty, billowing cloud.

Ketchum chuckled nastily to himself. "You know, this is good," he said. "I like this. Mousey Guy dreams of raping Fantasy Girl then hires Asswipe here to make his dreams come true. What do you know, Carlos? Turns out you're just a figment of your vic's imagination. Now he's dead, you'll probably up and fucking disappear." He chuckled again, a mirthless, throaty sound. "You're an interface, man, that's what you are."

Weiss had turned to the cop. No change in his heavy expression. He allowed a moment to pass. Then he said, "Ketch—I need to talk to the Identity Man."

On the instant, Ketchum's chuckle collapsed back into a scowl. "What're you talking about?"

"Whip Pomeroy. Soon. I need to talk to him as soon as possible."

Ketchum glanced sidelong at his old friend, his only friend. "What're you, kidding me?" Still, Weiss's expression didn't change. "The guy's PC'd up the wazoo, man. How the hell do you figure I'm supposed to get you in there?"

The car stopped precariously at the very brink of the hilltop. A cable car shuddered across the sky in front of them, ringing its bell. Ketchum took the opportunity to face Weiss full on. Weiss was still looking at him. His expression—that heavy, world-weary look of his—still hadn't changed.

Ketchum looked back out through the windshield. He shook his head once in disgust.

"I don't believe this shit," he sighed.

TWENTY-SIX

I had my feet up on the desk and the *Chronicle* spread open in front of my face when Weiss came into the Agency the next morning.

"I pay you for this?" I heard him say.

"Not that much." I scrunched the paper shut. Dropped my feet to the floor. "Anyway, I was just reading about your heroic exploits."

"All your doing, not mine."

"Me? What do you mean?"

"The Case of the Spanish Virgin. The killer—it was just like you said: It was an interface. He was real whether he was real or not."

I laughed and blushed at the same time. "All right, all right. I'm never gonna hear the end of this, I can tell."

"No, I'm serious. I'm gonna change the sign on the front door: BETTER DETECTION THROUGH MEANINGLESS PHILOSOPHY."

"I open up, I share, I try to contribute, what do I get?"

"OUR INVESTIGATORS ARE HERE FOR YOU WHETHER THEY'RE HERE OR NOT."

"Nothing but ridicule. Ridicule and disrespect."

Weiss stood over me, tongue in his cheek, hands in his pockets. Quiet a few seconds. He gestured with his chin at the newspaper crumpled on my desk. "So what do you think?"

"What," I said. "About Spender? Hell, I don't know."

"C'mon. You're the deep thinker. Was it some kind of psychological shit? He felt guilty about his fantasy. Wanted to punish himself for it."

I made a face. "Maybe. Tell you the truth, I think he probably just preferred death to reality. Most people do. They usually get there a little slower, that's all."

I was gratified when Weiss nodded thoughtfully at that. He began to edge away. But he said, "Oh, hey, listen: I'm giving you to Sissy on the Strawberry trial."

At first, I didn't understand him—or didn't believe what he was saying. Then, excitement went buzzing through me. "You mean to . . . ?"

"She needs background on a couple of witnesses."

He did mean it. Investigation. He was assigning me a real investigation for a real trial. I had never done anything like it before. It was a big step up for me. "Hey, thanks. That's great," I said. "That's great. Thanks. Really. Thanks a lot."

"It's your reward for cracking the Virgin case."

"All right, all right. Ha ha ha."

"Now I'm turning my back, okay? Don't go disappearing on me."

"Oh, shut up."

Off he rambled into his office. He left the door open and I could hear him in there. I heard him sigh heavily, heard him plunk heavily into his chair. I began to clear my desk for the work before me, smiling to myself. I heard his computer come on, the boops and beeps, the musical phrase. Then the three-note chime that meant he had e-mail. *Bishop,* I thought.

There was a pause. He must've been reading. I picked up the phone to call Sissy Truitt, to tell her she had a new op on the Strawberry trial.

Then Weiss's growl reached me from his office.

"Oh, for fuck's sake," I heard him say. And I heard what I guess was his hand coming down hard on his desktop.

Weiss. Situation here's unstable. Chris Wannamaker's coming apart. He and I had it out and Hirschorn definitely got the word on it. A lot of unknowable stuff: when Kathleen will crack and spill to her husband, how he'll react, which way Hirschorn will break. But I can't see another way in. From talks with Kathleen, my guess is Chris himself doesn't even know what the hell's happening. Only Hirschorn, if I can get close enough. Whatever they're planning, it's going down soon. Time's short, I'm doing my best. JB.

TWENTY-SEVEN

In Driscoll that morning, the light was pale and clear. It was early on, the heat of day had not yet risen. The neighborhood was quiet, the men gone off to work, some of the women too, the kids were at camp or wherever. A dog was barking. Lawn sprinklers made their chiggering sound from here and there. A mourning dove perched on a telephone wire sang its plaintive four-note song: *teroo-hoo-hoo*.

Bishop sat at his bedroom window and watched Chris Wanna-maker hit Kathleen. The couple was downstairs in the living room of their house next door. They'd been arguing for ten minutes and now Chris flathanded his wife along the side of her head.

"Ow! God damn it," she shouted. And she threw a fist right back at him, right for his face. He brushed the punch away with one hand. Then he was even angrier and he hit her again. This time, he connected so hard she tumbled sideways and went to the floor. The top of her head bounced against the padded edge of the sofa.

The corner of Bishop's mouth twitched when he saw that—which I guess coming from him was as good as a wince. But he went on sitting there, very still in the chair by his desk, watching, smoking a cigarette in the shadows. He had his bedroom light off. He had his window cracked open. He could see the Wannamakers very clearly and hear their voices too, the sounds of them and the words as well when they shouted loudly enough.

"I want him the fuck out of there! Now!" Chris screamed down at his fallen wife.

She screamed back up at him from the floor, screamed through her tears. "It's my goddamned house! I'll rent it to whoever the fuck I want!"

Chris's eyes were white with fury. He paced back and forth

above her. Even at this distance, Bishop could see how banged up he was. A red and purple bruise covered one whole cheek—that was where Bishop's elbow had caught him in their fight two nights before in the Clover Leaf. The bruise made Chris look twisted and monstrous, especially with him pacing there like a caged, hungry animal. Shaking his finger at his fallen wife. Snarling and snapping down at her.

He'd lowered his voice now but some words still reached Bishop: ". . . sniffing around you," he said.

Kathleen answered back. Bishop couldn't hear what she said but it must've been more sass because Chris lashed out at her with his foot. The tip of his boot caught the back of her thigh. She cried out and rolled away from him. She lay curled on her side, clutching herself through her jeans, gasping. Chris went on pacing over her, snarling at her. At some point, he shouted, "Whore!" Bishop could see Kathleen's body shaking with her sobs.

He took a drag on his Marlboro. His pale eyes, flat and cold, narrowed as the smoke drifted up around them.

Then his phone rang, loud and suddenly. Bishop grabbed it with one hand, crushed his cigarette in the ashtray with his other.

"Yeah?" he said.

"Am I speaking to Frank Kennedy?"

Bishop straightened in his chair. He didn't recognize the fine, clipped voice on the other end of the line but he guessed who it must be. He turned his back to the window so the scene below wouldn't distract him. "Yeah, this is Kennedy."

"Mr. Kennedy, my name is Alex Wellman. I'm Bernard Hirschorn's personal assistant."

"Okay. What can I do for you?"

"Mr. Hirschorn has asked me to arrange a meeting with you, if possible."

Bishop smiled tightly to himself, answered coolly, "Sure. When would he like to meet?"

"Noon today, his office at the Driscoll Foundation."

"I'll be there."

"Excellent. Thank you very much." There was a click. A dial tone. That was it.

Bishop laid the phone back in its cradle. He sat forward in his chair, his elbows on his knees. Thinking it over, taking the situation in. It was good, he thought, the situation was good. Hirschorn wanted to see him. That meant that maybe his plan had worked. Maybe when news of the brawl at the Clover Leaf had reached him, Hirschorn had started having second thoughts about Chris as a pilot. Maybe he was considering Bishop as a replacement too. *This is good,* he thought. *This could be good.*

Bishop sat up. Turned back to the window, glanced out again at the house across the way.

The shouting had stopped over there now. Chris had gotten down on his knees. Kathleen was lying on her back on the floor, her legs bent in self-defense. Chris was talking to her softly. His face was contorted and Bishop thought he might be crying. He moved his hands up and down as if he were trying to explain something to her or maybe pleading with her. Then he put one hand on her leg, on her calf. She drew away from his touch, but he followed after her. He moved his hand up onto her thigh and then into her crotch. He worked his body between her knees, forcing them apart. He tried to lower himself on top of her.

At first, Kathleen put her hand against his chest to hold him off. She turned her face away. But he kept on gently pressing down, talking quietly, trying to explain, pleading with her. Soon, her arm relaxed, her hand slipped up onto his shoulder. She had her face turned away but he kissed her cheek and her hair and then she turned and let him kiss her mouth and she reached up and touched the bruised side of his face. It was a sympathetic touch, even tender. She lay still for him as he moved down to work her pants off her.

Bishop went on watching them. He found himself wondering

what would happen to Chris if Hirschorn did decide to replace him. He found himself wondering if Hirschorn would kill Chris to make sure he kept his mouth shut. He decided: Yeah. Probably Hirschorn would kill him. If the operation was big enough, if Chris's silence was important enough, that was probably exactly what Hirschorn would do.

Kathleen continued to lie still on the floor and Chris came into her. He pressed his face close against the side of hers. She put her hand on his shoulder gently and held him like that. But she turned her head to look out through the window as if she were distracted, thinking other thoughts while he went on. She seemed to be looking up at Bishop's window, in fact, right up at the window where Bishop was sitting. She seemed to be looking right at Bishop himself, in fact, as Chris pumped in and out of her. With his lights off, and with the sun stationed where it was in the morning, Bishop doubted she could actually see him. He decided she was probably just thinking about him, that's all.

He went on watching. He thought about the phone call from Hirschorn's secretary. He thought about how Hirschorn would probably kill Chris if he replaced him. He looked down at Kathleen who, in turn, looked up at him. Chris heaved a final time and lay still on top of her.

Bishop looked down and wondered if Hirschorn would want to kill her too.

TWENTY-EIGHT

The motorcycle jigged beneath him as he rode over the long dirt road. It was dark and cool here under an arcade of oaks. Then the oaks were gone and the hot sun beat down on him and the land opened up in front of him and on either side. It was green, rolling land, like nothing else around it. Sprinklers showered it everywhere. Gardeners—there must've been eight or ten of them—stooped among violet flower beds or knelt on stretches of lawn. Ponds lay still and peaceful in the cruxes between hills and valleys. Some of the ponds burned blinding with the noonday glare, some reflected the mellow sky or the surrounding mountains. The mountains half ringed the place, smoky peaks against the big clouds, and even a few higher snowcaps etched flat and sharp against the distant blue. Hirschorn's buildings—the buildings of the Driscoll Foundation—the ranch house, the barn, the stables and so on—clustered in the piedmont plain, shaded by trees. It was, Bishop thought, quite a spread. Not just a local gangster's hangout. More like a big-time bad guy's piece of the good life.

The dirt road curled right. Bishop's Road King curled along with it and headed for the ranch house. The house came up before him, haughty and grand. It was yellow with white trim. It had three fanlit gables on the slanting roof above. Below, under the eave of the roof, a row of arching French doors opened onto a wraparound porch. There were pillars at the edge of the porch. Brick stairs led down between them to the edge of the road.

Bishop pulled up at the base of the stairs. As he killed the motor, the front door opened. A small, slender man stood stiffly in the entrance, waiting. He was haughty like the house but not so grand. His lips were pursed, his nose wrinkled as if he smelled something bad. *The personal assistant,* Bishop thought, *Alex Wellman.*

Bishop swung his leg over the bike's seat. He looped off his helmet and hung it from the handlebars. He climbed the stairs to meet the man.

Wellman led Bishop through the main room of the house. With all the French doors and with the picture window looking out on the mountains, the place was very bright. There were Spanish-style rugs. There was heavy oakwood furniture. There were small bronzes of horses and buffalo on the end tables and shelves. A Mexican maid knelt on the enormous stone fireplace, cleaning the cracks between the stones. Bishop's motorcycle boots clumped loudly as he walked by her.

They reached the library door.

"Mr. Hirschorn. Mr. Kennedy is here for your meeting," said Wellman stiffly.

Hirschorn was coming around the broad expanse of his desk, his hand extended, a smile on his tanned, moustachioed face. He was in shirtsleeves and slacks. He must've been nearly sixty, but he still looked very solid, very strong.

"Mr. Kennedy!" he said. He shook Bishop's hand vigorously. Looked him over and nodded, still smiling, as if he saw something in him particularly fine. "Come in. Come in. Please."

Bishop stepped over the threshold. Now he could see the goons. There were two of them standing side by side against one wall: the ape-armed, hatchet-faced monster from the Clover Leaf and another one, a little one, wired and jittery, all sinew and eyes.

Hirschorn lifted a hand at them, at the big one first. "You've met my chauffeur, Mr. Goldmunsen," he said. Then he indicated the smaller one, who was bouncing on his toes as if he couldn't contain himself, as if he might lift off through the ceiling any minute like a rocket. "And this is his associate, Mr. Flake."

Wellman, meanwhile, evaporated. He edged back into the shadows, then became a shadow, then was gone. The door to the library swung in mysteriously and clicked shut.

Hirschorn strode to one side of his desk, enthroned himself there in a hard, studded leather armchair. He didn't offer Bishop a seat and Bishop stood where he was in the middle of the room. The two goons stared at him.

"I'll offer you a seat in a few moments," said Hirschorn. "But first, Mr. Goldmunsen here is going to step forward and punch you very hard in the stomach. After that, you'll probably lie curled up on the floor and retch and gasp for a while."

Bishop smiled slightly. It was not a smile that came from his heart. He glanced at the grinning ape Goldmunsen and then back at Hirschorn. "You think so," he said tersely.

"Oh yes." The silver-haired gentleman laughed shortly. "I do think so. He will come forward and you'll stand there while he punches you. Otherwise, I'll ask Mr. Flake to draw his pistol and shoot you in the testicles. I'm sure you'd prefer the punch."

Bishop stopped smiling. Goldmunsen stepped forward. Bishop's eyes flicked to Flake. The little bouncing goon didn't actually draw his gun but Bishop took it on faith that he had one and that he'd use it if Hirschorn told him to. Goldmunsen stood in front of him. He grinned.

Bishop had to fight not to raise his arms to protect himself. He tightened his stomach muscles but it was no good. The fist at the end of Goldmunsen's gorilla arm was like a wrecking ball. The next moment, Bishop was lying curled up on the floor retching and gasping pretty much as Hirschorn had predicted.

"Thank you, gentlemen, that will be all," Hirschorn said to the goons.

After a while, Bishop became aware that Goldmunsen and Flake had left the room.

After another while, Hirschorn said, "Now you can have a seat, Mr. Kennedy."

Bishop crawled slowly to the sofa. He pulled himself onto it. It was leather like Hirschorn's armchair but soft. He sank into it deep.

Leaning against its arm, clutching his stomach, he had to look way up to see where Hirschorn sat enthroned above him.

"That dustup in the Clover Leaf the other night," Hirschorn said. "You understand: Chris Wannamaker is my employee. More than that, his father was my friend, we went all through school together, he worked for me until he died last year." He held up a hand as if Bishop were about to speak and he wanted to stop him. But Bishop was still in no condition to speak. "I understand that personal matters come up from time to time. These things have to be dealt with. We're all men. We all know the rules." He smiled and his blue eyes twinkled. But the twinkle did not seem to suggest that life was a merry cavalcade of mirth. It seemed instead to indicate that Hirschorn could easily have Bishop rubbed out as if he were a shit stain on his underwear. Bishop, half-lying there, gasping for breath, experienced the twinkle as if it were a slimy thing that had crawled up his spine.

"All the same," Hirschorn went on, "in this town—in my town—things are dealt with in a certain way—my way. And if you have a score to settle with one of my employees, personal or not, you clear it with me first. Because, as we've now learned, there are far worse things than a punch in the stomach. And if you annoy me, Mr. Kennedy, I'll have any number of those things done to you without batting an eyelash. Do we understand each other?"

Bishop dragged the heel of his palm across his chin, wiping away the drool. He managed to sit up straighter. He managed to nod. "Yeah," he whispered.

"Good." Hirschorn placed his hands on his knees and pushed himself standing. He went on in a brisker tone: down to business. "Now let's talk about what we can do for each other."

Hirschorn walked to the window behind his desk. He planted himself there with his hands clasped behind him. He looked out over his hills and valleys. He had his back turned toward Bishop and Bishop knew it was a message, a way of telling Bishop that he was now under Hirschorn's control, that he was not worth fearing. But

Bishop didn't need to be told that. He already knew that he was not worth fearing—not at the moment anyway. He collapsed back into the deep sofa. He sat there hollow-eyed, breathing hard, holding his stomach, waiting.

Hirschorn turned to face him. With the sunlight coming through the window behind him, his features were impossible to make out. He was just a silhouette surrounded by a glow. "A few weeks ago I took on an assignment from a . . . an associate of mine. A very big assignment from a very important associate. The assignment required a very well trained and experienced pilot."

"Chris," Bishop croaked. He put as much disdain into the syllable as he could.

Hirschorn lowered his chin. Bishop thought he might be smiling but he wasn't sure. "Chris, yes. Chris was my pilot. I was very pressed for time and, well, as I say, Chris was the son of an old friend who, frankly, needed a break. So I brought him on board." He spread his hands. "You try to be generous, you try to be faithful to your old buddies, am I right? Unfortunately, it doesn't always work out. As you seem to have noticed, Chris can be a little careless in his dealings with people. Especially when he's drunk. Which, it turns out, is a good deal of the time. So. The situation now is: I need a new pilot. In a hurry." He came forward, out of the light. Looking down at Bishop. "You said you wanted the job."

"Yeah . . ." Bishop drew a breath. "That's right."

"Well, that's good. Because your training and your background happen to make you perfect for it." Hirschorn moved away, sat down at his desk. He opened a folder that lay on the blotter. "Frank Kennedy. Born in Santa Maria, California, to Steve and Marcy. One younger sister, Susan. You were an Army brat. Moved around a lot, Texas, Louisiana. Blah, blah, blah. So on and so forth. Cut to the chase: You flew with Bravo Company in the Middle East. Awarded the DFC and the Silver Star. You've been a bit of a drifter since then. A little trouble with the law here and there. Arrested for aggravated assault in . . . let's see, Seattle . . . no, Phoenix. Charges dropped. Seattle was assault with a deadly weapon, reduced to a misdemeanor. Three months served. Your parole officer should be getting just a little annoyed by your absence right about this time." He looked up. Flashed his white, charmer smile. "I hope I'm impressing you with our intelligence-gathering operation here."

"Yeah," Bishop said more evenly. But the only thing that impressed him just then was Weiss. It was one of those moments when he felt a fierce, warm admiration for his employer. Weiss had a genius for creating these identities, for making them just right, just what was needed. And somehow he always managed to place the records of them into the system in such a way that other investigators would feel they had dug them up. Here was Hirschorn, rich and smart and powerful. With all kinds of resources at his disposal to do any kind of background check he wanted. And Weiss had fooled him. Bishop looked at Hirschorn and thought about what an arrogant ratbag he was and how Weiss had fooled him and how he, Bishop, was going to nail his arrogant ratbag hide to a wall and bring his head home to Weiss as a trophy. "Yeah," he said. "I'm impressed."

"Good," Hirschorn said again. He slapped the folder shut. "Good." He pushed off the desk with both hands. Stood up. "I hope you're beginning to see that I run a strong operation across the board." He came around to the leather armchair again. He sat down again where he could lord it over Bishop. "Because I'm about to ask you to join that operation in a way that could cost you your life."

He said it like that. Very melodramatic. Bishop raised an eyebrow. "My life is worth a lot to me."

"A hundred thousand dollars?"

"Yeah, that'd cover it."

"For a day's work."

Bishop nodded. "Fine."

"Fortunately, all the preliminaries have been taken care of. All the materiel and so forth that had to be transported—all that's been done. What I need you for is one flight, one last flight in two days' time. Are you up for that?"

"Can you give me any details?" Bishop asked.

"Not one."

"Okay. For a hundred thousand dollars, sure."

Hirschorn nodded. He was not smiling his charming smile anymore beneath the iron moustache. His blue eyes were no longer twinkling. He was watching Bishop, calculating, studying Bishop's reactions as he went on. "Here's what you'll have to do," he said. "Meet me at the airport at six tomorrow. We'll fly to a location. Once we're there, you'll be told more about what you have to do, as much as you need to know. Once you're told, you will not be able to leave the location or communicate with anyone outside for any reason whatsoever until the job is complete. You understand? I'm sorry to have to take all these precautions. I'm sure you're a good guy, very trustworthy. But I don't know you. I have to be careful. This associate of mine . . . Well, he has exacting standards . . . exacting standards," he repeated faintly. And something about this, about the way he said it, made Bishop take notice. There was fear in those words, he was almost sure of it. Hirschorn was afraid of this associate of his. Bishop remembered Weiss's e-mail: *There seems to be a connection between these people and a major whack specialist sometimes called Shadowman. . . .*

"Let's just say I'm uncomfortable making last-minute changes in an operation this complicated," Hirschorn continued. "For you the bottom line is: I'm letting you in on a good deal. But once I do let you in, I have to make certain you keep your mouth shut. That's the way it is."

Bishop nodded. He was thinking, *Jesus Christ, what a sucker play this is.* Because it was, let's face it. It was a sucker play right down the line. He was supposed to let himself be taken off to a secret location. Kept out of touch until the job was done. What the hell did he think they would do with him then, when the job *was* done? Pay him? Just hand him his hundred thou, let him walk away? A guy they didn't know, didn't trust? Bullshit. A hundred thousand dollars for a day's work is a lot of money. A single bullet to the brain was much cheaper, much safer all around.

Oh man, Bishop thought. *Weiss is going to go nuclear when he hears about this.* Weiss would pull him off the case the second he found out.

Well, he was just going to have to make sure Weiss didn't find out until it was too late to stop it.

"There's one more thing," Hirschorn said. He sat very still in the leather chair. He sat with his hands on his lap, his fingers intertwined. He sat relaxed. But Bishop sensed the tension in him. He sensed—could almost hear—the man's nerves thrumming like a bowstring. Hirschorn went on quietly: "If this is not something you want to do, I understand. There's no problem, no hard feelings. But the time to decide is now. Once I take you in, once I let you know the details of the assignment, there'll be no going back, no getting out."

Bishop sat sunk in the leather sofa, his hand on his aching stomach, his eyes deep, his face gray. *A sucker play,* he kept thinking. *A sucker play right down the line.*

"If you get on that plane with me tomorrow," Hirschorn told him, "you're coming home with a hundred thousand dollars in your pocket—or you're not coming home at all. Do you understand me?"

Again, Bishop nodded. He thought: *Jesus Christ.* He said: "Yeah, I understand you."

"Are you in?" Hirschorn asked him.

"Yeah," Bishop said. "I'm in."

TWENTY-NINE

That afternoon, Weiss drove down the coast to Half Moon Bay. It was bright and windy by the ocean. Forests of high pines dipped and swayed on the rolling hills all around him. Pearly clouds scudded over the dazzling sea, visible through the trees. But Weiss rumbled by in his gray Taurus, ignoring the scenery once again, grumbling to himself once again because Bishop and his latest e-mail—once again—were making a hellhole of his entire digestive system.

Situation here's unstable. Chris Wannamaker's coming apart. He and I had it out and Hirschorn definitely got the word on it. . . .

All of which was bullshit. Bullshit every word. Weiss had told him—told him in no uncertain terms: *Do not go undercover into Hirschorn's op; do not.* But—Weiss could read between the lines—that was exactly what the renegade op was doing. Why else would he have "had it out" with Chris Wannamaker if not to humiliate him in front of Hirschorn, to set himself up as a possible replacement? And then what? *A lot of unknowable stuff: when Kathleen will crack and spill to her husband, how he'll react, which way Hirschorn will break. . . .* Which, when translated into Non-Bullshit, even into Semi-Bullshit, meant the whole situation could explode any minute. If Kathleen decided she couldn't bear the guilt of her affair. Or if she wanted to use the affair to end her marriage. And if Chris found out she'd been feeding Bishop information. Or if Hirschorn found out . . .

Weiss wasn't sure which felt worse just then: his anger or his guilt. His anger at Bishop for endangering his own life and the lives of the people around him. Or his guilt because he, Weiss, wasn't going to stop it.

Time's short. That's what Bishop had written. And that was it, that was exactly it. Time *was* short. Weiss felt it too. Whatever was going to happen was going to happen soon. And while Weiss had no idea what the hell it was, there were other pieces of the thing that were starting to come together for him. And, the more he understood, the less he liked the look of it.

He had a strange, intuitive method of working, Weiss did. I've sometimes thought he was an artist in his way. He had this talent for getting into people's heads. Strangers, people he'd never even met. He could think his way into them, imagine what they'd done, what they would do. Then, almost without his knowing how it happened, a possible scenario would come to him, a narrative of past events or the events that might happen next.

It was that way with him now. The death of the wealthy criminal, Cameron Moncrieff. The suicide of Moncrieff's gardener, Harry Ridder. The possible suicide of Moncrieff's caregiver, Julie Wyant. The imprisonment of Moncrieff's lover, Whip Pomeroy, now trading away the secrets of his life's work to keep himself in protective custody, to keep himself out of the reach of the Shadowman. It was all beginning to make a kind of sense to Weiss, the individual minds and purposes interlinking to form a single picture.

And with that sense came a feeling of urgency, of fear. He wasn't sure why. In some way—some way he couldn't quite name—it had something to do with Julie Wyant. Even though she was supposed to be dead, even though the police were sure she was dead and even though he himself thought she was probably dead as well, he couldn't shake her, couldn't shake the thought of her. He had this image, this fantasy about her stuck in his mind. He saw himself running up a flight of stairs. He had to hurry. Every second counted. There was a door up ahead of him. Locked, bolted from the inside. He had to break it down, a single splintering kick. And then there she was. He was just in the nick of time to save her. She was lying on the bed with her red-gold hair splayed out like a halo around that angel face. She was gratefully looking up at him with those fathomless eyes. She was reaching out to him . . .

Well, anyway. That was what he felt. Just like in the fantasy. He felt he had to move, be quick, that every second counted. Which is why he would not risk taking Bishop off the case. Why he would live with the anger and the guilt both, not to mention the stomachache. And why, also, he was driving to Half Moon Bay.

Cameron Moncrieff's lawyer—the "good old-fashioned lowlife mouthpiece" Peter Crouch—had been surprisingly difficult to find. He was said to have retired after Moncrieff's death but no one seemed to know where exactly he'd gone to. More to the point, maybe, no one seemed to really care. Crouchy had no friends. He had never met a man who liked him. A potbellied, slovenly drone with a monotone voice and a face made slick and beady with avarice, only the drug dealers, pimps, extortionists, loan sharks and hit men he defended could tolerate him at all, and those just barely, just when they could use him. No one waved good-bye when he suddenly handed off his cases, packed up his office and left town, no one shed a tear or was even glad. It simply didn't matter.

But it had started to matter to Weiss. Crouch was there when Cameron Moncrieff had died. Just as Harry Ridder was there, as Julie Wyant was there. Crouch was the only one who was there and who was still, as far as anyone knew, alive. So Weiss needed to find him. And, being Weiss, he did.

He found his house at least. A modest remodeled farmhouse off the highway at the edge of town. Secluded, set back from a winding road on a patch of grass at the edge of a fallow pumpkin field. A homey old two-story clapboard with a swing on the front porch. The swing, wind-stirred, creaked and swayed comfortably as Weiss came up the porch steps to the front door.

He knocked on the door and waited. He had tried to phone ahead but there was no answer. A local police detective had told him that the farmhouse was unoccupied but that a handyman continued to keep the grounds and do repairs to the exterior. The handyman told him Crouch had the bank pay his bills automatically. As long as he got his money, he said, he did his job.

No one came to the door so Weiss tried it. Locked. He'd figured that. He drew a palm-sized leather case from his inside jacket pocket. Selected a pick from the case and worked it into the keyhole.

He picked the lock in a moment. Stepped inside. He was in the living room. It was dark and cool. The furniture stood quiet and cozy. Stuffed chairs with floral upholstery, sofas, a braid rug. An ottoman by the empty fireplace.

Windows were cracked open. The wind squeezed through. Dust balls stirred on the floor. Dust swirled in the air and tickled Weiss's nose. He heard things. Scrabbling. Mice or rats in the wall.

Some old cop instinct woke in Weiss and he went very still inside.

He stepped through doorways. A guest room, a dining room, a downstairs parlor. A kitchen with a southern window. A wedge of light lay yellow there on the green linoleum floor. Weiss could see rat damage in the tiles at the corners and where the legs of the brown kitchen table were gnawed white. He opened the cupboards. No food, nothing. He heard a gurgling. The refrigerator. Apparently the electricity bills were still being paid too. He pulled open the refrigerator door. Empty.

The whole floor was empty, the upstairs too. A bedroom with a bed neatly made, a study with dusty books, a dusty computer on a dusty desk. Nothing else. Just the pitter-patter in the walls. It kept running ahead of him like the footsteps of an escaping ghost.

Weiss would've left, in fact, if it weren't for that thing inside him, that still cop thing. It niggled at him and he stayed on, cruised through the rooms yet another time. That's how he stumbled on the trapdoor.

It was in the downstairs parlor. He felt it shift beneath his feet when he stepped on a little rectangle of shag rug. He kicked the rug aside, stooped down. Pulled on the iron ring.

Creaking hinges. A dark descent on rickety stairs. Another door. He had to fight to open it. When he did, he heard a little kiss of released air.

The big man had to bow his head low to duck through the entry. Inside, it was cool and very dry. He noticed that especially, how dry it was. He felt along the wall, found a light switch. The lights came on and then he understood. The racks, the bottles, the thermostat on the wall: It was a wine cellar.

That explained the state of the body.

After so many months, the atmosphere in the sealed room had had an ugly effect on the corpse of Peter Crouch. It had mummified him, turned his skin to a thin, brown leather. He looked like some kind of skeletal beast, especially the way he was hanging there, chained naked and spread-eagle to one of the wine racks on the opposite wall. His ribs had burst through their covering, the bones of his hands were also visible under the taut, shiny flesh. But his face was still weirdly alive, weirdly recognizable. The egg-shaped head, the stray wisps of hair in their lousy comb-over. The eyes as lifeless, black and hard as ever. The cheeks, though—the cheeks had been white and flaccid before and now they were taut and dark. At first, Weiss thought it was that—the tautness of the cheeks—that had pulled Crouch's lips so wide, that bared his teeth in that wild, mirthless grin.

But no. The longer he stood there, the more he considered the cadaver's condition, the more he came to feel that Crouch had been preserved exactly as he'd died: with his mouth jacked open to let out his screams.

PART THREE The Identity Man

THIRTY

The scotch tasted good and the whore was beautiful. But Weiss felt heavyhearted, unsettled, on edge.

He sat in the chair by the bay window. The chair was turned to face the room. His back was toward the night and the city. He was looking at the girl. For some reason, even her beauty rankled him.

Her hair was red, just what he'd asked for. Not golden silky red-blond like Julie Wyant's but still lightish red, as close as Casey could come on short notice. And she had the sweet face he'd wanted. A warm smile, fine, high cheekbones, a pixie chin. Weiss sipped his whiskey. Watched her as she began to undress. Watched with that saggy, hangdog expression of his. Unsettled, edgy. Afraid.

Afraid, that was the word. It was the dead lawyer that'd done it. Crouch hung up to dry in his own wine cellar. The coroner who came to take him away said it looked as if he'd been tortured. The cops were none too pleased about that. They were none too pleased that it was Weiss who'd found him either. They'd kept the detective around for hours, worked him as if he were a perp. And all the while the sense of urgency in him was building. Crouchy dead. Ridder dead. Julie Wyant . . .

He kept picturing himself charging up the stairs. Kicking down the door. Saving her in the nick of time. He kept thinking about that. And he was afraid.

The hooker peeled a strap down over her shoulder. She glanced at him sidelong. Licked her lips. It was supposed to be provocative but it just annoyed him. He never liked that phony, porno, come-hither shit. They were supposed to know that.

She began to breathe heavily. She caressed her own breast.

He made an impatient gesture, brushing the whole business away.

"You don't have to do all that," he said.

The girl dropped the act at once. "Oh yeah, sorry, they told me. I forgot."

"It's all right," said Weiss. "Just get undressed."

She did—quickly now, matter-of-factly, as if he weren't there. She tossed her dress carelessly over the arm of the sofa. Then, in her bra and panties, she spread her hands for him, a comic flourish: ta-da.

"How's that?" she said.

"That's fine," said Weiss. "Fine."

She shook her head. "You oughta just get married. You'd be a lot happier."

The ice in his scotch glass tinkled as Weiss shifted in his chair. He shouldn't have asked for the red hair, he thought. That was stupid of him, childish. He was bound to be disappointed. You couldn't imitate that color, not the real thing, that red-tinted gold.

"I was," he said. "Married, I mean. And I wasn't. I mean, happier."

"Well, you try again, that's all," said the whore. "Find some nice girl to take care of you and give a shit sometimes. A guy like you? Come on."

"I don't know. Maybe you're right."

"All the girls say what a great guy you are. I'm serious. You've got a really good reputation."

Weiss smiled faintly. "Well . . . That's nice to hear."

"You're a romantic, I'll bet that's what it is," the whore said. "One of these guys—you're into your fantasies more than you're into real life."

"Damn it," said Weiss. "I told Casey: No more psychology majors."

She had a pretty laugh. "Very funny. I'm going for my MBA, so ha ha."

She reached back and unhooked her bra. Nice breasts, excellent breasts, first-rate. Round, high, large pink aureoles. Weiss caught his breath, sure enough, at the sight of them. But even now he was distracted, half his mind on that flight of stairs, that locked door . . . Every second counted.

The whore came to him. Still in her panties but with her breasts bare. She knelt on his chair, her knee between his legs. Stroked the hair above his ears and kissed his face gently. Weiss put his scotch aside. Brushed the girl's flesh with his fingers. He was stirred down deep by the softness of her. But she whispered: "Hey, you, your mind's wandering." She crooked a finger under the big detective's chin, tilted it up till his eyes met hers. "I want your complete attention."

Weiss drew her down onto his lap. Hid his face against her and let her stroke him. Buried his face in the soft dark of her.

"Mm, now you're with me," said the whore, caressing him.

She stood up off him. Stood in front of him. Slipped her panties down and stepped out of them. Weiss was looking directly at the triangle of curls between her legs. The hair was black there. No hint of red at all.

And he thought: *She'd've bought a wig.*

At once, his heavy heart started beating harder. That was the first thing a woman changed when she wanted to hide herself: her hair. But Julie Wyant wouldn't have wanted to cut hers, or dye it. Long as it was, silky as it was, red and golden as it was. If she wanted to hide—if she wanted to pretend to kill herself and then run away and hide—the first thing she would've done was buy a wig.

His weary eyes grew bright as he looked at the black triangle between the hooker's legs. Someone would remember that, he thought: a girl with hair like hers buying a wig. Even now, even months later. That would stick with them.

The whore held her hand out to him. He took it. Rose heavily from his seat. He pictured himself, running up a flight of stairs, kicking in a locked door . . .

The whore led him into the bedroom.

THIRTY-ONE

Now up until this point, I've tried to keep my own presence in this story to a minimum. I know the misadventures of my callow youth can't compete with the business at hand. But for reasons that will become clear soon enough, I have to pause here a moment to tell, as briefly as I can, the poignant and instructive story of My First Investigation.

You'll remember that, as a reward for my "solution" to the Spanish Virgin case, Weiss had assigned me to assist Sissy Truitt in investigating the Strawberry trial. Theodore Strawberry, aged twenty-six, was our client, the defendant in the trial. He was no very sympathetic character. His mug shot, front and side, showed a baleful-eyed thug with a skewed face under a full head of slickly straightened hair. He was, in fact, an admitted crack addict and a convicted thief. This time out, he'd allegedly shot a Stanford student in the back while in the process of mugging him near an ATM. The student, Bill Mars, a second-string running back for the Cardinal, had been paralyzed for life. Strawberry's parents had hired Jaffe and Jaffe, the law firm upstairs from us, to take their son's case. Jaffe and Jaffe, in turn, had hired us, as usual, to do background checks on witnesses, confirm their testimony and so on. That's where I was supposed to help out.

Excited to begin my life as a private eye, I was loitering outside Sissy's door when she came in the next morning. Which made her laugh in that sweet motherly way she had. I held her armload of files and books for her as she unlocked her door to let me in. She had to bend over a little to fit the key in the lock, I remember. I took a half step back to better enjoy the view.

Now, as I said, Weiss was crazy about Sissy, and she was wonderful in lots of ways. But if you'd asked me, I would've said there was something kind of odd about her too. With those schoolgirl outfits of hers, the pleated skirts, the button-down sweaters and so on. And all that warmth and gentleness and maternal sweetness: It could get pretty treacly and smothering sometimes. I'd've been willing to bet she was neurotic as hell when you got her alone. But all the same, I have to confess, I found her incredibly attractive. She was ten years older than I was, if not more, but she still had the blond hair and delicate features, plus those blue eyes were so full of sympathy, that whispery voice sounded so caring. . . . Well, I was still a kid and I was three thousand miles from home. What can I say? I wanted her desperately.

So as we leaned over the files splayed across her desk, our heads bent together, I stole deep breaths of the scent of her. And whenever she looked up and our eyes met, I tried with all the power of my gaze to convey to her how incredibly available I was to serve as her youthful and energetic boy-toy for the price of a summoning phone call and maybe the cab fare home.

"Aside from the victim, there's only one actual eyewitness," Sissy said in her loin-simmering whisper. "But he's a strong one. A Catholic priest. Father Reginald O'Mara."

I gave a startled laugh. "*The* Reginald O'Mara? The governor's brother?"

"That's the guy. He runs a center for boys down in the mission. He was walking back to his rectory late, says he saw the whole thing. He's the one called the police on his cell phone."

I stared at her. Her eyes really were awfully nice, so sympathetic.

"A priest," I said again, "the governor's brother, a man who's won awards for his work with disadvantaged youths, eyewitnessed our guy, a crack-smoking two-time loser, shoot a college kid in the spine, and we're supposed to . . . do what exactly?"

"Find out if there's any information that might discredit his testimony, silly, what else?" Sissy said.

I laughed again. Then I stopped laughing. "You're serious."

"Well, a priest can lie, sweetheart, no matter whose brother he is.

And he might've just made some kind of mistake too. Our job is to make sure the justice system works properly by uncovering any evidence that shows he might not be the perfect witness he seems to be."

I heard little of this after the word *sweetheart,* the use of which on Sissy's lips had caused my separate self to begin uncoiling in the folds of my underwear. I simply floated off to my computer to—as we PIs say—"do the Background."

Which turned up exactly what you'd figure. Namely nothing. No arrests, convictions, bankruptcies, judgments, liens. No credit troubles, AKAs, or false job histories. The governor's brother had pulled down a big 4.0 GPA at Yale and then gone on to seminary. His work with the poor had been praised and recognized throughout the city—throughout the state—hell, even the president had shaken his hand. He was a source of pride and reflected credit to his governor brother, whom he advised on some matters concerning the Church and the poor. The guy was practically the right hand of God. As opposed to our client. Who was what we technically call in the legal business, a scumbag.

By lunchtime, I was back in Sissy's office. Standing over her by the window this time, gazing down at her with basset hound eyes full of longing.

"Tell our guy to pack an extra pair of pajamas," I told her. "I don't think he's going home in a big hurry."

She cocked her head and gave a lovely, loving laugh. Touched my cheek with a cool palm. "Off you go, check out his witness statements at the scene," she said. "When you're done, write up a report for the lawyers."

I walked as well as I could back to my desk.

Father O'Mara's statements to the police were—what else?—models of simplicity and directness. He had coached a basketball game at his center till 9:30 P.M. Stayed behind to walk home to his rectory, a strenuous constitutional up the city's hills, which he always enjoyed. Around 10:30, he was on Pine Street, near Nob Hill. That's where he witnessed the robbery and the shooting. He was standing on the opposite sidewalk but he said he saw our young Mr. Strawberry clearly in the security lights from the ATM. He described him as a "tall, light-skinned black man wearing an Army camouflage jacket. A limp, a bald spot, a broken nose," etc., etc. He said Mars, his back to the gunman, handed Strawberry his wallet over his shoulder. Strawberry rifled the wallet, cursed angrily and then fired twice into Mars's back. He then ran forward into the darkness and vanished. Later, Father O'Mara picked the guy out of a lineup without hesitation. It turned out our young Mr. S. had been arrested for armed robbery twice before. He'd pled down to lesser felonies both times but this was number three with a bullet: He was going to grow old behind bars unless Jaffe and Jaffe could save him. Which I hoped like hell they couldn't.

Still, Sissy had called me sweetheart and said something about the justice system—plus, did I mention she called me sweetheart?—so I guessed it was my job to help them try.

It was still early afternoon when I made my way to the Pine Street block below Nob Hill where the shooting had taken place. I was enjoying myself now, feeling very much the tough-guy gumshoe, even practicing a snarling curl to my upper lip and a knowing squint to my seen-it-all eyes, which I had brought along for the purpose. I stood across from the ATM and watched the passersby on the opposite sidewalk. I could make out their faces clearly. There was no doubt you could identify someone you'd seen from this distance. There was no doubt—in my mind anyway—that Father O'Mara was telling the truth.

I was about to head back to the office when, for my sins, a thought occurred to me. I stood a moment longer, watched the passersby across the street more closely. The mug shot of Strawberry. It showed, as I said, a man with a full head of hair. If the kid had a bald spot, as Father O'Mara had said he did in his witness report, you couldn't tell from the front or the side. The priest had never seen him from the back—he had dashed forward into the darkness after the shooting. So how had he seen the bald spot?

I turned and looked up at the bay windows of the apartment building behind me. I thought: He could only have seen it if he'd been looking down from above.

The mailboxes in the apartment building foyer showed ten names. There was a Murphy on the second floor. A fellow Irish Catholic maybe. I buzzed that one first. A man's voice answered and I said I was delivering flowers. The inner door unlocked for me. I felt very clever and detectivey indeed.

Mr. Brad Murphy was waiting for me in his doorway when I crested the stairs. He was a pretty young fellow and stood in a feminine pose, one fist pressed into his waist, his hip jutting.

"Mr. Murphy," I said, "I'm from Weiss Investigations, a private detective agency. Do you know a man named Father Reginald O'Mara?"

Mr. Murphy's pretty little face stared blankly at me for one second more. And then he burst into a fit of uncontrollable sobbing.

"Oh, I told him," he cried loudly, in a breaking, high-pitched voice. "I told him we could never keep it secret!"

THIRTY-TWO

Bishop now was in his bedroom, seated before the table, tapping at the miniature keyboard of his handheld computer.

Weiss. It worked. Wannamaker's out. I'm in. Six tonight, I fly to some secret location out in the forest somewhere. Once I arrive, they'll give me the details of the job. Soon as I know what's what, I'll make contact. With luck, we should be able to break it up without compromising . . .

"Turn around."

Bishop's hands froze in midsentence as the voice came suddenly from behind him. He didn't turn. He stared out the window, where the hot afternoon sun burned through the tree branches.

Again: "Turn around."

Quickly, he brushed his fingers over the keyboard. Saved the e-mail, closed it. Only then did he shift his chair so he could face her.

Kathleen was already in the room, standing just a few feet behind him. He didn't think she could've read the e-mail from there but he wasn't sure.

"How you doing, Kathleen?" he said. He kept his voice level but he was startled to see her that close, startled to see her at all. Ever since the fight at the Clover Leaf Chris had been watching her like a guard dog. She hadn't been able to sneak over for their usual meetings. The last he'd seen her, this morning, she and Chris had been leaving to go to work at the airpark.

But here she was, all the same, real as life, pissed off as hell by the look of her. She glared at Bishop, her arms crossed sternly beneath her breasts.

"Well, how the hell do you think I'm doing, Frank?" she said. "What's the matter, isn't Chris screaming loud enough? You must be the only one in the neighborhood who hasn't heard him."

"Uh, Chris . . . ?"

"What the fuck were you thinking, going into that bar, starting a rumble with him like that?"

Bishop felt relief. She hadn't read the e-mail. It was only this. "I guess we just got into it," he said.

"Oh bullshit, Frank. He told me what happened. You called him out. What the hell was that supposed to accomplish?"

"I don't . . . I don't know."

"I told you: You're not my white knight. No one asked you to be my white knight."

"I'm not your white knight. We just got into it," Bishop said.

"Now he's on me every second. He's saying you gotta leave, I gotta throw you outta here or else. He's got everyone in town watching me. I say the slightest thing, he goes off like some kind of bomb. If it gets back to him I was over here while he was flying, he'll fucking kill me. What the hell were you thinking?"

Bishop sat there, regarded her coolly with his pale eyes. What was he thinking? He was thinking that the time had come to dump her, that's what. He'd gotten what he wanted from her. He was in on Hirschorn's op. Her part in the deal was finished. It was time to press EJECT.

He hesitated though. He wasn't sure whether to tell her or not. A few more hours, he'd fly off with Hirschorn into the woods. After that, whatever happened, he'd be gone and she could find out for herself what was what, no tears, no mess.

He thought about it for another second. I don't know if it was conscience that finally decided him. Conscience or some code of his own he lived by. But the thing was: Kathleen was in danger. Hirschorn would kill her if he found out she'd been snooping on him, giving Bishop information. And Bishop did feel he had to warn her about that, give her a chance to save herself. Maybe it was just that he had liked being with her in the summer dark, that he remembered how his coiled mind would become easy when he lay with her there. But whatever it was, he couldn't just leave her behind in harm's way.

"Look, Kathleen . . ." he said slowly.

And she broke in at once: "Oh shit. Oh no."

"Listen to me."

"You're leaving? Oh shit. Oh . . ." She stomped her foot. "Fuck! How big an idiot am I? Oh, Christ. I should've known. You're leaving. Right?"

He looked down, nodded. He wished he didn't have to warn her. He wished he could've just left and skipped this part, the mess of it. "Yeah," he said. "I've gotta go."

Her nose wrinkled, her chin dimpled as she fought back tears. She kept her arms crossed tightly under her breasts. "Right. Of course. Obviously. How big a fucking idiot am I? Jesus!"

"Listen to me. . . ." he told her.

"So what was it, Frank?" she said. She sniffed. "Huh? Was it, like, convenience for you? Like, you needed a summer job and a summer house and a summer fuck, and I came in handy? Is that it?"

Bishop cursed under his breath. What the hell did she want from him? What was he supposed to say? That it was his job? "Just listen, will you?"

"Because it happened to be more than that for me, okay?" she said. "It was more than . . ." She couldn't go on without starting to cry so she stopped there. She squeezed her eyes shut. Pinched the bridge of her nose between thumb and finger. A single tear spilled out between her lids and spilled over her hand. "Shit."

Bishop pushed wearily to his feet. "Kathleen . . ."

She covered both her eyes with her hand now, her lips quivering. "I am so fucked," she said. "My life is so fucked. I can't go back there." She let out a gasping sob. "I can't go back to being with him. I just can't do this, keep doing this anymore."

She dropped her hand, exposed her mottled face to him. Beseeched him without restraint, without pride. "Why do you have to go? Why can't you stay? Why do you have to go?"

Bishop cursed again but silently this time. He went to her. Put his hands on her shoulders. Looked down into her swimming eyes, at the lines of mascara running down her cheeks.

"Kathleen, you've got to get out of here," he told her.

"I could make you happy, couldn't I?" she said. "We've been happy up here together sometimes, haven't we?"

"Listen to me!" he said again, more urgently. "He'll kill you, Kath. Hirschorn will kill you. He's had it with Chris, he's through with Chris. He's going to kill him and he'll kill you too."

She gazed up at him without comprehension.

"Do you understand what I'm saying?" said Bishop. "You need to get out of town until it's over, until Hirschorn's finished, until the whole thing is finished."

For one more second she gazed at him, yearned up at him. Then she heard what he was saying, saw that it was over. Her face went dark with anger again. She yanked herself away from him.

"Don't tell me that," she said. "Don't give me your grand advice and leave me here like that. Fuck you. Fuck you, Frank! Who the fuck are you to even pretend to care what happens to me?"

She bowed her head and cried. He stepped toward her. She waved him off. "Don't. Don't touch me. Stay away."

He did. He stood still. He watched her. He had done what he could—that's how he saw it. His code or his conscience or his sentiments were satisfied. He had warned her. He had done what he could. What else was he supposed to say? he asked himself. It was her life. What the hell else was he supposed to say?

Kathleen looked up, saw him standing there like that, watching her like that. She let out a laugh at first, a miserable little laugh. And then, crying, she shook her head at him. "Couldn't you just love me?" she asked him softly.

He didn't answer. He just stood there, just watched her. For a moment, he might have wondered . . . but no. He didn't love her. He didn't love anyone.

He was still standing there, still watching, when she walked out of the room.

THIRTY-THREE

As for Kathleen, she went slowly back to her house. She climbed slowly up the stairs to her bedroom. She lay down on her bed, on her back, and stared up at the ceiling. She stayed like that a long time. Some of that time she was crying. The light in the ceiling blurred and sparkled through her tears.

She was angry—angry with herself. And she felt like a fool, which was worse. She felt exposed in her foolishness, naked in front of the neighborhood, naked beyond recall, as if she could put on every piece of clothing she had and she would still be naked, naked and ashamed in front of everyone she met. In her shame, she was angry at the man she knew as Frank Kennedy also. She wished he were dead. She wished he would be hit by a truck and killed and no one would ever know about him and what had happened between them. But at the same time she was wishing that, she loved him too. She wished he was dead and she wished he would suddenly knock on her door and tell her he had made a mistake, he'd been wrong, he was humbly sorry, he wanted her back. It had been so good with him, in his bed, in his arms. She had felt she was beautiful because of the way he wanted her. When she lay with him afterwards, she had felt that her life was going to be different from now on because of him. Because of being with him, she could see clearly how bad everything was with Chris. She had seen it before but she hadn't seen it so clearly. Because Frank—the man she knew as Frank—was gentle and sure with her, she could see better how awful it was that Chris hit her and drank and wanted to prove himself by being with a criminal like Hirschorn. Resting in Frank's arms, she could see those things, but also she could feel that they were going to be different. Now though—now she knew they were not going to be different. She tried to believe she could change them herself, without Frank. She tried to believe she could leave Chris and start a new life on her own. But every time she tried to think it through, it just seemed impossible somehow and she knew she would be back with Chris again just like before and everything would be the same, day after day, forever.

She began to cry very hard now, the tears spilling down the sides of her face, dampening her pillow. She took a Kleenex from the box beside her bed. She held it to her nose. She thought about the man she knew as Frank, about the times she had had with him and she cried even harder and she thought, *Damn him. God damn him,* because of the way he had been with her just now. Standing there in his room and just staring at her, clueless and uncaring. He had been so different with her before, she thought, when they were lying together, when they were talking together in the dark.

Her crying began to slow. She crumpled one Kleenex and took a fresh one from the box, held that one against her runny nose. After a while, she crumpled that one and took another, then another and soon there was a collection of crumpled Kleenexes on the bed where the mattress sagged from her weight. She lay there staring at the ceiling and she thought about how different it had been before, about the things Frank had said to her, the sweet, soft things. Were they all lies? He had said such soft things and asked her questions about her life and listened to her as if he cared? Was it all phony, all an act? The way he had been concerned about what was happening to her, about what Chris was doing—he was always asking about that. He was always asking about Chris and his secret meetings with Bernie Hirschorn. In fact, every time they had been together they had somehow gotten around to talking about that. Every time.

Kathleen made a dull noise, stifling her runny nose. Without really realizing it, the tone of her thoughts had shifted. There was something . . . something that felt *wrong* to her now somehow. It was almost as if some kind of venom had entered her bloodstream, a cloudy venom spreading through her, making everything feel cloudy and wrong. Every time she had been with Frank, she thought, they had talked about Chris and Hirschorn. They had talked about them all the time. Frank had urged her to listen in on their conversations. *You have to find out what they're up to,* he'd said. *To protect yourself.* That's what he'd said, she remembered it clearly. And she had done exactly what he told her to do. She had listened in on Chris's conversations as much as she could. And then the next time she and Frank were together, well, she would tell him about what she had heard. And if she didn't tell him, he would ask her about it. Every time. Kathleen had thought Frank was helping her. She had thought he was concerned for her because of Chris and what he was getting himself into. He wanted her to find out more about the situation—*to protect yourself.* That's what he'd said.

Her eyes shifted back and forth now as if she were reading her own thoughts up there on the ceiling. Things were beginning to seem different to her, everything was. She was angry. Frank was leaving her and she was angry at him and now the things he'd said to her just seemed different. That cloudy venom of suspicion kept spreading through her. Spreading and spreading and suddenly she thought: *Wait a minute, what if . . . ?*

Her heart turned—that's what it felt like. It felt as if all at once her heart turned dark and sour and ashen in her chest. *What if . . . ?*

She sat up on the bed, her knees bent in front of her. Her lips parted. Her teary eyes, grown wide, kept moving back and forth, back and forth. Her streaked, tear-mottled face hung empty with shock and confusion. Too many thoughts, too many images, memories, all coming at once. The way Frank had ridden so conveniently out of the south. The way Ray had arranged it so he would rent the house from her. The way he had made a move on her so quickly . . . Yes, it had made her feel good at the time. She had felt flattered that he wanted her at the time. But now, now all at once, with the anger and the venomous suspicion in her, she began to wonder about it. And she began to wonder about some of the things he'd said . . . *I'm worried about you, Kathleen, I'm worried about what's going on in your house.* It had sounded sweet, it had sounded romantic to her. *You ought to make sure you know what they're saying. To protect yourself.* It had sounded as if he was concerned. She had thought he felt protective toward her, the way guys were supposed to feel, the way they felt about girls in the movies. But now . . .

Now all at once, all those things he'd said sounded wrong. They sounded like . . . well, they sounded kind of like bullshit. In fact, now she thought about it, now that she was angry and she really thought about it, they sounded like just exactly the same sort of bullshit men had been handing her all her life, the same stuff she had been falling for all her goddamned life.

Kathleen sat up in the puddle of Kleenex that had collected around her on the bed. She put her hand on her stomach. She felt sick, physically sick, as if she were going to throw up. She couldn't make sense of things. Too many thoughts.

And then, in a kind of lightless flash, all of the thoughts became one thought:

What if he's a cop? That's how it came to her, just like that. *What if he's a cop and he's after Hirschorn, after Hirschorn and Chris . . . ?*

She made a strangled noise, a strangled "Oh . . ." as if she had been punched. She felt exactly as if she had been punched. She felt sick and winded.

Quickly, she swung her legs off the edge of the bed, sat on the edge of the bed. Crumpled Kleenexes spilled to the floor at her feet. She stared urgently in front of her.

"Oh my God, oh my God!" The words came out of her in a tearful squeak. "What've I done?"

Then she heard a footstep. She turned.

Chris was standing in the doorway.

THIRTY-FOUR

Chris took one long look at her. His wife, sitting on the edge of the bed, crying on the edge of the bed. "What?" he said. "What is it?"

"Oh God, Chris," she blurted out. "Don't kill me. I think I did a really stupid thing." She covered her mouth with both hands. Her eyes filled again. She looked at him over her fingers. She knew she shouldn't just blurt it out like that, she should think first, try to consider what was best. But she couldn't think. She was too sick and ashamed and angry—starting to get really angry now at how she'd been used and betrayed. And here was her husband, who might be in real trouble—she might've gotten him into real trouble—and she had to do something. She had to warn him, tell him. She lowered her hands. "I swear to God I didn't mean it," she said. "He tricked me. The fucker! The *fucker*!"

Chris's mind, meanwhile, had been working too. Things had been happening and he'd been thinking and worrying. He had gotten a call from Hirschorn's office this morning. Not from Hirschorn himself but from that little faggot guy, that secretary, Wellman or whatever his name was.

"There's been a delay," Wellman had said. "Mr. Hirschorn wants you to wait for his call."

What delay? What call? What kind of delay? Wellman wouldn't tell him anything. And when Chris tried to call the inside number, there was nothing, just a machine, just Wellman's voice. "Leave a message and Mr. Hirschorn will get back to you."

So Chris was worried. His mind was turning over and over. And when he came into the room, when he saw the look on his wife's face, when he saw the crumpled Kleenexes on the floor, he was suddenly alert. The first thought that occurred to him was that this—his crying wife—was part of what was happening.

"What," he said again, drawing out the word. "What did you do?"

"Oh God, Chris," she moaned. "Please don't kill me. I thought he was just being nice. You know? Asking questions. Like he was concerned about me." She had to tell it differently from how it really was, of course. She couldn't just tell him that she and Frank had been sleeping together. "It was like you said," she went on, finding her way. "It was just like you said all along, Chris. You were so right. He was sniffing around me. But not the way you thought, he didn't want what you thought. Oh God, Chris, I am so, so sorry. I was worried, y'know. You wouldn't tell me anything and I was worried about you and I just thought . . ."

Chris clenched his fists at his sides. The muscles in his bare arms knotted. The bruise on his face where Bishop had hit him had grown yellow but the purple came back into it until it was livid and horrible. Oh, he was more than worried now. He was frightened now, good and frightened. But of what? What the hell was she saying? "Damn it, Kathleen. Just tell me, willya. Just tell me what happened. What did you do?"

And she did. She left out the part about sleeping with Frank but she told him all the rest. How she had listened in on his conversations with Hirschorn and passed the information on to Frank. The names she had heard, the hints she had picked up, everything.

"And I think . . . I think he might be a cop, Chris," she said when she was finished. "I'm so sorry."

Chris's mouth had come open while she talked. It hung open now. "What?" he whispered.

She pounded her knee with her fist. "Damn it! *Damn* it! I think he might be a fucking cop."

The big man shuddered as the fear exploded inside him, tightened around him. He felt as if he was choking on it. "A cop?" he barely managed to say. A cop. If that was true, if it was true and Hirschorn found out about it . . .

Quickly, he stepped to the window. He stared through the trees at the house across the way. Behind him, Kathleen was wiping the tears from her face, making noises, blowing her nose.

"Is he there now?" Chris asked her. "Kennedy. Is he over there now?"

She nodded. He had to glance back to see it. "Yeah. I mean, I guess. Is his bike still there?"

"Yeah."

"Then I guess he is."

Chris stared out the window. Stared at the house. Then a thought struck him and his eyes flicked to the street in front. Just a small stretch of it was visible at this angle between the houses, through the trees. He eyed it nervously. Did Hirschorn know? he wondered. Did Hirschorn already know? Were they already coming for him? Were they already on their way?

Chris's mouth went very dry. He dragged his hand across it. No. No, Hirschorn couldn't know yet. Why would he? He stared at the house again, up at the upstairs window, the bedroom window. He was sick and strangling on his fear but his voice was steady, soft, distant, as if it were someone else who was speaking for him.

"I gotta get over there," he said. "We've gotta get that son of a bitch to go out so I can get over there. I mean, I gotta. I gotta find out what the hell is going on."

THIRTY-FIVE

Just then, Weiss found the shop he wanted. He was rapping on the glass door. Pressing his nose to the cold surface of it to peer inside. MOSTLY YOU, the place was called. WIGS AND HAIR EXTENSIONS. The sign said it was closed for lunch until two o'clock. But Weiss had been in the coffee shop across the street and seen the man go in.

The shop was on the border of the Haight. Right between a smoke shop that served the last of the local stoners and a Century 21 that catered to the incoming gentry. Another investigator would've felt less eager coming here, would've figured it was just another stop in a long, half-hopeless canvas of the city's stores. But Weiss, with his weird instincts for other people's minds, had gotten used to being right about such things. He knew he was getting close.

He knuckled the glass again. A round white face appeared mistily in the shop's inner gloom. The man in there put on a mime show, shaking his hands, tapping his wristwatch: *We're not open yet, go away*. Weiss rapped heavily again, insistent. Rolling his eyes heavenward, the man inside came toward him down the aisle.

The man in the wig shop was the owner, it turned out. Patrick Fandler. What Weiss thought of as a standard-issue city homosexual: crew cut, hipless, blandly handsome, the slacks and pullover painted on.

"What does the little sign tell us?" he said, annoyed, as he cracked the door open. "Lunchy-time. It's only a wig store, after all. Whatever you need, I'm sure it can wait." Then, taking a glance at Weiss's sloppy salt-and-pepper hair: "Or maybe not. I wouldn't want to turn away an actual emergency."

Weiss pushed a card through the crack in the door. "My name is Weiss. I'm a private detective."

"Are you? Just like in the movies?"

"Pretty much. Except not. Could I come in and ask you a couple of questions?"

Fandler considered the card another moment. "*Mi casa es su casa,*" he said then, and he stepped back and pulled the door wide.

Weiss followed the man up the aisle to a counter in the back. The remains of a tuna salad sandwich sat in its wrapper atop a display of weaving extensions. The bizarrely curled stretches of brown and blond hair lay under the glass like the trophy tails of hunted animals. Weiss set the photograph of Julie Wyant down on top of them.

Patrick Fandler took a single glance. "Oh yes," he said. "I could never forget that hair."

Weiss nodded. He had hoped for as much. No one, as far as he was concerned, could ever forget that hair. He kept his hangdog expression in place but he could feel his inner systems ratcheting up. He was excited.

"And that face!" Fandler went on. "She was so beautiful she almost made me wish I was a lesbian."

Weiss lowered his chin by way of acknowledging the joke. "This is about three months ago?" He wanted to be sure.

"Yes, about then."

"And did she buy anything?"

"Well, yes, that's why I remember. She bought a wig."

Weiss managed to keep his deadpan. But he had to breathe deep to steady himself. "A wig."

"Yes, and I mean, why would a girl with hair like that want to cover it with a wig?" said Fandler.

"Right," said Weiss. And he thought, *She's alive*. He was sure of it, suddenly, standing there in the little shop. Julie Wyant was still alive. She had faked her suicide, disguised herself with the wig and run away.

"She bought three, now I think of it," said Fandler. "One blond, two brunettes, one with sort of auburn highlights. She tried them on right in here."

He led the way down a narrow aisle to a curtain. Pulled the curtain back. Weiss looked into a cluttered changing room. A stool, a vanity table, a lighted mirror. He gazed at them. The stool, the mirror. She had sat right there. She had looked at herself right there. It made his old heart go thumpety-thump just to think about it. And she was still alive.

"She said the funniest thing," said Fandler.

Weiss glanced at him. "Yeah?"

"She was trying on the blond one I remember. I just gave a little peek in to see how she was making out, you know. And she was studying herself, turning this way and that with the wig on. So I said, 'Is everything all right?' And she looked just . . . so sad, for a moment. So terribly sad. There were absolute tears in her eyes. And she said to me—I remember this so clearly—she just looked right at me in the mirror and said, 'Well . . . I'm still me anyway.'"

Weiss turned again to look at the stool, at the mirror. Thinking about her, his heart thumping.

"'I'm still me,'" Fandler repeated softly.

Jarring, Weiss's cell phone rang. He blinked, came to himself. Drew it from his jacket pocket.

"This is Weiss," he murmured.

"It's Ketchum," said the Inspector's voice. "Get over to SFO jig time. I just got you in to see the Identity Man."

Weiss only nodded. Slipped the little phone back into his jacket. Stood another second, staring at the vanity table.

I'm still me, he thought.

Julie Wyant was alive.

THIRTY-SIX
Just a couple of hours later, Weiss was looking out the window of a twin-propeller de Havilland as the plane descended through a thin mist. Below, there was nothing but forest—blue-green forest, and the sparkling sea.

"I hope you appreciate what I'm doing for you here, Weiss," muttered Ketchum in the seat beside him. "I had to call in favors on this I haven't even done yet. Had to practically get down on my knees to the FBI and I hate those Feeb motherfuckers."

His complaints fell away to inaudible muttering. Which was fine. Weiss wasn't listening anyway. He went on looking out the window, his nose propped on his fist. Outside, the last tendrils of mist parted. There was the airfield up ahead, two crossed runways at the ocean's edge.

Shadowman. The mist in Weiss's mind—the swirl of impressions, facts, deductions—was parting too, the sense of everything coming clearer to him. The urgency he felt was now almost frantic—as frantic, anyway, as his sturdy nature would allow. Like the video loop of Julie Wyant beckoning, his fantasy repeated itself almost obsessively. Running up the stairs. Kicking in the locked door. The girl lying on the bed. Every second counted.

Shadowman.

"Oh, man, and I hate this shit," Ketchum started up again a while later, when they were off the plane, when Weiss was guiding their rented Cavalier up the coast road. "Look at this." He gestured at the windshield. On the other side of the windshield was a spectacle of surf and stone, sunlight through spindrift, a sky of robin's-egg blue above the winding highway. "These back roads. Make me sicker than the damn plane . . ."

Shadowman. Weiss had been one of the first detectives on the scene after the so-called South Bay Massacre. He had watched while police divers pulled the children's bodies to shore. He remembered one little girl, her face shot half-away, her body half-devoured, but one profile still whole, still sweet, just sleeping.

He had told me that the media invented a criminal to fit that scene. Jeff Bloom of the *Chronicle*—"he had, like, one unnamed source"—had been the apparent author. The character Bloom created—a fantastical monster, really, melodramatic name and all—was an unstoppable killer, feared even by his criminal employers, a man who could find anyone, get in anywhere, in order to carry out a job. Weiss had told me all of this.

But he had never told me—I had only heard it rumored—who Bloom's unnamed source was, the *true* creator of this diabolical creature: a police detective at odds with his willfully blind department, a detective who was unsure himself whether he had invented the Shadowman or simply traced his living outline in the fabric of events.

And now, Harry Ridder was dead, a suicide. And Peter Crouch was dead, murdered in his wine cellar. And Julie Wyant was gone, was missing.

The Shadowman was real whether he was real or not.

"Here we go. Into the woods," Ketchum went on, scowling.

This now was the northern wilderness. The road had curved away from the coast. Hills of forest were closing in on either side of it.

"Look at this shit," Ketchum said.

Weiss did look. After a few miles, he saw the screen of trees growing thinner by the roadside. The coils of razor wire growing visible through the trees. Towers rose against the sky, the shadows of riflemen inside them. Concrete cages jigsawed together on the ground below. Nothing seemed to move anywhere, not one thing. No sign of a living soul.

"It's the asshole of the world," Ketchum growled miserably. "You've dragged me straight into the asshole of the world."

THIRTY-SEVEN

There were identity checks at the gate and again in the entry chamber. Grimly efficient guards searched them. They went through metal detectors so sensitive the iron in your blood could set them off. Then more pat-downs. Then a wood-faced officer the size of a mighty pine thumped along a hallway with them, led them to the first barred gate.

The officer stood rigid while a scanner read the patterns in the iris of his right eye. There was an ear-piercing buzzer. The gate slid open. The officer hung back. Weiss and Ketchum went into the cinder block corridor alone.

The gate slid shut behind them like a sprung trap. They walked down the colorless corridor side by side. Experience had hardened Weiss to the desolation of these places but it pressed on him all the same, more so with every step. It felt to him as if they were descending away from the light and air into a cave of suffocating blackness.

Ketchum felt it too. He shook his head. "Man oh man," he muttered, "This is about as far from your mother's tit as you can get."

Video monitors watched their every step. They did not see another living officer until they reached the steel door of the visiting room. There was a Lexan-enclosed control booth here to their right. The control booth officer nodded at them, unsmiling, through the booth's thick windows. Another deafening buzz. Weiss pulled the steel door open.

They came into a small concrete room. One wall—the wall in front of them—was transparent, Lexan like the control booth. There were plastic chairs against the walls to their sides. Weiss and Ketchum each drew one up and sat down.

They sat without speaking, looked through the Lexan wall. There was a single metal chair on the other side of it. It was bolted to the floor. Now, a steel panel behind the chair slid open. Two guards came in holding a shackled man between them. Each guard held one of the man's arms. They led him to the chair. They sat him down in it. They knelt and chained his shackles to bolts in the floor. Then the guards withdrew. The steel panel slid shut. Weiss and Ketchum sat facing the man chained to the chair: Lenny "Whip" Pomeroy.

He was not the usual prison thing. Very slender, almost delicate. Delicate hands with long, thin, fidgeting fingers. A long, delicate face, damp, sorry eyes and thin, delicate lips that were constantly moving, moving. It seemed as if his inner monologue was steadily leaking out of him in an inaudible whisper.

For the past two months or so, he had been trading with state and federal lawmen: the false identities of escaping felons in return for high-level protective custody. He had barely seen the sun in all that time and he was paper white.

"All right, Pomeroy," said Ketchum. "I'm Inspector Ketchum of the San Francisco Police Department. This is Weiss of Weiss Investigations, a private agency. He's got some questions for you."

The convict's eyes ping-ponged between them. They seemed to choose Weiss finally—not to rest on him but to hover around him like a hummingbird around a flower. He gave a quick shake of his head. "No. No. Three months we said." His voice was a nervous breath. The voice-activated mike made it sound metallic and staccato in the speakers above the Lexan. His shackles rattled, pulling taut as the fingers of his two hands twined together and untwined. "No more, no more for three months."

"This isn't about that," Weiss said quietly.

"Three months, that's what we agreed to." Fingers twining, fidgeting.

"We're not asking you for any more AKAs."

"We had an arrangement, a deal. You said. You told me . . ."

Weiss cut in on him. "We're looking for Julie Wyant."

The effect of the name on Pomeroy was instantaneous and

dramatic. Weiss wouldn't've thought the guy could get any paler but what color there was in his cheeks drained out. He seemed practically transparent sitting there, except for those eyes, big and bright now in the see-through outline of the man.

Weiss couldn't tell if Pomeroy was shaking his head—no, no, no—or just spasming in his agitation. The detective spoke in the same quiet voice. "I don't work for the Shadowman," he said. "I'm trying to stop him."

The bright hummingbird eyes hung around him. "Yes . . . Well . . . Well . . . You'd say that, wouldn't you? I mean . . . But how do I know? You see what I'm saying? How do . . . ?" It trailed off. His lips went on moving, moved even faster, but nothing more came out.

Weiss ignored the question. "I figure it this way," he continued in a firm, calm voice. "Something happened when Cameron Moncrieff was on his deathbed—he said something or did something that affected the Shadowman. Exposed him maybe in some way. Julie Wyant was there. And Moncrieff's lawyer, Peter Crouch. And the gardener, the kid, Harry Ridder, what was he, outside the window? Eavesdropping? Or just passing by?"

"Tending the roses." It seemed as if the phrase were part of his ceaseless monologue made suddenly audible, like a word suddenly highlighted, suddenly visible in a jumble of letters. "Early Heart of Gold roses under the bedroom window. He just overheard, just overheard, that's all."

Weiss nodded his encouragement into the bright, frantic gaze. Leaned forward, his hands clasped between his knees, his big body hulking in the little plastic chair. "So what was it, Pomeroy? What happened the day Moncrieff died? Tell me. I need to know. For Julie's sake."

Weiss and Pomeroy regarded each other through the transparent wall. Ketchum said later it was like some kind of exorcism was taking place, as if Julie Wyant's name had put a spell on the prisoner and was forcing the information to come out of him against his will.

The lips in the white face went swiftly on and again, after a while, some of the words he was whispering grew loud enough to hear. "You can't understand. You can't . . . You don't know her."

"Well, you explain it to me. How about that?" Weiss said. "Moncrieff told her something, didn't he? He told her something the Shadowman doesn't want her to know. Or gave her something he doesn't want her to have or . . ."

"No!" Pomeroy hissed. "No, no, no, no. You see? You can't understand. You can't. You think it's about . . . about things, about . . . about *things*. But you don't know. You don't know Julie." He drew out the syllables of the name tenderly, with a tone of exaltation.

Weiss didn't like the sound it made. A queasy sort of sound. It sent a heavy, queasy feeling over him. He had thought he was pretty close to figuring out this whole scenario. Now he wasn't sure. Now he wasn't even sure he wanted to figure it out.

"She changed things," Whip Pomeroy went on in that same overly sweet, overly elevated tone. "She changed . . . everything. Everyone. She was like . . . oh—oh, an unreal creature. Like paintings you see. Or daydreams you have. She was the way people never are. You know? You can't know."

Weiss grew queasier, heavier. Staring through the window at the pale, nervous man shackled to his chair on the other side. Judging by the high expression that had now come over Pomeroy's delicate features, he seemed in danger of going into some kind of rapture over the missing woman.

Weiss gave a gruff shake of his head. As if he didn't get it, didn't understand. But in truth, he feared he was beginning to.

"She talked to you as if you were the only person in the world," Pomeroy whispered ecstatically. "And when she put her hands on you . . . You see? She changed things. . . . She changed . . . everyone."

"Moncrieff, we're talking about," Weiss said finally. "You mean she changed Moncrieff."

"Oh, Cam—Cam worshiped her. We both did. Everyone . . . And after Cam took her in, the way she cared for him when he was sick, the way she was with him, it . . . It changed him, that's all. He wanted to . . . to do something. You know?"

, Trying to shake off the queasy feeling, Weiss fought to focus instead on the emotional logic of the scene Pomeroy was describing. Moncrieff, the old pimp and smuggler, on his deathbed. The weight of his sins on his chest like so much bullion. The impatient fingers of hellfire scrabbling up the sheets to get at him. "He wanted to do something good, you mean?"

Pomeroy's head went up and down. His shackles pulled tight and rattled loose as he fidgeted. "Something for her," said Pomeroy. "Something . . . to save . . . her."

"To save her." *From her prostitute's life,* he thought. "He wanted to save her. So he gave her—what? Some money?"

"Money, yes. Cam didn't really have very much money in the end. He gave her what he could but really . . . it was me. It was, you know, the AKA."

"The identity. Moncrieff told you to give her a new identity."

Pomeroy's eyes wandered around the room as if following the flight of a mosquito. He whispered, whispered, whispered inaudibly, then whispered, "It was what I could do for her. Cam knew that. No one . . . No one's ever traced an identity I made. No one ever has unless I told it to them."

"Okay. Okay," said Weiss. "I've got all this. Moncrieff gave Julie Wyant money and a new ID so she could start a new life. What I'm asking you is: What about the Shadowman? What does he want? Why does he have to find her? What does she know, Pomeroy? What did Moncrieff tell her or give her that he . . . ?"

"Aaah . . ." The air came out of Pomeroy like that. He descended from whatever lofty heights. And now he had a new look on him, a look, Weiss thought, as if someone had run an electric wire down his shorts. His teeth were bared, his eyes were all scrunched up, his whole face was all tensed and scrunched up. As if it pained him, just pained him to listen to Weiss's speculations. "You see, you see?" he said. "Because you don't know her. So you don't think it's all *things*. Just money she might have or something she heard or witnessed. . . . You don't believe there's anything. . . ."

Then his lips continued moving, but his voice was gone, was silent. And Weiss still couldn't get it. He was still sitting there with this half-formed, inarticulate suspicion and he couldn't give it shape, make it clear.

"All right. All right, let me do this again," he said slowly. "Moncrieff is on his deathbed. And he's sorry for his sins and so on. And he wants to do something nice for someone. So he gives Julie Wyant some money and a new identity. . . ."

"Yes. Yes. Exactly."

"And the lawyer's there, Peter Crouch."

"Yes."

"And Harry Ridder, the gardener, is outside the window tending the roses or whatever and he overhears this."

"Yes."

"And you were . . . where? You had to be there too, didn't you?"

"I was there. But I left right after Cam died so no one would know."

Weiss gave a big, slow nod. "Right. Right. Because you were the only one who knew the new identity, who knew what it was."

"Yes."

"And that's it then. That's everything. The whole story."

Ketchum pinched the bridge of his nose between his thumb and forefinger, shook his head. "Unbelievable," he muttered.

But Weiss pressed on, playing the scene through in his mind. "Okay. So—let me just make sure I've got this. Moncrieff realizes the kid, the gardener, Harry Ridder, is eavesdropping."

Pomeroy's nervous eyes flickered back and forth. "Crouch. It was Crouch who realized it."

"Okay. So then what? After Moncrieff dies, Crouchy says to the kid—what?—'You're in big trouble, kid. If anyone finds out you overheard this, you're a dead man. You better run for your life before the Shadowman gets you.' Right? Something like that?"

"Yes."

"And he throws in some horror stories about the Shadowman for good measure. To scare the kid or whatever. Only he scares the kid so much, the kid blows his brains out in sheer terror."

Pomeroy nodded, his lips moving, his eyes wandering.

"And now the Shadowman does show up. And it's Crouch he comes after. He tortures Crouch to death in order to get the whole story about what happened around the deathbed. And you—that's panic time for you. You could be living in a suburb of Cleveland or something on Witness Protection but instead you get yourself arrested and have yourself locked up in the deepest, darkest hole you can find. . . ."

Pomeroy hardly seemed to be listening anymore. He was studying the ceiling, whispering something inaudible. But he nodded.

Weiss sighed. "And it's all because . . ." He hadn't known how he was going to finish that sentence, what he was going to say, but as the words came out of him, his inner resistance broke. Suddenly he knew what it was he knew, knew why the heavy queasiness had come upon him. He swallowed once. And then he said, "It's all because of her. That's it, isn't it? That's what the Shadowman is after. He's after her."

It seemed to take a second or two for this to register on Whip Pomeroy's brain. But then, as if startled, he glanced at Weiss, at Ketchum, at Weiss again. And he whispered, "Yes. Of course. Of course. Yes."

"That's it. Just her. Not . . . money. Not some secret that she knows or he wants to know. Just . . ."

Ketchum let out a short bark of a laugh and the delicate Pomeroy jumped at the sound as if it were a gunshot. Weiss was also thinking—telling himself—that it was nonsense. Craziness, nonsense.

"The Shadowman's in love with her," he said slowly.

Now a weird and dreamy stillness seemed to drift down over Whip Pomeroy. His shackled hands sank motionless to the chair arms and his pale face went slack. His lips stopped moving, hung parted. The damp, enormous eyes stared. Weiss waited for what seemed to him a long time before the prisoner's mouth began its quivering again. He waited what seemed a long time more before Pomeroy said, almost wistfully, "He's the worst man in the world, you know. Maybe the worst man ever. I told Cam. I always told him. But Cam said he had to use him sometimes. In business sometimes. He had to." Now, as if providing accompaniment to his lips, his hands began to twine and fidget again too. "And one day, he saw her. The man . . . You know, I never knew his name. Not his real name. He had so many. Different ones each time. The Shadowman—that's what the newspapers called him. That's the way I came to think of him after a while. We both did, me and Cam. The Shadowman. And one day, he . . . he saw her. He set eyes on her. And that was that. He would never stay away then. We couldn't make him stay away. He kept coming back and back. He kept coming back to see her. And she told him . . . she told him she didn't . . . want him there . . . but he wouldn't stay away. Nothing could keep him away. And one day, he . . ."

Pomeroy was silent and Weiss was silent. He was silent, thinking about her. The beckoning woman in the video. Her red-blond hair, her face like an angel. *I'm still me.*

"He hurt her," whispered Whip Pomeroy. "He hurt her. I heard it all. I was in the next room. I heard it all. He wanted her to be with him and she wouldn't. So he hurt her. And then . . . then when he was finished, he started to say things . . . things . . . things a person can't say, things no one can say and still be human. He told her all the things he would do to her unless . . . unless she was his now. He wanted her to be his now. And I heard him. In my room next door. He needed her, he said. He said she was the only thing he had ever needed in all the world, the only thing he had ever wanted his whole life. And he would do anything—anything he had to to have her in the end. He would have her in the end no matter what, he said. He said these terrible things and then . . . then he began to cry. I heard. I . . . He began to cry and he begged her. He begged her."

My God, thought Weiss. "You heard . . ."

"I was in my room, the room next door. I heard it all."

Well, why didn't you stop him, you wimpy piece of shit, he thought, he almost said aloud. But of course, he knew better. He fought the words down, the anger down. "And now you're the only one who knows where she is," was what he said. "The only one who knows who she is."

"I'm the only one," whispered Whip Pomeroy.

Ketchum had not interrupted up to this point. But the wiry little cop had had enough. His scowl twisted into an even deeper scowl. He said, "Are you trying to tell us you had yourself locked away in this hellhole—that you *bargained* to have yourself locked away in this . . . this *hellhole*—because you created this girl's new identity and now you're afraid this so-called Shadowman character is going to come after you and make you tell him what the identity is?"

"Oh, he'll come," Pomeroy answered. "You don't know him. He'll come. He tortured Crouch. You see what I'm saying? When he realized Julie was gone, when he realized that Crouch had been there in the end, he tortured Crouch and Crouch would've told him everything. Crouch would've told him about me and the false identity. So he knows. You see what I'm saying? He knows I'm the only one who can help him."

"Yeah? So?" said Ketchum in his rasping growl. "So why don't you? I mean, what the hell, right? You're a scumbag. Why don't you just tell him? What the hell do you care what happens to her?"

Pomeroy lifted his chin a little as if trying to look noble and exalted again. But Weiss said, "Because the Shadowman will kill him anyway." And Pomeroy dropped the noble act. His chin sank at once to his chest. "The Shadowman has to kill him no matter what," Weiss went on. "Because he heard him. He heard him beg. He heard him cry to Julile Wyant that he needed her. Isn't that right, Pomeroy?"

"No," said Whip Pomeroy forlornly. "No. Not because I heard him."

Weiss closed his eyes a moment. Now he saw. Now he had all of it. "Because you heard *her*," he said. "Because you heard her answer him."

Pomeroy nodded slowly. "He has to kill me no matter what," he whispered in a near singsong. "Because I heard her laugh."

There was another long quiet in the room after that. Sometimes the mike in the prisoner's booth picked up the rattle of Pomeroy's shackles as he twitched and shivered. Other than that, there were just the three men sitting there, sitting there with this bizarre thing in the air between them, this bizarre story. The worst man in the world had fallen in love. The worst man in the world had fallen in love with Julie Angel.

"You've got one chance, Pomeroy," said Weiss after a while. "Your only chance. You've got to tell us now. Tell us where she is. Tell us the name you gave her, the identity, so we can track her down. We'll protect you. You and her both. Me, the police, we'll all protect the both of you. I promise."

"Protect us?" Even Weiss recoiled a little as Pomeroy's head came suddenly forward, as the bright eyes in that transparent face found him, as those bloodless, ceaseless lips curled into a painful grin. "You can't. You can't protect me. You can't protect her. You can't protect anyone. Not from him. Nothing stops him in the end. Nothing. Ever. He can go anywhere. Get to anyone. And he will. For her. He will." Pomeroy drew back, drew away as if fading into himself. His lips moved a moment more before the words whispered out of him. "He can't be stopped. Nothing can stop him. Ever."

THIRTY-EIGHT

When the guards had come again, when they'd unshackled Pomeroy and hauled him back to his cell, Weiss sat where he was a while. He sat in the plastic chair, his hands clasped between his thighs. He stared through the Lexan at the empty booth where the prisoner had been. Ketchum watched him without speaking.

"Damn," said Weiss finally with a sigh.

"Well, there's one thing," said Ketchum. "He may not tell us the name, but as long as he's in this place, our friend the Shadowman sure as hell can't get to him either."

Weiss nodded heavily, with no joy. What Ketchum said was true, it made sense, but somehow . . . somehow that urgency wouldn't leave him. That fantasy of running upstairs . . . the locked door . . . That sense that every second counted.

Still, there was nothing to do. He pushed off his knees, rose heavily. He went to the door with Ketchum beside him. The video camera watched them. The door buzzed loudly. Weiss pulled it open.

He paused. He looked back at the empty chair on the other side of the Lexan wall. "I guess you're right," he said. "I guess he's safe for now."

They left. And, for a while, the room, Visiting Room Three at North Wilderness SHU, remained empty. Empty and silent half an hour, forty-five minutes, no more. Then the door buzzed again. Opened again. A man walked in. He was a slender man in an expensive charcoal gray suit. His hands were clasped in front of him, his elbows pressed tight to his sides. He seemed a fastidious and disdainful character. He moved to one of the plastic chairs.

Bernard Hirschorn's assistant, Alex Wellman, took a seat and waited. Another minute passed. Then the door on the other side of the transparent wall opened. Two guards came in. They led a shackled prisoner between them.

It was the man called Ben Fry.

THIRTY-NINE But back to my own somewhat less thrilling adventures.

When we last saw our intrepid hero—namely me—I was on the horns of a moral dilemma. Through my brilliant investigative work, I had uncovered the ugly little secret of Father Reginald O'Mara. To wit, at the time he witnessed our client rob, shoot and paralyze a college student, he happened to be in the process of butt-fucking one of his parishioners. Now I'm not a Catholic—in fact, I'm not a moralist of any kind. I don't care who butt-fucks whom as long as it's all friendly and on the level between adults. But I realized right away that not everyone would share my broad-minded view on this subject. Which is to say I realized that Father Reg was now in what I believe the theologians call "deep shit." Basically, if I handed my report in to Sissy as I was supposed to, I would destroy the career of this good man who helped the poor and so forth in order to free our client who, as I believe I mentioned before, was a scumbag—a scumbag who very much deserved to be in prison, where the priest's eyewitness testimony would surely put him with no problem if you leave out the butt-fucking part.

But I couldn't leave it out and still be said to be doing my job. So here was my moral dilemma. On the one hand, there was that stuff about the justice system and Sissy calling me sweetheart and so on and the fact that, in my fantasy life at least, this was my chance to prove myself as a gumshoe like the heroes in the novels I loved growing up and thus get more assignments with Sissy and thus, ultimately, take her to bed. Which counts for a lot with a fellow. Whereas on the other hand, this ruin-the-good-priest-to-free-the-evil-scumbag scenario was not entirely working for me. So I worried at it and worried at it and after a while I figured: Well, if you have a moral dilemma, who do you call? A priest, right?

Brad Murphy—the butt-fuckee—arranged for me to meet with Father O'Mara outside the Palace of the Legion of Honor. Right next to the *Thinker* statue, in fact, which was appropriate enough as I was desperately trying to think my way out of this sucker before I had to get back with my report to Sissy.

The Palace, for those who've never been, is a pretty grand and majestic-looking place. A neoclassical arch flanked by stately colonnades. An elegant temple with a small glass pyramid before it. A reflecting pool beyond the wide courtyard—just then catching the dramatic image of a sky that had grown low and heavy and steel gray as the afternoon wore on. And beyond that there was a stand of towering eucalyptus. And beyond that were the waters of the everlasting Pacific. All of which majesty and grandeur and so forth only served to make me feel like just that much more of a scurvy knave. As if the Sam Spade, Philip Marlowe type I'd set out as a couple of hours before had been magically transformed into the sort of slimy dickhead who peeks through keyholes at other men's dirty secrets.

Speaking of which, here came Father O'Mara. Stern face lowering like the sky. The guy was fifty, maybe six feet tall, broad-shouldered, trim-waisted. A chiseled face with a dignified shock of silver hair. He wasn't wearing the black priest suit or the backward collar or anything. Just a gray turtleneck, slacks. I stuck out my hand as he approached. He sniffed at it: actually looked disdainfully at my hand and went *sniff* and glanced away without offering to shake. Which *really* made me feel like a scurvy knave, a very *small* scurvy knave, a little scurvy miniknave about two inches high.

There was a gaggle of Japanese tourists taking pictures of each other in front of the *Thinker,* so we moved off toward the courtyard archway. We walked side by side, but he never looked at me. He just gazed straight ahead, speaking as if confiding his thoughts to the air.

"You want money, I assume," he said.

I rolled my eyes. "I don't want money. Jesus. I'm trying to help here."

He snorted in such a way that I no longer felt two inches high, not even in boots. We were at the arch, under it, our footsteps echoing on the stone.

"You're trying to help," he said.

"That's right. I didn't know I was going to come up with this." We emerged under the low-hanging clouds. Our voices lost their resonance. "I was just trying to make sure your statement checked out. That was my assignment. Now I'm stuck with this sh—crap," I amended in light of his priestlitude.

We drew up at the edge of the reflecting pool, both of us staring determinedly across the water, out through the trees at the low sky over the roiling sea. Finally, he relented; glanced over at me. I only caught it from the corner of my eye but I got the sense he was trying to take my measure.

"What a surprise," he said mildly after a moment. "A private investigator with a conscience."

"Yeah, well . . . I'm new," I said.

"Ah, right." He looked out at the ocean again and nodded. "I see the difficulty. It's a pretty little problem."

"Look, you seem like a really good guy, Father. I don't want to bring the roof down on you. But I can't let my client take the fall, go to prison."

"Why not? He shot someone."

"I know but . . . he's my client," I finished lamely.

"Ah, right," he said again—and that was all.

A cold wind came in off the Pacific. I slipped my hands in my pockets, hunched my shoulders against it. Faced him. He was frowning out into the middle distance. Staring down the coming catastrophe, as I imagined. He looked kind of noble doing it, in fact. Noble and sad.

"I don't suppose you would consider standing down," I said finally.

"What do you mean?"

"You know. Maybe you didn't see what you thought you saw. Maybe you're not sure. No witness, no need for witness background."

He got it. Lifted his chin. Smiled a little at nobody in particular. "You want me to lie to save myself. Let this man go free."

"No offense, Father. But you already did lie."

He looked at me, still smiling. I think, to be honest, if I read him right, he pitied me: a young man caught up in more than he could handle. "I saw it as a harmless fib at the time. My mistake and I'll correct it. In any case, it wasn't to save myself, though I don't expect you to believe that. There are a lot of people who depend on me, on the work I do. And a lot of people who . . . who would be hurt by the scandal, even though they'd done nothing wrong themselves."

"Right," I said. "Right." I could see all that: the kids he helped off the streets, his brother the governor. They'd all go down with him one way or another. It was official: This sucked.

He caught the expression that must've been on my face about then. He actually laughed. "What can I tell you? I guess you're on your own."

"Oh wonderful. What the hell kind of priesting is that?"

"Are you a Catholic?"

"No."

"Oh, then you're really screwed."

I laughed too. Feebly though—I didn't feel much like laughing. I dug my way even deeper into my pockets. Brooded into the clouds on the surface of the pool.

"How old are you anyway?" the priest asked me.

"Twenty-two," I said morosely.

"Janey Mack! A baby." I didn't even have the heart to protest. I was just glad neither Weiss nor Bishop could see me now. "Well . . ."

The priest reached out and clasped my shoulder. "Here's a news flash for you: You're a better man than you know. You'll figure this out."

I watched him stride off toward the parking lot under the darkening sky.

Great, I thought. "Shit," I said.

FORTY

By now, it was—I don't know—five o'clock, let's say. And Jim Bishop—or, that is, the man Chris and Kathleen knew as Frank Kennedy—still hadn't left his house. Chris felt sick and weak with the suspense of waiting.

"Damn it," he said. He was peeking out the bedroom window again, watching for any sign of the man. "We *gotta* get him out of there. If he's a cop, I gotta find out."

Kathleen, brooding on the bed behind him, answered nothing. She thought about it a moment, then just picked up the phone and dialed. Chris could hear Kennedy's phone ringing faintly in the house across the way.

"It's Kathleen," he heard his wife say then. "I have to talk to you."

Chris drew back from the window quickly. There was Kennedy now, a dim figure at his own window, holding the phone to his ear, gazing over at them as he answered her.

"No," Kathleen said. "It's about Hirschorn, Chris and Hirschorn. It's important. I can't tell you on the phone. Meet me in front of the Kmart in the River Mall in ten minutes. Hurry."

She hung up without another word. She made a move to join Chris at the window but he waved at her behind his back. "Stay down, he's looking this way," he said.

Kennedy had put the phone down but he was still standing there, still watching their house. "He'll see the truck," Chris whispered—whispered harshly, as if Kennedy were close enough to hear him. "He'll see the truck, he'll know you're here."

Kathleen spoke clearly. "He knows I take the bus when you're not around. Hell, I walk to River Mall sometimes."

"He's doing something."

As he watched, Kennedy faded back from the window, faded into the shadows of his room. A long minute passed. Then Chris, excited, said, "Look! It's working! There he goes."

Kathleen sat on the bed. She stared at the floor. The Kleenexes still lay there from when she was crying. But she wasn't crying anymore. Now she was just dark and hard inside. Kennedy had humiliated her and it had made her dark and hard. She wanted Kennedy to get hurt the way she was hurt.

"There he goes, there he goes," whispered Chris, triumphant.

Kathleen heard Kennedy's motorcycle, heard its engine sputter and roar. The bike went into gear. The noise of the engine quickly grew fainter and fainter. Then it was gone.

"Go on," she said aloud. "He'll be back any minute when he sees I'm not there. Go on and search the house. The key's in my bag on the kitchen table."

Chris obeyed her in a big hurry. Kathleen could hear his footsteps stampeding down the stairs. She just sat there—just sat there, dark and hard, staring down, frowning down at the Kleenexes on the floor.

Fuck you, Frank, she thought.

FORTY-ONE

Outside, the sun was in its long summer descent, but the heat of the day was full. By the time Chris crossed the lawn to reach the house next door, he was sweating hard. His gray cut-off T-shirt had gone wet and dark at his chest and between his shoulder blades. His smooth face was glistening.

He let himself into the house with Kathleen's key. Took the stairs fast, his long legs stretching over two and then three steps at a time. He was panting, pouring sweat as he stepped into the bedroom.

The air-conditioning was still on in here. Which meant Kennedy was planning to come back soon. The hollow sough of the machine made Chris nervous, made his throat tight. He would never admit it—not even to himself—but the idea of confronting Kennedy again scared him to his toes. He knew he had to act fast, before Kennedy's return.

He let his eyes travel once around the place. The room was shadowy but sunshine was falling through the window, through the trees. It lay in patterns on the floor. By its light, Chris saw Kennedy's traveling bag on the bed. It was packed full of clothing. Kennedy was getting ready to go. For good, by the looks of it.

Chris stepped to the bag. It was unzipped. He pulled it open. Even with the air-conditioning on, the place felt airless to him, stifling. Maybe it was just fear. Anyway, sweat dripped off his temples as he bent over, dug through Bishop's clothes. He felt down deep, along the bag's lining. It didn't take him long to find Bishop's handheld computer.

He'd never worked one of these little gizmos before but it wasn't hard. He was a pilot. He knew machines, computers. He had it open on the desk, had it booted in a minute. Wiping the dripping sweat off his face with one hand. Glancing up at the pale day through the window now and then, watching for Bishop's motorcycle, listening for its engine. He poked the handheld's buttons. He worked quickly through Bishop's files. Notes, Names, Mail . . .

Chris panted through his open mouth as he read the tiny screen. He couldn't breathe in this damn place. He felt as if a hand were on his throat, choking him. But his mind was working as he read. If this Kennedy was a cop, he thought, if he had used Kathleen to get the goods on Hirschorn . . . well, there would be hell to pay. Hirschorn's vengeance would be swift and sure. On Kennedy, yes, but on him and Kathleen too, unless . . . Unless he could warn Hirschorn first, if he could tell him about Kennedy, if he could save the day in the nick of time. Then maybe Hirschorn would be grateful. Then maybe he would be forgiving. He would still be angry but maybe it wouldn't be so bad. Maybe he would be indulgent about it. Maybe he would just say something like, "You ought to keep a closer watch on your wife. . . ."

Chris felt his cheeks burn. *Your wife.* He felt an acid anger eating at his groin. Sometime in the last hour or so, it had occurred to him that Kathleen was not telling him the whole truth. He had been so worried at first about Kennedy being a cop, so frightened about what would happen when Hirschorn found out, that he hadn't really thought about anything else. But slowly, all the same, it had begun to occur to him that Kathleen was lying about Kennedy. She had fucked him. That was the true story. She had eavesdropped on Chris's conversations with Hirschorn and then told them to Kennedy. They had talked about him while they were lying in bed together.

Chris was sure of this now and the acid anger bubbled in him and flamed. He had to force the thought away. Concentrate on what he was doing.

He growled. "God damn it." The fucking handheld was useless. There was nothing in the files. Names, numbers, e-mail addresses. They didn't mean shit to him. How the hell was he supposed to know who was who?

But this was all he had. He kept going, kept reading. Now he moved to the e-mail folder, called it up on the screen.

There was an unsent e-mail on file, just one. Bishop was usually so careful about these things. He never saved the mail he sent. He always deleted the mail he received. But Kathleen had interrupted him as he was writing his latest to Weiss. Bishop had saved it—and then he'd forgotten it. He hadn't finished it yet and he hadn't sent it. Chris opened the file.

Weiss. It worked. Wannamaker's out. I'm in. Six tonight, I fly to some secret location out in the forest somewhere. Once I arrive, they'll give me the details of the job. Soon as I know what's what, I'll make contact. With luck, we should be able to break it up without compromising . . .

Chris stopped breathing, stopped thinking even. He just stared, dumbstruck. His heart beat hard in his chest. His pulse sounded loud, incredibly loud, in his head.

Wannamaker's out. I'm in.

Jesus. Jesus. This was even worse than he'd thought. This was the worst thing ever. There was only one way to be "out" with Bernie Hirschorn. If he was "out," then it was only a matter of time before Hirschorn's men came to get him. They would come and take him away to make sure he didn't talk. He had to hurry. He had to warn Hirschorn about Kennedy. He had to save the day in the nick of time so Hirschorn wouldn't kill him.

His eyes went desperately over the e-mail. His mind tried desperately to take in the words. *Weiss,* he thought numbly. He had seen the name before. In the phone files.

His hand was trembling now but he forced it to work the keyboard. He brought up the name. *Weiss,* that's all it said. And the number. A San Francisco area code.

Chris picked up the phone. Picked out the buttons with an unsteady finger.

A ring. He waited. Breathing again, breathing hard, the sound of his own breath drowning his heartbeat.

Wannamaker's out.

Another ring. *Come on,* he thought. Then a woman's voice: "Weiss Investigations."

Chris couldn't speak, couldn't get his throat to open.

The woman said, "Hello? Weiss Investigations."

"You some kind of detective agency?" he asked in a croak.

"Yes, this is Weiss Investigations, we're a private detective agency. . . ."

Chris's mind was racing, racing. Kennedy was a detective, a private detective. Spying on him. Using Kathleen. Now going off to fly with Hirschorn. Jesus . . .

"How can I help you?" said the woman on the phone.

But now . . . Now, as he stood with the phone to his ear . . . Now, there was a sound outside. Chris glanced up. An engine. Kennedy's motorcycle, was his first thought. But no. This was a car. He saw it through the window, through the branches of the trees.

The sweat streaming down his temples turned cold. The back of his neck turned clammy. Slowly, slowly, as if in a trance, he lowered the phone to its cradle.

"Sir, how can I . . . ?" he heard the receptionist say distantly. And then he'd hung up.

He'd hung up and he was standing there with his jaw slack. Weak with fear. Helpless and sick with fear. Staring down at the car. A BMW, sleek, dark. One of Hirschorn's cars, he was sure of it. And it was pulling to a stop. Pulling to a stop by the curb in front of his house.

Chris watched, stared, not breathing, pouring sweat. His head felt light. The airless room seemed to be smothering him. Two men were getting out of the car, out of the front seats. At the sight of them, Chris groaned aloud.

They were Hirschorn's men. The big one with the long arms, Goldmunsen, and the little nervous one, Flake. Chris had heard stories about Flake. Goldmunsen used a gun, people said, but Flake was a knife man. He liked to carve on people. He enjoyed it.

The two men were walking up the path to Chris's house. They had come to take him away in their car.

Chris stood frozen, stared down through the tree branches, helpless, smothering, weak in the legs. Goldmunsen was ringing the doorbell.

"Don't answer," Chris whispered, urging Kathleen.

But he caught a movement out of the corner of his eye. His glance shifted. He saw Kathleen crossing the living room, going to answer the door. Distantly, it occurred to him that Kennedy had been able to watch her from here too. He could watch both of them right through their windows. He would've seen Hirschorn. He would've seen everything. The anger bubbled and flamed in him again. He had a flashing thought of Kathleen and Kennedy in the bed, talking about him. . . .

Kathleen opened the door. Chris watched through the window. Goldmunsen spoke to her. The jittery Flake bounced on his toes. Goldmunsen seemed to speak politely, calmly. He smiled, a slick, toothy smile. But Flake—Flake could hardly contain himself. He bobbed his head this way, that. Tried to peer in past Kathleen, around her, over her, into the living room. To see if Chris was there.

The sweat streamed freely down Chris's face. It stung his eyes. He couldn't breathe. He was suffocating. If Kathleen turned . . . If Kathleen turned and pointed at the house . . . If she told them, "He's right next door," then it was over, they would come for him, they would take him away.

Chris heard himself whimper—a sound he'd never heard himself make before, a terrible sound. He stood paralyzed with fear, tortured by a wild, helpless rage. He hated his wife—*hated* her. Because she'd fucked Kennedy and because right now she had his life in her hands. All he could do was stand here and watch her, so helpless and so afraid.

But Kathleen did not betray him. She didn't turn or point. Chris could just see her, just her arm and her hair and a bit of profile. He could see she was shaking her head. She was telling Goldmunsen no. She was telling him that she didn't know where Chris was. She understood. She saw what was happening. She knew why they had come. She was lying to protect him, to keep him alive.

Chris saw Goldmunsen nod. He believed her. Flake bounced on his toes. Kathleen went on telling them . . . something, some bullshit. That Chris was at the bar, or out at the airpark or that she didn't know. Something.

And now—yes!—the two goons were turning away. Walking back down the front path. Back to the car. Chris waited for the car to move. He felt as if he were hanging suspended in the thick air, waiting. Then the car did move. It pulled away from the curb. It was driving off. Chris had the dizzying sensation of falling and falling out of nowhere back into his own body. Suddenly he was breathing again, panting. Suddenly his pulse was loud again and pounding in his ears.

The car was gone. Kathleen stood another moment in the doorway. Chris saw her come forward a step, away from the house. Then she turned. She looked up—up at the window, up at Chris. Her face was pasty. Her eyes were lost and afraid.

Chris grimaced down at her. He wished he had his hand on her throat at that moment.

He came back to himself. He glanced around, started moving. He snapped the handheld shut. For a second, he made as if to pocket the thing. He would show the e-mail to Hirschorn, he thought. He would warn him. He would save the day and the goons wouldn't take him away in their car. Maybe he would even get his piloting job back. He would be in again instead of out. . . .

But now he stopped. The plan was no good. If he stole the

handheld, Kennedy was sure to notice. He'd know he'd been discovered. He'd call in the cops, the real cops. That would ruin everything.

No. Things were going too fast here. He had to think. Scared as he was, he had to be smart. He didn't need the handheld. That's right. The e-mail didn't prove anything. He could've typed it himself. The handheld didn't matter. Hirschorn was no fool. When he heard what Chris had to say, he'd check it out himself. He'd see that it was true. He just had to get to Hirschorn. Fast.

Sweating hard, breathing hard, Chris carried the handheld back to the traveling bag. He stuffed it back in, down deep, right where he'd found it. He looked at his watch. Five-thirty almost. Kennedy was flying into the woods with Hirschorn at six o'clock. If Chris hurried, he could get there first. Tell Hirschorn everything and save the day. Then Hirschorn's goons would come for Kennedy. It would be Kennedy who was taken away in the car.

For a moment, he stood still, sweat draining down his cheeks in rivulets. For a moment, his eyes grew distant and glistening like the eyes of a daydreaming child. Kennedy had taken his wife. He had taken his job. He had taken his dignity when he beat him up in the Clover Leaf Bar in front of his friends. Kennedy had stripped him of everything that made him a man. Now, just as Kennedy thought he had the upper hand, it was payback time. Now Chris would tell Hirschorn the truth and it would all be turned around.

He had to move. Hirschorn wouldn't answer his phone calls. He had to get to him in person, get to the airpark before Kennedy did. Get to Hirschorn before the plane took off.

He headed for the door.

FORTY-TWO

The rumble of Chris's truck was just fading from the neighborhood when Bishop's motorcyle came down the road from the other direction.

Bishop turned in beside his house, dismounted. He jogged to the door, in a hurry. He didn't even spare a glance for the other house, Kathleen's house. He didn't even wonder much about why she hadn't met him at the mall. He had gone because she said it was about Hirschorn, because he couldn't take the chance of missing something important. But he didn't really believe it was anything important. He believed it was just some scheme she'd hatched to try and get back together with him. When she hadn't showed, he shrugged it off. He didn't have time to worry about it now. He had to get to the airpark. He had to meet Hirschorn, find out what he was doing.

Inside, he took the stairs quickly, several at a time, just as Chris had done. He went quickly into the bedroom. To the traveling bag sitting open on the bed. He zipped it shut. Took hold of the handles. Paused to let his eyes sweep once around the room.

But he was in too big a rush. He didn't notice that anything had been disturbed. He didn't remember the e-mail he'd forgotten to send to Weiss.

He hoisted the traveling bag. He snapped off the air conditioner on the way to the door.

A minute later, his motorcycle roared again and he was gone.

FORTY-THREE

Chris reached the airpark first. His pickup made a screeching swing across the hangar doors and he leapt out of the cab to the tarmac. His boots cracked on the concrete hangar floor as he strode to the twin-engine Aero Commander parked inside.

Ray Grambling was standing by the plane in his overalls, bent into the open cowling with a wrench. Another mechanic, Wilson Tubbs, was lying down inside the cockpit, his feet sticking out the door.

Chris was on them fast. Ray was just starting to look up when Chris grabbed him. He grabbed the front of Ray's overalls, forced him back hard against the tool chest behind him. The chest's wheels were locked. Ray winced and grunted as the chest's open drawer hit him in the spine. He stumbled back as the drawer rattled shut. Before he really knew what was happening, Chris snapped the wrench out of his hand and raised it over his head. Then Ray—the bald, craggy older man—was goggling helplessly up at the angry young face, twisted and bruised and terrible, hovering above him.

"Where's Hirschorn?" Chris said.

"Jesus, Chris, Jesus, Jesus . . ." Ray said quickly.

"Come on, you piece of shit! You brought him in, didn't you? Kennedy. You set him on my wife. I oughta kill you where you stand. C'mon!" Chris raised the wrench higher as if to strike.

"I didn't . . ."

"You brought Kennedy in. Right? You did this whole thing."

Tubbs—the mechanic in the plane—had only just now figured out that something was going on. He was trying to wriggle backwards out of the cockpit.

Ray had his hands up uselessly at his chest. "I swear to God," he babbled. "I swear to God . . ."

"Where the hell is he?" Chris shouted. "Where's Hirschorn? Which plane are they taking?"

"Please, Chris, I swear to God . . ."

"Hey!" It was Tubbs. A little guy in his thirties, quick and scrappy. Out of the cockpit now, at Chris's shoulder. He grabbed Chris's wrist, tried to wrestle down the wrench. "Hey, what the hell are you . . . ?"

Chris yanked his wrist away, pistoned his elbow into Tubbs's nose. Tubbs flew back against the plane. He sat down hard on the hangar floor and then tipped over onto his side, clutching his bloody face.

Chris brandished the wrench over Ray Grambling's head. "You tell me which plane they're taking now or I'm gonna split your skull like a fucking walnut, you . . ."

"Chris, I . . ."

Behind them: another screech of tires. Chris's head snapped round. He looked back over his shoulder through the hangar doors.

And now it was his—Chris's—eyes that went wide with terror. Out in the parking lot, the sleek, dark BMW had just pulled in. It had followed him. Waited near the house for his truck and then followed him here. Goldmundsen and Flake—Hirschorn's goons—were already pouring out the doors. In an instant, Chris's face changed from scowling threat to fearful quiver. His bark became a squeak down in his throat.

"Oh God," he said.

Ray Grambling fell back against the tool chest as Chris released him. The wrench Chris had been holding clanged as it dropped to the floor. And just like that, Chris was gone. He'd bolted. He was running for his pickup.

Out in the parking lot, the big goon, Goldmunsen, spotted him, shouted. Flake, the little electric goon, froze like a pointer dog, then darted for the pickup too.

Chris reached the truck, the passenger side. He grabbed hold of the door. He looked up through the window. He saw Flake running at him, Goldmunsen running behind Flake. They were five steps away. They were going into their jackets, going for their guns.

Chris had no time. No time to get into the truck. He stopped on his heels. He pushed off the pickup door. Spun full around. Darted back into the hangar.

Ray Grambling in the hangar was frozen where he stood. He saw Chris coming right at him, coming at him like a speeding bus. He rolled away from the tool chest, pinned himself against the Commander's cowling.

Chris sped past him, looking back over his shoulder, back at the goons racing around the pickup to come after him.

Chris faced forward just in time to see the tool chest. Then he plowed into it. He hit it hard. The top of it went into his gut. The breath coughed up out of his diaphragm. Even with its wheels locked the chest gave way, tipped up, went over. It smashed into the hangar floor with a hellacious, rattling bang. Chris, winded, tumbled in the other direction. Staggered and fell, his shoulder bouncing off the concrete.

From down there, Chris twisted around to see the wired Flake charging at him. Chris screamed, a high-pitched scream like a woman's. He scrabbled for purchase like a bug on its back. In another second, he was on his feet. He was running, frantic, for the small door on the hangar's opposite wall.

The door was shut. There was a window in the top of it. Chris could see through the window out to the airpark apron. He could see the blue sky and the heat rising off the black tarmac, waves of heat rising past the wings of the parked planes.

Chris knew the door would be unlocked and flung himself against it. For one second, his face was pressed to the window. He saw the sky, the apron, the planes, the heat, all wild and tumbling to his panicked mind. And then, in that one second, there was one thing, one image he saw that mattered, that counted for everything.

Hirschorn. He saw Hirschorn through the waves of heat. The silver-haired man was standing by five-zero-four, the twin-engine Cessna. Standing casual, with his hands in his pockets. Just looking off absently toward the mansions gleaming in the far-off hills.

Even in his fear, Chris's heart rose up. He'd made it. He would get to Hirschorn. He would tell Hirschorn about Kennedy, that Kennedy was a PI. He would save the day—and Hirschorn would keep him alive and kill Kennedy instead.

Chris did not look back—there was no time. But he knew that Flake was several steps behind him. He would not catch him now. He had made it. He shoved against the hangar door. It started to swing out.

And then the window went black as Goldmunsen stepped up to the other side and slammed the door shut in Chris's face.

Chris gaped through the glass at the hatchet-faced thug who had come round the outside of the hangar to block his way. The hatchet-faced thug grinned.

Then Flake had him, had Chris, had the cold muzzle of a Glock pressed hard against Chris's neck. Chris could hear Flake panting in his ear, could feel his hot, wet breath against his neck.

"Tag you're it, motherfucker," said Flake. He dragged Chris back away from the door.

Ray Grambling watched in fear as Goldmunsen pulled the door open and stepped into the hangar.

"Wait," said Chris, his voice high and breathless. "I gotta talk to Mr. Hirschorn, I gotta tell him . . ."

Goldmunsen drove that wrecking ball fist of his into Chris's stomach. All the way across the hangar, Ray Grambling heard Chris grunt. Then, groaning, Chris sank down on buckled knees.

Goldmunsen grinned at the crumpled man. Then he looked up. He grinned at Ray Grambling. Ray looked away quickly.

Chris knelt there, swaying. He was trying to talk. He was trying to tell them what he had found out. But all he could do was gasp and drool.

Still grinning, Goldmunsen lifted his fist high, up by his ear. He swung it around like some great hammer. It drove into the side of Chris's head with a thud. Chris's eyes rolled crazily. He pitched forward onto his face, unconscious.

Goldmunsen took hold of Chris by one arm, wrapping his big hand around the *Born To Raise Hell* tattoo. Flake took hold of Chris by the other arm. Chris's feet scraped over the concrete floor as the two goons dragged him back through the hangar.

Ray Grambling kept his eyes down the whole time. Wilson Tubbs had pushed himself up on one elbow. He looked around and saw what was happening and then he turned his eyes down too. He watched the blood falling from his broken nose onto the concrete.

Neither Tubbs nor Ray Grambling looked up again as Goldmunsen and Flake hauled Chris out into the parking lot. Neither of them looked up at all until the two thugs had driven Chris away with them in their sleek, black car.

FORTY-FOUR About two minutes later, Jim

Bishop's Harley bounded into the parking lot. The bike skidded to a stop, gravel spitting out from under its tires. Bishop dismounted. He came toward the hangar quickly, his flight bag slung over his left shoulder, his traveling bag clutched in his right hand.

Ray Grambling had helped Tubbs to his feet by now. Tubbs was holding a rag to his bleeding face. "Fuck me!" he was in the midst of saying for about the fifth time. "Did you see that?"

Ray looked over the other man's shoulder and saw Bishop coming toward them. "Tubbs?" he said. His voice was shaking.

"I mean, fuck me, did you . . . ?"

"Tubbs!" Tubbs glanced at Ray around the rag. And Ray said, "Go get yourself looked at, y'hear me. You tell the doctor you bumped into the wing of the plane. You understand?"

"Ray, what're you . . . ?"

"Do it, Tubbsy. Nothing happened and you bumped into the wing of the plane. Now get the hell outta here and don't tell nobody. Go on."

Dazed, Tubbs nodded. Ray's tone made him start moving. By the time Bishop stepped up to Ray Grambling, Tubbs was limping out of the hangar, nursing his face, bleeding into his rag.

Bishop glanced at him, then at Ray. "What happened?" he said.

"They took Chris away," Ray said in a shaky whisper. He swallowed hard. Bishop was wearing his aviator shades. Ray couldn't make out his eyes. He couldn't tell what his reaction was. He rushed on. "He knows, man. Chris—he knows you're a detective. He knows I brought you in. He came in here looking for Hirschorn, to tell him. But these two goons got to him, they wouldn't listen. They just took him away. They just came in here and knocked him out and took him."

Bishop said nothing for a long moment. Then he nodded slowly. "They knocked him out."

"Yeah, but if he wakes up, man. If he wakes up and tells them, tells them about you and me, I'm dead," Ray went on. "I know Hirschorn. He'll kill me. He'll kill my whole family, he finds out about this. I knew I never should've done this. Damn it, I never should've. What are we gonna do, Bishop? What're we gonna do?"

Bishop stood there, stood there with his pale eyes hidden by his shades and said nothing. Ray was right. If Chris regained consciousness and convinced the goons that Bishop was a detective, Hirschorn would kill him. He'd also kill Bishop on the spot.

"I mean, what're we gonna do?" said Ray again. "We can't go to the cops. In this town? Hirschorn'd find out the minute we got there. Oh, I never should've done it. He wakes up, they'll kill me. They'll kill my wife, my kids. They'll kill you. They'll kill everybody. What're we gonna do?"

"Nothing." Bishop spoke quietly. "There's nothing we can do. We're gonna have to take our chances."

"But what if he wakes up, man? What if he wakes up?"

"Pull yourself together," Bishop snapped. "He's not gonna wake up. You hear me? That's why they knocked him out, that was the point. By the time he wakes up, he'll already be dead."

Ray Grambling started to say more but Bishop wouldn't listen. He pushed past him, heading for Hirschorn and the plane.

FORTY-FIVE

The woods three thousand feet below were deep green in the gathering twilight. The Cessna tilted in the air as Bishop guided it northward through the dusk.

Hirschorn's voice came over Bishop's headset. "It's a whole lot of nothing down there, isn't it?"

Bishop nodded, rolling the plane out of its bank. Flying on straight and level at the heading Hirschorn had given him.

"No way in. No way out," Hirschorn went on. "No roads. No phones."

"No runways either, far as I can see," said Bishop.

He heard Hirschorn's chuckle, cold and mechanical over the set. "You getting nervous?"

Bishop barely smiled.

The sun had dropped behind the western hills but the cool blue of the sky held on. Bishop drew off his aviators, slipped them into his pocket. Now, by the last light of day, he spotted something below. A glimpse, through the treetops, of a winding line, too brown for a river, too narrow for a road.

Hirschorn saw him looking. "Yeah, that—" he said over the engines. "—That's a dynamite road. There used to be a mine down there in the gold rush days. They'd use that road to cart dynamite to the mine from camp. Not much use on the ground anymore. Just a track—twenty mountain miles from anything. But from the air— well, just follow it along and you can start to bring her down."

Surprised, Bishop glanced at him. As in: *Bring her down where?* But Hirschorn only showed the white teeth beneath his steel moustache. He was a chilly dude was old Hirschorn, you had to give him that.

With a shrug, Bishop throttled back. He felt the plane pitch down smoothly. He banked as they descended to follow the dynamite road.

"Hell, you can land in the trees, can't you?" Hirschorn said with a laugh.

And in fact, for a long time, it looked as if they would. The Cessna sank lower and lower. The crowns of the oaks and the points of the pines rushed toward them, swept under them and stretched out before them. The only break in the sea of green was that snaking brown miner's track that Bishop kept just off their right wing. Even that was hard to see after a while as the darkness deepened, and the evening drew on. The blue sky turned indigo. The green of the leaves was submerged under colorless shadow. The dynamite road became a gray wisp.

"There!" said Hirschorn.

Where? Bishop peered through the gloaming. He saw nothing. Nothing. Then—yes—for a swift second—the runway at his one o'clock . . . and it was gone. Just like that, they had flown past it.

Bishop pursed his lips. Hirschorn laughed again. "Not much to land on, is it?"

It sure wasn't. Two thousand feet of packed dirt, if that. With tall pines and oaks crowding it on both ends and either side. It would've been tough to drop a chopper in there let alone an airplane.

"Think you can handle it?" said Hirschorn.

Bishop didn't even bother to answer. He wound the plane back around. Slowed her as she dropped even closer to the treetops. He ran back the length of the runway, measuring the strip of dirt with his eyes. It wasn't easy. The runway too was disappearing now into the dark.

"Chris blew out a tire first time he did this, nearly spun us right into a fucking tree," said Hirschorn merrily. "You can see why I needed a top-notch pilot."

Bishop brought the plane onto final approach. Lowered the gear. Could almost feel, in his imagination, the tires scraping the branches. The beams of his landing lights dissipated in the rising forest mist. He could barely see ahead of him now, could just make out the strip through the dusk. In his mind, he was all flaps and low speed and just a pure silent hum as the dim shadow of the rising runway filled his consciousness. He picked his spot a yard or two beyond the trees. Cleared the last oak and pulled the nose up. The Cessna dropped in. Dropped like a flying brick, almost straight down. The cockpit jarred as the gear whomped against the ground. And Bishop was wrestling the nose high, pulling a wheelie, keeping the front tire off the soft earth as long as possible. Then, as the speed bled off, as the danger of a skid or noseover eased, he lowered her, pressed his feet against the brakes, steady and sure.

The last light died down here beneath the trees. The plane kept rolling. Bishop stared hard through the windshield. The forest up ahead was only a darker mass on the dark. Then suddenly, out of the shadows, there it was, a broken wall of stout trunks rushing toward him.

But the Cessna was under control. The night slowed around it. Stopped. The plane sat quietly on the runway, the engines chugging. They had landed.

Bishop allowed himself a sigh. He glanced over at Hirschorn, just a silhouette in the seat beside him.

"You like that?" Hirschorn said. Bishop didn't answer. Hirschorn laughed, a jovial laugh. He reached across the pilot and plucked the key out of the Cessna's ignition. "Wait'll you see what you're going to fly next," he said.

FORTY-SIX

There were lights moving in the forest as Bishop stepped down from the cockpit. There were footsteps approaching on the fallen leaves. Another moment and two men emerged from the trees, came onto the runway. The men were wearing fatigues and watch caps. They were carrying Stinger flashlights. Each had a Heckler & Koch MP5—a machine gun—slung by a strap over his shoulder.

It was a lot of firepower out here in the middle of nowhere. Even Bishop, fearless as he usually was, felt suddenly very alone, very far from any chance of help, any avenue of escape.

"Let's go," said Hirschorn.

Bishop got his traveling bag out of the Cessna's backseat. At a nod from Hirschorn, one of the gunmen started back into the woods. Bishop and Hirschorn followed him. The second gunman brought up the rear.

There was no trail. Patches of tangled roots sprung from the night under the swinging beams of the gunmen's Stingers. Patches of forest in patches of swirling mist. Then those lighted places sank away again, were replaced by others in a confusing, moving jumble. Bishop couldn't always make out where he was stepping. But the lead gunman moved fast. There was no choice but to march after him, to stumble after him, deeper into the trees.

It was cooler in the woods than in the town but muggier too. Bishop's T-shirt hung damp on him within minutes. His face felt slick and clammy. As they went, the mosquitoes found them. Sometimes, in a flashlight's outglow, Bishop could see them swarm. He heard their wearying high-pitched whisper of attack. He cursed at them. He swatted at his neck and cheek, smeared himself with his own blood as he dragged their corpses off his skin.

But the walk wasn't long. Ten minutes, maybe less. Then the rumble of a generator reached him. Dangling vines and twisted branches appeared, black against a ghostly white glow, a light in the distance filtering to him through the rising mist.

Even with that warning, though, it was startling to arrive at the campsite. There was no clearing. Not much of one anyway. There were just a couple of instant buildings, set up and wedged between the trees. One building was a two-story barracks: two rectangular boxes of steel stacked one on top of the other. There was one window on each side of each box and even a stairway slapped onto one end of them. The windows were curtained and only that dim, ghostly glow escaped from them, seeping into the forest vapors and carried away in their slow, rising spiral.

The other building was larger, a shed. It was completely dark.

As he approached, marching with the little band, Bishop glanced upward instinctively. He saw one star, one jagged sliver of blue-black sky. The rest was blocked out by the canopy of leaves. And over the shed, where there was a wider break in the treetops, there was some kind of cover—mosquito netting maybe—hung to act as camouflage. *You could fly over this site at two hundred feet,* he thought, *and never spot it.* Especially in the dark. There was no question about it: If he didn't make it out of here on his own, no one would ever find him.

The lead gunman stopped. Bishop and Hirschorn stopped. So did the gunman behind them. Now, as the crunch of their footsteps ceased, there was only the rumble of the generator, and the burr of crickets and the rattle of cicada and the bleat and belch of peepers and bullfrogs in the thickening night all around.

Hirschorn wiped his chiseled features with a white handkerchief. Bishop could just make him out in the light of the Stingers. The silver-haired man still looked elegant and composed as he daubed the sweat off his neck and forehead. Then he gestured with the handkerchief toward the shed.

"I'll let you get washed up and settled in a minute," he said, "but first I want to give you a look at my baby."

He lifted his chin to the lead gunman. The gunman went to the front of the shed. At another gesture from Hirschorn, Bishop followed.

The gunman wedged the flash under his arm. By its unsteady light, Bishop could see him working the shed latch. Then the gunman drew one-half of the shed front open. He returned and drew the other half open the other way.

Bishop stood in front of the wide-open shed. He looked in. He saw the gunman's flashlight jouncing here and there, but beyond that he made out nothing but blackness. Then with a queasy feeling, he began to distinguish a darker darkness, a blacker black hunkering in the shed's depths.

The gunman slipped inside the steel box. He threw a switch. A pair of fluorescent lights attached to the shed's sides began to work their way on. In that flickering blue light, Bishop saw what was in there.

He whistled. Hirschorn laughed, delighted by his reaction.

Bishop tried to think of something to say. He couldn't. All he could do was whistle again. And finally he managed a stunned murmur: "Man oh man oh man."

FORTY-SEVEN

All Weiss was after at that moment was a drink. He was driving the Taurus home from the airport, home from his visit to Whip Pomeroy in the prison upstate.

While he'd been gone, the weather down here had turned crummy. The wide sky over the ballpark and the bay was thick with clouds. There had been no sunset. Night had just dropped as from a gallows high. Now the lights of Oakland across the water were blurring in a closing mist. He watched them idly. The traffic north was slow. The cars along the freeway ahead of him glared red and went dark and glared an angry red again.

It was what the drinking man calls *time*. As in, "It's time!" As in, "The time has come." Weiss could practically taste the scotch. He could practically smell it. His mind was practically crying out for a measure of greater stillness. It would be greater stillness than this anyway, this agitation, this obsessive imagining: the stairway, the locked door, the angel-faced girl in the halo of her own red-gold hair, blah, blah, blah. *Oh, thank you, thank you, you saved me, saved me . . .*

"Oh, for fuck's sake," muttered Weiss as he drove.

Shouldn't he have felt reassured at this point? Julie Wyant had made her escape, hadn't she? Sure she had. She'd vanished in her wig, taken on a whole new identity. No one would ever find her now. The only person who had the faintest notion of who she'd become or where she'd gone was the man who'd given her the AKA, Pomeroy. And Pomeroy had himself locked up so tight and deep that even if the Shadowman were as unstoppable as the newspapers made him out to be he could never get to him. So for now, at least, Julie was safe. There was no urgency. No stairs, no locked door. No every second counts. What was he so goddamned worried about?

The SUV in front of him went red and slowed. He braked the Taurus. The traffic congealed and horns started honking here and there like geese passing over it. Weiss tapped his finger on the steering wheel impatiently.

Jesus, he thought. Jesus, who was this woman anyway? This Julie Wyant. Was she really that special? Was anyone? Where did she even come from? The cops had searched for her—so had he—and she seemed to have no past, no family, no one who really knew where she'd been before the moment she turned up in Moncrieff's stable of girls. She seemed to have shimmered into being out of nothingness and dissolved again back into the nothingness whence she came. All that was left behind was a picture of her, a video of her, beckoning. And all those men, of course, in love with her. Obsessed with her. Her johns. Moncrieff. The Shadowman . . .

A flush crawled up Weiss's neck as he thought about it. It was a flush of embarrassment, of shame. Because what about him, after all? Him and these daydreams of his, these feverish longings he felt at night? What about that prostitute he'd hired with the red wig? Talk about obsession. Jesus.

The traffic started moving again. The red brake lights along the freeway went out in swift sequence, like dominoes falling. As the Taurus edged forward, Weiss saw a clutch of cop cars with flashing racks on the shoulder of the road. Two civilian cars had collided, denting each other. An accident; a bottleneck. The Taurus squeezed through it. The traffic fanned out on the far side and he accelerated. To his left, in the murk of cloud and mist, the weary, yellow lights of the city skyline finally rose. That first sip of whiskey was as good as on his lips, the heat of it as good as in him. It was time.

But just then, something occurred to him. Occurred to him, that is, in the Weissian sense. That is, he felt a separate presence in his thoughts, the logic of another personality. That was his way, his Weiss-like way. People, their emotions, the progress of their emotions just came to him, just took up residence in his inner space so that suddenly he understood things, things they would think, things they would do, without exactly knowing how or why.

He had been thinking about Julie Wyant. And then about the Shadowman. And then he had been thinking about himself and then . . . and then there it was. This poisoned heart. The logic of this poisoned heart. Its rage—tremendous, living rage—rage like a second soul that worked its will in a man until his every act was just the rage in motion.

It was a weird thought. It was frightening. Because you didn't think of a character like that falling in love. Sure, Weiss had known hit men who were good to their wives, mob bosses who were kind to their kids, even a serial killer who was sweet as hell to the old lady in the apartment next door. But the violence and the decency seemed to come from separate places in them. They loved whom they loved and killed whom they killed and it was not all one thing.

But somehow—he had no idea how—somehow, sitting here in his car, he had felt his way into the mind of the Shadowman and there was no separation there. That heart of poison that had shot those children to death off China Beach, that was the self-same heart that wanted Julie Wyant now, that needed Julie Wyant. Pomeroy had misunderstood what he'd overheard. The Shadowman hadn't hurt Julie and then begged her to be his: It had all been one thing. Hurting her had been his manner of courtship and his love . . . His love would be an act of destruction; the destruction of her would be the token of his love. It was as if Rage itself had come to adore someone, as if Murder itself had, as if the Devil had. Weiss snorted softly at the melodrama of that thought. But it was unsettling. The Devil in love. What would the Devil do on his wedding night, after all? And what *wouldn't* the Devil do to claim his bride?

He cursed. His car slid down the freeway ramp to the misty base of the skyline. Angrily, he turned the wheel, turned it hard so that the tires squealed under him. He headed along Market Street—but not to his apartment now, not to the scotch he was way past ready for. He headed to his office. To his computer, to his phone.

Because now, slowly, finally, it was beginning to come to him. He was beginning to understand what would happen next.

PART FOUR Hellfire

FORTY-EIGHT

It was dark when they reached the killing place. They had been driving a long time.

Chris Wannamaker was just now coming around. Slumped in the BMW's backseat, he was just beginning to feel the motion of the car. His eyes came slowly open, slowly closed. His big, muscular body felt floaty to him, strengthless. His head lay heavy against the window, too heavy to raise. His jaw hung loose, too heavy to shut. His eyes came slowly open again. He stared out at the night.

Flake was up front, behind the wheel. Goldmunsen was sitting behind him. One of Goldmunsen's apelike arms lay lax across his middle. At the end of the apelike arm was an apelike hand. In the apelike hand was a gun, a Glock, pointed at nothing. Now, as Chris stirred, Goldmunsen smiled, the way people do when someone wakens. He shifted his hand to point the Glock at Chris.

Chris shifted again. He moaned. His head was starting to throb. He had a vague sense that something terrible was happening to him. He wanted it to stop. He wanted to close his eyes and open them and be at home in his bed. He tried it, closed his eyes again, opened them again. No. He was still in the car. The car kept moving. The miles unwound. The night closed in.

Chris tried to focus. He tried to see what was outside the window. There wasn't much. He could make out the shapes of trees pressed black against the edges of the twisting road. Now and then he could see a paler black, a strip of sky, above them. They were in the forest somewhere. He was starting to feel afraid, more and more afraid. Something terrible was going to happen to him in the forest. There was something he had to do to stop it. There was something he had to do in the nick of time.

But time was up. Flake was turning the car off the road. Chris felt the tires bounce over dirt and gravel. He was jolted in his seat. Punch-drunk, he lifted his heavy head. He looked around him. He saw Flake driving. Goldmunsen smiling down at him. He saw the gun in Goldmunsen's hand.

"Oh," he said thickly. "No . . ."

It all swam back in on him. He was going to his own execution. Terror shuddered through him and his limbs went weak.

"No . . . no," he said. "You have to . . ."

"Just park it here, this is good," said Goldmunsen to Flake.

"Let me get a little more in, some CHIPs asshole doesn't see us from the road," said Flake over his shoulder.

"Yeah," said Goldmunsen. "Okay. Go more in."

Chris moved his hand to his throbbing forehead. For a moment, the interior of the BMW receded into fog and silence. Then it snapped back again, sickening and real.

"Oh God. Oh . . ."

"Hey, shut him up, will you," said Flake.

"No, wait. Listen," said Chris, holding his head. "This is . . . Listen to me."

"Just take it easy," said Goldmunsen amiably. "It'll all be over in a couple of minutes."

"But you've gotta . . . you've gotta listen." Chris held his head. He tried to think. Something he had to do. The nick of time. The pain pulsed in his temple like a living thing and he couldn't think and he was so afraid. "Listen."

"It ain't gonna help, my friend. We have our orders," said Goldmunsen. "You know how it is, right? Just stay cool. We'll make it real easy on you."

Chris looked at him, blinked at him. The smiling gorilla face. "Goldmunsen," he said. "Listen to me. Please . . ."

"Hey!" said Flake sharply, glancing up at Chris in the rearview as he drove. "What did the man just say to you? Huh? Shut up already."

Goldmunsen shrugged. "See what we're dealing with?" he said to Chris. "We don't want to get Flake here angry. You know? He gets pissed, he starts in with the knife, it'll get very messy."

"Oh God, please . . ."

"I'm serious, you won't like it. Just be a man about it and I'll take care of you. Okay?"

A new wave of fear and weakness washed down over Chris. He swallowed hard. "You don't understand," he said.

Goldmunsen laughed. "Oh, we understand."

"No, no, it's . . . Oh God, you have to listen. I don't want to die!"

"Well, you have to," said Flake. "So take it like a man and shut up. Jesus." He muttered, "Knock this fuck out again, would you?"

"Eh," said Goldmunsen. "Then we gotta carry him all the way out there? Fuck that shit."

The car stopped. Chris's eyes went wide. He looked around the darkness desperately. It came back to him now. Fragments coming together in his mind like jigsaw pieces. "Wait! Please," he whined. "It was Kennedy! That's what I have to tell you. It's all Kennedy."

"I'm gonna cut this fuck, so help me," said Flake.

"All right, all right," said Goldmunsen. "Let's all just try to stay cool and get this done in a professional manner. Pop the lock back here already, wouldja?"

Flake hit the switch. The back doors unlocked. Goldmunsen gestured with the gun.

"You get out on my side," he said to Chris.

"It's all Kennedy, I swear!"

But the hatchet-faced gorilla ignored him. He nudged the door open. Slid out of the car carefully, keeping the Glock on Chris the whole time. Flake got out too.

"Listen!" said Chris. "Kennedy! He did all this. He . . . oh . . ." He held his head. He tried to put the pieces together.

Goldmunsen beckoned with the gun. "Come on," he said.

"Hurry the fuck up about it. Don't make me climb in there," said Flake. "I mean it. Let's go."

Chris stared wildly at the black bore of the gun barrel. He was too limp with fear to move, too limp even to speak anymore. But somehow there he was, sliding across the seat toward the beckoning gun as if he were a charmed snake.

He stood up into the cool mountain air. He was trembling all over. Dazed and weak.

"This isn't right," he managed to whisper. "This . . . It's not right. It's a mistake. Not . . ."

They were standing in a clearing in the forest. They were in the thick of the forest, and yet it was strange. In the moonlight, the things Chris saw confused him, disoriented him even more. Buildings. There was a line of what looked like old brick buildings, like the main street of an old Western town. They were two stories tall, most of them, with crescents rising at the top, or with indentations like a castle battlement. But, in fact, these were only the fronts of the buildings. Their windows were as hollow as the eyeholes of a skull, they went straight through, straight into the black woods behind them. It was just the shell of an old gold rush town left intact for the tourists but to Chris it seemed like the landscape of a nightmare, unreal. With his concussion, his terror, the weirdness of the place, he couldn't put everything together.

"Let's go," said Goldmunsen.

"Wait," said Chris. "Listen. Kennedy . . ."

Casually, Goldmunsen slapped him with the gun. Chris staggered, went down on one knee. The sky, the trees, the buildings wheeled around him. His thoughts scattered like startled crows.

"This guy," said Goldmunsen. "He's just not paying attention. You know?" With a good-natured shake of his head, he clutched a handful of Chris's hair and hauled him to his feet. He prodded him hard in the ribs with the gun barrel. "So now let's go. All right?"

Chris's mind reeled. Everything was confusion and terror. He began to stumble weakly toward the buildings. He began to whimper. "Please. Listen to me. Please. It's a mistake. You have to listen. . . ." He could barely speak, barely make his voice loud enough to be heard. He was whimpering and murmuring as if in prayer. "It was Kennedy. He was doing it the whole time. Kennedy and Kathleen."

"What do you think?" said Goldmunsen behind him. "Think we can still get back before Lucky's closes?"

"I don't know," said Flake. "I can't think at all with this blabbering fuck going. Getting on my nerves. I got a mind to take a blade to him, really take some time about it."

"He was spying on us," whimpered Chris. "Somebody has to believe me. You have to. The whole time. Him and Kathleen. We gotta tell Mr. Hirschorn."

"What blade? What're you talking about?" said Goldmunsen to Flake. "Fuck the blade. I'm hungry. We do this, we go to Lucky's, we get some prime rib. You can take a blade to that."

"Eh," said Flake. "I'm just saying."

"You're always saying. You got sadistical tendencies. I mean it. You should have that looked at."

"Eh."

Chris was remembering now. It was coming back to him. The handheld computer. The e-mail. He found the right words. "He's a detective. That's it," he said under his trembling breath. "Kennedy's a private detective."

He tried to look around but Goldmunsen stuck him with the gun again. "Keep going."

Chris stumbled forward. "No, but listen, Goldmunsen. Flake. Listen. Kennedy's a private detective, that's what I'm trying to tell you."

"Jesus Christ, somebody shut this fuck up already," said Flake.

"Ah, leave him alone," said Goldmunsen. "Think of it from his side."

"I mean it though. I won't be responsible. What the fuck is he saying now?"

"I don't know. He says Kennedy's a detective."

"Oh, right. What're we, idiots?"

"Let him talk."

"He thinks Mr. Hirschorn didn't check him out?"

"He's gotta say something. Leave him the fuck alone."

"Sheezus!" said Flake.

The skull-eyed brick storefronts closed around them. An owl hooted in the woods beyond. Crickets and ciccadas set up a steady chirp all around them. And just as steady now, Chris's whimper ran on.

"No, it's true! Listen, listen. Kennedy's a private detective. Please. He's with an agency. Um . . . Weiss. The Weiss Agency down in San Francisco. It was on his thing, his thing, his machine, his little computer. He sent them an e-mail."

There was a break in the line of buildings, a jagged gap in the brick. Chris stepped through it, prodded by the gun against his spine. Goldmunsen stepped through after him. Flake stepped through.

"Listen to this shit," Flake muttered. Then: "Hey, fuckhead, what're you talking about? What e-mail?"

"Jesus Christ, leave him alone, would you," said Goldmunsen. "You're just tormenting him."

"No, no, I want to hear this," said Flake, amused. "Just how stupid does he think we are? Kennedy sent an e-mail?"

Chris managed to raise his voice a little. "To the Agency. The Weiss Agency. I swear it to God."

"Oh, you swear it to God, huh?" said Flake ironically. "What, he showed you this? You saw this?"

"It was on his handheld."

"Oh right. His handheld. So where's that? Let's see. You show me now."

Chris's terror deepened. His muscles felt like water. Why had he left the handheld behind? How could he have done that? What had he been thinking? "No, but see, I thought, I didn't . . ."

"Oh, oh, you thought, you didn't, you thought," said Flake with a laugh. "You thought what? You thought you'd bullshit us 'cause we're idiots. Listen to this fuck. Can you believe this?"

"Hey, what time you think the kitchen closes at Lucky's?" Goldmunsen wondered aloud.

"What?" said Flake, distracted. "I don't know. Ten? How the fuck should I know? Forget Lucky's. You got your brain in your fucking stomach."

"My brain in my stomach," said Goldmunsen. "Get me some fucking prime rib, I'll put my brain back in my dick where it belongs."

The ghost town fell away behind them. The tree line loured only a few yards before. Chris approached it, step by stumbling step. It was a black maw, a thousand-mile grave, waiting to swallow him. He went on babbling out his story. He hardly knew what he was saying anymore. They wouldn't listen. Everything just kept happening. He couldn't make it stop. His wide eyes darted here and there. Whatever they fell on seemed weirdly sharp and clear. The trees: the trunks, the branches of the trees. The starry indigo of the night. The grass and his feet moving on the grass. And under the pale silver moonglow: an opening into the woods. Waiting to swallow him. A trailhead. The path to his place of execution.

They reached it. Chris wanted to stop. He wanted to turn, to fight—to run, at least—before the woods took him in forever. Instead, he just shuffled miserably down the trail. The forest closed dark and cool around him. It all just kept happening and he couldn't stop it.

"It was Kathleen," he said bitterly, his voice breaking, a line of spittle spilling from the corner of his mouth, tears spilling from his eyes. "It was my wife. She's the one. She was listening. You gotta believe me. She told him everything. That's how he knew."

"This is good," said Goldmunsen after a while. "All right, Chris, you can hold up. This is far enough."

Chris obeyed as if he were hypnotized. He stood there crying, his broad shoulders slumped, his muscular arms hanging limp. Through his tears, he saw the tangled forest. It looked so wonderful to him, so wonderfully real. The air was so cool and crisp and the night so deep. All he wanted out of life just then was more life. The tears and snot ran down his face. He waited to be shot in the back of the head. He babbled, "She went to bed with him, that's what happened. See? He'd fuck her and she'd tell him, that's how he knew. That's how he knew all along. Oh please, please . . ." He began to blubber wordlessly.

Then suddenly, the snap of the Glock behind him as Goldmunsen checked the round in the chamber. Hot piss went down Chris's leg, soaked his jeans. He shook and sobbed.

"Please, please, please, oh, please, I swear to God . . ."

"Wait a minute—what?" muttered Flake.

Goldmunsen hoisted the gun. Pointed it squarely at the nape of Chris's neck.

"Hoh! Hoh, hoh, hoh!" said Flake. "Wait a minute? Did you hear that?"

"Hear what?"

"What he just said. Did he just say what I think he said?"

"I don't know. What did he say?" said Goldmunsen impatiently, pointing the gun. "He said, 'Please, please, please.' What's he gonna say?"

"No, no, no, no, wait, wait, wait," said Flake. "Kennedy was fucking his wife? Is that what he said?"

"I don't know. Who gives a shit? Can I do this already?"

"Hold on a minute, hold on." Flake held up a hand to keep Goldmunsen from firing.

Goldmunsen rolled his eyes. "Shit." He gestured with the gun. "I'm fucking starving here."

"Hey," Flake said to Chris's back. "Hey, asswipe. What're you fucking talking about? Kennedy was fucking your wife, is that what you're saying?"

Chris heaved a breath. He slumped with his mouth open, sobbing hard. Waiting for the gunshot, he stared through his tears, entranced with the beautiful moonlit woods. The seconds were so long he began to hold out hope that one of them would go on forever. "Fucking my wife," he murmured distantly, answering Flake without really knowing he was. "That's how he knew, that's right. That's how he knew."

"So Kennedy's a private detective and he's fucking your wife and she's telling him what you and Mr. Hirschorn are talking about. That's what you're saying," said Flake, leaning forward as if he didn't trust his ears. "That's what you're telling me?"

"We could save the day," Chris whimpered to himself. "We could save . . . Mr. Hirschorn . . . would be happy . . ."

"Hey!" said Flake. He slapped Chris in the back of the head.

Chris thought that was it—the gunshot. He cried out in a high-pitched voice, stumbled forward and fell to his knees, weeping. He was surprised to find he was not yet dead and thought wildly that now they would shoot him again and finish the job and he hoped they'd do it quickly before there was any pain.

"Hey!" said Flake again. He grabbed Chris by the ear. He yanked Chris's head back until the bigger man was staring up at him. The wiry thug sneered down at Chris, his psycho eyes bright. "I'm talking to you, you dipshit. I'm asking you a question. What exactly are you saying here?"

His mouth hanging open, his face smeared with snot and tears, Chris stared up into the killer's corkscrewed features. It took a moment, but then he understood. Flake was listening to him! Flake was listening and Chris was still alive! He gaped at Flake as if he were his loving mother.

"That's right!" he cried out to him through his tears. The cicadas went silent as his voice rose up into the trees. "Kathleen and Kennedy. He's a private detective."

"And he's fucking your wife?"

"He was fucking Kathleen and she was spying on me and Mr. Hirschorn and telling him everything. I saw an e-mail. In his computer. To the Weiss Agency in San Francisco. He said he was in, he was in and I was out, and he was going to find out all about the operation."

Flake took a moment to digest this. Then, with a hard shove, the little man sent Chris sprawling into the dirt. Chris covered his head with his hands. "Please don't. Don't," he said. "I can help, I swear. I can save the day. Please, please."

Flake stared down at him, panting with irritation, considering. Finally, in an outburst of rage, he kicked Chris in the thigh.

Chris shouted in pain. Writhed in the dirt, clutching his leg.

"Fuck!" Flake shouted.

Goldmunsen let his long arms hang down in despair, the gun barrel tapping his thigh. "What?" he said. "You're gonna believe this shit now?"

With his hands on his hips, Flake scowled at the earth. "Fuck, fuck, fuck!"

"Mr. Hirschorn checked Kennedy out," Goldmunsen insisted. "He made sure. He's clean."

"Did you hear this guy? He says Kennedy was fucking his wife," Flake shot back.

"So? So what? Who gives a shit what he says? He'd say anything."

"Not that. He's not gonna say that. Someone's fucking his wife? A guy's not gonna just say that. Would you say that?"

"Oh, come on!" Goldmunsen gestured at the cowering, crying Chris. "Look at him."

Flake glanced at him, disgusted. But he shook his head. "He's not just gonna say that. That another guy's fucking his wife. It's not human nature. He's not just gonna make that up."

Goldmunsen threw his hands in the air. "Oh, Christ. So what's that? What the fuck does that mean?"

Flake jabbed at the dirt with the point of his shoe. "Well, for one thing," he said. "It means you can forget about going to Lucky's."

FORTY-NINE

"Man oh man oh man," said Bishop again.

He came forward slowly into the big shed. His eyes traveled inch by inch over the machine where it squatted stark and vicious under the fluorescent lights.

"Is she beautiful or is she beautiful?" said Hirschorn behind him, smiling.

Bishop didn't answer. But *beautiful* was not the word. Out here in the middle of this forest wilderness, what it looked like more than anything was some sort of enormous locust, some sort of cosmic monster insect bristling with malice to suit its size. The crew station windshield, dead-eyed with the reflection of the night, seemed to watch him warily as he approached. The great drooping main rotors and the short, stiff wings seemed, even in repose, as if they could lift the thing at any second into a ferocious attack.

It had been a long time since Bishop had stood up close to one of these: an Apache Longbow AH-64D—an army attack chopper. Complete, he noticed, with missiles. Fucking missiles. Four of a possible eight Hellfire fire-and-forget air-to-ground missiles under each wing. Not to mention the 30 mm automatic chain gun sticking out like a Stinger from under the fuselage.

Bishop stood up by the nose. Still gripping his traveling bag in his left hand, he lifted his right and laid it gently on the cool armor. He shook his head a little. It must've cost Hirschorn millions to get this, taken him weeks to smuggle it in here. He glanced back—with some admiration—at the silver-haired gangster in the shadows beyond the shed lights.

"What are you, Hirschorn, some kind of terrorist?" he asked quietly.

The smaller man's body stiffened. "Hey, hey, hey. Careful who you're talking to. I'm a hundred-percent American, all the way."

"Well, then, if you don't mind my asking, what the fuck do you want with one of these?"

Hirschorn relaxed, laughed again. "Patience, my friend. It'll all be made clear to you. A simple mission, out and back. And I'll be right there with you all the way."

"Simple," Bishop echoed. He looked at the helo again, that tongue-in-cheek expression on his face. "Mind if I check out the cockpit?"

"Not at all," said Hirschorn expansively. "Go ahead. I want you to be comfortable with it."

Bishop did not let go of his traveling bag but swung it up onto one wing. Then he hoisted himself after it. Popped the hatch. He tossed the bag ahead of him onto the floor by the cyclic. Lowered himself into the raised backseat—the pilot's seat. He closed the hatch after him. And sat there a moment, looking out through the windshield at the gunmen's flashlight beams, at the silhouette of Hirschorn with the black forest hunkering behind him.

"Jesus H. Christ," he said aloud. "Jesus H. Christ."

Another man's heart might have misgiven him now. Another man might've asked himself: What the hell had he gotten himself into—and in the middle of nowhere too? But Bishop was calm, even confident. Whatever "out and back mission" they were planning to pull off with this flying war machine of theirs, he figured he'd already scuttled it—for tonight anyway. He was the only pilot they had on hand and, say what you will about the man, they could shoot him dead before he'd take this thing up into his home skies. Trouble was, if he refused, or if he flew it off in the wrong direction, they actually *would* shoot him dead. So what he really needed to do right now was get the fiddling fuck out of here and let someone know where this monster was hiding.

Of course that wasn't going to be so easy with these two machine gunners watching him—plus whoever else was stationed around the camp. So, cool as he was, just in case, Bishop lowered his hand—already beneath the eyeline of the thugs outside—down to his traveling bag. He began to work the zipper open. As he did, he scanned the helo's systems. He noticed they were incomplete. Wherever they'd bought or stolen this from, they hadn't managed to get the full warfare suite, the radar warning, jammer, the infrared countermeasures and so on. But the GPS seemed to be intact, plus the TADS and FLIR for easy targeting. It looked like they were really planning to go after something with those Hellfires.

"Jesus H. Christ."

The bag was open. Bishop's hand slipped into it. He found his handheld, drew it out. He nestled it in his crotch, turned it on. But he also kept moving his head back and forth, stretching his free hand out over the systems. Making a show, in other words, of examining the controls and whatnot. He figured Hirschorn was proud enough of his baby here to have a little patience while he checked it out.

As soon as his handheld came on, he worked it to the e-mail with one fingertip. It was the first time he saw that he'd forgotten to send his last e-mail to Weiss. The realization jolted him a little. He cursed Kathleen in his heart for distracting him from his business. Now even Weiss didn't know he was out here.

But on the other hand, having the letter there sped things up a little. He opened the e-mail on the screen.

Weiss. It worked. Wannamaker's out. I'm in. Six tonight, I fly to some secret location out in the forest somewhere. Once I arrive, they'll give me the details of the job. Soon as I know what's what, I'll make contact. With luck, we should be able to break it up without compromising . . .

With the smallest movements he could make, he tapped the keys with his fingernail and added:

a150kmnwah-64d

That was all he had time for. He saw Hirschorn wave him out with a grand gesture.

"Come on, Kennedy! You'll have all the time to play with her you want. We have work to do."

Bishop closed the e-mail and pressed *send*. There was a pause—a long pause it seemed like—as Hirschorn stood outside waiting for him to come down. Then a message began blinking up from the handheld: *waiting for signal . . . waiting for signal . . .* That was that. Bishop knew it would wait forever out here in this wilderness. It would keep trying to send the e-mail until its batteries died.

He set the handheld on the floor. Shoved it under the seat out of sight, well hidden. Still trying to send.

A moment later, he stepped down from the aircraft with the traveling bag in his hand again. He walked back to Hirschorn while the two gunmen looked on.

"Just wanted to get a feel for her," he said.

"Oh you will," said Hirschorn. He slapped him on the shoulder. Smiling with his bright teeth. Feeling good. "Believe me. You will. Chase, show Mr. Kennedy to his quarters."

Chase was one of the gunmen. He stepped up to Bishop and made a gesture with his Stinger, holding his HK lightly with his left hand.

"After you," he said in a deep rasp.

Bishop started walking. Hirschorn and the other gunman stayed behind to shut off the lights in the chopper shed and close the doors.

Bishop moved slowly through the trees with Chase behind him tracing the path with his flash. Chase knew what he was doing and stayed too far back for Bishop to turn on him. Bishop was thinking about that, about turning on him, getting his weapon, heading for the trees. If he could get to the Cessna, he could jump her engine, fly her back to town. Warn the cops about the Apache. But Chase was too cautious, too alert. Bishop had to wait.

So he moved on through the trees by the Stinger light, made his way toward the other building, the two-story barracks with the stairs on the side. He was still cool, still more or less easy in his mind. He figured it was all right to wait for a better shot at escape. He figured he still had time.

As long as Chris was dead, as long as they'd shot him before he'd come around and told his story, Bishop figured he still had plenty of time.

FIFTY

At this point, Weiss stepped into the Agency offices, and he knew right away that something was wrong. His racing mind went quiet, wary. He paused in the doorway, watched the dark.

The shop was closed up for the night—it was after eight. All the lights were off. All the rooms were silent. Still, Weiss had a sense—that cop sense again—that he wasn't alone in here.

The big man moved lightly when he wanted to. He trod down the hallway without making a sound. He approached the little nook that was our mailroom. In the city glow coming in through the windows, he could make out the dinosaur shadows of the copying machine and the fax. And there was my desk on one side. And there was me, in fact, collapsed on top of it.

Weiss slowed when he saw me. He found the light switch, flicked it up. Now he could see: I was seated in my chair, unconscious, my head on the desktop buried in my arms. A look of annoyance passed over Weiss's face. His thoughts—his effort to outguess the Shadowman—had been interrupted. He sighed. Collared the bottle of J&B standing by my elbow. He lifted it, looked it over. Not even half-gone. Well, he figured I probably wasn't quite dead yet. So he shook me roughly by the shoulder.

"He's clean!" I shouted, sitting up suddenly, blinking wildly in the light.

He waved the bottle at me. "I taught you better than to drink this blended shit."

I gaped at him. Weiss? Hey, what do you know, it was Weiss. "Weiss!" I said groggily. I squinted at the bottle. "No, no, no, iz okay. I'm done."

"Yeah, you're pretty done all right. I'd say you're well-done."

"All finished, I just thought I'd . . ." I tried to think what it was I just thought I'd do.

"Pass out at your desk?" Weiss suggested. "That's good, we encourage that. It gives the agency a certain flair."

I let out an idiotic laugh, waving in my seat like a cornstalk in the wind. What a great guy that Weiss was. Wonderful, wonderful guy. What the fuck was he talking about, I wondered. Must be some kind of thing.

"I checked him out," I tried to explain to him. I blinked some more. "Wrote my report. He's good, he's clean."

Weiss set the bottle back on my desk with a clunk. "This is the Strawberry case we're discussing here?"

"Yeah." I dragged my two hands over my face, trying to polish my brain. "The priest. The governor's brother."

Weiss lifted his chin. It was beginning to fall into place for him. "And he's clean. His testimony checks out. That's what you're saying."

"Oh yeah," I said, waving my hand so broadly I almost spilled over. "O-o-oh yeah. Way clean. Way checks out."

"Uh-huh." Weiss nodded. He picked a sheaf of papers up off my desk. "It's all in your report, right?"

"Absolutely. All in my report. Right there, smack in that report. Yesiree-bobbo."

Weiss checked his watch. Blustered. "All right, Bobbo, you've got about twenty minutes before you start puking your guts out. What-say you give the cleaning lady a break and just sort of mosey on home."

I moseyed. No easy task. Just getting up from my desk was no easy task. Weiss stood in the hallway watching me wend my way to the door. I shuffled nice and slow but I still brushed my shoulder against first one wall and then the other, finally tilting over completely so that I had to push off a picture frame to right myself again.

Weiss stood and watched me go. Holding my report in one hand, tapping its pages against the other. He smiled with one corner of his mouth. He snorted. He felt a little disappointed in me. He had thought I was sharp, showed promise. He had figured for sure I would catch that bit about Strawberry's bald spot, find out where the priest had really been standing when he witnessed our client shooting Mars. Probably the good father was in some girl's apartment, that was his guess. Or some guy's, if it came to that, this being San Fran. Anyway, he'd have to tell Sissy in the morning I'd screwed up my first investigation. She'd have to check the witness statement herself, find out what the real story was.

I managed to open the door. Managed to weave my way through it. Managed to stumble down the hall, tumble into the elevator. I rode down with my head resting against the elevator wall. My eyes slipped shut, jerked open as the darkness started spinning. The elevator landed. I spilled out into the lobby. Staggered headlong to the door like a man pushing against a strong wind. I shouldered my way out onto the misty streets of the city.

Head down, hands in my pockets, I shuffled across Market. Headlights pierced the thin rain. The spark and rattle of a streetcar jarred against the steady whisper of traffic. I left the busy avenue behind, headed up the darker side street. There was darkness in my gut as well. The whiskey dulled my feelings, but not enough, not half-enough. I don't think I actually sensed Weiss's disappointment, but I didn't need to. I was plenty disappointed on my own. More than that. I was disgusted with myself. With my weakness and my nice morality. Letting Father O'Mara off the hook like that, lying for him, clearing him like that. I had failed miserably as a hard-nosed private eye. I had hoped, when I started drinking that night, that it would dull my shame in that. But it hadn't. I thought I would never forgive myself.

With bitter, sentimental self-pity, I turned and cast what I imagined was a final farewell glance up at the Agency, the eighth floor of the concrete tower with the red mansard roof. I still remember what

I saw there. I don't suppose I'll ever forget. It was Weiss. Framed massive in the massive arched window. Standing with his hands in his pockets, looking down on the city, on the traffic, on the pedestrians passing beneath him, the people hurrying off into the night and their mysterious lives. The computer must've been on at his desk because most of the room was dark but there was a white glow and it cast him into partial silhouette. In my hazy state, I even thought I could make out some of his features, some of his ugly, sagging, sorrowful and compassionate face. I thought I could see the glint of his eyes as they peered down intently through the churning mist.

I paused there, looking up at him, at his looming, brooding stillness. Even in the toils of my self-loathing, I felt a fierce thrill of admiration for him, and felt with it a dim glimmer of inspiration rekindle in me, a dimly remembered idea I mean of the kind of man I wanted one day to be.

After a long moment, I turned away and headed off into the darkness.

And with that I pass from this story and good riddance to me. But as I staggered home to puke massively and collapse on the bathroom floor, that fierce feeling of admiration remained and made my heart warm with excitement. I didn't know it at the time, of course, but looking back, I think I must've somehow intuitively understood that Weiss as I had just seen him, right then, right there, so perfectly motionless in the big arched window, was actually operating at his very highest level, at his most ferociously just and unstoppable. That was the man at his best: right then, right there, so perfectly motionless—and yet in fact, as I found out later, hot on the trail of the Shadowman.

FIFTY-ONE

They came for Kathleen not too long after that, almost nine o'clock. She was in the den at the back of the house. She was slumped on the sofa, staring at the TV. She'd been doing that, staring at the TV, for the last two hours. Eating Cheez Doodles out of a plastic bowl, drinking Budweiser out of the bottle. Lighting Marlboros and snuffing them halfway through in the ashtray she held loosely at her waist. She barely knew what show she was watching.

Too much garbage in her head, that's why. Too much crud and blackness in her heart. Kennedy and how he'd tricked her, how he'd dumped her. Chris and the thugs who were looking for him. Hirschorn. She was disgusted with the lot of them. How the hell had her life come down to this shit? She was disgusted with the whole fucking thing.

She was disgusted, but she wasn't afraid, not yet. Kennedy had warned her but that was crap, she didn't take that seriously at all. The thugs had come and gone already. They were looking for Chris, not her. She figured they would work Chris over a little for drinking too much, talking too much. Served him right. And Kennedy—he was the one who ought to be scared. When Hirschorn found out Kennedy was a cop . . . well, it served him right too, whatever happened. The hell with him. With all of them. She didn't care.

She stared at the TV. Drinking her beer, lighting her cigarettes and snuffing them out. Some sort of game show was on now. One of those shows where they did outrageous things to the contestants. Now they were dumping a bucket of snakes onto this one woman. If she could endure it, she would win some money. *What the hell was so hard about that?* Kathleen thought. That woman would probably stick her head in a bucket of shit if you gave her enough money. Fuck her if that was all she cared about. Idiot bitch.

She thought of changing the channel but she couldn't be bothered. She went on staring at the show. Where she was, at the back of the house, of course, she didn't see the sleek, dark car pull up to the curb outside. She didn't hear her own front door open. She didn't even hear the footsteps coming down the hall until the last minute. Then she glanced around and saw her husband moving into the doorway.

Startled, she sat up straight. Jesus, he looked bad. Really bad. Gray-faced, crazy-eyed. There was a dark patch just drying on his pants—and was that the smell of piss on him?

She had just lit up another cigarette. She quickly screwed it into the ashtray, set the tray on the coffee table. She found the remote on the cushion against her thigh. Pressed the MUTE button. The sound on the TV went off.

"Hey, Chris," she said uncertainly.

The windows were open to let the smoke out, to let the night air in. With the TV silent—just some bland fathead on the screen flapping his grin now—she could hear the noises of the backyard and the neighborhood. The crickets, the O'Connors' yapping rat of a Chihuahua, the thump of a plastic garbage can lid at the Paynters' house next door.

Chris stood another long second, kind of unsteady and wavering, kind of smiling in this eerie, distant way.

"You okay?" she asked him.

"Yeah," he said finally. His tone of voice was eerie too. Small and dreamy. "Yeah, I'm okay. I'm fine. But we gotta go now, Kathleen."

"Go? Where the hell we gotta go?" She looked at her watch. "It's, like, nine o'clock . . ."

"I know," he said in that same voice. "But we gotta. Mr. Hirschorn says we won't be safe here. He's sent some guys to take us.

They're gonna take us to where it's safe until all this is over."

"All . . . ? Chris, what're you talking about, I don't get it, all . . . ?"

And then she knew they were going to kill her.

The fathead on the TV went on talking and grinning with glittery eyes and the crickets outside went on chirping and that goddamn little Chihuahua dog went on yapping and maybe there was a footstep in the backyard grass that tipped her off or maybe it was just the weird way Chris was talking but all of a sudden she just knew that the men in the BMW were here. She knew they were going to take her away, take her into the woods somewhere. When she was found her hair would be matted with blood around the hole where the bullet went in. Her face would be half in the dirt with leaves and twigs sticking to it.

And here was Chris. That was the part that sucked, really sucked. Chris had come to give her over to them. Her own loving husband. He was here to coax her outside so she would go quietly, so the neighbors wouldn't know what was happening and there wouldn't be a fuss. She didn't think anything could hurt her anymore but that hurt her. That made her sick just about to death. She was his own wife and she didn't mean shit to him. He'd just hand her over. Like the game show, for money. Anyone would do anything for money in the end. Nobody meant shit to anyone.

She stood up—stood up slowly, even as she felt everything inside her sinking down, caving in.

"Jesus, Chris," she said.

"We have to go now," her husband told her dreamily. "Mr. Hirschorn sent some guys to take us."

Hot tears welled in her eyes. "I mean, Jesus. What're you doing?"

"Come on, Kathleen," he said. "It's all right. No one'll hurt you. We have to go."

She flung herself at him. She cried out in her rage and despair and tried to hit him with both fists at once. When he grabbed her wrists, she tried to claw at him with her fingernails, to tear his cheeks. She was sobbing and her tears burned her eyes like acid. Somehow her despair and her fury made her tears burn.

Chris wrapped his powerful arms around her. He held her close. She couldn't get free to strike at him again. She struggled and twisted. She smelled his rancid sweat and his urine and some other smell she didn't know that was rank and dead and awful. She struggled—and then finally she collapsed against him. She pressed her face against his chest and sobbed. He put a hand on the back of her head and patted her gently. He kissed her hair.

"It's all right," he said in the same strange tone. "We just have to go away for a while. It's no problem. No one'll hurt you. It's just until all this is over."

Kathleen sobbed into his shirt. "Oh, Chris," she said. "Oh, Chris."

"Come on now," said Chris. "It's all right. Really." He guided her to the door of the den.

Behind them, a commercial had come on the TV. Dad was home for dinner and Mom was putting a hearty bowl of soup on the table for him and one for Junior and one for smiling Sis as well. It was all in silence, only the crickets for a sound track and the yapping Chihuahua and Kathleen's sobs against her husband's chest.

Chris led her out of the den into the hallway and the men were there. Flake had come in through the back, through the kitchen, and Goldmunsen through the front. That way they had both ends of the hall blocked off in case she tried to run for it.

But she didn't run for it. She didn't give a shit what happened anymore. Why should she? She let Chris take her down the hall. Out the door. Into the warm night. She balked a little at the sight of the BMW. The sleek, dark car. She hesitated a little when she saw it, trying to hold up on the front path of her house. It was just so horrible somehow, the car and the way Chris was leading her to it with his arm around her. She tried to stop but he kept his grip on her. He drew her gently but firmly on.

"It's all right, Kathleen," he said dreamily.

The three men put her into the car and they drove away with her and she didn't care anymore what happened.

FIFTY-TWO

Out in the forest, meanwhile, Bishop waited for his chance at the man with the gun. They were in the barracks now, in the room on the second floor. It was a long room, without much in it. A couple of air mattresses. A square card table. Chairs. A bare bulb that hung down from a wire.

Chase, the gunman, sat at the card table, tilted back in one of the chairs. The bulb sent a circle of glare down over him, cast him in stark light, dark shadow. He was a squat powerhouse of a man. His torso was the shape of an upside-down triangle and his head was like a boulder perched on top of it. He never took his meaty hands off his HK. He never took his beady eyes off Bishop.

Bishop was facing him, leaning against the opposite wall, his leg bent back, his foot pressed flat against the wall's surface. His hand rested lightly against his midsection and a wisp of smoke trailed up from the cigarette he held between his fingers. He was thinking, wondering. Wondering what a mutt like Hirschorn was planning to do with an attack helo. Wondering if he could get out of here in time to stop him. Wondering if he'd have to kill this Chase guy when he got the chance and made his move.

After a while, he pushed off the wall. Strolled over to one of the two windows. He drew the blind aside a little. Peeked out into the night. The second gunman, a black man, six-foot-four, was standing guard outside the ground-level door. There was some kind of meeting going on down there, it sounded like. Bishop could hear voices coming up through the floor. He could make out Hirschorn's voice and at least two others. Which meant there were probably at least four gunmen in all. Whatever he did up here, it was going to have to be quick and quiet so as not to alert the whole gang of them.

He let the blind slip shut again. Let his eyes wander around the steel box of a room. There was only one door. It led to the stairway outside. The stairway led down to where the black gunman was posted. There was no way to get around him. It was a nice little puzzle.

He glanced over at Chase.

"How about I step out on the stairs and get a breath?" he said.

"How about you don't," said Chase in his deep monotone rasp. "How about you just breathe in here." He rocked back and forth on the hind legs of his chair. He never took his eyes off Bishop.

Bishop strolled toward him. Chase watched him with a thin bouldery smile on his big bouldery face. It amused him to think that Bishop might make a play.

"What the hell is this?" Bishop said. "Am I a prisoner here?"

"Only in the sense that if you try to leave the room I'll kill you," said Chase.

"Oh," said Bishop. "For a minute there, I was starting to get worried."

He turned before he came within reach of the gunman. No way to angle in on him with him as watchful as that. He strolled to the other side of the card table. Chase's eyes followed him and his gun barrel followed him.

"To tell the truth, I don't think killing me's all that smart," Bishop said.

"Hey, don't criticise my ideas," said Chase. "It damages my self-esteem."

Bishop came around behind the chair across from him. He put his hands on the back of it. He wondered if he was fast enough to lift it, swing it at the guy's head. He might've been, but he thought Chase would probably shoot him dead if he tried it. Which seemed a major drawback to the plan.

"I mean, it'd be kind of tough for your boy Hirschorn to find a new pilot on such short notice, wouldn't it?" he said.

"Yeah," said Chase. "But it'd be kind of tough for you to come back to life too."

"I see your point." Instead of swinging the chair, Bishop pulled it from under the table and sat on it. He shuffled his cigarette pack out of his T-shirt pocket and tossed it down on the tabletop. "Help yourself," he said. He thought if Chase reached for the pack, he might be able to break his arm, then his neck.

But Chase didn't reach for it. His bouldery smile grew wider. "Hey, you know what I think?" he said.

Bishop considered the question. "No," he said then. "What do you think?"

"I think you're looking for ways to take me."

"Really?"

"I do."

"That's startling. Why would I?"

"Hey, don't ask me," rasped Chase. "If you're smart, you'll just sit tight and smoke your cigarettes. Give yourself cancer—you'll live longer."

Bishop smiled himself a little. Lifted the last of his smoke into the smile and sucked the flame down to the filter. Then he dropped what was left to the floor, twisted his shoe on the ember, crushed it out. All in all, he thought, yes, he might well have to kill this guy. The gunman was too good to take a chance on.

The two men's eyes met across the card table. Chase knew what Bishop was thinking. He knew and it didn't stop him from smiling. Which probably wasn't a good sign.

But no matter. Whatever Bishop was planning, he didn't get to pull it off, not just then. Because just then, there was a sound outside, a rhythmic beating of the air. A chopper, a little Jet Ranger or something by the sound of it. Coming in close and low. Too close, too low. It had to be landing on the nearby runway.

"You expecting someone?" Bishop asked.

Chase didn't answer. He didn't have to. Bishop could read his expression: He was surprised.

Bishop's mind raced. Who would show up here unexpected? The

helo sounded too dinky to belong to the cops. No one else would be able to find this place. And that meant it must be one of Hirschorn's friendlies. And that meant they were bringing news, surprising news that couldn't wait.

And that meant Chris must've woken up, must've gotten his chance to tell them who "Frank Kennedy" really was, what he'd been up to.

And that meant, finally, that Bishop's time had just run out.

FIFTY-THREE

Weiss went on standing at the big arched window, went on looking down at the misty city. Hands in his pockets, shoulders low, chin sunk nearly to his chest. He let his eyes follow the slow progress of a motorcycle as it wove its way through an intersection thick with cars.

A pale white light played over the room behind him. The computer was on at his desk. There had been no e-mail from Bishop. The long silence was like fuel on the fire of urgency in him. Knowing Bishop, it meant he was out of touch. Which probably meant that, against Weiss's specific instructions, he had worked his way into Hirschorn's confidence and was moving toward the heart of his operation. *Whatever they're planning, it's going down soon. Time's short, I'm doing my best. JB.*

Time's short. But how short? And what were they planning? And what the hell did it have to do with Whip Pomeroy, with Julie Wyant, with the Shadowman?

Weiss stood at the window, stood still, looked down. He watched a man in a black raincoat as he walked swiftly along the sidewalk. The man came under a streetlight haloed in mist. His figure was etched clearly for a moment, hunched against the rain. Then he was gone into the haze and darkness. Weiss stood gazing at the place where he had been.

His mind wandered back to that moment in the car, that moment when he had felt the presence of the Shadowman, felt the poison in him, felt the logic of his monstrous rage. He remembered what Bishop had said about Hirschorn, how he had left *a lot of dead bodies on his way to the top.* What if it had been the Shadowman who arranged for those bodies to become dead? What if Hirschorn owed the Shadowman something—or owed him everything? And feared him, as anyone would fear him? What if the Shadowman had called in his debts? It would be the nightmare of Hirschorn's life. Hirschorn would probably do anything to make the hit man go away again.

But what? What had the Shadowman wanted him to do?

Weiss let his thoughts play over it. Pomeroy. Whip Pomeroy was the key. Pomeroy with his secret: Julie Wyant's new identity, her name. Pomeroy, who had overheard the Shadowman's humiliation. Weiss knew the Shadowman would have to kill Pomeroy for that. Torture him to find out about Julie and then kill him because he had overheard. Pomeroy knew it too. He knew it and was so terrified he was willing to barter away his clients' identities if the law would only keep him locked up in the most secure prison in the country—and then he was still terrified. *Nothing stops him in the end. Nothing. Ever . . . You can't protect me. You can't protect her. You can't protect anyone.*

Weiss made a soft noise, his head moving slightly. His focus shifted upward from the people and the traffic on the street below. He saw instead the mist coiling and turning above them. *No one can protect me.* It was ridiculous, he thought. North Wilderness SHU was impregnable. If the Shadowman, if anyone, could get close enough to Pomeroy to make him tell his secret, well, then Weiss was king of Romania.

And yet . . . And yet he felt that rage, that poison, that unstoppable rage. Rage itself in love. What wouldn't it do? Weiss peered down into the mist and thought; *Rage. Rage in love.*

And so he began to consider. If it could be done, how could it be done? If your rage and your love compelled you. If Julie had to be found. If Pomeroy had to die. It was a complicated thing. You couldn't just bribe a guard or another prisoner to take Pomeroy down. No. You'd need access, real access, real time to work the secret out of him. You'd have to look in the man's eyes for yourself and know when he was finally telling the truth.

Weiss frowned into the night, unseeing now. The easiest way

would be to threaten Pomeroy's family, his friends, let him know you would hurt them if he didn't give over. But that was no good. Weiss remembered what Ketchum had said. *Moncrieff was the only friend he had, the only anything he had, family, friend, anything.*

Weiss's big chest lifted on a breath. Then there was only one other solution. The Shadowman would have to get into the prison himself. He would have to get a job there as a guard or something. But even as the thought occurred to him, Weiss gave a small shake of his head. He remembered reading that the North Wilderness guards were specially chosen. They needed years of experience, extra months of training. You could fake the credentials but not the references, the recognition. It would take too long, be far too uncertain.

"Ach," he said softly. The whole thing was impossible. A crazy idea, just Pomeroy's paranoia.

But that rage. That poison he had felt in the car. The logic of that rage. He stood with his hands in his pockets, unmoving. He came back to himself, focused on the mist again. He stared down into that swirling, shifting mist. Saw the silhouettes and shadows moving underneath it, the lights, ringed and rainbowed, breaking through.

The image of Julie came to him. Those deep and distant, dreaming eyes. That beckoning gesture from the computer screen. For a moment, he was with her by the Golden Gate, watching in suspense as she ditched her car, put on her wig, picked up the new car, the new papers Pomeroy must've arranged for her.

And now he was with Pomeroy in his prison cell. Waiting, afraid.

And now he was with the Shadowman. That rage . . .

There was only one other way into that prison, he thought. The easiest way. The surest way. The way everyone else got in.

Finally, Weiss raised his eyes, raised them until he was gazing, not outside anymore, but into his own reflection.

"For fuck's sake," he whispered.

Then, quickly, he turned away from the night-blackened window and moved into the glow of his computer.

FIFTY-FOUR

Now there were noises outside. Voices calling. A gruff reply. Bishop got to his feet again.

Chase, tilted back in his chair, tightened his grip on the machine gun. "Stay where you are," he rasped.

Bishop ignored him. He went back to the window. Looked out through the blinds.

There they were. Approaching the buildings through the trees. Chris and Kathleen. Hirschorn's asssistant, Alex Wellman, with the flashlight. And the two goons, Bishop's old pals Goldmunsen and Flake, shepherding them from behind.

The black gunman was waiting to meet them by the barracks. And now Hirschorn stepped through the door to meet them too. Two more gunmen, complete with fatigues and machine guns, followed him out. He flung gestures at them this way and that, and they hurried away, out of Bishop's line of vision. Hirschorn continued forward to meet the others.

Chris was already moving his hands, talking fast as Hirschorn approached him. His voice drifted up clearly to the room above. Almost at once, Bishop heard his false name spoken: Kennedy. So that was it. The certainty dropped like a stone in his belly. It was over. His cover was blown.

Bishop figured it would take Chris maybe two minutes to convince Hirschorn of the truth. Maybe only ninety seconds. Twenty seconds after that, they'd be on their way up here to kick his head in by way of interrogation. Or maybe they'd just shoot him dead, who could say. Either way, it seemed like a good time to get out of here.

That cold blood of his came in handy now. He somehow managed to turn smoothly from the window. He somehow managed to play it easy and calm.

"Just reinforcements, it looks like," he said. His voice was as relaxed as that. "What the hell are you boys planning tonight, an invasion?"

"Just sit back down," said Chase quietly. He kept the barrel of the HK rock steady, trained on Bishop's chest.

Bishop shrugged. Outside, Chris was telling the whole story. How Bishop had seduced Kathleen, how she'd eavesdropped on them, whatever else he knew. Right this minute, the truth of it all was slowly dawning on Hirschorn, everything was suddenly making sense to him. Bishop knew that—and all the same, he strolled back to his chair as casually as he'd strolled to the window. The barrel of Chase's machine gun followed him every step of the way.

Bishop reached his chair. Did he have a minute left? Forty-five seconds? Less? He sat down with a casual sigh. Any moment, he would hear the footsteps coming up the stairs. Any moment, the door would burst in . . . He smiled at Chase with one side of his mouth.

"You look tense, son," he said quietly. "You ought to . . ."

And as Chase listened to hear whatever smart-ass remark Bishop was about to make, Bishop shoved the card table at him, hard. The massive gunman, his chair tilted, flew backwards, arms and legs wheeling, hands flailing for purchase. The table, the chair, the gunman—all went down to the floor together. Bishop had to fling the table aside to get at the man. In that single instant, Chase wrapped his hands around his gun again, opened his mouth to let out a roar.

Bishop hammered down on top of him. Drove the weapon against his chest with his knee. Pincered the front of his throat with one hand. Chase made one soft, strangled sound—and that was all, it was finished. The pincer of Bishop's hand snapped shut. His arm pistoned back with brutal swiftness. A bloody chunk of the gunman's throat and a section of his esophagus were ripped away.

Chase's body arched like a bow then fell back spasming. Bishop knelt on him while he thrashed. It took only moments. Then the gunman flopped against the floor, a corpse. With a grimace of disgust, Bishop flung the piece of his windpipe down beside him.

He climbed off the dead man. Took his gun—worked the strap of it over his head and shoulders. Only a fifteen-round magazine. He ran his hands over the still form, looking for a reload. There was none.

He stood up, the weapon in his hand. Listened. Nothing. No footsteps on the stairs. Not yet. The whole thing—knocking Chase over, killing him—had taken maybe ten seconds all told. Aside from the soft thump of the gunman falling, the mild clatter of the lightweight card table and folding chair, there had hardly been any noise to it at all.

Now, moving quickly, Bishop returned to the window. He pressed against the wall. Peeked out through the edge of the blind. Moving slightly side to side, he could make out the scene below. Chris had been driven to his knees somehow. He was kneeling on the ground, hanging his head. Kathleen was held fast by the hatchet-faced thug, limp in the grip of his ape-long arms. And Hirschorn . . . Even at this distance, even in the forest shadows, Bishop could see: The man had gone deathly pale. He knew.

"What a cluster fuck, it's a cluster fuck!" he heard Hirschorn shouting. The criminal's hand went up through his coiffed silver hair. Those handsome chiseled features seemed slack and lifeless. He was angry at what Chris had told him. He was angry—and he was afraid.

Suddenly, he looked up—looked up at the window. Bishop pulled back quickly, pressed against the wall, gripping the HK close to his chest. He took a glance over one shoulder at the door. No way out there. He'd be stepping right into the line of fire. Carefully, pressing his head tight to the wall again, he peeked out again through the blind.

Hirschorn was looking down at the kneeling Chris. His pale features were growing dark red with fury. He snarled. He slapped Chris hard across the side of his head. Chris cowered, weakly lifting his arms to shield himself.

Hirschorn sneered. "Looks like you'll get your chance to fly after all," he said. "Ya dumb fuck."

Bishop heard Chris answer through tears. "I will, I swear, I swear I'll . . ."

Hirschorn hit him again. "Shut up." His compact frame rose and fell with a breath. He lifted his chin at his assistant, Wellman. "Take him inside."

The slender factotum reached down. He took Chris under the armpit. He was too slight to actually lift the bigger man but just his touch was enough: Chris lumbered to his feet, keeping his head hung down. The two men moved together toward the building.

Hirschorn, disgusted, spat on the earth. He ran his fingers through his hair again. Bishop, watching from above, could almost smell the man's fear. *This associate of mine has exacting standards.* Whatever mission he was supposed to accomplish for this associate, there was no room in it for failure or delay.

Hirschorn glanced at Goldmunsen where he held Kathleen. He glanced at Flake, who stood bouncing on his toes. He took a breath, trying to gather himself. "All right," he said, more quietly now. "Take this little cunt to the swamp. And just do her, don't diddle with her, understand? Then come right back here. Give him the flash."

This last was to the black gunman, who handed his Stinger over to Flake. Goldmunsen, meanwhile, slung Kathleen around and gave her a push to start her walking. Her movements were limp and sullen. The big thug had to shove her again and then again to keep her shuffling forward into the woods. Flake shimmered off just behind them, lighting the way.

Bishop stood there—could only stand there, pressed to the wall, could only watch as Kathleen was taken into the forest, into the darkness. Out of sight.

When they were gone, Hirschorn lifted his chin at the black gunman. "Go take care of that son of a bitch upstairs," he said. "And make it quick. We've gotta get this show on the road."

The black gunman moved to the stairway. Bishop pulled back again, hard against the wall.

"Jesus," he heard Hirschorn mutter. "What a cluster fuck!"

Then there came the heavy footsteps, charging up the stairs. Then the black gunman burst through the door.

FIFTY-FIVE

The black gunman burst through the door and Bishop shot him. He pulled the trigger twice, three bursts each, and the man sat down against the doorframe, dead.

Bishop was already moving as his target fell. Leaping over the body. Stepping out onto the stairs.

It was bad out there. The shots had been heard, the killing had been spotted. The other two gunmen were coming for him through the trees. One came from the chopper shed to his left, one from the deeper forest to his right. Both were in full charge, swinging their weapons toward him.

Bishop grabbed hold of the stairway railing. The gunmen opened fire at him. He vaulted over the railing into the air. The stuttering blasts cut through the night as he sailed down into darkness. He hit the ground. Dropped, rolling, blind. Bullets thudded and sang against the steel walls of the house beside him. Bishop jumped up, fired a wild burst at his attackers and ran.

He was around the corner of the building, among the trees at once. Breaking back and forth as he ran, dodging for cover behind the oaks and pines. He lost the moon, the light, could hardly see. Stinger beams pierced the tangled vines and branches, crisscrossed all around him. There were shouts. Another stuttering burst of gunfire. Tree bark spat against his face as a bullet sent it flying. He heard— felt—the ground kick up too near his feet. He dropped to the dirt again, rolled again, flattened. Prone, he let off another three-round burst. He saw the shadow of a guman duck among the forest shadows. Then suddenly, a flashlight pinned him where he lay. He fired at it. The beam rolled up crazily over the woods, vanished into the sky.

He seized the moment of confusion. Was up again, running through the dark. He tried to let off a rearguard burst but that was it for the magazine. The HK was spent. He cursed and tossed the weapon away. Ran, lifting his feet high, trying not to trip, stumble, go down.

He heard more shouting behind him but it was farther away now and fading even farther. They didn't know he was out of bullets so no one was in a big hurry to follow him into the forest. With luck, he could beat them to the plane. Get out of here, spread the word about the helo.

He ran. But something nagged at him. Kathleen. Out there somewhere behind him. With Goldmunsen, with Flake. They were taking her to a swamp. They were going to put a bullet in the back of her head. Bishop didn't have much in the way of an imagination but he could imagine that. He could see her lying facedown, trailing blood and brains into the murky water.

Still, what was he supposed to do? He'd warned her to get out, hadn't he? He'd told her things were going bad, that she had to save herself. His conscience was satisfied on that point. Whatever code he lived by was fulfilled. It wasn't as if he was going to turn around and go back for her. He couldn't. Not the way he saw it. He had to get to the Cessna. He had to stop the helo, make sure Hirschorn went down. That was his assignment. Kathleen was not his assignment.

What the hell? he thought. She was probably already dead anyway. Her body was probably already facedown in the swamp.

He pictured that—that body he had held—and he ran on, dodging quickly through the dark wood.

FIFTY-SIX

Weiss by then had almost found what he was looking for. Sitting in his dark office at his computer with only the monitor-shine for light. All the information he needed was right in front of him.

His search engine—a service for licensed investigators called Endgame—contained over five hundred databases, including records from criminal and civil courts, law enforcement agencies and corrections departments around the country. He quickly worked up a list of men who had been transferred to Pelican Bay within the last three months, since Pomeroy had himself PC'd there. It was a long list, over a hundred and fifty names. But most of those had been in one prison or another for many months or even years before that. Only twelve had been on the outside when Julie Wyant disappeared.

All twelve of these new inmates were murderers, of course. If you wanted to get into North Wilderness, murder was the only place to start. Weiss began searching the database for details of their crimes. Gang killings, random shootings, the slow dismemberment of a girlfriend in LA . . . He went through each of them, not just the cop records, newspaper stories too. The truth was, he could have had his answers a whole lot faster but he didn't trust his own instincts and revelations. He was very much the modern man in that sense. He went forward hesitantly, like someone making his way through a strange room at night, groping for the furniture. He wanted everything to make logical sense.

His big hands rattled at the keyboard. He peered into the scrolling screen, his hangdog features bathed in the white glow. He made his eliminations painstakingly. For instance, before returning to his cell, Pomeroy had given him and Ketchum a rather vague description of the Shadowman so Weiss knew his target was white but he was afraid to eliminate Hispanics, fearing the killer might use a disguise. He crossed blacks off the list. And he knew the Shadowman was in a hurry to get into prison so he crossed off suspects who had allowed their cases to go to trial, those who had been arrested after long investigations, even those who had been arrested more than two or three days after they'd killed.

So it was all very scientific and all that, but it was a pure waste of time. If he had only believed in that illogical insight of his, he would've already had his man. Because Weiss, in his peculiar way, was practically thinking along with the killer, was even out-thinking him. He knew exactly what kind of crime would've suited him. The killer, he felt, would've deceived himself, would've believed he'd picked his victim at random. Why not? He could've killed anyone and accomplished the same thing. But there would be more to it than that, Weiss thought. There'd be an accidental signature, a mark of the murderer's personality, like a fingerprint unintentionally left behind. There would be, he thought, a kind of muffled sadism, a repressed, sniggering thrill. The killer would think he was being cool and efficient, performing a necessary operation in a businesslike way. But without meaning to, he would embed a horrible kind of humor into the proceedings, sneering, giggling irony. He'd choose a young victim. A woman probably. Attractive, intelligent, wholesome. Either a new mother or, better yet, a girl recently engaged. Someone who was cherished, promising, sure to be missed. She'd have a job that gave her a certain status—not too much, nothing too challenging or complex—the killer wouldn't want anyone too quick-witted or resourceful. He'd just select a sweet, happy creature making her way in the world. That way, when he snuffed her out, he would experience all the hilarity of her slapstick collision with sudden death.

Weiss knew this—but he didn't really believe he knew it. It wasn't solid or logical enough for him. Just a feeling, too much like superstition or a hunch. He would spend precious minutes now reviewing the crimes of each of his murderers. But from the start—and to the end—he kept coming back to one.

He called up a newspaper article on the murder of Penny Morgan. He read how the twenty-three-year-old San Francisco woman was shot dead during a robbery in her apartment. She had recently become engaged, the article said. She was described by friends as "sweet," "cheerful," "loving." And she'd been shot in the face at close range. Neighbors called the police when they heard the gun go off. The police arrived on the scene to find the perpetrator was only just leaving. He was trying to make off with a small take of cash and jewelry and credit cards. He confessed to the crime within an hour of his arrest.

Weiss tilted back in his chair. Out of reach of the monitor's glow, he faded into the room's shadows. He read the article again to the very bottom. He would check and double-check the other killings until he had eliminated every other possibility. But even now, his voice came murmuring softly out of the dark.

"Ben Fry," was all he said.

FIFTY-SEVEN

Out in the woods, Kathleen stumbled on. The big thug, Goldmunsen, was right behind her with his gun. The wiry psycho Flake moved along beside her. Flake kept the flashlight trained on the ground ahead of them so the little group could make their way in the beam.

Kathleen didn't look at either one of them. She just went on, watching the ground, uncaring. She didn't give a damn about the dying or any of it anymore. The only reason she was crying the way she was was because her life had turned out to suck so much and now it was over, which also sucked, and it was all because of men, who sucked worse than anything. Men were bullies and cowards, the lot of them. Chris crawling like a bitch to Hirschorn. Frank Kennedy with his I-don't-give-a-shit eyes. All she'd ever wanted was for one of the little bastards to love her. What the hell was that anyway, a crime in this state?

She dragged her forearm across her dripping nose. Trudged on through the thick duff. Kicking through the undergrowth. Downhill over the uneven ground. They'd been walking for a long time. The swamp was not far off now. Kathleen could hear it—the bullfrogs and the peepers and the bugs. It was loud, a real racket, getting louder. They were very close. Step after heavy step she went. The tears poured down her cheek. The snot poured out of her nose. Her pace slowed as she wiped her face again. Goldmunsen prodded her in the back with his pistol. It made her stumble forward. She tripped on something, a root or a rock. She had to pull up a second to keep her balance, reaching out to steady herself against the trunk of a tree.

Goldmunsen said behind her, "Keep moving."

"Oh, fuck you," muttered Kathleen.

Flake giggled crazily at that.

"And fuck you too," she said. "Psycho asshole."

"Hey!" said Flake. "Watch your mouth, bitch." He backhanded her in the face—or he tried to. Kathleen blocked his arm with both her own. Threw him off with a furious gesture, staggering sideways as she did. "Hey!" he said again, nearly falling himself.

"Just get the fuck away from me, you sick fuck." She spat the words out. Because fuck him, fuck both of them. They could kill her if they wanted but she'd be damned if anyone hit her anymore. None of these assholes was going to hit her anymore ever. "Just get the fuck away."

Crying, she stormed off ahead of them down the hill.

For a second Flake just stood there, amazed, stunned, looking after her.

"Come on, let's go already," said Goldmunsen. "Jesus. Let's just for once do what we're supposed to do tonight and stop complicating things. Fucking mosquitoes are killing me out here."

"Did you see that?" said Flake. "Did you see what that little bitch . . . ?"

He went after her, caught up with her, moved beside her, shining the flashlight into her eyes to get her attention. She brushed at the light as if it were a bug or something but that was it. She didn't even turn to look at him.

"You think I won't cut you?" he said.

"Oh, shove it up your ass," she told him.

Flake stopped dead, stood still again, his mouth open.

"Come on already!" said Goldmunsen as he passed.

"Did you . . . ?"

"Come on!"

What could Flake do? He followed the two of them, seething. Lighting the way with the flash.

Now Kathleen felt the ground grow spongy under her feet. The mosquitoes swarmed and harried her. The noise of the frogs and the water bugs grew louder—screaming loud all around her. Then there was a spark in the blackness, a ripple of glitter: The flashlight's beam had struck water.

Kathleen felt a jolt of fear. Here they were. The swamp. She swallowed. God, this sucked. She wished it would just be over.

Another step—and her foot sank into bog. The cold water seeped in over her tennis shoes, soaked her socks. She stopped, standing in muck up to her shins. There was nowhere else to go. This was it. This was the end of it.

A shudder went through her. She crossed her arms beneath her breasts, defiant and resigned. A mist of flies and mosquitoes settled around her head but she didn't even bother to try to chase them off. Let them have her. Why not? Her life ought to be good for something.

She stood and stared out across the expanse of water. There was open sky above and some moonlight though the moon was low. She could make out the shapes of reeds and cattails. She could make out the shifting water, the reflection of the stars. All of it—everything— blurred by her tears.

She shook her head at the night, frowned bitterly at it. What the hell good was any of it anyway if no one loved you? Christ, maybe she should've asked a man to abandon her like her father had or beat her like her husband had or lie to her like her lover. Maybe then, you know, if she'd asked him for it, he'd've been faithful and kind and true just to spite her. Just to throw her for a loss. Who the fuck knew? Who the fuck knew anything anyway?

She shivered again, getting cold. *Jesus, let them do it already.* What the hell was taking them so long?

She turned around to face the bastards. But she had marched so fast there at the end that they were still lagging behind. Goldmunsen was just coming down the slope, just galumphing down on his bowed ape legs with one dangling ape arm swinging, the other clutching his gun. Another day, another murder for Goldmunsen, that's how he was. And Flake was pulling up to the left of her, hanging back from the water to keep his shoes dry. Bouncing on his toes there, looking like he was just about to blast the fuck off from pure psycho energy. He trained the flashlight on her. His face was glowing in the light, glowing with anticipation. His mouth was corkscrewed into a little smirk at the thought of what would happen to her now.

The two of them—Goldmunsen and Flake: just like the rest, bullies and cowards. They pissed her off, every goddamned one of them.

"Look at you fucks," she burst out. She hated that she was crying in front of them but she couldn't stop. She was too scared and miserable to stop. "Look at you."

The two murderers actually obeyed her, actually glanced at one another like the idiots they were. She'd've laughed if she could've worked herself up to it.

"If I was you I'd be ashamed to breathe it'd be such a waste of air," she said. They stared at her. Anger twisted her face. "Come on, already, you dumb fucks. Shoot me for the love of Christ. What're you waiting for? I'm sick of the sight of you."

Flake could hardly believe his ears. He gaped at her, gaped at Goldmunsen. He couldn't get his mouth shut, that's how shocked he was.

"All right, that's it!" he said finally. With a muttered curse, he shifted the flashlight from his right hand to his left. Now his right hand was free to pull his switchblade out of his pocket. He snapped it open. "I'm . . . I'm . . . I'm gonna cut her." He could barely get the words out.

Kathleen sneered at him, him and his switchblade. "Oh yeah, big fucking man," she said.

Flake started toward her. But Goldmunsen had had it with Flake. This had been a long day for poor Goldmunsen. He'd already been through this whole business once already with the bitch's husband. Twice to the killing place in one day and nobody was even dead yet. Well, that was enough. Enough of Flake, enough of this whole business.

"Hold it, Flake! Just hold it!" he said.

The tone of his voice made Flake hold up. He stood at the edge of the water. He glared hate at the woman in the swamp.

"Just stay the fuck right there," Goldmunsen said. "And keep the goddamned flashlight steady. Let me get this over with. Christ."

Flake hesitated, still trembling with outrage.

"Come on!" shouted Goldmunsen. "Remember what Mr. Hirschorn said. No diddly-shit now, let's go."

Hirschorn's name decided it. Flake breathed down his anger. "All right, all right," he muttered. "Shit." He jerked the flashlight up until the beam caught Kathleen full in the face. She flinched at it, holding up her hand. Then she squinted straight into it, still sneering at them through her tears. Flake couldn't understand it: How the hell could Goldmunsen just take that shit from her? How could he just let it go and kill her without wiping that sneer off her face, without making her scream for mercy?

But Goldmunsen didn't care a fart about the look on her face or what she said or whether she screamed or anything. He just wanted to take her out and get this over with. In fact, he gave a little snort of admiration for her.

"You got more balls than your old man does, I'll say that for you," he told her.

Then, with one smooth motion, he lifted his gun and aimed it squarely at her chest.

And Jim Bishop leapt at him, flying out of the darkness like a panther.

FIFTY-EIGHT

He had cut it too close. Even running as fast as he could in the darkness, he had found the swamp only then, only at the last possible moment. There was no chance for ambush, no chance to plan his attack. He just leapt, hoping to reach the ape-armed gunman before the bastard pulled the trigger.

He did—he did reach him—with an instant to spare. He slammed into the thug's midsection and the Glock fired. There was a spurt of flame angled up at the sky. The bullet went wild. Tangled together, Bishop and Goldmunsen went sprawling into the mud.

For a second, Flake froze. Completely surprised, he stood staring, knife in one hand, flashlight in the other. He saw the two men struggling with each other, rolling over and tearing at each other. He could hardly understand what it was he saw.

Then he did understand. He charged toward the fight. He tried to fold the switchblade as he ran. He couldn't. He threw it away. He dug into his shoulder holster. Fumbled out his Glock.

He was there, right on top of the battle. Bishop rose up—rose up over Goldmunsen's fallen form. For that moment, he presented a perfect target. Flake, not a yard away, pointed the Glock at Bishop's forehead.

Bishop shot him. He had snapped Goldmunsen's gun from his hand. He had come up, looking for the second man. Found him—right there, right in front of him. Flake was just taking aim when Bishop opened up, sweeping the gun barrel across the little thug's torso, squeezing off shot after shot. Three crackling explosions in the night. Three bullets in the psycho's chest. The jolt of it made Flake stagger, made his hand go loose on the gun before he could fire back. But in the next instant, he tightened his grip again, ready to pull the trigger.

Bishop raised his weapon and sent another round into Flake's face. The thug's features exploded, and his body collapsed under him. He was dead on his back in the mud. The flashlight in his left hand landed on top of him, lay on top of him, shining up at the black-and-red mass where his face had been.

Now Goldmunsen heaved up under Bishop and sent the smaller man flying.

Bishop rolled on the soft earth. Sprang to his feet. He tried to bring the gun to bear in the darkness. But Goldmunsen was too fast. He unleashed a side-kick, caught Bishop's wrist. The Glock spun free, lost in the night.

And Goldmunsen kept coming. Turned sidewise by the kick, he drove his right fist straight into Bishop's jaw. Bishop had no time to block or dodge. It was a full hit. It sent him reeling backward. There was no pain but the force of it stunned him. Before he could get his feet under him, before he could even think, Goldmunsen struck again. Crouched low, he stepped forward and, with all the strength of his ape arm, he powered his left fist into Bishop's solar plexus.

Bishop grunted as the air rushed out of him. He doubled over. He couldn't think. A moment of helpless anger, frustration. Then Goldmunsen lifted his right fist high in the air and hammered it down on the back of Bishop's head.

Bishop's brain was knocked blank. He felt himself drop to one knee, felt himself topple over onto his side but that was all he understood of it.

He lay there in the leaves and mud. He saw Goldmunsen step to Flake's body. He saw Goldmunsen bend down, reach down for Flake's gun. Vaguely, he understood that this was the end of things, that he had to get up or he'd die.

But he couldn't get up. His mind was thick and dull. His center was emptied, his strength was gone. All the same, by dumb will, he pressed a hand against the earth and tried. He shifted a knee under him. He started to raise himself.

That was as far as he got. He was caught like that—half-raised on one hand, on one knee—when Goldmunsen lifted Flake's Glock and brought it round to train it on the bridge of Bishop's nose.

Bishop looked up, looked into the black barrel of the gun. No chance to get it. He was dead.

Shit, he thought.

Then everything was gunfire. Two slow, shattering blasts. The night quaked with them.

Panting, still lifted on one hand, on one knee, Bishop looked up at Goldmunsen. Goldmunsen looked down at Bishop, his chest heaving. There was an expression of confusion and concern on his hatchet face. He was finding it hard to figure out what exactly had happened.

Then he staggered forward. He went down slantwise, sending up a puff of leaves as he dropped to the forest floor.

Bishop looked up over the thug's dead body and saw Kathleen. She had recovered the gun he'd lost. She was holding it out in front of her with both trembling hands. Her eyes were wild, her face was mottled and tear-stained and contorted with rage.

Slowly, Bishop looked from her to the thug, back to her again. Slowly, he understood that she had killed him. He nodded. That was good. Better than what he was expecting anyway.

He began to work his way to his feet.

"Don't you fucking move, you son of a bitch," said Kathleen. And she pointed the gun at him now. "You're next."

FIFTY-NINE

"Wait a minute," said the man on the telephone at the same time. "Let me get this straight."

Weiss rubbed his eyes. How late was it already? After ten sometime. His office was still dark. The computer was still on. On the screen now, the video of Julie Wyant was playing, the ten-second loop that showed her crooking her finger at the viewer, beckoning. Weiss had started it going and each time he looked at it, looked at her, he felt something clutch his heart, squeeze it. She was out there somewhere. The Shadowman was after her. Every second counted.

"You called me at home at this hour of the night to inform me I have a killer locked up in my maximum security prison," said the man on the phone. His name was Roger Nelson. He was the warden of North Wilderness SHU. He had a dry, crusty voice, and sounded as if he had lived long and seen much. He also sounded as if he was not very happy Weiss had called. "This may surprise you, sir, but in fact I have a very large number of killers locked up in my prison. It's generally considered one of my best personality traits."

"Yeah, but this prisoner—Ben Fry—*arranged* to have himself locked up," said Weiss. "He's planning to break in on a man you're holding in protective custody, Lenny Pomeroy. He's going to torture Pomeroy for some information and then kill him. And then escape."

The woman on the monitor leaned forward, one hand behind her back. She crooked the finger of her other hand at Weiss. Weiss gazed soulfully at her otherwordly expression. He thought she had eyes as deep and searching as any he had ever seen.

Nelson, meanwhile, laughed. "Well, that's a diabolically clever plan if I ever heard one, Mr. Weiss. It sure is. Only flaw in it, far as I can see, is that it happens to be completely impossible. Have you got any idea what security in our prison is like? Even if any of this were true, which I kind of doubt, he couldn't do it."

"He can," said Weiss, his voice tightening with frustration. "He will."

"Uh-huh," said Nelson. "And you know this how exactly?"

Weiss raised his face to Heaven for help but no help came. This was the question he was afraid of, the one he had no answer for. How did he know what he knew? His hunch? His intuition? Even he wasn't sure.

"I have a source," he lied finally.

"Who?"

"I can't tell you that."

"Good night, Mr. Weiss," said Nelson.

"Superintendant Nelson . . ."

"Mr. Weiss," the warden said wearily, "let me repeat one more time before hanging up very loudly that you and every other tax-paying pain in the ass in the state of California can sleep well tonight knowing that your Department of Corrections is doing everything in its power to protect you from the malefactors under its protection. All right?"

Weiss opened his mouth to answer but there was no chance. Down came the phone on the other end. The dial tone quickly followed.

Weiss put his own phone down. He dragged his palm across his parched lips, thinking.

The girl on the monitor beckoned him, her red-gold hair glistening.

Weiss reached for the phone again.

SIXTY

And again, Kathleen screamed, "You're next, I swear it!"

Beaten stupid, Bishop stood. He swayed on his feet like the mast of a ship at sea.

"Don't, don't move, don't you move!" Kathleen's voice was raw and hoarse. Night birds fluttered up out of the swamp at the sound of it. Even the chigger of bugs grew quiet.

She took a step toward Bishop. Holding the gun on him. Her teeth were bared in her rage. She was choking on her own sobs.

Bishop stared distantly at her. Stared at the gun. Watched her take another step at him. Saw her face, considered her face. Looked around him, dazed.

Bizarre—it was a bizarre scene. Flake dead on his back with the flashlight shining on his gory mask. The shape of Goldmunsen huddled dead in the outglow. The suddenly quiet night, and the trees against the sky and Kathleen in the starlight coming toward him with the gun. For another second or so Bishop was too punch-drunk to take it in, to understand that she might really shoot him. Then, slowly, he forced his mind to clear. He remembered how he'd treated her, what he'd done to her. He began to realize that, hey, she just might shoot him at that. She just might.

Kathleen thought so too, she thought she just might shoot him too. She sure as hell wanted to. She had shot that other man, Goldmunsen, after all, and she had felt really good about it. If she shot Bishop she thought she would feel even more good. Shooting people seemed to work for her. In fact, she was sick and tired of not shooting people.

She clasped the pistol tight—so tight her hands shook violently. She saw Bishop through her tears.

"You *suck!*" she said. "You know that?" Her voice almost vanished beneath the sobbing. "I was going to love you. I was going to *love* you and you were all just . . . lies. You were just lies. You *suck!*"

Bishop looked at the gun. At Kathleen. He nodded. It felt like the right thing to do.

It wasn't. "*Shut up!*" Kathleen shouted. "Don't you nod at me! You were just lies. You suck so bad."

"Look," he said dully. "You're right. I did lie to you. . . ."

"*Don't tell me I'm right, you son of a bitch!* I was going to love you." She kept coming toward him. Coming toward him, pointing the gun. She was gripping the gun so hard her knuckles were white. Her trigger finger was white. "And you were all just . . . *lies!* How could you be like that? How could you do that to someone? How would you like it if someone did that to you? If I killed you, you'd be sorry, wouldn't you? I ought to kill you right fucking now, you son of a bitch."

Bishop winced. This was beginning to give him a headache. Something was anyway. Maybe it was the side of his face, the spot where Goldmunsen got in that punch. His cheek was swelling, throbbing there. Sharp pains were knifing up from it into his skull. Then add to that Kathleen yelling at him. Which he hated—he always hated the part when women found out what he was and got all crazy and started yelling at him. And then add to that the gun—hell, the gun would've given him a headache all by itself.

And now . . . Christ, now there was a new noise. Off in the forest somewhere. Back in the camp. A cough, a pounding disturbance in the wind. Bishop glanced in the direction of it.

Oh hell, he thought.

"*Look at me! Don't you turn away, you look at me, you bastard, I don't care!*" shouted Kathleen.

It was the helicopter, Bishop realized. That noise, that fillip in the wind. It was the Apache. They had started up the Apache.

Kathleen took another step and another and she was really close to him. Close enough for him to see her face clearly in the dark. Close enough for him to see the anger and hurt in her eyes. Close enough for him to grab the gun probably. If he was that fast. If he wasn't too deadheaded and he was faster than her finger which was already squeezed white and tight against the trigger.

Right now, he was pretty sure he was nowhere near that fast.

Kathleen shook her head sadly. "I'll bet your name's not even Frank," she said. "Shit, I was gonna love you and I don't even know your name."

Another jolt of pain went up his skull. He massaged his temple with one hand. He sighed. He really did hate this part. "Bishop," he said. "It's Jim Bishop."

The sound of the helo altered. Steadied, grew louder. The Apache was lifting off.

"And you didn't love me at all," said Kathleen. "Did you?"

Bishop shook his head, flinching at the ache of it. "No," he told her.

The thunder of the Apache grew louder still.

"God damn you," said Kathleen.

She gave a strangled growl of fury and grabbed him. She grabbed a fistful of his hair and yanked his face down to hers. She pressed the gun hard against his belly. She pressed her lips hard against his lips. She kissed him. His swollen face throbbed with pain and it stung where she kept holding fast to his hair. He felt her tongue warm in his mouth. He felt the barrel of the Glock digging into his flesh. He wondered if she was going to kill him, if he'd die like this, kissing her. He lifted his hand and touched her hair as they kissed. All around them, all around the starlit swamp, all above the dead men lying at their feet in the flashlight glow, the air trembled with the sound of the rising Apache.

Then, with a harsh jerk of her hand, Kathleen forced Bishop away from her, forced him out of the kiss and let go of his hair as if flinging him away. The gun was still against him though. She stared into his eyes.

"Why did you come back?" she asked him. She had to raise her voice above the noise of the chopper now. "Why did you come back for me?"

Bishop's gaze moved over her. The helo beat the air. The pain pulsed up his temple. He tried to smile at her with one corner of his busted mouth. "Damned if I know," he said.

A quick laugh surprised Kathleen, burst out of her. What was it about guys like this? What made them so goddamned attractive? She shook her head. "Jesus. You're a genuine prick, you know that." She lowered the gun to her side. She laughed again. Shook her head again. "I gotta say that for you anyway, Bishop. Some guys are just trying, boy, but you are the real deal."

A moment later, they both looked up. The chopper was gliding into sight above them. It hovered in the indigo air over the swamp for a moment, a black shape etched in the starlight and the low moonlight. With its blades whipping round and the Hellfire missiles hanging from its stunted wings, it really did look like some malicious insect, the Great Mosquito of Wrath, risen out of the cattails and the murky waters.

It was up there maybe two hundred feet, not high. The pulsing sound of it enveloped them. They could feel the rotor wash on their lifted faces.

"You think that's Chris?" Kathleen shouted over the noise, squinting up at the machine.

"I guess," Bishop shouted back. "He must be flying it."

"You think I'll ever see him again?"

"Nah. Any way this plays out, he's a dead man."

"I guess I won't be needing this then," Kathleen said after a moment. She tossed the Glock to the ground.

The two stood shoulder by shoulder, peering at the monster in the sky. Inside it, beneath the pilot's seat, Bishop's handheld computer was still searching for a signal, still trying to send its warning message to Weiss.

All it needed, Bishop thought, *was a little more altitude.*

Just then, with startling quickness, the Apache tilted skyward and shot up and away into the night.

SIXTY-ONE

Suddenly, the man called Ben Fry opened his eyes.

He was lying on his cell cot. He was under the blanket, fully clothed. He had slept—for a minute—five—he wasn't sure. There'd been a nightmare. He'd dreamt he opened a closet in his mother's house and it had been full of butchered bodies. As he woke, his heart was beating fast, his breath was trembling. But it was all right. He remembered where he was. Calm settled over him. His hour had finally come.

Now it seemed to him that he became himself again. The meticulous, unemotional precision of his thoughts seemed to grind back into motion after a long lapse. Images like the one in his nightmare—and a million even uglier images from an entire lifetime—seemed to scrabble back into their recesses like rats scattering from a burst of flame. He could climb down from his tower now and they wouldn't trouble him. All he had to do was follow the plan.

The capsule, that was the first thing.

The man called Ben Fry glanced at the clock—a plastic digital stopwatch he kept strapped to his cot. He had set it to time the pictures in the control booth video monitors. Forty-eight cells, each displayed for ten seconds. An eight-minute cycle. In one of his trips to the visiting room, he had seen his own cell come up and he'd begun the count from there. He waited till it was his cell's turn to be shown. Waited till the turn was over. Then he waited a little longer to be sure. And even then, he was careful, just in case. He rolled over on his side to face the wall.

The blanket hid his hands as he worked them down under the waistband of his pants. His fingers probed the tender flesh on the inside of his thigh. He found the scar, the place where he'd cut himself. He took several deep breaths, gazing at the whiteness of the white wall. Then he grabbed a hunk of flesh between his thumb and forefinger and began to squeeze.

He squeezed hard. White flashes went off in front of him, an explosion of white pain then sparks of it sprinkling down like fireworks. The man called Ben Fry stared at the wall, his teeth gritted, his eyes bulging. A pocket of encysted pus had formed around the capsule inside him. His fingers were pushing the cyst upward. He could feel the object itself—not with his fingers but from within. He could feel its sharp edge lancing through layers of flesh toward the surface. He squeezed harder. The capsule was forced up with the pus, slicing through his interior. A wave of red agony washed down over his eyes, red agony dancing with the sprinkling white flashes. Even the man called Ben Fry was amazed at how much it hurt.

Then, with a gloppy, squirting sound, the flesh of his thigh burst open. Just like that, just like popping a pimple. He tugged the blanket aside so he could peek down and see. He saw the yellow pus burbling down over his leg. It soaked into the green fabric of his pants, a spreading stain. Making a noise down in his throat, the man worked his fingers in deeper. As the pus ran out of him, he could start to feel the capsule itself pinched between his fingertips. The gouts of pus kept coming. He couldn't believe how much there was. Then there was blood, watery and pale. And in the middle of the red-and-yellow gush, the dark tip of the capsule itself poked out of the torn skin.

With his other hand, the man called Ben Fry caught that small tip, pinched it between thumb- and fingernail. Tears poured from his eyes as he slowly drew the thing out of his body.

The capsule was slick and slippery with his fluids. He tamped it dry on the bedsheet so he could get a grip on it. Then he took the thing in his two hands and snapped it in half. It broke pretty easily. It was designed that way. Now it was in two pieces, one shaded blue, the other red. Each piece had one sharp end and one end that was flat. Using the sharp end of one half, he poked a hole in the flat end of the other. Like poking an opening in a tube of glue. He repeated the process on the other side.

He had about six minutes left before the video camera went on in his cell again. It was plenty of time.

Ignoring the burning pain in his thigh, he rolled off the cot. He crouched down at the cell door. He used the blue half of the capsule first. Squeezed it four times, once each where the lead section of the door latched to the upright, once each where it connected to the computerized sliding mechanism. At each spot, he left a dab of viscous blue fluid. Then he used the red capsule the same way, in the same places. The red fluid and the blue fluid mixed.

The man called Ben Fry moved back across the small cell. He squatted, his back to the door, his hands covering his neck, his head down. Positioned like that, he watched the red bloodstain spreading slowly over his pants leg. He was conscious of a small hum of excitement all through him while he waited, but nothing more. He wasn't afraid. He had planned this out in his mind, every step of it. His plans were perfect—they always were. Now it was just a matter of making them happen.

A second went by. Another. The blue fluid and the red fluid from the capsule mixed on the cell door. Finally, there was a quiet, sizzling hiss—a near-silent explosion that blew the door free of its locking mechanism.

The instant he heard it, the man called Ben Fry leapt back to the door. He seized it by the mesh, shoved it back. The door didn't budge. For a moment, the man felt dazzled, confused. This was not the plan. But he shoved again. And the door did slide back this time exactly as it was supposed to—not a lot, just a little. Just enough.

The man called Ben Fry squeezed through the narrow gap and stepped into the pod gallery.

He was out.

SIXTY-TWO

Weiss was on the phone with Ketchum when it happened. Ketchum's deep mutter had become an angry, guttural growl.

"What the hell do you want me to do, Weiss? What the hell do you think I can do?"

"At least get them to put the prison on some kind of high alert."

"I already talked to them. There is no high alert, they're always on high alert. You saw the place. How much more fucking alert can it be?"

"Haven't they got some kind of emergency escape response?"

"Hell yeah, they got an escape response. Automated steel doors, alarms, all that shit. What're they gonna do, set the whole thing off 'cause my private eye friend says he has a hunch?"

Weiss deflated with a sigh. Stared glumly at the woman beckoning from his computer screen. "At least they could put a guard on Ben Fry," he said hopelessly.

"There already is a guard on Ben Fry," Ketchum answered. "There's a guard on everybody. It's a fucking prison."

Weiss's head rested heavily against the telephone handset. When he didn't answer, Ketchum went on a little more gently, as gently as he knew how anyway:

"Look, man, they've got resource problems the same as everyone. What'm I supposed to tell them? I mean, maybe with more time, we can convince them to put this Fry on some kind of twenty-four-hour watch or something, I don't know, but the way it is . . . You don't even know when this is supposed to happen."

Weiss nodded, staring at the screen, at the image of Julie Wyant, answering nothing. It was true: He didn't know. What he did know

was that he'd lost contact with Bishop. What he knew was that
Bishop said it would be soon. Soon.

He heard Ketchum sigh back at him over the line. "The trouble
is, you got the warden thinking you're crazy now. The way he sees it,
there's no way . . ."

But Weiss was hardly listening. Just gazing at the image of Julie
Wyant in that hangdog way he had. His elbow on the chair arm, his
head resting against the phone. That squeeze he felt in his heart at the
sight of her—it'd become a steady ache, an ache of helplessness and
frustration. He was stuck here, in this city, on this phone, while
almost three hundred miles away the man who was hunting her was
getting into position to learn everything he needed to track her down.
And Weiss couldn't make anyone believe it was happening . . .

Ketchum's low voice muttered on and on somewhere in the background. Weiss continued gazing at the woman on the screen. And as
his wandering mind began to dream itself into the amazing deeps of
her mysterious eyes, a little song came to him suddenly, a little three-
note tune.

Weiss straightened, blinked in surprise. It took him another
moment before he realized what it was: an e-mail.

". . . because the whole place is geared to keep that from happening . . ." Ketchum was grumbling.

"Hold it, Ketch," said Weiss with a faint energy coming back
into his voice. He clicked the e-mail icon. The picture of Julie Wyant
disappeared behind the screen. He saw the mail.

"What," said Ketchum over the phone. "What now?"

"I got something from Bishop."

"Bishop? What the hell's he want?"

*Weiss. It worked. Wannamaker's out. I'm in. Six tonight, I fly to
some secret location out in the forest somewhere. Once I arrive,
they'll give me the details of the job. Soon as I know what's what, I'll*

make contact. With luck, we should be able to break it up without compromising . . . a150kmnwah-64d

"Well?" said Ketchum after a second.

Weiss didn't answer. He was reading, thinking. *Six tonight. Bishop must already be out there. a150kmnwah-64d. He must be under guard. He couldn't type out a full message. a150kmnw. Approximately 150 kilometers northwest . . .*

"What the hell is AH-64D?" he asked aloud.

"What?" said Ketchum. "AH-64D? What the hell is that?"

Weiss only shook his head. And Ketchum kept at him, "Hey. Weiss? What're you talking about? AH-64D?"

AH-64D. Weiss called up his everyday search engine. Tapped the initials in. A website came back at once. "Army Technology—AH-64D—Attack Helicopter."

"You're kidding me," whispered Weiss. He swallowed hard. He felt something inside him begin to come apart.

He saw it. He saw the whole thing at once, the whole picture came to him. Too late. Useless and too late.

"Weiss, what the hell's going on, are you there?"

"Ketch," he said. "I think they're sending a chopper."

"What?"

"I think . . ."

Ketchum snorted. "Forget it. To the prison? No chance. There's chopper wire strung up all over the place. There's no way to land one of those things. . . ."

"They don't have to land it," Weiss said. "It's an attack chopper. It must be armed. Son of a bitch. That's how he's gonna escape. He's just gonna blow the place open."

Ketchum was silent a long second. "Weiss," he said then. "Now *I* think you're crazy."

Weiss stared at the screen. Pressed the phone so hard against his ear it hurt. He felt a cold sweat forming on the back of his neck. Too fucking late.

"Weiss," said Ketchum. "Weiss."

Weiss grunted, "Yeah?"

"I can't tell them he's gonna blow the place open with an attack helo, man. He's gonna break out of his cell—which he can't do—and break into Pomeroy's—which he also can't do—and then attack the place with an army chopper? I can't tell them that, Weiss."

Weiss licked his dry lips. He tried to swallow again but couldn't. "No," he murmured hoarsely.

There was a pause. Then Ketchum asked, "When the hell is this chopper supposed to attack?"

Weiss gave a silent, sickly laugh. If Bishop was 150 klicks into the wilderness, there was no way his handheld could've gotten a signal on the ground. And if Bishop were in a plane, he would've radioed the cops. Weiss understood this too: He'd put the handheld right into the helo itself so that when it took off . . .

"It's already airborne," he said hoarsely.

"What?" said Ketchum. "What?"

But Weiss, as if he were in a dream, slowly set the phone down in its cradle. Too late. He had been too late. All of it, everything he had figured out, was useless.

He sat staring into space, defeated.

SIXTY-THREE

As for Chris, this was the moment of his life. His past had fallen away like four walls falling. He felt balanced on the pinpoint of the wind. The low moon was sailing with him. The very horizon line was in the power of the stick between his legs. The beat of the rotors above him, the beat of the engine in his bones, the familiar sight of the green world through the helmet's targeting monocle . . . It was all he had ever wanted. All he had ever wanted was to be like this, like an Army pilot. He felt as if the sky were carrying him in its arms.

Seated below and in front of him, in the gunner's seat, was Hirschorn. Chris could see his fine face reflected on the windshield. He could hear his voice in his headset, now and then murmuring a new direction in his ear. Every time he looked at the man, he experienced a great wave of feeling for him, a great wave of devotion.

He was so grateful to be back in his employer's good graces. Only a few hours ago, he had stood waiting for Hirschorn's goons to fire a bullet into his brain. Only forty-five minutes ago, he had knelt in the mud while Hirschorn slapped him, while Hirschorn ordered his wife to be taken away and shot. Ever since the Army had cashiered Chris, things had been that way for him. Bad juju, nothing right. But now, Hirschorn had given him another chance. Hirschorn had put him in the pilot's seat. He would have died for Hirschorn then. He loved him.

The Apache swayed low above the oak tops. They were moving at a solid night speed, about seventy-five knots. Chris watched the featureless landscape scroll by on the GPS readout.

"We should be about thirty-five miles northeast," said Hirschorn in his ear.

Chris nodded. "Roger that."

They were half an hour away from the prison.

SIXTY-FOUR

In the prison, no one suspected a thing. No alarm had gone off when the man called Ben Fry blew open his cell door. There was no alarm for a blown cell door because a blown cell door was not considered a possibility. A discreet little red square on one of the control booth readouts went on to indicate that a door was disengaged; that was it. Unfortunately, the control booth officer wasn't looking at the readout at the time.

The control booth officer was named Mike O'Brien. He had a rough but friendly face. Wispy red hair. Canny Irish eyes. He was short and stocky, still muscular, but getting a little paunch around the middle. He was thirty-four years old.

Mike had drifted into corrections work after getting out of the Army. He had been happy enough at first to go from job to job but then he'd gotten married and he wanted something steadier. Corrections turned out to be it. It wasn't the greatest work in the world but it was regular and secure. And the fairly dependable schedules made it possible for him to plan his life and to spend time with his wife and daughter, which was the main thing to him. His wife, Maura, was just a slip of a thing but she ran Mike's world with a firm hand and he revered her. Their two-year-old daughter was named Caitlin and Mike loved her as if she had strung the stars.

When the red light went on, Mike was turned away from the readout, dutifully running a monitor scan and thinking idly about a tavern called McGill's. McGill's was the place in town where the married COs generally hung out—as opposed to Blinky Mae's where the single guys went to try to hook up with a local girl for the weekend. McGill's had a family room, with tables to eat at and a pool table and video games for recreation. There was a karaoke machine too. Mike was crazy about the karaoke machine. Sometimes, when things at

McGill's got friendly, he would allow himself to be talked into singing along with one of the tracks. He had a fine natural tenor and though he nursed a weakness for the sentimental Irish ballads his father had taught him, he could be a boogie-down dude when he had to be. Give him a couple of beers, a couple of chicks going *doo-wa* for backup, there was just no telling how far down he could get. Some of the black COs liked to kid him about it. "You a pasty Irish bastard to behold," they'd say, "but you a brother in disguise, man." Mike loved that stuff, loved it.

So he was thinking about McGill's. Scanning the monitors, smiling to himself. Beginning to hum the first few bars of "Danny Boy" under his breath. And the red light went on and he didn't see it. And then, almost soundlessly, the barred door to B Gallery blew.

The man called Ben Fry had been able to see Mike working in the booth. He had waited, flat against his cell, until Mike wasn't looking and then come swiftly down the gallery to the barred door. He had mixed his chemicals on the door and edged back against another cell where he was difficult to see. There, again, he waited. A second, two.

Mike didn't hear the hiss of the chemicals mixing. He didn't see the barred gallery door inch open. But when it swung shut, he caught the movement from the corner of his eyes. He glanced over at the door through the control booth window. The door was closed. He could see right through it into the gallery. No one was moving in there. (By now, the man called Ben Fry was pressed against the control booth itself, beneath the window, out of Mike's line of vision.) Mike saw nothing unusual at all.

Mike turned away again—and that's when he spotted the discreet little red square, the indicator that a cell door was open . . . and now, suddenly, another light, a second light, went on, to indicate that the door to B Gallery was unlocked as well.

What the hell? Mike narrowed his blue eyes at the pair of red lights. *Gotta be a glitch,* he thought. *Gotta be.* He felt a little rabbity skip in his chest as it flashed through his mind that he might accidentally have tripped a couple of doors or something. But he reviewed it in his mind, it wasn't possible. It had to be a glitch.

He looked at the door to B Gallery again. It seemed the same as always. It had to be the same as always. How could it be any other way?

Then, a creeping doubt. Mike squinted for a better look. It wasn't possible the gallery door was slightly ajar, was it? And yet it almost looked to him as if it might be.

Mike lowered his eyes to the red squares on his monitor, raised them again to the gallery door on the other side of the thick Lexan.

Then the door to the control booth itself was ripped outward. Startled—flabbergasted—Mike spun round. Even now, he could not comprehend what was happening, what could possibly be happening. There was the inmate known as Ben Fry right in front of him, right there.

Mike didn't think, he just lunged for the panic button, reached to slap his palm down on the red disk that would sound the alarm. It was too late. The man called Ben Fry was on him so fast. Too fast for Mike to react. Mike could only watch as if from a distance. Watch the inmate grab his hand, watch him twist it away from the button and snap the wrist. It was that fast. Mike never even had time to feel the pain. Even as his lips were parting to let out a shout, the man called Fry swarmed over him. Mike saw nothing but that face without emotion, those eyes without light: a man at work. Then Mike was dead.

The man called Ben Fry lowered Mike's corpse to the control booth floor, went down with it, so he was below the window, out of sight. Quickly, he stripped the body of its khaki shirt, of its creased green pants. He stripped his own T-shirt and prison pants off. Mike's clothes were a little big on the killer but that was all right, that was no problem. The belt cinched the pants tight, held them in place. That was good enough.

Next, the man called Ben Fry leaned down close to Mike's head.

The Irishman's rough, friendly features were disfigured now. There was a red hole in the center of them where the killer had driven Mike's nose cartilage up into his brain. But the blue eyes were still intact, open, staring. The man called Ben Fry dug his thumb deep into the corner of the right eye. He was going to need that eye to get through the retinal scan.

When he was finished, he wiped his hands on his prison clothes and stood up. He turned to the control booth's main panel. He took a moment to orient himself, but he'd already studied the schematics, he already knew what he wanted to do. Everything had been perfectly planned, just like always. The man called Ben Fry knew exactly where he was going to go next. And there was nothing to stop him now.

SIXTY-FIVE

Then Weiss sat forward in his chair. Sat forward quickly. In the depths of his frustration, waiting helplessly for news of the disaster, his glance had fallen on something, something at the edge of the computer's glow. He took it in his hands now. My report. The pages of my report on Father O'Mara. He hadn't given much thought to it before. He had been too busy working out the Shadowman's plans. But suddenly now a string of connections flashed through his brain. The way I hadn't lived up to his expectations, had missed the discrepancy he was sure I'd see. The way I'd been sitting in here drunk, loudly insisting that the priest was clean . . . The whole picture—the whole picture of me—came to him at once, as these things did. He realized that I *had* lived up to his expectations, that I'd gotten drunk not because I didn't know but because I did know and had lied.

At the same time he realized these things, an idea came to him. It was only half-formed but he couldn't wait for the rest of it. There was no time. He snapped the phone up once again. Reading from the top of the report, he punched in a number quickly.

The man who answered sounded wary, as if he weren't used to receiving calls this late at night and suspected it might be bad news.

"Hello?"

"Father Reginald O'Mara," Weiss said quietly.

"Yes, speaking. Who's this?"

Weiss leaned farther forward, staring, intense. His heavy features glowed in the monitor light. The rest of his hunched, urgent figure was sunk in shadow.

"My name is Weiss. I run a private detective agency."

There was a long silence. "Yes," the priest said finally. "I spoke to one of your operatives this evening."

"You did?"

"Yes."

Weiss held his breath a moment. It was pure bluff but he had nothing else, he had to try it. "I want you to know we've decided to keep your little secret to ourselves," he said. There was no answer. Weiss's stomach dropped. Was it a mistake, a bad guess, a desperate guess? "My client will probably be convicted and go to prison, where he belongs," he went on. "And the people you want to protect, including your brother, the governor, will be safe. Do you understand?"

"Uh-huh." O'Mara was still wary—still not sure it wasn't bad news after all. "And what do you want in return, exactly?"

"I want a favor," Weiss told him at once. "And don't get me wrong—this isn't blackmail."

"Oh no?"

"No. I understand you wouldn't go for that. Whatever you decide to do, your secret's safe. Consider it a gesture of goodwill."

"All right," the priest said. He sounded as if he was beginning to relax a little. "What do you want then?"

"I want you to listen to me," said Weiss in the same even tone. "I want you to listen to what I have to say—and then I want you to get me through to the governor."

SIXTY-SIX

Later, the California Department of Corrections convened a Board of Inquiry to try to reconstruct what happened next, but after nearly three months of investigation, no one was ever completely sure. The man called Ben Fry had to pass two more control booths to get to Whip Pomeroy's cell. According to an internal systems check, he accomplished this in little over half an hour. And yet the officer in the first booth, booth four, claimed never to have seen him. And as for the control booth in the priority watch pod, it couldn't even be approached but through a complex protocol involving a retinal scan and a double key lock. There were no signs of a forced entry there but both the booth officer and the security officer were found dead at their posts. Obviously the man called Ben Fry had borrowed the retina he needed from Mike O'Brien. But how he got hold of the keys remained a mystery, as did the killer's ability to travel through the galleries unseen. Whatever speculations the CDC Board came up with were never made public for "security reasons." Likewise, the exact type of explosive the killer used to get through the doors was revealed only in a classified section of the report. It was apparently a pretty simple mixture and the authorities didn't want to spread the word.

But this much, at least, was publically agreed on: Once the man called Ben Fry breached the control booth in priority watch, there was nothing to keep him from the Identity Man. Whip Pomeroy might never even have seen him coming if he hadn't been startled awake by the sound of his prison door sliding open. When it did, Whip sat up on his cot. His delicate fingers started fidgeting at once. His delicate lips were already mouthing their silent monologue and his damp eyes were darting this way and that. His heart beat wildly. His mind raced to find an explanation. Afraid, he struggled to his feet unsteadily.

And then—incredibly—there he was: the man called Ben Fry. He stepped to the door of Pomeroy's cell as if it were the usual thing, as if it were not amazing for him to be there. His expression was like that too, matter-of-fact, businesslike, competent and calm. That expression terrified Pomeroy more than anything. The man called Ben Fry was simply here, he was simply going to do what he was going to do. There was not a possibility on earth that anyone could get in his way.

In the wild panic of his fear, Whip Pomeroy let out a sob. He flung himself back into the corner of his cell. He sank down the wall, sank to the floor, his fingers working themselves together in a frenzy. His lips moved even faster and out of his inaudible whisper he sobbed again and cried out, "*I won't tell you! I won't tell you!*"

"Oh yes," the man called Ben Fry said simply. "You will."

He took a step toward the cowering prisoner.

And at that moment, by a peremptory order from the governor of the state, the prison's night warden set off the emergency escape response, and the screaming, deafening sirens overwhelmed everything.

Weiss had gotten through.

SIXTY-SEVEN

It was then the Apache came within range. Chris checked the fire control radar and saw the prison's cruciform pattern moving to the center of the screen. He glanced at the GPS. Eight thousand feet away, seven thousand, six. He scanned the horizon with his free eye and made visual contact. A little more than a mile distant, the white halo of the place shone out of the black woods and up into the black sky.

Working the rudders with his shoetips to keep the helo steady, Chris slowed her to a hover and pressed hover control. The big bird hung steady, moon high above the forest.

Hirschorn checked the flight clock. "We've still got two minutes."

"I'll acquire the target," said Chris.

Hirschorn just nodded. He was sitting in the gunner's seat but he was no gunner. There was nothing for him to do. He had only come along for the ride on the orders of the man called Ben Fry. That way, he could keep the operation secret until the last minute and make sure that it was carried out exactly as planned.

But when it came to setting up the missile attack, Chris was on his own. He had to reach forward awkwardly into the gunner's well in order to activate the Hellfires and prepare them for lock-on before launch. But when that was done, he only had to sit back and look out through his helmet monocle. The helmet monocle—the Helmet and Display Sighting System—was the greatest part of the Apache for Chris. It had taken him a long time—eighteen hours of training—to learn how to use it but man oh man, once you got the hang of it, it was uncanny shit indeed. The HADSS was slaved to the Apache's Target Acquisition and Designation System so that all you had to do was look through the eyepiece at what you wanted to destroy and the fire-and-forget Hellfires would know right where to go. Lock-on became like a body function. Which made Chris feel as if he were the monster head on top of some mythical whirling creature—a flying dragon of some kind, ready to reach out and strike with its fire-dealing claws.

There was a word for what he felt just then but he couldn't think of it. It was a kind of glow inside. He hadn't felt this way since he was in the Army. No. He had never felt this way. Never. Not until now.

Chris raised his head and turned his monocle on the prison. He focused the green ball on the northeast gun tower.

"I've got the target," he said a moment later.

"One minute," said Hirschorn.

They waited. At that distance, and with all the chopper noise, neither of them could hear the sirens going off below. But suddenly— and they could see this—the halo of light around the prison grew brighter, stronger. It began to sway and reach and probe the dark.

Hirschorn's voice was in Chris's headset again. "Spotlights."

That's what they were. They could see them through the windshield. Going off everywhere around the prison's perimeter. Their broad beams wheeled this way and that, covering the yard around the prison buildings.

"What the hell's that about?" said Chris.

Hirschorn didn't answer. He didn't know. And the heat of the lights scotched any chance for the FLIR to pick up any of the action on the ground. They couldn't see the men running to their emergency stations. They didn't know the armory had already been unlocked. Warned of the approaching Apache, specially trained officers were shouldering Stinger-style missile launchers as others scanned the skyline with night scopes, searching for the invader. But Chris and Hirschorn didn't know.

Nervously, Hirschorn checked the flight clock. "Thirty seconds," he said.

"Jesus," said Chris staring out at the lights below. "I think they might be looking for . . ."

"*Fire 'em!*" Hirschorn shouted. "*Fire! Fire!*"

Chris hesitated. It was still too soon. But then the order sunk in. Quickly, he flicked the guard up, brought his thumb down on the button. The Apache jerked as if startled by the missile's release. Chris fired the second one even as the first was sizzling through the night air.

The explosions came one on top of the other. A bright orange plume of fire rose up over the legs of the prison gun tower, then another fireball right away, just beyond the first, ripping through the innermost fence. Chris forgot everything else at the sight of them. By the light of the second blast, he could see the silhouetted gun tower sink down heavily, then tumble into the flames. He fired a third missile, and a fourth. He still had four more to go. He felt as if his heart were pumping electricity through him. He let out a whoop, a roar, a laugh. It was the happiest moment of his life.

"What the hell is . . . ?" Hirschorn started to say.

Chris's mouth was still open on that laugh as a blinding ball of light detached itself from the fire on the ground and came streaking straight toward them above the trees.

SIXTY-EIGHT "Mr. Weiss?"

"Yes," said Weiss huskily into the phone.

"This is Norman Kamen at the governor's office."

"Yes," Weiss repeated. He held his breath.

"The governor wanted to let you know that the emergency response systems at the prison have been activated. Apparently a National Guard helicopter has confirmed the presence of an incoming aircraft. The guards will be armed accordingly."

Weiss's eyes gleamed in the computer light. He clutched the phone hard, his palm sweating. "And the prison's shut down?"

"Completely. No one is going to escape tonight, believe me."

Weiss nodded, staring at nothing. Staring, unseeing, at the girl on the screen.

"Mr. Weiss," said Norman Kamen, "the governor wants to thank you for your information."

Weiss went on nodding, hardly listening. When he'd hung up, he still sat forward in his chair. His sweaty hand closed into a sweaty fist. A small smile played at the corner of his sorry features.

"Got you, you son of a bitch," he whispered.

SIXTY-NINE

But it was another long moment before the man called Ben Fry took the full measure of the catastrophe. It was just too hard for him to accept the fact that this plan of his might fail, that the only thing on earth he had ever really wanted might slip from his fingers at the last instant.

He stared with burning eyes at the convict cowering in the corner—at Whip Pomeroy, the one man who could lead him back to Julie Wyant. He stared at him but, like a vapor, like a momentary faintness, it was another face, her face, that passed before his eyes. Her laughing face.

He had no words for how he felt about her, what she'd done to him, how he'd altered inside from the moment he'd first seen her. That moment, he remembered still, it was as if some dream he hadn't even known he'd dreamed had been ripped out of him and into the world, full-blooded suddenly and real. He knew, at the single sight of her, that her image had been growing, all these years, inside his brain, that she had burst forth now into reality, his creation, part of him in some way. In some way, she was the part he loved most and she was also the part he most wanted to shred and savage. It was all one thing in some way, the savagery and the love.

He had no words for it, no words. Just the things his flesh was driven to do to hers. The cries he needed to extract from her, the tears he needed. The tears. When he hurt her, when he made her cry, he wanted to catch those tears in a bottle, he wanted to inject her tears into his veins, he wanted to wander into high mountains and live on her hurt and tears until the end of days.

He had tried, one time, that one time when he could no longer control himself, he had tried to tell her all of this. But he had no words. And she laughed at him. With that angel face he'd dreamed into existence and her red lips. Even crying, even bleeding, even naked and beaten at his feet, she laughed. Which only made it worse. Which only made him need to hurt her more and love her more. He stood in front of her, naked himself, humiliated in his need and his nakedness, and she laughed.

Pomeroy had heard her. Pomeroy had been in the next room and had heard it all.

And now here Pomeroy was. Cowering there at the back of his cell. The man called Ben Fry knew he would need no more than thirty seconds to extract the necessary information from him. To get what he needed and then destroy him and so destroy his memory of Julie's laughter. Then the man called Ben Fry would be gone, on his way to finding her again, to having her again. This time, he would take her somewhere, somewhere away. This time, he would have her until it didn't matter to him anymore, until he was fat and woozy and satiated with her pain. And then it would be over finally. She would be part of him again and the helpless humiliating naked desire would be over and done. Thirty seconds. Thirty seconds and he'd have everything he had come for.

But as the sirens and alarms sounded all around him, all through the prison, everywhere, it began to dawn on the man called Ben Fry that thirty seconds was a lot more time than he had.

Even as he stood there, steel security doors were beginning to slide shut, cutting off his retreat along the galleries. Guards were grabbing rifles and securing the perimeter. For all he knew, they had been tipped off to his identity, they were converging on him right that second. If he didn't start to move—if he didn't move now—he would miss his rendezvous with the chopper, miss the ropes that would be thrown down to him. He would miss his chance to escape and he would be caught in this place, this place of endless nothingness, forever. Forever and alone and with the image of her laughing face.

He tore his gaze away from Pomeroy. He ran.

The sirens were unbelievably loud. The noise seemed to expand inside his head, to shiver his thoughts to dust. He dashed past the priority watch control booth, overstepping the body of the security guard he'd murdered coming in. He turned the corner.

And there they were, fifteen yards from him down an empty gallery: steel doors, sliding toward each other automatically.

What was the gap between them? Five feet? Four? Less and less every second that he raced their way. The siren hammered at him and his mind reeled. And now too he heard the bump, felt the rumble of the Hellfires hitting home. He knew as he ran that this was it, this was everything. If he could make it through that narrowing gap there was a chance he could reach the chopper. If those doors closed . . . He knew how it would be. Stuck here with his mind stagnant and vulnerable. Desperately imagining his high calm tower while, slowly, slowly, day by day, those horrors that had scrabbled away from him like rats crept in on him again, began to devour him.

The steel doors slid toward each other. The man called Ben Fry stretched like a racer. The siren . . . his panting breath . . . his pounding heart. The gap was small, already too small, it seemed, for him to fit through.

But then he was there. Forcing himself between the two halves of the door. Pressured in between them. Certain for a second he'd be cut in half. And then squeezing through. His arm, then his hand trailing behind. Then all of him out, as he pulled free, stumbled to the ground. Lay on the ground watching the steel doors finally clang shut.

The next explosion rocked the white corridor around him. Even with that deafening siren screaming, the man called Ben Fry could hear the falling debris. He was on his feet again. Running again. Turning another corner.

And there, before him, just as he'd planned—the shattered wall. A hole opening onto the night, onto the yard, onto the free world beyond.

The man called Ben Fry tripped, stumbled over the flaming rubble. He felt the open air touching his face. There was fire, madness, all round him. Blinding lights, deafening sirens. A tower fallen. Leaping flames. Men with guns, running to their positions, cutting off his escape. Machine guns in those towers that were still standing, sweeping the yard, looking for anyone, looking for him.

How could this have happened? How could they have known? There was no one alive who had the courage to betray him. Someone would have had to have figured it out, to have out-thought him, out-smarted him. It was impossible. Nothing like this had ever happened to him before.

The man called Ben Fry stood in the debris, staring into the night sky, searching for his only hope.

He saw it. The chopper, the Apache. He saw its lights, hovering over the forest, not a mile away.

"Come on! Come on!" he growled.

It was early yet for the rendezvous. Everything was thrown off schedule. But he couldn't just stand there, exposed like that. He started running forward. Running into the yard, into the spotlights. Risking the machine guns in the tower, risking the guns of the guards everywhere.

The lights made him squint. The sirens pounded and pounded at him. The flames from the missiles leapt and crackled here and there, on every side. But the man called Ben Fry ran, his eyes raised upward, lifted to the Apache. He willed the craft to come forward, to make the rendezvous, to pull him out.

The first missile was launched from the ground even as he ran. He watched in shock as its green-white trail spiraled upward over the black silhouette of the woods, lighting the treetops as it rose. The shot went past the helo, climbing into the night. A second crossed the trail of the first and also missed.

The man called Ben Fry pulled up short. He saw the chopper start to turn, start to fly. Was it leaving him? Horrified, he watched as a third missile snaked up from the ground after it. This one slammed full force into the base of the Apache's rotors. In the light of the explosion, he could see the mangled blades, like the crushed wings of an insect. Then the whole mechanism was blown apart.

"*No!*" the killer shouted, his voice lost beneath the shrieking sirens.

He froze, powerless. The Apache heeled over like a breached whale. It plummeted nose down into the forest. He could not hear the blast beyond the noise of the prison. But the ball of flame bellied out of the trees and turned the black sky red.

The man called Ben Fry stood openmouthed and watched the helo die. The spotlights crisscrossed over him. The sound of the sirens filled his mind. From every direction, men with guns were running toward him. And yet everything seemed very still somehow, as if he stood on the edge of a limitless valley in which nothing lived or moved or changed but just went on and on forever.

SEVENTY

Nearly three hundred miles away, on the eighth floor of the concrete tower with the red mansard roof, in the office with the large arching windows and the midnight sounds of Market Street trailing up from below, Weiss shifted slowly in the shadows. When the phone rang again, he snapped it up quickly.

"It's over," Ketchum growled.

"Have they got him? Have they got him?" Weiss heard a streetcar pass below in the long silence that followed. Too long a silence. His heart went dark.

"It's still kind of chaos up there," Ketchum told him finally. "They're not sure how things shake out. I'm having a hard time getting anybody to tell me anything."

"You're saying he got away? How the fuck could he get away?"

"I'm saying I don't know, Weiss. Okay. No one knows."

"Shit."

"He was wearing a CO's uniform," Ketchum pushed on. "He killed a guard, took the guy's clothes. There's a possibility he might've mingled with the rest of the guards in all the confusion. He could've slipped out somehow." Weiss said nothing for a while and Ketchum added in his low angry voice, "Look, it's not like he's going anywhere. They've got dead guards up there, man. They're angry. They've got dogs and helicopters combing the area for this asshole. You saw the place. It's all trees and rocks and shit. Where the hell's he gonna go?"

"What about Pomeroy?" Weiss asked.

"You saved him. You did it, Weiss. He's scared as shit and shaken to his toes but Fry never touched him."

"He didn't get any information out of him?"

"Not a word. Whip swears he didn't tell him a thing. The alarm went off just in time."

Weiss's body rose and fell on a breath. That was something any-way. Maybe it was the main thing. Wherever the man called Ben Fry was, he didn't know any more now than he did before. He didn't know any more than Weiss did.

"But he'll still go after her," he said softly, as if to himself. "He'll never stop hunting her until he finds her."

After that, for a moment, there was no sound in the office but the fading traffic noises from the street.

Then Ketchum answered, "Tell you what, Weiss. My money says you find her first."

Weiss snorted softly. He set the phone down. He tilted back in his chair. He peered into the light from the computer—still the only light in the room. On the monitor, the beautiful woman with the red-gold hair was beckoning, beckoning, the video loop playing over and over. In her high-collared white lace, somehow prim and sexy at once, she bent forward slightly. Weiss watched her—her bottomless eyes, her dreamy, distant expression. Slowly, he leaned closer to her. The glow of the computer etched deep lines into his heavy, sagging, ugly fea-tures. He watched the beckoning woman for a long time.

You find her first, he thought.

And he reached out and touched her image, tenderly.

EPILOGUE

Weiss was still at his desk when I came in the next morning. Still staring at his computer. But he was reading an e-mail now. Bishop had sent it to him from a terminal at the California Highway Patrol's Driscoll air barracks.

Weiss. Glad to hear word reached you about the helo in time. I had to stay in woods to stop whack on Kathleen. Have to answer cop questions for a while due to bodies. See you in a day or two. JB.

As Weiss read, his mouth curled up in an exceptionally goofy smile. Bishop had risked blowing his assignment to go back and get the girl. Weiss wasn't exactly sure why, but he found this piece of news incredibly gratifying.

And in fact, Bishop had not only retrieved Kathleen from the swamp, he'd also flown her out of the woods to safety. Hirschorn's gunmen had stood guard over the runway for a while after Bishop's escape as they'd been ordered. But as the night dragged on, they got bored and returned to camp to join Alex Wellman, who was anxiously watching for his employer's return. Bishop and Kathleen, hiding in the nearby trees, saw their chance and made their way to the plane. Bishop got it started and took off. They reached Driscoll in one of the dark hours of morning.

By that time, the first reports of the attack on North Wilderness were going out over TV and radio news. So when Bishop showed up at the California Highway Patrol's chopper station near the airpark, the police were very interested to hear what he had to say. Bishop found the Dynamite Road on the sectional chart of the area and used it to lead the cops directly to the forest runway. Wellman and the remaining gunmen were in custody before the sun rose.

Bishop had killed three people out there in the woods and Kathleen had killed another. This troubled the police—a little. They kept the two of them around town for questioning for a couple of days. Most of that time, Bishop and Kathleen spent together upstairs in the house he'd lived in. As events unfolded and the full story was revealed, it became pretty clear that the killings they'd committed had been done in self-defense. They were told they were free to go and that no charges would be filed.

Bishop bid Kathleen a tearless farewell at the airpark. Then he mounted his Harley and rode off into the sunset.

News continued to come out of North Wilderness for several weeks afterwards. By the final count, five corrections officers and one prisoner died in the attack on the SHU. The man called Ben Fry was suspected of killing three of them. The other three, including the prisoner in his cell, were killed by the Hellfires.

Two other people also lost their lives that night: the pilot of the attacking Apache and the man in the helo's gunner seat. It was another day or so before they were identified as Chris Wannamaker and Bernard Hirschorn.

With his death, over time, the full extent of Hirschorn's criminal organization began to become public. His stranglehold on the town of Driscoll was only a small part of it, it turned out. He was also responsible for a good deal of the trafficking in drugs, weapons and human beings throughout the Pacific Northwest. It was an organization built on murder—twenty-five murders at least, some of fairly high-level bad guys who had tried to stand in Hirschorn's way. It remained Weiss's belief that the Shadowman had been hired to commit many of these killings and that in doing so he had become the one man who could easily destroy Hirschorn's business and Hirschorn himself. He knew where the bodies were buried so to speak, and Weiss thought he had used this leverage to convince Hirschorn to act on his behalf.

Anyway, on the basis of testimony from Alex Wellman, local and federal authorities were able to close down much of Hirschorn's network from Driscoll clear up to the Canadian border. Which—as a comical sidelight—made a hero out of Ray Grambling: the honest FBO owner who'd hired detectives to investigate what Hirschorn was doing with his planes. The detectives themselves refused to be interviewed at any length and so the press quickly lost interest in them.

Whip Pomeroy killed himself. Weiss, being Weiss, had known that he would. He'd tried to get the prison to put the man on suicide watch. He'd tried to get in to talk to him again. But officials at North Wilderness were furious with the detective for going over their heads to alert the governor about the incoming Apache. The fact that he'd turned out to be right only made the matter worse. So they didn't listen and, about ten days after the attack, Pomeroy chewed through his wrists and bled to death in his cell. He just couldn't stand the suspense anymore, Weiss thought. He knew—he believed with all his heart—that if he stayed alive, the killer was sure to come back.

As for him—the killer, the man called Ben Fry—he vanished without a trace. Search parties, choppers and dogs crisscrossed the wilderness surrounding the prison for two weeks but couldn't come up with a single sign of him. His mug shot appeared in newspapers, on TV, but no one had seen him anywhere. After a while, the authorities began telling the media that the escapee was almost surely dead, lost in the forest or maybe drowned trying to make his way along the coast. What they neglected to mention was the fact that, the more they studied the records, the more they began to understand that there had never been a man called Ben Fry at all. His identity, his fingerprints, even his face on closer study, seemed to have been a construct, a fake. But no matter. Their story—that he was dead—became the official version of things. Most reporters seemed satisfied with it.

With one exception. Jeff Bloom, the guy from the *Chronicle*, the guy who'd done the original stories about the Shadowman after the South Bay Massacre. Jeff claimed to have a secret source who said Ben Fry was the Shadowman himself, or at least was believed to be by the people who knew him. He wrote an article describing the entire incident at the prison as one chapter in a kind of twisted love story, a killer's attempt to reclaim the woman who had captured his unspeakable heart.

The *Chronicle* editors didn't believe that one for a second. The article never ran.

And so that appeared to be the end of it. But there was one other incident that seems to me worth describing. I'll leave it to the reader to decide whether it's part of this narrative or not.

A few weeks after the attack on the prison, an early heat wave hit San Francisco. Temperatures rose over a hundred for three days running. Men stooped as they walked to work as if they were shriveling into the pavement. Women went disconcertingly bare and their skin glistened.

Then, one midnight when the heat lay on top of us like a dead horse, when it seemed as if there would be no relief from it forever, the blessed fog came in. It rolled down street after street like some kind of heavenly cavalry that stirred up a cooling dust with its silent hooves. As streetlamps and building facades vanished underneath it, the temperature dropped thirty degrees, just like that, on the instant.

"Thank God," said the whore in Weiss's apartment. She stood at the open window in her underwear. She let the chill air blow in over her. She held back the hair of her red wig with both hands to expose her features to it. "Thank God."

Weiss sat in the easy chair in the bay, holding a scotch glass in place on the chair's arm. He smiled faintly at the girl, only faintly. He was ready for her to go.

But then, when she was gone, Weiss grew despondent, as he often did when these trysts of his were over. He lifted the Macallan's bottle from the floor beside him. He refilled his glass. Another hooker with another red wig. It made him feel low and dirty somehow.

He sat alone, sipped his scotch. Set it down. The billowing fog lay hard by the windowpanes. The people in the street below were merely shadows. The cars passed in smears of dull yellow light. He started to raise his glass to his lips again.

And he stopped, his hand half-lifted. A violent shudder went through him. All at once, a clammy sweat began to collect on the back of his neck just under his shirt collar. He felt cold, as if he had come down with a fever.

But it was not a fever. It was something else, something strange. Weiss was afraid. Really afraid and for no apparent reason. The cold, damp fear felt as if it were suddenly eating into his bones, spreading through him, weakening him. Something—something on the periphery of his vision—had brought a presence like death into the room. He shifted his gaze—slowly, reluctantly, as if he were terrified of what he might see.

There, on the corner across the street, in the jaundiced beam of a streetlamp lost in fog, he made out the shape of a man. A man wearing a dark raincoat, standing very still. Looking up at his window. Watching him.

Weiss felt his breath catch. He stared down at the figure, unable to turn away. His mouth went dry. He slowly dabbed his lips with his tongue and swallowed—swallowed what tasted like ashes. He made to set his scotch glass back down on the chair arm, but it tipped, slipped from his fingers. It fell on the rug with a ringing thud, spitting the last of the fine whiskey into a flame-shaped stain.

The man in the fog stared up at him, stared and stared. Weiss stared back helplessly, as if hypnotized. He thought of his gun, the old service revolver he kept in his desk drawer. But he couldn't bring himself to rise, couldn't find the strength to take the three steps across the room to retrieve it. He was like a man in a nightmare whose will is screaming to escape but whose muscles have turned to mud. He couldn't explain it even to himself. He simply sat locked in the dim figure's gaze and felt the chill pressure of terror rising in him and rising until it seemed it would become unbearable and then . . .

And then the phone rang. The sudden sharp trill of it jolted Weiss where he sat. It broke the spell—only for a second, but he seized that second and stood quickly from his chair.

He strode to the desk. Grabbed the phone with one hand. Stooped and pulled open the lower drawer with another. He was drawing his gun out even as he spoke.

"Weiss," he said.

"Hello, Mr. Weiss." The woman's voice was low and warm. He had never heard it before.

Weiss looked around him, confused, sweeping the gun over the room uncertainly. The sweat was still cold on the back of his neck, but the fear had receded as quickly and mysteriously as it had come. He felt dazed now, as if he really had been in a nightmare, as if he'd been awakened from a deep sleep. He began to wonder if maybe that was it. Maybe he'd dozed off in his easy chair and had a bad dream.

"Who is this?" he said thickly into the phone.

"I just wanted to say thank you, Mr. Weiss," the woman answered softly. There was something otherworldly, almost unreal in the way she spoke, a lofty, distant quality. "Maybe one day I'll be able to thank you in person."

Weiss shook his head, trying to clear it. "Who . . . Who are you?"

"I can't come to see you now. Do you understand that? It's too dangerous now. And you can't come to me either. Do you understand? Do you?"

"No, I . . . I don't . . ."

"You would only bring him with you. You see? He'll be watching you now all the time, every second. And if you come to find me, he'll follow you and he'll find me first."

Weiss was breathing quick, breathing hard. Suddenly the things she was saying seemed to make sense to him. "Maybe I could help you," he blurted out. His voice was soft, almost plaintive. "Maybe I could . . ."

"Please," said the woman. "Please listen. You can't, you can't come. Don't look for me. He'll follow you. He'll find me."

"But . . ."

"And be careful, all right? Please. Be very, very careful, Mr. Weiss."

The line went dead. It was over. Another moment and the dial tone started. With an unsteady motion, Weiss set the phone back in its cradle. He looked around him. He must've fallen asleep, he thought again. That had to be it. He'd fallen asleep and had a dream, that's all. He half believed he was dreaming still.

He was about to put the pistol back in the desk drawer but he hesitated. His eyes went to the window again. He held on to the gun. Walked back across the room. He looked out through the glass bay, out and down into the yellow glow of the streetlamp.

There was nobody there now. Nothing. Only the shadows. Only the fog.

ACKNOWLEDGMENTS

I have to take a few lines to say thank you to the many people who helped me with this book. Some of their names and titles were lost in a tragic computer disk accident but I reconstructed as many of my notes as I could. My apologies to anyone missing, untitled or misspelled.

Private Investigator Lynn McLaren has been unendingly patient with my questions and generous with her answers. Raymond McGrath of the Institute for International Criminal Investigations sat for a long interview and follow-up calls. Audrey Schutte and all the good people at Hillside Aviation in Redding, California, showed me the ropes of an FBO and Andrea Read of Spitfire Aviation in Santa Barbara was always available with information about planes and flying. Ty Blasingame, a pilot with the Army National Guard, taught me the ins and outs of an attack helicopter. I also received help from Airman First Class Christopher Miller of the Air National Guard and Lieutenant Colonel Robert "Nash" Cooper of the Air Guard's Office of the Adjutant General. David Brunk gave me an excellent, not to mention frightening, tour of Lompoc Federal Prison—be careful in there, David. Lt. Rawland Swift, administrative assistant to the warden at Pelican Bay State Prison, was also extremely helpful, as was Tom Hansen at the California Department of Corrections and Colonel Dennis Sarkeijian from the Office of the Adjutant General. Fred Gardner from the San Francisco District Attorney's Office and Sherman Ackerson of the San Francisco Police Department both made themselves available for procedural questions, as did Lieutenant Nick Katzenstein, formerly of the Santa Barbara PD. Dr. Lesley Wallis, Assistant Miami Medical Examiner, walked me through the gorier parts of the Shadowman's evil plan. And my thanks also to Larry Mousouris for teaching me how to work Bishop's motorcycle.

On a more personal level, my deep thanks to Robert Gottlieb at Trident Media Group; Brian Lipson at the Endeavor Agency; Tom Doherty, Robert Gleason and Brian Callaghan at Tor/Forge; and my excellent researcher, Wendy Miller, AKA Vendybar. And on an even more personal level, more thanks than words alone can say to Ellen, the best wife a boy ever had.